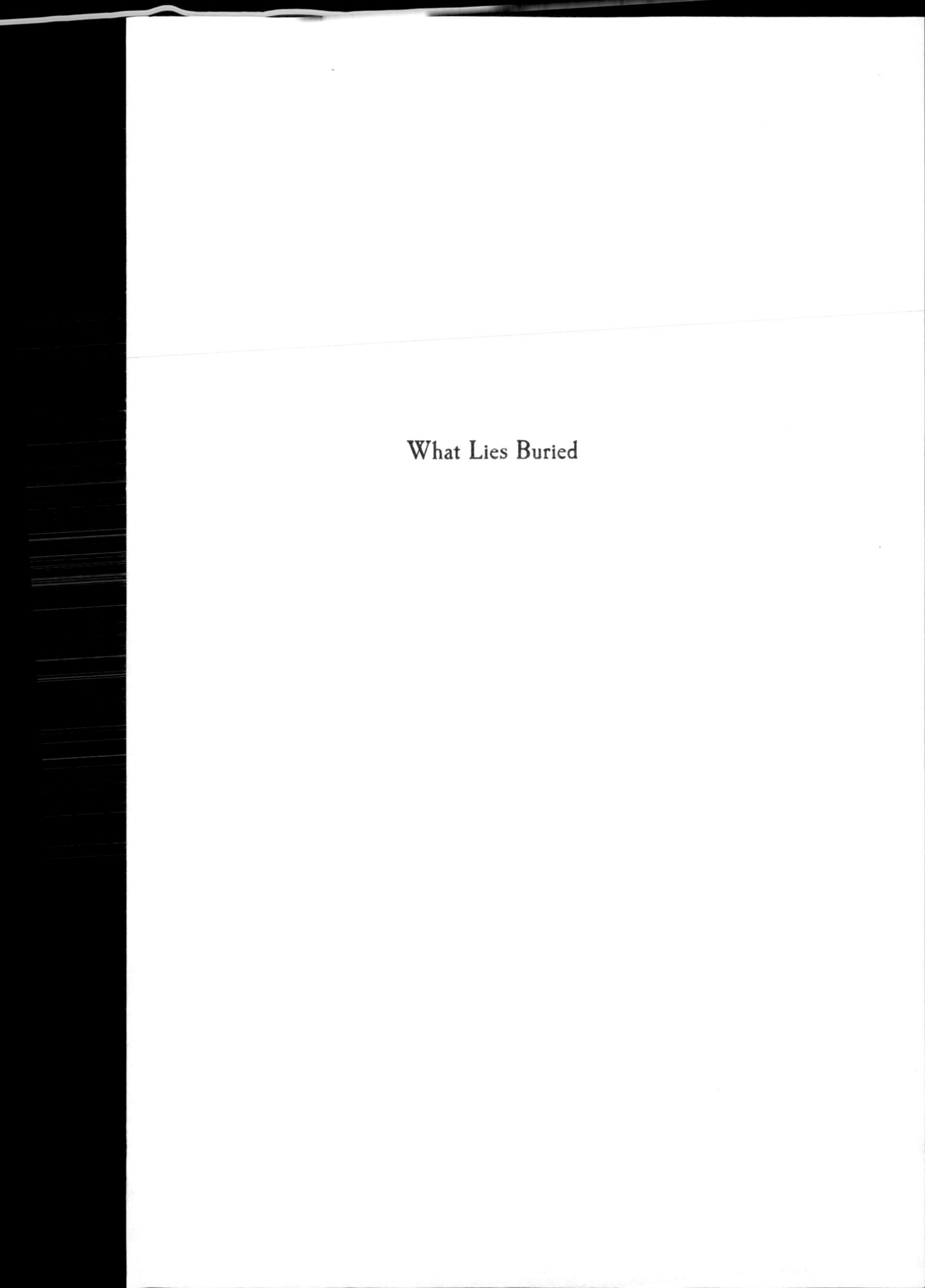

What Lies Buried

What Lies Buried

A Novel of Old Cape Fear

by Dewey Lambdin

McBooks Press, Inc.
Ithaca, New York

Published by McBooks Press 2005

Cover photograph: Live Oak on Drayton Hall Grounds, ca. 1976–1977, © David Muench/CORBIS.

Cover and text design: Panda Musgrove.

ISBN: 1-59013-116-9

Library of Congress Cataloging-in-Publication Data

Lambdin, Dewey.
What lies buried : a novel of Old Cape Fear / by Dewey Lambdin.

p. cm.

ISBN 1-59013-116-9 (alk. paper)

1. North Carolina--History--Colonial period, ca. 1600–1775--Fiction. 2. Cape Fear River Valley (N.C.)--Fiction. 3. Fear, Cape (N.C.)--Fiction. I. Title.

PS3562.A435W47 2005

813'.54--dc22

2005007274

Distributed to the trade by National Book Network, Inc.
15200 NBN Way, Blue Ridge Summit, PA 17214
800-462-6420

Additional copies of this book may be ordered from any bookstore or directly from McBooks Press, Inc., ID Booth Building, 520 North Meadow St., Ithaca, NY 14850. Please include $4.00 postage and handling with mail orders. New York State residents must add sales tax to total remittance (books & shipping). All McBooks Press publications can also be ordered by calling toll-free 1-888-BOOKS11 (1-888-266-5711).

Please call to request a free catalog.
Visit the McBooks Press website at www.mcbooks.com.

Printed in the United States of America

9 8 7 6 5 4 3 2 1

CAPE FEAR

. . . *As pleasant and delectable to behold as it is possible to imagine.*
—Giovanni Verrazano, 1524

. . . *the goodliest Soile under the Cope of Heaven.*
—Ralph Lane to Sir Richard Hakluyt, 1585

DEDICATION

Thanks to fellow author Deborah Adams of "Jesus Creek," Tennessee, for putting the flea in my ear of trying to write a "Hist'ry-Myst'ry."

Call it a "Love Song" to the Coastal Carolinas.

For Glenn and Beverly Tetterton, and the New Hanover County Library; for Stan and Nancy Colbert, Jack Fryer, and Phil Gerard; for Ellyn Bache; for Diane Cobb Cashman and her *Cape Fear Adventure* that I got by serendipity; and for ol' James Sprunt, the youngest purser on any Wilmington-based Confederate blockade runner, for his *Chronicles of the Cape Fear.*

And to all the rowdy folks I met at The Raw Bar, Dock Street, the Oceanic, the Bridge Tender, King Neptune's, the "M.O.I." and Wally's, or Pusser's, or whatever they call it now.

And Kefi's Bar, whose location I will never tell to any *turista* or Yankee for any price. If you go, Do *NOT* Feed The Seagulls At Your Table!

Chapter 1

THE TAFFRAIL LANTERNS and nighttime riding lights of the many ships alongside the piers, or anchored out in the stream, lit only a bit of the evening, shimmering like molten yellow gold over the broad expanse of the Cape Fear River, which glinted like a ripply sheet of black glass. Across the river on Eagle's Island lay a weak smear of light from fires that burned low and sullenly amber-red under the try-pots and rendering works to keep their contents soft and workable for the morning. Up-river, down-river—beyond the marshes and the rice beds west of the island, Alligator Creek and the narrower Brunswick River—primeval, stygian dark ruled, as far as the Piedmont uplands.

Ebony blackness and vast tracts of forest surrounded the tiny seaport town of Wilmington on the opposite bank, the cape side. North, south and east dark mastered the named streets that climbed the river bluffs and the numbered streets that ran north-south. It was a rare homeowner diligent enough to light a porch lantern much past suppertime unless expecting company. Wilmington was small but industrious, and its residents were mostly "early to bed, early to rise." Even on a night during Quarterly Assizes, Court Sessions and the corresponding militia muster, and market day to lure plaintiffs, planters and humble settlers to town, when its population could double, the borough was already snoring at that middling hour. Mostly.

Near the Courthouse, though, there was Widow Yadkin's Ordinary, and there was light aplenty. Two lanterns shone in the coach yard in front, where men chuckled and joshed, comparing the merits of horses they had brought to town for the races; two more burned on the deep front porch of the log-cabin tavern, where other men smoked pipes and sipped from tankards, taking the cooler night airs, sitting on the log benches with their heels up on railings or planter-boxes.

A visitor in search of meat, drink and joy would espy Widow Yadkin's and be drawn like a moth to that wee oasis of brightness, be lured by Sirens'

Song, by the merry sounds of fiddles from within doing a lively "Rakes of Mallow," perhaps. He would turn the reins of his humble wagon, fine coach or mount over to the towheaded lad who served as ostler, and relish his entrance, perhaps pausing for a while to survey the sprawling, added-upon-so-often establishment, take cheer from the flung-open windows along the front, nicely framed by gingham-checked curtains within and fresh-painted shutters without, and all the amber candlelight that spilled out of them. And smile to himself as he cocked an ear to the genial hum-um of its patrons' voices commingling in good-natured banter, or raised in songs of merriment and glee:

Come, let us drink about, and drive away all sorrow.
Come, let us drink about, and drive away all sorrow.
For, 'haps we may not, for 'haps we may not, for 'haps
we may nnott . . . *be here to drink, tomorrow!*

There was a talented young Alston on violin, an older Harnett plucking a lute and an Irish sailor whom no one exactly knew off one of the anchored ships piping on a flute. The song, though, was being bellowed out by Harry Tresmayne, who stood atop a stout wooden bench and waved one arm to lead the others, his left akimbo against his hip.

"This'un's for you, Matthew," Tresmayne called down from above to one of his table companions, "you abstemious old rascal!" reaching down to ruffle the fellow's shock of reddish hair.

Wine, wine, it cures the gout, the spirit and the colic!
Wine, it cures the gout, the spirit and the colic!

"Aye, top him up there, a brimmin' bumper!" cried Mr Osgoode Moore, a younger member of their set at the table.

Hand it to a-all men, hand it to a-all men,
hand *it to a-all men! A very specif-physick!*

Harry Tresmayne bugled in high spirits. "Drink, drink, drink! Show us heel-taps!" he instructed.

"Drink, drink, drink!" the others hooted and cheered, and their current "victim" was forced to tilt back his wineglass and gulp down the whole thing, before lifting it high, upside down, to show that not a drop remained, which garnered a further cheer, and a thunder of fists pounded on the tabletop.

"And the next is you, Thom Lakey!" Tresmayne shouted, pointing to a slim and distinguished-looking planter of some means. "What? *Hiccup* is it, Matthew? More wine's your cure fer that, too!"

"Have mercy!" Mr Matthew Livesey cried in mock distress, one hand to his chest. "Mercy, I beg you, and 'let this cup . . . *hic* . . . pass from me'!" Which quotation raised a cheerful growl from his compatriots, and more drummed fists.

Spotting what Lakey was drinking, Tresmayne skipped a verse, moving on to:

But, he that drinks small beer, goes to bed quite sober.
He *that drinks small beer, goes to bed sober.*

And they all joined in on,

falls *as the leaves do fall,* falls *as the leaves do fall,*
falls as the leaves do fall . . . he'll rot before October!

Thom Lakey upended his pint tankard of small beer in a few gulps, then goggled at them through the glass bottom to show manful; without even a stifled belch.

Finally, the last "victim" exhausted and the song done, Tresmayne sprang lithely down and took his seat on the bench again, the amateur musicians launching themselves into the lively "Flowers of Edinburgh."

"A toast, gentlemen," the dashing and handsome Harry Tresmayne offered, waving for their serving maid to come attend any who lacked spirits.

"Lord, spare me," Livesey tried to demur.

"Aye, God's sake, Harry. I've a plea to make in th' mornin'," Osgoode Moore mildly protested. "Politics in th' afternoon, too, so . . ."

"I've the chandlery to open . . . early," Livesey added.

"We've the 'barons' to confound," Thom Lakey fussily stuck in. "An' thick heads'll not carry th' day. Your *oration* after all . . ."

"He'll toast a round dozen things, like he always does," a Mr Ashe said to Livesey from 'cross the table. "But the one glass this time, Tresmayne, and make it a combination."

"Oh, very well then, ye pack o' tea-drinkers," Tresmayne said, with only a slight sign of disappointment. "A combination, then. And never fear about th' speechifyin', Thom. My address is all but writ, and a mornin's polish'll put a high gloss on it. We'll roast our opponents, and serve 'em up well-done this time. Top-ups all 'round, me girl!"

"You'll touch upon autonomy, as we discussed?" Thom Lakey asked in a whisper, leaning closer to Tresmayne. "*Gently* I trust . . . In his last letter to me, even Samuel Adams in Boston said he feared raisin' *too* much Hell 'gainst th' Crown. Time's not ripe . . . average people aren't ready for *too* much talk o' change an' upsets, so . . ."

"Bosh, Thomas," Tresmayne blithely objected as the maid returned with a full tray. "Boston 'Bow-Wows' mayn't have th' bottom t'dare be outspoken, but we Carolinians are possessed of bolder spirit, after all. And no, I'll *not* cry out for too much, too soon, Thomas. We are loyal Englishmen merely callin' for th' *rights* o' free Englishmen t'govern ourselves but a *tad* more. A Parliament of our own, *this* side of th' ocean. Though, one without a House of Lords, pray God! Else we'll end held in thrall forever by self-styled landgraves, white *caciques* and barons, are we ever *that* successful, hah! Are the *current* leadin' men ever given patents of nobility by the King, well . . . !"

"Never happen," Thom Lakey snickered. "They refused good Colonel Washington th' right t'even *apply* for an Army commission, e'en could he afford t'buy colors *ten* times over—"

"And him one of th' most talented soldiers Virginia's produced," Tresmayne interjected, "the American *colonies* have produced, too. Those of ye who went north with me in the militia will surely vouch for that!"

"As I said," Thom Lakey went on, "if Colonel Washington's too crude an' rustic t'soldier with their elevated arses, then it's long odds any colonist'd ever win a *knighthood* much less be made th' merest baronet, hah! We're not thought quite as good as *home*-raised . . ."

"And those who served know th' truth o' *that!*" Harry Tresmayne energetically agreed. "And that's th' whole problem in a nut-shell. They look down their long, top-lofty noses at American-born Englishmen as if we were little better than Red Indians. And do we *not* stir th' pot an' make 'em take notice of our bein' their *equals,* then they'll never have t'face th' matter, and things'll *never* change. Ah, thankee, me dear Betty. Glasses topped? Let us lay our toast, and bow like a Chinaman to our betters yonder, hmm?"

With a fresh glass of wine at last in hand, Harry Tresmayne held it aloft in a silent and sardonic salute to the gentlemen congregated at the other end of Widow Yadkin's public rooms, to those richer, and longer-settled, in the opposing faction: "Prince Dick" Ramseur and his son, a gaggle of the Moore clan, and others allied with the original developers who'd come up from Goose Creek, or Charleston from the South Carolina colony, those more-elegant with real aspirations to nobility from down south of the Pee Dee River, who had naturally segregated themselves from the "upstarts" and "parvenus."

"A toast!" Tresmayne cried, with a devilish glint of merriment in his eyes. "Success to our endeavors . . . profit to our commerce . . . untold bounty for our crops . . ." He knew he had the barons' attention as he concluded with, "and, by the Grace of God, all th' liberties of loyal Englishmen be granted to *American* Englishmen!"

His companions lustily cheered his toast, and his characteristic boldness, tipping their glasses back to heel-taps, again. The sentiment was shared, and glasses were raised, among a fair majority of the ordinary's other customers as well.

The musicians had, in the meantime, done "He that Would an Alehouse Keep," changing the words to twit Mrs Yadkin, and just finished the sentimental "Over the Hills and Far Away" from *The Beggars' Opera.* Then, at the urging of Mr Richard Ramseur, Esquire, himself, they launched into a tune of his choosing. His son, possessed of as fine a voice as Harry Tresmayne's, stood to lead them.

Here's a health to the King, and a lasting peace.
To faction's *end, and our wealth increase.*
Come, let us drink while we have breath,

for there's no drinking af-ter *death.*
And they *that will this health de-ny,*
down among the dead men, down among the dead men,
down, *down, down, down,*
down *among the dead men, let them lie!*

Tresmayne lifted his significantly *empty* glass to them, a broad grin and a quick laugh on his lips, and made an exaggerated, wide-armed bow from the waist, congratulating his opponents for their sly choice of a song, and the quick wits that had twisted a genial drinking song into a pointed comment in riposte.

"Didn't think they had such drollery *in* 'em!" he snickered as he sat down, his voice lowered to be shared only among his tablemates.

"My apologies, Mr Livesey," Osgoode Moore said as he slid a pew or two closer, "for I've not, as yet, inquired of you how Sam'l and your charmin' Bess keep. They thrive, I trust? And mine and Anne's best regards t'both, I hope ye'll say for me."

"Main-well, sir, main-well," Livesey replied, struggling to get a long, clay, church-warden pipe lit.

What *else* passed, he could but dimly recall after: a *smatter* of his conversation with Osgoode, vague memories of more wine than was his usual wont taken aboard, more songs, some jocular tales told by others (though exactly what they'd been quite escaped him!) and a last reverie of stumping homeward, more dependent on his walking stick than usual, down the inky darkness of Dock Street, grunting "I'll Fathom the Bowl" under his breath. Or, had it been "Nottingham Ale"? Either one, it did not signify, for it had been a rare, and most convivial, evening.

Chapter 2

SHALL I HELP you with your leg, Father?" Samuel asked from beyond the bedchamber door.

"I shall manage." Matthew Livesey replied, testily. A rare free night had left him "headed" and grumpy. But he could picture his tall, athletic son, so anxious to please, so eager to contribute, and modified his tone. "Thankee kindly, my boy, but I rose early. I'm all but afoot."

It was a kindly lie, and after a long moment, Livesey could hear Samuel clumping down the short hall to the front rooms, gangly and loose limbed. And loud!

Too loud for this morning, Matthew Livesey grumpily thought, as he cursed again his lack of control the night before. Any other night, the chandlery would be closed by seven, and he'd have dined at home in sober domesticity. But he had let himself be seduced. Life had been hard for the Liveseys, the past few years, and he'd been little more than a drudge, six days a week from sunup to sundown at the chandlery, the sawmill or rendering works, so little in the till for *any* frivolities that he'd quite forgotten the simple joys of the coffeehouses or taverns.

Liveseys were stern Scots-Presbyterian stock, too, supposed to be immune to folly. Though they *were* listed on the parish rolls of St James's as *somewhat* Church of England, now. But it was the *only* church in Wilmington, so what could one do? Had Anglican ways rubbed off on him, at last, resulting in his seduction into frivolous doings?

"Damn, Harry . . . you old pagan," Livesey chuckled as he pulled up fresh white cotton stockings on his legs, seated on the edge of his high bedstead.

Matthew Livesey's head was paining him. Not with the cotton-mouthed thudding of youthful excess, but with that maze-y, disoriented, semi-bilious, and when once attained, seemingly *eternal* sort of "head" that God retains for those who know better, but indulge anyway. And refreshing sleep had not stayed long enough to temper the slightest bit of it; he had awakened to a cock's crow, perhaps, certainly to the dry snap of the firelock on the tinderbox as Bess put light to the kindling of the hearth before sunup.

He had at least had wit enough to lay things out about him as he would on a righteous evening. Wash-hand stand, basin and pitcher were beside the headboard on one side, his own tinderbox with new flint and singed rag with which to light his pre-dawn candle on the other side. His clothes laid out at the foot of the mattress where he could reach them easily.

And, That Thing.

Satisfied that the end of the right stocking was well-padded with fresh wool batting and drawn snug against his stump, he pulled on his breeches, with the good leg and foot braced against the short bed-ladder, almost standing but not quite. Not yet.

He had already managed a clean shirt, attained stuffing the tails into his breeches, and did up the buttons and buckles. Then, with a put-upon sigh, he at last reached for It.

That Thing was, he had to grudgingly admit, a devilishly well-made appliance and a right handsomely decorated bit of carpentry. Though the militia surgeon had left him three inches of stump below the knee, he didn't trust it, so the glove-leather-lined cup was deep enough to reach well above his right knee, like a dragoon's knee-boot flap. The cup was of a handsome burl-wood, trimmed with silver inset wire and ivory. Below the cup it was oar-wood, solid and unyielding ash that tapered to a vaguely foot-shaped block which was long enough in the "toes" to give him better balance erect, some support in a custom-made off-side stirrup so he could still ride, and let him prop himself to the windward side of his little shallop even when going close-hauled down-river to Brunswick or New Inlet to fish.

Still, That Thing was the most hateful device ever he'd laid his eyes upon.

"Damned foolishness," he muttered as he snugged the last buckle in place. "Then, and now. God, Harry," he reiterated.

It had been the dashing and rake-hell Harry Tresmayne of his one and only year away at Harvard College, who had stayed in touch as his father's Philadelphia firm, Arnott Livesey & Son, was going under.

But then it had been Corinthian, brothel-haunting Harry who'd almost ruined that one and only college year with the threats of expulsion; Matthew had gone home before the term ended, short of funds. Harry *had* been expelled!

Yet it had been Harry who had lured him to the Lower Cape Fear country with his tales of Brunswick and Wilmington becoming the naval stores capital of the world, cheap land, cheap timber and a better life for him, his dear wife, Charlotte, and his two children. Harry Tresmayne who'd introduced them into Society and Trade hereabouts, and had steered him right the first few years to a modicum of comfort and financial security.

Without Harry as a guide, they could never have made sense of all the factions, the clans, feuds and alliances; who was tied to the landgraves, "barons" and *caciques* who'd held power under the old Lords Proprietors; who of the original Goose Creek, South Carolina, families mattered now under the Royal Governor; and who supported him. And who could be trusted on credit, and who was "aristocratic" but penniless.

But—there always had seemed to be a "but" whenever one discussed Harry Tresmayne—it had been Harry, too, who'd seduced Matthew into accompanying the local militia up north in the recent war, after that pleasant social organization had been called to arms. To serve, even as their commissary officer with the 2nd North Carolina Regiment, might gain him more social acceptance among the gentry and might gain Matthew Livesey, Chandlery, more custom once they were home again.

Matthew Livesey was certain to the depths of his neglected Presbyterian soul that his crass, pecuniary motives had cost him his leg, that bright winter morning in the revetments facing Fort Dusquesne near his native Philadelphia. Greed, Pride—he'd been guilty of a whole slew of sins. And, he'd paid for his scheming, vaunting *hubris.*

He'd gone forward with the salt-beef and biscuit rations, just for a glimpse of real fighting. As his sergeant and victualers doled out the day's supplies, he had walked up to chat with the redoubtable Colonel Innes from his adopted colony, now in command of all of the Colonial Militia forces. Gay as spring robins, they'd been, especially after Harry—Major Harry Tresmayne—had come up, too, chortling over some new witticism he'd just heard, accompanied by Colonels Ashe and Waddell, and the young Virginian, Colonel Washington.

A desultory bombardment had been thumping away from the guns of the British Royal Artillery all night, into the dawn. Perhaps the knot of staff officers had been a too-tempting target for revenge for those besieged French, for Fort Dusquesne had belched a few barks of ire in reply—their first of the morning.

Round shot from hotter barrels might have reached them, but the salvo from cold iron tubes fell jeeringly short. But one round cannon ball had skipped or rolled farther than the rest; a twelve-pounder shot, it had been, four inches across, trundling across dun winter grass in playful little hops and twirls, spinning as harmlessly as a child's ball at the end of a weak kick. And Matthew Livesey had thought to get himself a memento for his mantel, or a doorstop. So, he put out a foot in its path to stop it, oblivious to a chorus of warning shouts.

Twelve pounds of solid iron, still rolling at a slow walking pace, had taken his foot off in a twinkling, shattered both the bones in his shin, and spun him head-over-heels, stupefied—into this Hell!

But me all your buts 'bout Harry, Livesey thought as he got to his feet, wincing at the dull ache which would be his companion to the grave; *'twas Harry held me, stifling my urge to howl and un-man myself before the others. Harry who saw me to the surgeons and gripped my hands so I never uttered a weakling's screams as they sawed that ruin away, even when I was near senseless from rum, fear and pain.*

But! It had also been seductively glib Harry who'd assured him he deserved a night out, a bought supper 'stead of home cooking, and a pipe or two among the excitingly rancorous political talk. And much too much claret, for a man old enough to know better!

Sliding free of the bed's support, Matthew Livesey assayed a few stiff-legged paces about his tiny bedchamber. He went to the one small window and threw up the sash, but it was still dark out, barely gray enough to espy the glint of the river sliding by in the sliver of view he had of Water Street. Warm as it would be this day, the morning was a touch cool, still, tanged with low-tide aromas, that particular stale-salt effluvia of a lowland seaport, much like his native Philadelphia. And it was humid, making not only his leg, but diverse other joints ache slightly. Matthew Livesey did not consider himself as old—not yet, pray God—still, what were these croupy twinges he felt lately?

He stumped back to the wash-hand stand and basin to wash his face and comb back his long, unruly and wiry hair into a queue and tie it off with a bit of black silk ribbon. He peered into the smoky indistinct reflection of the small mirror.

"Not too bad, consid'rin' . . ." he mused half aloud as he decided that his stubble could go another day before shaving. His hair was still thick, reddish blonde. And if it *had* receded, it had revealed a well-formed, intelligent brow. Perhaps his visage *had* widened and thickened, and furrowed a might, but what could one expect for a man who'd gone through so much . . . and was only four years shy of a half century, hmm? "No, not too awful a phyz. Better'n most."

He donned and tied his neck-stock, then hitched up another much put upon sigh of resigned determination. It was time to put on his "Publick Phyz," to go out and meet the day a steady and reliable man of means, a credit to his town and a joy to his family.

Even if he did feel like the Wrath of God.

"Hear him come in?" Samuel Livesey asked, eyeing the skillets with a famished dog's longing. "Half-seas-over, he was. 'Least, when I come back in from caterwauling, I take my shoes off."

"Oh, Sam'l!" his sister Bess chuckled as she turned bacon with a long-tined fork. "You, *Rake's Progress?* You sneak out your window! And the only reason you come back shoeless is you can't remember where you left 'em. I'd love to see the day you go out the front door," she snickered, turning from her chore to mimic him, hitching up a shoulder in a caricature of Samuel's meek stooping when confronting their sire.

"Well, Father dear, I'm off to drink and scratch up Hell! If ya don't mind, that is? Ooh, Father forgive me, *do* forget I said it!" She cringed as if switched. Samuel cringed, too—at the accuracy of her portrayal, and the idea of *ever* saying such. "Oh, don't cane me so, I'll be good!" Bess went on. "Not my ears, Father, don't box 'em!"

"Oh, bloody . . . !" Samuel grumbled, fed up with her mocking him. "I'm a man grown, Bess! Don't see why I can't, if he can. It's not as if we're so 'skint' any longer, either. 'Prentices and 'dentured servants get their nights off. Hard as I've been working lately . . . Oww!"

He'd tried to sneak a strip of bacon off the serving plate, but Bess had rapped his knuckles with the side of the turning fork, leaving him only a tasty but greasy smear to suck at.

"You'll get your share, no more, no less, Sam'l," Bess warned.

"Hard as you've been working . . . spare us!" she went on, vexed at last. "How much work do you *do* at the sawmill or the tar-pots or the docks? When there's hired men and overseers who know what they're about? All you do is gawp and pretend. Dear Lord, I do allow a 'prentice clerk, fresh off-ship from England, could do better. *And* spare us victuals!"

"We could marry you off to some piney-woods hog drover, and not miss you the slightest, either, Bess! And ne'er hear your venom, again!" Samuel shot back, wounded too easily, as he always was, by her tongue. "As far away as possible. It's Livesey & *Son* Chandlery, now, ye know. I do my share, like he expects o' me."

"Your share!" Bess groaned. "Sneaking off whole *days* to hunt or fish with that shiftless pack of hounds you call friends, when work is wanting," she snapped, in full scold. "Lookee here, Sam'l, we're not so well off yet, and what little ahead we are took hellish effort. Now it *is* Livesey & Son, he expects you, he *needs* you, to pitch in as hard as he does. To shoulder things, so he *can* have the rare night free. Pray God *not,* but should anything happen to Father, where'd we be if it becomes Samuel Livesey's Chandlery? A little freedom from a camel's load o' cares isn't a jot on what he deserves, after all he's done . . . for us, Sam'l!"

"I do all he asks," Samuel sulked, spraddle-legged on a chair turned back-to-front. "I just wish . . . !" He choked on his own unformed wishes; on that very fear, of inheriting *all* the burdens; of living a life he *knew* he wasn't cut out for. Samuel had known, since coming to Wilmington, and the edge of North Carolina Colony's tantalising wilderness wonders, that what *he* wanted from life, and what was *expected* of him, would have a hard time co-inciding.

For a time, they'd had *land,* which they'd planned to farm, land where a beguiled Samuel Livesey had dreamt of hounds, blooded horses, spirited hunts and bushel baskets filled with fish, of crops ripening in orderly rows nigh to the horizon in fields he'd cleared himself.

Samuel *knew,* early on, that he wasn't *quite* his father's son; he'd never been a prodigy at ledgers and accounts, felt imprisoned by sun-blocking shelves of goods and naval stores, and what ins and outs of business acumen his father had tried to instill in him made as much sense as conversing in nothing but Greek, from his hopelessly abandoned school textbooks. Nor did Samuel feel as glib and facile with clients or customers as his father, even as comfortable as Bess seemed to be, when she helped out at their chandlery. The second-hand allure of the sea meant little to him, either, when *supplying* the needs of far-roving merchant ships—but not taking *part* in visiting seafarers' adventures—felt pointless and empty.

Pray God! Samuel moodily thought; *Acres, again! Jesus, just one* middlin' *little farm! Then, the courage t'tell Father what* I'd *rather!*

How to say, someday, that he preferred the smell of manure, and cow barns, of haylofts and corn bins to hemp, tar, oakum and pitch!

"I try, Bess, I truly do," he sighed, feeling hangdog under her pointed stare—whether she was staring at him or not.

"I'm sorry, Sam'l," Bess relented, fearing she'd gone too far. "I wash for you, so I know how hard you work. You pitch in as manful as any hired hand. And the way you tend the garden, our flower beds, is a marvel, better than anyone could, so we've our own food on the table. Sorry for natterin' you, so early in the morning."

She left the hearth to stand at the edge of the dining table by his chair and tousle his hair. "Father appreciates all you do, and so do I, Sam'l, but Lord . . . 'tis hard t'keep your mind on it, sometimes," she concluded with a wry expression. "Here, mighty hunter . . . a bacon strip . . . Nimrod!"

Samuel brightened and laughed softly as he took her peace offering, opening the mustard pot to smear it down to his taste.

"One more good year, and we will have plantings again, Sam'l," Bess assured him, turning back to the hearth to lift out the last bacon strip, and begin to crack eggs into the skillet. "A country house, and land . . ."

"Pray God, let it be tomorrow morning!" Samuel said with heartfelt longing, as he got to his feet to transfer the plate to the table.

Livesey & Son had not been a grand establishment before the war, not as big as some longer settled in the Cape Fear. They had moved to Wilmington in 1755, seven years before, when Samuel was twelve and Bess was ten. What could be salvaged of the Philadelphia chandlery had been little, after it had finally gone under. But it had bought a town lot and this small house, a shop and a warehouse on Water Street. There had even been enough for the sawmill and renderings on Eagle's Island, in a borough where a little coin went a *long* way. And two hundred forty acres of bottom land on the Northeast Branch near Point Pleasant on the Duplin Road.

But they'd done little more than clear it of timber, pine long gone for roofing shakes, lumber and barrel staves, before the French and Indian War broke out. Bess's father had left his business in care of her mother Charlotte, assisted by a talented apprentice overseer, whose indenture contract they'd bought.

And by the time he'd come home so cruelly wounded in '60, that apprentice had run off to the Georgia Colony with a fair amount of the ready cash, and the damning ledgers he'd kept, which would have proved his duplicity, his low cunning at withholding monies owed and inflating sums paid out. Her darling mother had gone down with ague, taken abed with chills and fever that Dr DeRosset suspected was malaria. After lingering for days, she had died, and Bess's father had been forced from his own sickbed, clumsy and swooning upon his first crude prosthesis, to sell or auction off almost everything, to sell plantings and hopes for landed respectability to save a failing business, just as he once had with his own father's firm in Philadelphia, where she'd been born.

For two frugal years, there'd been no hope of extras. Not one horse of their own in the yawning-empty stables, nor carriage, nor a single hired servant to help out. Two penurious years, Bess ground her teeth in embarrassing reverie, as she stirred the eggs a trifle harder than really necessary.

Two years when food on the table, enough food to keep body and soul together, was almost a luxury, and 'twas signal times when it went beyond sweet potatoes, hominy, garden beans or peas, and actually included meat.

That, and charity. Bess swiped at her unruly hair once more as she gave the eggs a furious spanking about the pan. Well meant though she was sure it had been, to be clucked over . . . ! To be talked about as if she wasn't there, when the neighbor ladies had come from church or their own kitchens with gifts of food, simpering and purring, with all outward, seeming concern for a fellow Christian. Told that they'd cooked too much, and could you use it . . . knowing it was left-overs from the night before. Such usually would go to the chickens they cooped at the back of their yards, or slopped to their hogs!

She'd come to dread those gentle raps on their door, those soft voices so full of pity. With her mother gone, and Samuel off with her father to learn the business, it had been her lot to keep the house in order, to receive their "callers"—and take their cast-offs: food, sometimes; articles of clothing ready for the rag bin, that children or husbands had "outgrown," at other times. She'd curtsied to her benefactors, cooed and simpered and purred right back, measure for measure, in feigned delight, and adopted their own liquid, flowing Low Country accent, her voice pitched just a tad higher and softer.

When what she'd wanted all those two miserly years was to yell at them like a Philadelphia fishmonger's wife, put up her nose high in the air and pridefully tell them all to go to the Devil!

"Such a lovely young miss," they'd cooed, "and isn't it just *such* a pity . . . poor li'l thing?" Once they thought they were out of earshot. Behind her back in church at Saint James's, or when she was out to market with her few scrimped coins. "Why, bless her heart!"

Oh, things were better, now, Bess had to admit. They could not yet aspire to a matched pair of horses, or a carriage, but Father had restored a *measure* of their fortunes—and their respectability. Folk admired him for his persistence, and his modest success. Business now came to the chandlery more for his fair dealings than from pity. With a mere modicum of restored prosperity, Bess no longer got those pitying looks about town, no longer was cooed at and simpered at. Not to her face, certainly, and rarely behind her back anymore, she also suspected. It had taken time, but they had been re-accepted in Society's bosom. All it took was time. Time, and money enough to make the proper show.

Certainly, there'd never again be a hired apprentice, nor would there be indentured workers. Her father had taken on a few new workers—men he could trust who'd been small hold farmers, who'd also fallen on hard times—but their wages weren't charity. Indentured folk were rare in North Carolina—leave that for Virginia, South Carolina or Georgia. Or slaves—not only were they horrendously expensive, far beyond the means of the Liveseys even now, even the price of a single house maid and cook to help her out—but as far as her father would go toward *owning* people was to contract other slave owners for labor gangs at their sawmill or at the tar, pitch, resin and turpentine renderings on Eagle's Island across the river.

They might be welcome in the homes of the gentry once more, but she was still doomed to make do. Things were better than they had been, yet there was still a long way to go to recapture those first few heady years after arriving at this small village perched on the edge of a great wilderness, when their dreams for a prosperous future were unbroken. Or of the days she now could only wistfully recall back in bustling Philadelphia, as a doted-upon child of middling fortune with so little demanded of her!

Eggs done and turned into a warming pan, Bess poked at her cathead biscuits, then swung the copper kettle nearer the tall flames to hasten the tea water's boiling. She sat on a stool by the hearth for a welcome moment of ease. She turned her head to look at Samuel, who was standing four-square by the front window, munching on his strip of bacon, hands in the small of his back, and contemplating the weather.

She *knew* it was termagant of her to take things out on him, but God in Heaven, he was a slender reed! He *did* toil hard, when *put* to it, but merely followed, never seemed to lead, and the idea of Samuel taking charge of the struggling businesses, even *decades* later, gave Bess a chill which the hearth fire could not ease. He had no head for Commerce, and when it came time for Father . . .

She put that thought firmly out of her mind. Father was not yet elderly, far from it, with many productive years left him! Lamed as he was, he let nothing stop him! Just to walk again took more determination than a dozen gentlemen could boast! Failure, the dire shame of poverty—the shame of being *needful* of charity!—rolled off their father's stout shoulders like water off a duck's back. Even the cruel and heartless japes from children in the streets, idlers and ne'er-do-wells, the taunts of "Hoy, Board-Foot!" and "Hallo, Mr Hop-kins!" could not faze him. He merely laughed and shook his fist or his stick at them, joshing them back in like manner, then dismissing it as merely a thoughtless, minor burden to be borne, and had never uttered a single word of frustration. Bess wished she had her father's forbearance and ability to cope, or his strong faith to bear such insults in a truly Christian manner.

More admire than jeer, she assured herself, was forced to smile a wee trifle, considering the glances her father had been getting lately, those he drew from the widows and elder spinster ladies at church.

The war and his disability had thinned him painfully, and going about in his everyday exertions, as regular as a full man should, had made him strong and fit. Liveseys, so he'd confessed to her when she had asked about her grandparents, had always run a tad stocky, appeared solidly square-built, and her father had been weathered down to a fine figure of a man for his age.

One who deserved better, she gloomed, poking at their breakfast fire to speed the boiling. A dutiful son who'd shoulder the burdens a business demanded. A daughter more supportive and cheerful, she chided herself, too. But it was so hard not to yearn for those better times, so hard not to *want* . . . ! A real house servant, 'stead of the old free-Negro woman who came once a week for a day. Daily garden help, 'stead of the old woman's husband and his white-whiskered mule, who came even less often to plow or weed, do chores, nail things back together . . .

Hands other than hers to do the tatting and repairing, so their clothing was presentable. Hands other than hers to do the washing and ironing of their threadbare garments and bed linens: altering and letting out to fit her sprouting brother until they'd saved up enough for one precious bolt of cloth, from which she so dearly wished hands other than hers—just the once!—could run up new!

If Samuel feels like kicking over the traces, he hasn't a patch on the way I *feel,*

Bess sighed, squirming and blushing at her selfish, ungrateful, rebellious and un-dutiful, un-Christian feelings of wants. Surely it was Woman's Lot to do for her loved ones. Yet Bess ached for just a *few* luxuries, for just a few more idle hours in her days, for a tiny jot or tittle of wealth. Other Wilmington girls, in or above her own station, seemed so much better off to her. There were only six hundred or so white settlers in the borough, and only about a third of them could be considered well-to-do. Thankfully, the Livesey's *earlier* prosperity, and the warm sponsorship of the Tresmaynes—"Uncle" Harry and "Aunt" Georgina—had eased their entry into that elevated third of the colony and its social doings. Even their bankruptcy hadn't ended that, for "There But For The Grace of God Go I" could so easily strike any or all, seemingly at whim in a single hard season.

Other girls her age could seem so *idle,* could tat lace or entertain, gossip and titter over such inconsequential things, their hands unsullied or roughened by actual *labor.* Goose-silly some of them were, at times, yet Bess *burned* to be that idle, to have time to read a whole book without interruptions . . . to be able to afford a *new* one!

Grateful to still be included, yet awkward and secretly sullen, *envious,* imagining that her invitations to join her sisters was more of the same shameful *charity* . . . ! Could a body really crave the ability to glide through Life dumb, giddy and carefree, she asked herself ruefully? *Then here, Lord, is one . . . God help me,* she thought.

The tea water began to bubble in the copper pot and she darted a hand out to swing the rod away from the flames with her usual quickness, then scowled in wry amusement at herself.

Long before, she'd been told by her mother and grandmothers that a young *lady* of her station (back in Philadelphia when she'd had one) must always comport herself gracefully. One *glided,* not tromped; one's hands and gestures must always be languid and flowing. Breeding was expressed by one's elegance in all things, every waking moment, if one expected to be a credit to one's family . . . and catch the eye of a suitable young man.

Bess, though, seemed doomed to wave expressively when she spoke, to be chirpy and a bit *too* vivacious when engaged in an exciting conversation, to dart . . . to even sometimes *point!*

"I'm a trull," she whispered over her failings. "A common drab."

"I agree, wholeheartedly," Samuel piped up from the window.

Perhaps it was the frontier that debased all her mother's hopes; Bess stuck her tongue out at her brother. "Bless me, Sam'l, but I had no idea you *knew* words that big. Break teeth, did it?" she cooed.

"Termagant trull's more like it," her brother grinned back, sure that her nagging was at an end. "Poor Bess. No hope *a'tall* of weddin' you off, long as you spit fire and nettles. I s'pose we're stuck with you. At least you know how t'cook."

"More talk like that, dear brother, and it'll be the *last* meal you'll eat," Bess snickered. "'Less you learn to fix for yourself."

"Good thing I love game-meat, then," Samuel responded quickly, coming back to the table.

"Charred on a stick, with the hide and hair still on . . ." Bess suggested.

"Nothing better!" Samuel declared. Their bickerings were over; this was their normal repartee, 'twixt elder brother and bright sister.

Bess sifted the tea leaves with the mote-spoon for twigs, dust and such, then poured the boiling water over them into a large "company-come" china pot, using a larger, stronger measure of leaves than usual economy might dictate. Father would be in need of bracing, if he had stayed as late at the taverns as she suspected.

As she hung the copper kettle back on the fire-rod, she heard his door open, heard the careful thump of his footsteps in the narrow hallway from the rear of the house. Bess took a moment to swipe at her forehead with a dishclout and tuck her raven-black hair into tidier order 'neath her mob-cap. She put a proper daughter's smile upon her face, even a welcoming twinkle in her blue eyes, and presented herself absent of any judgment or amusement over her father's night of Falling From Grace. She willed herself, a long day's chores notwithstanding, to be the cheerful, helpful and dutiful daughter that he had a right to expect.

Not without at least a *wee* bit of teasing, though.

Chapter 3

AT LEAST *they've gotten over whatever plagued them,* Matthew Livesey was happy to note when he took his place at the head of the table, after dutiful hugs and a peck on the cheek from Bess. In a wood house as small as theirs, one could not help hearing voices raised in pique.

"Tea, Father?" Bess offered.

"Bless me, yes!" He enthused, as much as his head would tolerate, at least. "We were hard at it last night at the Widow Yadkin's. Moores, Ramseurs, all the barons and their lot. Harry and his crowd, all the young sparks, going at it hammer and tongs. Deuced polite, they were . . . consid'rin'. Politics, Lord save us!"

"And did the wine flow?" Bess inquired with a grin.

"I expect it did," Livesey allowed, shrugging innocently as he spooned sugar into his tea and added a dollop of cream.

He looked up at his daughter as she took her seat at the end of the table, marveling again at how much like her mother she had become. The same clear skin, the same pert and tapering face, the same shining hair and eyes. Taller by an inch or two than Charlotte; he imagined that was Livesey blood, but the Fairclough side showed through. It was only lately, though, as she had matured, that Bess had developed her mother's unconscious gestures, her wry wit and her side-long, quirky smile that lifted one corner of her mouth, along with the raised eyebrow that had been Charlotte's "dubious" expression. The one Bess wore now.

"Thomas Lakey was there, too," Mr Livesey told her, intent on teasing her in turn. "And his nephew Andrew Hewlett. Young Hewlett expressed the wish that I convey his respects to you, Bess."

"Did he indeed," she replied, composing her face to "placid."

"A well-set-up young fellow. Nice enough, I suppose. Should we be setting out the good china for him anytime soon, hey?" Livesey inquired with a bland innocence of his own.

Bess snorted in amusement. Whether that meant she thought Andrew Hewlett a fine catch someday, or an abysmal lout, he could not discover. But her eyes sparkled with merriment as she quickly deflected his query with her own. "And did Widow Yadkin give you her best respects, too, Father?"

"God rot th . . ." Livesey began to say, blushing as he caught himself. "God forbid, I meant to say. Poor, pop-eyed mort."

"Pop-eyes for you, Father, haw haw!" Samuel said with a snigger of delight. It was no secret that Barbara Yadkin needed a new husband to help her keep and run her inherited ordinary. She was an acceptable enough woman of middling height, years and features; but for the unfortunate way she blared her eyes in any state but sleep, or could be found staring—unblinking for so long it made peoples' eyes water in sympathy—as fixedly as an alligator. And had declared to anyone unlucky enough to have to listen to her rather ewe-like, bleating voice that she thought Matthew Livesey a likely prospect, now his year of mourning was done.

"Not being able to decipher your words through that considerable cud in your mouth, Sam'l, I shall pretend you made no comment." Livesey pretended to huff up, leaning away from his son in mock disgust, and wishing (not for the first time) that Samuel had merely a moiety of Bess's cleverer humor. "We taught you better, surely. And before I say grace? Is it this clime, bad influences in town? We never heard the like of old, I'm bound. Poor manners, a father mocked by his own children! What *is* the world coming to, I ask you?"

He ended with a laugh, his first of the day, and was amazed it didn't pain his throbbing skull as much as it might have. He took a long sip of hot and refreshing tea. Half the maze-y cobwebs seemed to clear of an instant, restoring his humors. Then, he opened the *Book of Common Prayer* which was always by his plate, and found a suitable Collect to read before he asked for a blessing on their breakfast. As he did so, the low-mounted bell at St James's around the corner on Market Street began to toll the hour, as did the smaller bell in front of the courthouse, chiming both the hour and the end of the night curfew for freedmen blacks.

As they ate, he laid down his instructions, as a father must. Samuel to get the barges ready on Chandler's Wharf, instead of going to the sawmills, for they had a ship to load out for the West Indies this morning; for Bess he offered a free day, once the breakfast items were done. He left off further admonitions for Samuel to keep at it. He'd be under his eye today, and Bess had (he had overheard) put the word on him already, so he would not have to hector him like a puppy who'd soiled their one and only decent carpet.

Matthew Livesey garbed himself carefully in sober brown tailcoat and buff colored waistcoat, black tricorne and his long walking stick. He stepped out onto his front stoop and looked about with a pleased grin. The sun was barely up over the eastern rise of Fifth Street and the trackless pine barrens that led to the ocean across the cape, but the sky was clear and blue already. It would be a fine day. A deuced fine day! The street was dry, making for good footing in the light, sandy roadway. A few pushcarts were already at their labors as tinkers, flower vendors, ragmen, milk sellers and vegetable mongers cried their wares. Drays were out as well, heavy wagons drawn by ox teams, or rare and solid draft horses. Mules were in abundance. So too, unfortunately, were pigs and chickens, running free and only partly claimed; and dogs and cats and geese were two-a-penny.

He levered himself down off his high stoop to the road with a wince and a puff, and made his way down the slope of Dock Street, for the waterfront, crossing the roadway which ended above the actual dock which gouged into the foot of the bluff's hill like a rectangular indentation, in which one of the coastal trading schooners from farther up north was being cleaned of barnacles and weed. Being re-stocked, too, with naval stores, with hemp and manila rigging purchased from his stocks, her sails patched with canvas from his own bolts of cloth.

He stopped to savor the sight, as if seeing it all for the first time all over again, as he did almost every morning of his existence.

For there was the river, the Cape Fear, flowing brown as tobacco juice from the Piedmont, stained brown by the pine forest saps, leaf-moldy and rich. Sweet water was the Cape Fear, this high up above the tides, death on the *teredo* worms and ship-borers which ruined vessels. That made Wilmington a much more desirable port than poor, dying Brunswick, sixteen miles down-river near its mouth. Especially after that hurricane of last

September of '61 which had aimed direct for Brunswick, and had ripped the New Inlet open, making a channel a quarter-mile wide and eighteen feet deep at the low tide.

He increased his pace as he neared Water Street which ran along the life-giving river's banks. Eagle's Island on the opposite shore, before the wavering salt-marsh lowlands, smoked with the fumes of the distilleries and rendering try-pots set among the few surviving trees and the wire-grasses which bowed in marshy surrender to the insistent currents and tides, the new sluices and dikes which fed fresh river water to burgeoning rice fields behind them.

And, the Thoroughfare! Not as grand or as broad an anchorage as old Philadelphia, but filled with coastal schooners or corn crackers from up-river settlements, with brigs and even small three-masted ships. Ships from New York, Philadelphia, Boston and New England ports, from Charleston, Georgetown and Savannah, from Port Royal and Beaufort and little Plymouth on the Outer Banks, from New Bern and Edenton along the Albemarle or Pamlico Sounds. Ships from Bermuda, up from the Bahamas, the Salt Isles of the Turks, even from Jamaica and rich Sugar Isles of the Caribbean—timber-hungry, pitch- and tar-needy vessels from the Danish Virgins, the Dutch Antilles, the West Indies and England, too, come for salt-beef, salt-pork or salt-fish, cloth, barrel staves, cut lumber, naval stores and tobacco.

And the in-bound cargoes, now free of the Pratique Grounds by Brunswick, down-river, certified sickness-free, at last! Ships laden gunwale-deep with sugar, rum or molasses, with bolts of cloth, lace, iron, nails or glassware, coffee or tea, with whole carriages, books and newspapers, or fine china and strong brandies, with wines so fine they went down the maw like smoke, Italian marble and New England oak, Hamburg knives, anvils and clocks, English thread or ribbon, shoes or boots . . . Trade! The sinews of Commerce from the whole civilized world were gathered in this struggling but boundless little seaport!

Matthew Livesey had always stood in awe of ships and their goods, from his earliest days toddling 'twixt his father and grandfather along the immense spread of bustling wharves of Philadelphia, with the ships' beakheads spearing to heaven over his head, and every unloading he had witnessed then had felt like the Magi come bearing their gifts for the Baby Jesus. Early on, he'd fallen in thrall at the sight of spars and masts and rigging laced against the clouds, of sailors' cries in dozens of languages and the esoteric foreign tongue of the sailor's trade itself, of the chanty songs of men set to pulley hauley, the jaunty lilts of fiddlers' and fifers' tunes at fore bitters or idle hornpipes, the husky voices of black dock workers in call and response choruses when lading a vessel bound out for somewhere distant.

He stood in awe of such things, still. There had even been a time when he'd thought to flee a fretful teen's drudgery of chandlery work for the life of a jolly sea rover, himself! Like a well-set fore tops'l, Matthew Livesey had felt the press of wide open ocean breezes that led to exotic horizons, and had signed aboard a stout merchantman out of Liverpool . . . for a day. One thrilling day, he had had, before his father had come for him, nigh dragged him down the gangplank by his ear to set him back on his Proper Course before the lines could be cast off, returned him to the role *expected* of him . . . with a shameful bout of lecturing on Familial Duty and Responsibility delivered just before a painful caning! "When I was a Child, I spake as a Child . . . when I became a Man I put away all childish . . . !"

This morning, the Thoroughfare, that safe haven under his adopted town's low bluffs, was aflutter with new-day life, with swooping, keening seagulls and terns. Shoals of mewing herring gulls, so pristine white and gray, or spotty brown piebald pariahs. Here and there his favorites, scoffing like jesters, the black-headed laughing gulls perched on bollards and spars. Snowy egrets across the river, fluffed up and flying like a passing blizzard, and blue herons stalking the marshes. Cormorants on their long, narrow wings, gyring about the swirls and eddies cross-set by current and tide. And the comical spotted brown pelicans which wafted crank-necked round the sterns of ships, looking for a morsel of edible jetsam. He felt like shouting glad greetings to them all.

How could a man of Commerce, he asked himself, allowing himself a moment of almost boyish happiness—how could *any* man gaze upon this, and *not* be inspired by both its beauty and the possible fortune it might represent?

He shooed off a brace of mongrel dogs, and an imperious gander, with his walking stick, shook a good-natured fist at a street-vendor's boy who was miming his gait, and turned south into Water Street to the uneven, graying cypress piers, towards Chandler's Wharf. Who could say, he told himself; this might be the day he'd reap that fortune!

Chapter 4

"SHE CRAB! Blue crab, missus! Soup's on t'night!"

"Fraysh s'rimp, mistuh, big's ya thumb, ten t'the poun'!"

"Scallions . . . wil' onions . . . ha'penny a peck!"

"Bloody Hell," Captain Prouty grumbled at the intruding hawkers' cries. Matthew Livesey shuttered the windows of his small rear office and diminished the volume at least a trifle, so they could continue to conduct their business. "Thankee, Mr Livesey. Loud enough t'wake the dead, damme'f they aren't."

"As you were saying, Captain Prouty, sir." Livesey smiled back, hiding his wince at the sailor's salty language deuced well. "Or, as you were attempting to say, hey?"

He stumped back to his desk and sat down heavily in a chair behind it, the bad leg extended. A bottle of rum stood between them, a good Demerara. Though Prouty tossed it off like mother's milk, and had done so repeatedly for the last hour, Livesey's glass contained a mere dottle of his first pouring in the bottom.

"Lookee here, Mr Livesey," Prouty continued, leaning forward chummily. "Roof shakes an' barrel staves be a fair bus'ness, an' we've turned a goodly profit afore, have we not, sir. But here's my thinkin'. There's 25 pound sterlin' a ton fer sawn lumber, seasoned an' dry, delivered. Teak, Madiera-oak, scrub pine, cypress'r mahogany, those buggers in th' West Indies'r so wood-shy they'd buss yer blind cheeks fer *kindlin'*, damme'f they wouldn't!"

"Granted." Livesey nodded sagely, hiding another wince. While he was not a stranger to blunt, Billingsgate language, he thought of himself as a cultured Christian and strove ever to avoid it, as the mark of a gentleman who had read enough to find other ways of saying *much* the same thing. And had taken the hide off Samuel more than a few times when he heard him practice it.

"Saw it." Prouty beamed, tapping his noggin with a sage wink of one rheumy eye. "Twelve foot, eight foot'n trim. An' keep trim damned spare, short's a whore's promise, get me, sir? They take it pre-cut, they save payin' t'have it done. Three pound more per ton, we could get, me Bible-oath on't! An' not just pre-cut it, oh no!"

Prouty leaned a little more forward on the table, looked about the small, dim office, as if he were plotting mutiny in the fore-peak cable-tier of a "whippin' ship," to whisper his last with the glee of the about-to-be-revenged. "Pre-paneled, sir! Think on't!"

"Hmm," Livesey replied, scrubbing his stubble dubiously.

"Goddamme, sir! They need houses, we send 'em houses!" Prouty sniggered, reaching for the rum bottle. "Twelve foot by eight, eight foot by eight, studs, framin' an' clapboardin' altogether! Forty or more pound a ton we'd fetch, with nailin' an' bracin' included, an' all they'd have t'do is stand 'em up-right, bang 'em t'the roof beams, an' clap on th' roof. A snug little house, up in a week, sir."

"I would suppose doors and window frames would go over as well," Livesey wondered. "But our cost, Captain Prouty . . . the gangs to make those would . . . dear to make, perhaps too dear to vend."

"First inta the market with 'em, an' we'd be rich, sir," the sea-captain intoned. "*Stap* me if they wouldn't eat 'em up like plum duff!" he insisted, banging a fist on the desk for emphasis.

"You'd try a ship-load?" Livesey asked quickly. "On a wager, as it were? To front the venture entire would break me if it failed."

"I'd bear the carryin' charges meself." Prouty cooled, leaning back from Livesey's lack of ardor.

"The cost of nails, of skilled labor . . . hmm . . . your *Lapwing* is two-hundred-tons burthen, that's . . ." Livesey speculated at the number of board feet it would require. "Why, it may cost me upwards of an hundred pounds to run up a ship-load, even *with* cheap timber."

"God's Teeth, yer a slim-parin' bugger, Livesey," Prouty said. "Afore we warp down t'the Dram Tree an' cast off fer Nassau, I'll let ya have me letter o' credit fer . . . thirty pounds. An' twenty pound more o' coin. You put up fifty pounds in lumber, nails, an' what it skelps yer purse t'have 'em run up. I carry th' goods fer free, an' we split even. We judge wrong, well, we're neither out so much. If we judge right, though, an' I drop hook off the Cape fer quarantine with a barricoe o' gold for ya, then ya c'n reckon sure as shite do stink we're onta somethin'. Wot say ye, Mr Livesey, sir?"

"I'd have to work out the costs first, Captain Prouty. Perhaps not this voyage, if you're casting off on the morning tide to fall down-river," Livesey stalled. It was a most promising notion, as seductive as . . . He almost shivered, considering how he'd been seduced the night before into a rash act.

"Run up some, whilst I'm gone, an' see. If ya do bring 'em in fer ten pound a ton, we're hotter'n a fresh-fucked fox, damme'f we're not!" Prouty guffawed, offering his hand in agreement.

Livesey wasn't sure about labor costs, wasn't sure if hired slave gangs could do carpentry work, but if they could . . . for decent fees . . . he stuck out his hand to shake with Prouty. They might just be onto something!

It had been a profitable day, anyway. The last shipment that *Lapwing* had run to Nassau and the Turks had shown nearly five hundred pounds net gain, and the rum, molasses and salt, the tortoise-shell, sugar, whale oil and such that Prouty imported through him would yield more on top of that. Less debts, less wares-left-owing he had sold or warehoused, he might end up two hundred pounds free and clear!

"A dram on it, Captain Prouty. To our new enterprise," Matthew offered, reaching for the bottle. He was interrupted by a rap on the door to the front counters.

"Father?" Samuel called out, sounding a touch tremulous, much like he might if he'd sunk a barge loaded with perishable goods, and Livesey cringed.

"Yes, Sam'l? What is it?" He knocked wood, hopefully.

"Bess is here, Father. With Mr Osgoode Moore? They need you to come out," Samuel implored. Yes, he definitely sounded distraught and imploring.

"Excuse me, Captain Prouty," Livesey said, rocking forward to lever himself erect with the good leg under him, and both hands gripping the heavy desk. He stumped to the door and stepped out into his display hall, among the ship's and bosun's stores, the imported goods and frivolities.

It must be damned . . . he thought; *deuced bad,* he corrected himself. *Bess has been crying. And Osgoode looks like a hanged spaniel.*

"Attorney Moore, sir, good day to you, sir. You wished to see me on some matter?"

"It's Harry, Mr Livesey," Moore almost moaned. "He's dead."

"Dear Lord." Livesey paled. Death, sudden death was no stranger anywhere, most especially in the Cape Fear, where the marshes gave out foetid miasmas, and the heat struck down so many each summer, or the fogs and humid conditions took so many to bloody flux, grippe or quinsy. "But we saw him just last night, Mr Moore, and he was . . ."

"Not took sick, Mr Livesey." Moore grimaced, swallowing as if to stop his bile. "They found him out on the Sound Road, the one that goes to Masonborough? He'd been shot, Mr Livesey. He was murdered!"

"Mur . . ." Livesey gasped. "Shot, you say!"

"A . . ." Osgoode frowned, darting a glance at Bess. Livesey understood, and walked down the counter out of her hearing. "A freedman found him just about sunup, sir. Ran to tell the constable. I was told he'd been, well . . . peppered, Mr Livesey. With a fowling piece. Dear God, his face was gone! And . . ." Moore shuddered. Harry Tresmayne and Osgoode Moore, scion of a cadet branch of *The* Moores, had been political allies in the law courts, borough affairs and the General Assembly. Osgoode Moore had been Harry Tresmayne's trusted attorney as well. "Shot twice! Once in the heart, sir! His very heart!"

"Merciful God." Livesey sighed. "How awful for you, Osgoode. Your dearest friend! And, I know, mine as well. Did you see . . ."

"No, sir. Only told, so far. I thought of you, soon as I heard," Moore muttered on. "The constable came into the courthouse and announced it not a quarter-hour past. I ran into your daughter on my way here. Word had reached the markets, I suppose, so she had already heard, and was coming here, too. I would not like you to think I discomfited her with such horrid news."

"Any clue as to who . . . did it?" Livesey asked. He could not bear to say "killed him" or "murdered him" yet. He could not yet, in fact, grasp the idea that the brilliant, cultured and devil-may-care Harry Tresmayne, a friend for half his life, was even dead.

"Constable Swann threw the nigger in the cells, the one claimed he *found* him," Moore grumbled. "Probably robbed him. Just shot and robbed the first rider he came across. Damn his black blood!"

One thing that Philadelphia-born Matthew Livesey could not get used to in his adopted colony was this constant suspicion of anyone of color—curfews, slave-catchers, whippings and hangings—or the cool, dismissive way the owners looked down upon the owned. No matter how profitable, his father had never invested in the trade, never bought shares in any ship on the Middle Passage; though many of their business associates had. Sons of Ham, that much-fallen dusky tribe, but were they not mentioned in the Bible as people? Not his kind, but still . . .

"Where would a freedman get a fowling-gun, I wonder?" Livesey speculated. "Aren't there laws against it?"

"Well, certainly, Mr Livesey, but . . ."

"And you say Harry was shot twice?" he inquired. "If in head or heart, *once* would have been enough, Lord save us."

"Mayhap the first shot did not suffice," Osgoode said, looking ill. "And when he went to rifle his clothing, he . . . reloaded, then shot again, so there'd be no witness against him. Oh, God . . ."

"Here, Mr Moore, sit you down, sir!" Livesey urged, seeing the young man sink into a half-swoon. "Sam'l, fetch a tot o' that brandy, from the little keg on the counter yonder. Quick, lad!"

Moore put his head on his knees, trembling hands agrip about his temples, running fingers through his hair to his neck, and back again. He sipped the brandy thankfully, and after some few minutes began to resemble a human pallor once again.

"We must see to Georgina," Livesey realized aloud after Moore had regained his feet.

"Oh Lord, Mr Livesey, she doesn't know yet, I'm bound!" Moore exclaimed. "She didn't come into town for Court Sessions with Harry this time. She's still out at Tuscarora."

"Better one of us than the constable or sheriff, Mr Moore," Livesey decided as the elder man. "Better from a long-time friend, or a man from the old regiment."

"I know." Moore sighed heavily. "I'm . . . quicker on a horse than you, sir. Sorry. I'll be the one to ride out."

"Thankee, Osgoode. I'll . . . uhm . . . I suppose someone should see to the . . . uhm . . . remains." Livesey winced. He didn't know which odorous task he disliked least. "I'll send some runners to people who knew him in our regiment who are still in town. We'll care for him."

"Better let me have a stirrup-cup then, if you would, Mr Livesey," Moore requested. "'Tis a ride I'll need to liquor my boots for."

"I'll have one with you, Mr Moore. Sam'l?"

Samuel poured two tots full this time.

"To Harry," Livesey offered.

"And his memory," Moore rejoined sadly.

"And catching the bas . . . the person who did this," Livesey concluded, grim, before they tossed off their drinks.

Chapter 5

COURT SESSIONS, church, militia musters . . . and death . . . were the calls for gatherings, Matthew Livesey mused. The Romans, and the London 'prentices and clerks, had their burial societies to care for departed members, as Masons might gather to inter a fellow brother of a lodge. In Wilmington, it was the militiamen who saw to Harry.

His townhouse was on a verdant half-acre lot at the corner of Princess Street and Second, a prosperous two-story home with a broad front piazza and upper balconies supported by wooden columns turned and carved by local craftsmen to resemble classical Greco-Roman marble. To guard against fires, which swept the tiny wooden town in the middle of pine thickets regularly, Harry Tresmayne had insisted on ballast stones from un-loading ships for the front face and the first-floor walls. It was a genteelly elegant manse, filled with furnishings as fine as any the town could boast, with a personal library of over one hundred volumes—reflecting Harry's discriminating taste, as well as the hand of his wife, Georgina.

It also held a superbly wrought wine cabinet filled with such fruits of the vine as would make a statue sit up and beg.

Sergeant Zebedee Howe was a take-charge, neck-or-nothing sort—which had earned him his half-pike and sash during the War—so he had led the charge when the pony-trap had brought Harry home, past the horrified and grieving house servants, into Harry's wardrobe for burial clothes, the hot-water to bathe the corpse—and some refreshments for the fellow militiamen who had come to render honors to their dead compatriot.

It being a rather warm day for only middle spring, and the task a sad one, they had needed to un-cork a few, and were now almost done—and almost as convivial as an Irish wake.

". . . potted that injun, in the end, after lettin' him take two shots at him," Howe reminisced fondly. "Bowed from the saddle, he did, took off his hat and let him have second honors. Told the bugger that he couldn't shoot worth a tinker's damn. And he was right!"

"Fearless, Major Harry was," Private Moseley interjected, with a firm nod. "A gallant an' fearless gen'lem'n."

"A mite reckless, now an' agin," chimed another. "Not with the lads, now. Not sayin' that. With hisself, he was."

"Them as show no concern for dyin'," Zebedee Howe pointed out, "they live a charmed life. Remember Hoskins now, always mopin' and sighin', turnin' pale as milk? Hung back, God rest his soul. And he got it after all, day we broke that French ambush. He'da charged 'em with us, he'd be alive, 'stead o' gettin' cut down with the others when they volleyed from our right, an' mowed our slow'uns down."

"He lived larger than life," Livesey felt required to say. "He was bolder than any of us. Life'll be dull without Harry around."

"Aye, he *was* grand!" Moseley agreed with enthusiasm. "An' amen t'dull, Mr Livesey. Reckon you got that right."

"Quieter, that's fer certain." Constable Swann sighed. "In the courts, fer sure." Swann had served with distinction as a lieutenant, though not in Harry's half-battalion of their regiment.

"Quieter for the likes o' Moores an' Ramseurs," Moseley sniffed, stifling a belch. "Quit-rents'll still be owin'. Poll taxes'll still be so high a body can't vote. 'Thout Major Harry, who's goin' t'speak fer the small holders an' tradesmen, I ask ye?"

"There's still yer Osgoode Moore, Lakey and his crowd," Swann grumbled. His family was allied with Moores and Ramseurs and the big land owners, the longest-tenured landgraves. There was so little real crime in New Hanover County or Wilmington that Swann's post of Constable was more ceremonial than real: officiating at Court Sessions or serving notices, collecting fees and overseeing unruly ordinaries and the prices they charged, with little real law enforcement.

"He could raise up a power o' good cheer," Moseley sighed as he looked down on the corpse, laid out on a bed coverlet on the floor. "Raise up a power o' storms 'gin them 'at'd oppress us, too." Moseley, in his morose, liquored state, had trouble with saying "oppress." "I just wish t'God he'da been able t'give as good's he got. Drawed his pistols'r somethin'. Not shot down like a dog, way he was."

"He wasn't armed," Constable Swann told them, as they all took a moment to contemplate Harry Tresmayne's body. "Oh, there was his knife in a saddle bag, but he wasn't armed. That Cuffy shot him out of the saddle too quick, and I don't think he was expecting trouble."

"Shot with what, sir?" Matthew Livesey questioned. After one night of weakness—and sociable but abstemious tippling with Prouty, just to be polite—he had limited himself to one well-watered tot of rum, so his acuity was not awash. "Did the freedman have a gun?"

"Hid it, most likely," Swann dismissed easily.

"And where would a freedman black get a gun?" Livesey went on. "Osgoode Moore told me such was against the law. Surely, someone had to have seen the fellow walking about armed before, and told you or the sheriff of it. By the way, just who was he, Constable Swann? I don't recall you naming him."

"Name's London. One of old man Ashe's slaves. Freed him back in '58."

"Why, London's upwards of sixty, if he's a day, and blind in one eye, sir!" Sergeant Howe exclaimed. "All he's good for is crabbin'. Why, damme, everybody knows he's meeker'n water."

"And Mr Tresmayne knew him, too," Constable Swann replied, sulking a bit to have his notions questioned. "Mayhap that's why he was able to get so close. Then even a man with one eye could shoot as well as any."

"How close?" Livesey asked.

"Damn close, Mr Livesey." Moseley shuddered, kneeling at the side of the body. "Lookee here. You boys recall how gritty we could get on the firin' line, firelocks poppin' in our cheeks for hours, 'til they got so hot we had t'pee on 'em t'cool 'em off? We couldn't scrub his face much as we'da liked. Lord save us, there ain't much face left! Major Harry's powder-burned 'round where all them pistol balls struck him, peppery as a gunner'd get. Peppery as we got after awhile."

"Ahum," Samuel said from the corner of the room where he had sat for the last half-hour as the attendants peered morbidly down at the ruin of Harry Tresmayne's once-handsome and distinguished face. He was a young'un—the older men had dismissed his presence, but for sending him on errands to fetch and tote with the house slaves.

"Father?" Samuel said, after being ignored a piece more.

"Yes, Sam'l?" Livesey prompted, displaying patience.

"Well, Mr Harry's coat and things . . ." Samuel blushed. "Mr Moseley's right. His shirt and waistcoat, I recall when you took them off him, they were charred with gunpowder. Little bitty holes like a moth'd been at 'em? And some half-spent powder smudges on his shirt. Had to have been real close, whoever shot him. Maybe no more than a sword-length? Maybe even closer?"

"Bless you, Sam'l, I do believe you're right, my boy!"

Matthew Livesey found occasions to praise Samuel so rare that he made the most of this one, and Samuel straightened from his usual hunched, deferent posture, and positively glowed with unaccustomed delight.

"Major Harry knew the bastard who kilt him, all right," Moseley agreed, swallowing against a hiccup. "Let him get right up to 'im."

"The Cuffy," Constable Swann announced. "To rob him."

"To rob him, sir?" Matthew Livesey scoffed, a trifle more loudly and forcefully than he planned. *Damn all this sociable rum,* he sighed! "Of what, sir?" he continued in a mellower tone. "Here's Harry's watch and fob. Here's his purse, full as it seemed when he left the Widow Yadkin's last night. His silver snuffbox, his gilt shoe buckles and all . . . I see nothing of value missing."

"Mebbe somebody come along an' interrupted London, before he'd had a chance," Swann replied, bristling a little. He was a vain coxcomb, and used to having his own way, and the last say.

"Oh, horseshit, sir!" Zebedee Howe hooted. "Ya shoot a feller, twice! Wake the night, then run off when somebody comes along, *then* trot inta town to report it?"

"And if London did it for loot, then why not go back to the . . . the body, and rifle the clothes after this alleged somebody passed by?" Livesey asked. "No one else reported shots, or finding Harry's body, did they? No, sir. I do believe Mr Howe is correct. This London is a gentle old fellow, so I'm told. He had no gun. And he had none of Harry's valuables on him. And he came direct to you to tell you of it. Now, does that sound like the work of a scheming murderer, sir?"

"Well, now, sir . . ." Swann gargled, turning a pale purple as he contemplated how wrong he might be, how dead-set his friends and neighbors were on the black's innocence—and how much work would be involved in finding the real perpetrator, work which might well be beyond his deductive powers. Swann was rich; that didn't mean he was smart. His place was a sinecure so his wealthy compatriots could control as many county and borough offices as possible.

"Oh, turn the poor bugger loose, will ya, now, Swann?" Zebedee Howe implored wearily. "Old London's a simpleton. He's lucky t'outsmart a crab'r two, but he's no killer. Ashe'd never have made him free, else."

"'Ere's no tellin' how many scoff-laws'r hauntin' the Sound, yonder, Mr Swann," Moseley said, getting back to his feet just a trifle unsteadily. "Stede Bonnet an' Blackbeard's buccaneers, not fifty years back? Rogue Injuns? Highwaymen passin' through, down the New Bern Road? 'Tis a wild, lonely place, here t'the little islands an' the sea, north t'the Holly Shelter swamps. Plenty o' room fer all sorts o' black-hearted rogues t'wander about."

"I'll vouch for London, Constable," Howe offered. "I'll take him on at my place, to keep him close if you find out he's the killer later. Though I can't feature him doin' such, never in a million years. Let the poor ol' feller out, why don't ya?"

"That was well said, Mr Howe," Livesey congratulated him. "A most Christian act."

"Well, thankee, Mr Livesey." Howe flushed red. "Weren't no more nor less'n I'd do for anyone, white or black."

"Well," Constable Swann dithered, gnawing pensive on a knuckle. "Right, then. You take London over t'your place, Howe. I'll remand 'im to ye 'til this is solved. Now, though . . . what'll we do with . . . Harry?" he asked, gesturing at the corpse. "Dress him? Or just wrap him in a windin' sheet?"

"Dress him," Moseley insisted. "In 'is uniform, if ya ask me! Let 'im go inta the ground the brave soldier he was, I say!"

"His face, though . . ." Howe grimaced, tossing off a last gulp of hock. "Town's full, and lots o' people'll turn out for the buryin'. Folks'll wish t'see the body. Better a closed casket, consid'rin' . . . ?"

"Uniform, but with a cloth coverlet over his face, perhaps sirs?" Livesey suggested. "So they remember him the way he was, not . . ." He darted his eyes away queasily. Plum-colored bruises, reddish-black at the center of the many wounds, revulsed him. Livesey more than most wanted to remember Harry Tresmayne the way he'd last seen him, too. There was no face. And the mortal remains left in a hideous relict were now puffy and mottled with rapid decomposition.

Their sad discussion was interrupted by the rattle and clop of a carriage outside, the squeaking and groaning of axles and straps.

"That'll be the coffin comin' from Taneyhill's, I 'spect," the constable said, going to the door to peer out. He blanched, shut the door, and spun to face them, panic-stricken. "Cover 'im! Cover 'im, quick, boys! It's Osgoode Moore, back with the widow. Good Christ A'mighty, Georgina's here!"

Chapter 6

THERE HAD NOT been room in little St James's for all of the mourners, so the doors had been left open, and the vicar, Reverend McDowell, had had to speak up louder than usual. The square little building as yet had no steeple, no belfry but for a ship's bell in a cradle resembling the public stocks, low to the ground. It had been started years before, but still was not finished. The well-to-do of the parish were seated in oak "double-pew" boxes by families; the rest took crude benches in the back, or clustered by the gaping openings that faced Market Street, the river, or the graveyard. Those better-off up from Brunswick, pledged to even tinier St Philip's, sat in carriages or heavy farm wagons outside, fanning off the heat, amid the common folk who'd walked to town.

Samuel and Bess stood on the western lawn, unable to get a seat on the back benches, too poor yet for the purchase of their own pew box. They could see their father, though, up front by the immediate family, dressed in his dark blue and buff colored captain-of-militia uniform, which now hung on his frame like sacking. Too unsteady to lift the coffin as the other militia pallbearers could, he was to bear Harry's sword to the grave.

"Thought we'd be early enough for a seat, anyways," Samuel said, choking in his only formal suit of snuff-colored broadcloth. "They sure turned out early."

"And so many, too," Bess muttered back, pivoting slowly to eye the large crowd. She spotted many faces she'd seen the night before, when she'd gone to Georgina's house to help at the lying-in.

Cape Fear funerals were so different from Philadelphia ones, Bess thought. The larger cities made knowing neighbors harder. But here in the South, *everyone* was a neighbor, expected to "do" for the grieving family. She'd whipped up a hurried sweet-potato pie, a skillet of corn bread and a platter of crab cakes the afternoon before, soon as she had gotten home. It was simply the expected thing to do. Compared to some of the dishes she'd seen, fetched in by friends and neighbors with slave-help in their kitchens, her offering might have looked meager. But, she comforted herself, it was the thought that counted. This *wasn't* charity, she assured herself, and could not ever be taken for it. This was neighborliness: to fill a house with food or drink, so the survivors would not have to bother with mundane things, like cooking, for awhile. They would take care of all earthly cares, to spare the bereft so they could get on with their grieving, and the cares of Heaven.

Grim-faced older women had come running—widows themselves, or weary matrons who had lost beloved children and knew all about grief. They'd commandeered the house and its order from the mistress. They'd flung themselves with sad practice into arranging chairs, or borrowing from others if there weren't enough. The hearth-fires had been slaked, the clocks stopped and draped in black. Mirrors and framed portraits were covered. They'd brought daughters or servants to help with last-minute cleaning, took charge of the house slaves, sent their menfolk or boy children off on errands for whatever was needful, so the house would be prepared to fend for itself, on at least a week's largesse in store. And handle enough left over for those who would come—would surely come—to view the newly dead, and make their shame-faced contact and pay their respects to the bereaved, and sigh most guiltily to be glad it wasn't any of theirs who had been taken—not this time.

The gentry would surely come. But there were others, as well, who'd flock to town to note the passing of one so famous and beloved. Small land owners, tradesmen and hardscrabblers, dockmen and laborers, and their families, who didn't really know Harry, but had known *of* him, and had respected him.

Most were English-born; people who'd been indentured long ago and sold into temporary bondage sometimes as harsh as any the Negroes suffered, far back in the piney woods. A few "transported for life" as criminals who'd fallen shy of being hung—which was the fate of most in the Mother Country—who slaved and scratched a meager living from that trackless wilderness, inland. There was a sprinkling of the defiantly Highland Scots, dressed in a polyglot of tartans and wide, slanted bonnets sporting hackle or wing feathers, with *sporrans* at their waists, *skean dubhs* in their hose-tops:

those who'd been transported after the Rising of '45, come in chains to a new world; or those who'd fled over the seas after giving their Bible-Oath to their conquerors; and their kin who'd followed them to unlimited horizons and larger acreage. It was a murmuring, sometimes roughly guttural, sometimes musical, Gaelic they spoke.

And even more Irish, or Scotch-Irish, clad in rough home-spun, and flax and hemp. Some even garbed in deer leather whose least words sang with Cymric rhythms, over from the nearby Welsh Tract from South Carolina. A few freedmen Negroes, here and there, too. But for the most part, these backwoods folk, these near-town folk, were not slave owners, or at best had only one or two. Most depended on their own sweat, or that of their many children.

Bess had been amazed to see these work-worn, sun-baked, dry-as-apple-face-doll folk come shyly to that stately house the night before to queue up and wait for hours for one last look at the legendary gentleman, Harry Tresmayne.

There, that old man yonder! she noted. He'd touched the wood of the coffin on its bier with a tentative hand, a hand gnarled by a lifetime of hard labor, ungainly and nut-brown; and as shyly as if it had been one of his own who'd passed over. There, another fellow, in poor-fit home-spun, who'd gone to bow to Aunt Georgina and nod, crying real tears as he'd mumbled out a barely intelligible, raw, unpolished, but genuinely heartfelt expression of loss to her.

Bess noted there were few of the true aristocrats present, not in the outside crowd, at least, or listening from the rare, well-made carriages. Some had come to the house to pay grudging respects. Oh, but they were a prideful, testy and irascible lot, and Harry Tresmayne and his clique of younger men had gored them sore, been their bug-a-bear! They were a thin-skinned, touchy folk, jealous of their honor and privileges as the first, and best-off, settlers. And held their grudges, Bess sighed, with the tenacity of wild Indians.

"Even unto the grave," Bess murmured to herself.

"Hhhh?" Samuel asked, drawn by her whisper from ogling those prettier of the common-folks' daughters crowded close about them.

"Nothing." Bess shrugged. It was politics; it was men's doings, and there was nothing a mere woman could ever hope to say about it.

Though it was an early morning service, it was already humid, and warm. It had rained the night before—merely a passing drizzle—now and again, and the damp churchyard and lawn almost steamed in the springtime heat. A fitful breeze, which was much cooler, now and then came from the southeast, off the ocean. She looked heavenward, envying the birds who could be reached by that breeze, the pine tops and swaying oak boughs in the forests close at hand. Thankfully it was clear, the sky such an incredible hue of blue, set off by high-piled banks of stark white clouds which loomed over the distant ocean, over the sounds to the south and east. Farther back in the Piedmont, higher up and closer to God, she'd heard some settlers who hailed from there call it Carolinas Blue. As if that hue presaged a benign and merciful God's blessing on all who walked beneath it. Bess hoped that was so. Her father was worried, his brow furrowed far beyond his grief—worried about what Uncle Harry's murder boded. They might soon be in need of a blessing.

"Into Thy hands, O Merciful Saviour, we commend Thy Servant . . . Harry Tresmayne. Acknowledge, we humbly beseech Thee, a sheep of Thine own fold, a lamb of Thine own flock, a sinner of Thine own redeeming . . ." the elderly Rev. McDowell pronounced in sad conclusion, his voice soft and echo-ey from within.

Now what's so funny 'bout that? Bess wondered. She flushed hot with indignation as she heard the faint sniggers from the crowd, which was pressed so hound-warm around them. She turned her head to peer, to see both men and women wearing sly smiles, half-shaded and shared under wide brims; waggish looks, thrown cutty-eyed.

". . . let us go forth, in the name of Christ!" the vicar ended.

"Thanks be to God," Bess murmured, as she crossed herself with the rest. A great many of the mourners of the humbler sort were satisfied that they'd seen their champion into the ground, proper, and were beginning to thin out, to wander away as the burial party left church behind the coffin, for a new-dug grave. Her father marched behind the coffin, sheathed sword held level. Behind him came Osgoode Moore and Thomas Lakey, to either side of the widow Georgina.

"She's bearing up main-well," Samuel whispered as they moved closer, down into the graveyard.

"Poor lady." Bess nodded. Georgina was at least fifteen years younger than Harry had been, as were her escorts. Harry Tresmayne's first wife had been nearer his age, nearer their father's age, but she had died in '57, two years after they'd moved to the Cape Fear. Once home from the War, Tresmayne had married Georgina in '60.

Bess had been to the wedding, since Harry had been like a distant uncle to her. They had made a most handsome couple.

Grieving though she was, Georgina Tresmayne was still a most handsome woman. She was slim and trim, poised and elegant, with a languid, willowy demeanor, cool green eyes and golden hair. In her dark blue sack gown, bereft of white lace or satin trim for the sad occasion, and a dark hat and veil, she was still poignantly lovely as she walked bravely to the grave, not depending on the offered arms of Moore or Lakey, almost crushing her small prayer book in trembling hands.

The graveside service was mercifully brief: a spoken prayer, the sandy soil cast down as uniformed militiamen lowered the coffin, and the committal. They recited The Lord's Prayer, and Rev. McDowell read the shortest blessing before dismissing them. Bess and Samuel waited for their father to join them as the thinner crowd of mourners milled past them.

"Timin's ev'rything, don't ye know," one of the younger sons of the Ramseurs, who held acres below Wilmington on the long cape-land near Myrtle Grove, said with a sly snigger to his wife as they strolled past. "He couldn't have had a larger audience if he'd had his heart set on't. Theatrical to the end, he was."

"Sir," Mr John Burgwyn interrupted, full of pique. "Slur the dead, would you, sir?" John and Margaret Burgwyn farmed The Hermitage near her father's plantation, Castle Haynes, up north. Burgwyn was the most respected, the most civilized, man New Hanover County could boast, and usually showed the world a genteel and unruffled face.

"Mr Burgwyn, sir." The Ramseur scion blushed. "I find it most like poor Mr Tresmayne's gestures in life, that he passed over at a time when most of the Quality would be in town to attend the funeral." Blushing or not (most likely at getting caught being snide, Bess thought) Ramseur was bristling with indignation at being called down.

"And I would expect . . . *sir* . . . that Harry Tresmayne's passing would have brought out the same numbers, were he interred in a full-blown hurricane," Burgwyn replied in an arch tone, the sort of high-nosed pose only a graduate of Eton *and* Oxford could manage. It was said in a very calm voice, but it pricked like a rank of bayonets.

"For shame!" Bess found herself saying, and almost gulped in fright at her boldness. *Damme,* she thought; *I've gone and done it again!* Not only could she not manage "languid," she had difficulty with keeping properly demure. And silent in men's affairs.

"I believe Mistress Livesey speaks for all of us," Margaret Burgwyn added. "And deuced well said, too. For shame, sir, indeed."

"Errp," Young Ramseur rejoined at last. "I . . . hahumm! Mean no disrespect, I assure you, ma'am . . . sir. You will excuse us . . . ?"

"Compliments to your father, sir," Mr Burgwyn said in parting, lifting his hat and making the slightest "leg" for a departing bow as the Ramseurs fled, most un-genteelly and un-languidly.

Matthew Livesey joined them, plucking at the warm wool uniform he wore, and fanning himself with his cocked military hat. His eyes were still pink and moist with final tears.

"Good day to you, Mr Livesey."

"Good day to you as well, Mr Burgwyn," Livesey offered in kind. "Ma'am. I don't recall you meeting my children before? Allow me to name to you my son, Samuel. My daughter, Elisabeth . . . Bess."

"A bold young lady, sir," Mistress Burgwyn commented. "And an honest one. A credit to you, sir. And a joy, I'm bound."

"I must have missed something?" Livesey shrugged hopefully. His generation didn't approve of young ladies anywhere *near* "bold"! But a quick recital of events reassured him, and he beamed approval at Bess, of her sentiments and her bravery, as it ended.

Good-byes were said, and a vague invitation offered as they bowed or curtsied, then the Burgwyns were off down Market Street on the short walk to their in-town residence, and the Liveseys were left to make their own way home.

"How dare anyone scoff, or speak ill of the dead?" Bess asked in a huff. "Of *anyone* barely in the ground, not just Uncle Harry! I should think, at a funeral at least, people might set aside their grudges. Granted, Mr Tresmayne . . . Uncle Harry, rowed them beyond all temperance by championing the common folk, but surely . . . !"

So like dear, departed Charlotte, Livesey was pleased to admit again; the same upright furrow between her brows, a tiny departure from placid perfection that only someone familiar with her, or her angers, would ever detect. Or know for what it was.

"He was building a constituency, Bess," Livesey told her. Bold young ladies might be disturbing to him, but ignorant women were a deal worse in his estimation, so he was open with her. "I think he'd begun before the War. Perhaps even as long ago as Harvard. Then, there were things we experienced up north. Hmm, let us say we Colonials, not just militia forces, were poorly regarded at best by people out from England, officers or rankers alike. Top to bottom, there was an arrogance from them. Open signs of our . . . inferiority." He smiled briefly.

"The same sort of arrogance our 'barons' display here, Father?" Bess inquired, lifting an expressive brow. Yes, her mouth had curled up at one corner, Livesey noted, just like Charlotte's used to.

"Exactly so," he replied with a sardonic grin of his own.

"So it was most opportune . . . for someone . . . that Uncle Harry died, before any up-start constituency could arise, is it not?" Bess asked. "Was faction the reason for his death, do you think, Father?"

"Dear Lord," Matthew Livesey groaned. He was still having devilish trouble accepting the fact that Harry Tresmayne had been killed, and had been thinking more along Ezekiel Moseley's line: a random murder by a scoff-law or highwayman. Yet if faction, and politics, and expanding the franchise by lowering the land and property values necessary to qualify as a voter, or the minimum yearly income requirements—or legislating a two-shilling poll tax instead of the present five or six shillings—was the motive, then the murder of Harry Tresmayne was even fouler a deed than mere robbery or hot-blooded anger.

Christ save us, Livesey gloomed, getting a chill as he imagined that one of the aristocratic planters who had just left the funeral, and had wept a dram of "crocodile tears" in public, was secretly a murderer! Or had paid some dock worker, shipyard or sawmill bully-buck to do it! The actual murderer might have come riding postillion, as coachee, or "catch-fart" valet to his master, to gloat over his crime!

"That could be why, Father," Samuel ventured to opine. "It was his enemies did him in, to keep their control, surely."

"It does bear thinking about," Matthew Livesey grudgingly rejoined. "But . . . I adjure you . . . both of you," he said, drawing them to a halt. "Some things might best be held in the mind, but never said in public. If powerful men would stoop to such a dastardly deed . . . and mind you, I only said 'if' . . . then those who speak such suspicions might draw the same sort of attention upon themselves. An excuse to a duel for you, Sam'l."

"I'm not afraid, Father, of any . . ."

"Do you heed what I say, lad!" Livesey stormed up, taking his son by the shoulders. "Until it's proven, and indictable in a court of law, it's a rumor, an ugly rumor. Sheer, spiteful gossip, and calls for a defense of one's honor, even from an innocent man. And if true, but unprovable, a reason for whoever had it done to send a pack of hellhounds to silence the accuser."

"Or cause whoever did it," Bess wondered aloud, "to become so careful and guarded, they could never be discovered?"

"Bright lass!" Livesey nodded in continuing agreement. "So you will *not* bruit this about. Cleave your tongues to the rooves of your mouths, hear me? Don't mention this to anyone. And if somebody else does say it, you do *not* have to pipe up and agree with 'em! Have you understood that, Sam'l?"

"Yes, Father," he replied in a small, chastened voice.

"And you, Bess? You'll guard your . . . bold . . . thoughts for me? Just this once?" He frowned, though with less fear for her discretion.

"I will, Father," she swore.

"Good," he relented, with as much peace of mind as a father could rightly expect. "Another reason, beyond safety, is that we're not so long in the Cape Fear that we've call to accuse people we don't know well. And . . . venal as this may sound to you . . . we live or die on the good will, and *custom,* of our neighbors. Perhaps of the very people, or person, who might . . . Lord!" He realized at once. He might have had dealings in past—might deal this very afternoon—with his friend's murderer! The idea gave him a queasy chill under his heart. "Forgive me, it *does* sound venal and low of me! Oh, how I wish we were landed again, so we could close up and retire to the country until Harry's murderer is found. If it is one of our own customers, I don't know how I will be able to live with the idea of trading with the . . . with him."

"They could ruin our business, by withdrawing their custom?" Bess summed up with a cool logic, though posing it as a question so she didn't sound too interfering. "But to close up just when all the ships are returning after winter, for fear we might be tainted, would that not be ruin just as certain, Father?"

He looked at her sharply, one eyebrow raised.

"Forgive me, I know 'tis none of my concern . . . you and Sam'l are the men of the house, after all, but . . ." She blushed. *Damme,* she thought, *now I'm beyond "bold"—I sound like a mercenary harridan! And a heartless one! God, take my tongue out by the roots before I do something horrid with it!*

"It would be foolhardy, yes," Mr Livesey gloomed. "Do nought for Harry's memory . . . look like cowardice on my part . . . and ruin our hopes for the future. No, much as it pains me . . . life . . . and business, must go on. We'll all have to keep mum . . . wear a fool's face like a 'Merry Andrew.' Else we lose all we've built back up, and have to start over somewhere new again. And I don't know as how I could."

"You could do anything, Father," Bess assured him, wishing to cheer him. And atone for her previous comment.

"Well," Mr Livesey sighed. "Back home. A cold collation, a change of clothes. Then back to work. Heartsick or not, there is business doable before sundown. We'll take a day o' rest of a Sunday."

Chapter 7

BETWEEN HARRY TRESMAYNE'S Wednesday burial and the Sabbath, little Wilmington stirred like an anthill with rumor or speculation. What Matthew Livesey had warned his children never to speak of was thrown up to him across his sales counter daily! In ordinaries or taverns, or the lone coffeehouse, men of every social stripe kicked their heels over claret, or cheap persimmon beer, and winked grimly to each other as they imparted their particular slant on the murder.

Some thought Arthur Dobbs, the Royal Governor, who presided over the colony at his manse—Russellborough—down-river near Brunswick, had ordered Harry killed to squash the so-far small group of independent-minded thinkers who chafed at far-off London's disdaining, lordly grip on them.

There were others less canny who thought Dobbs *responsible* for it. But they were the ones who were rock-ribbed certain that Dobbs's recent engagement to a fourteen-year-old girl, young enough to be one of the seventy-two-year-old dodderer's granddaughters, a sign of such licentiousness that God would hurl a bolt at Wilmington again. They were also the same who thought that the New Inlet hurricane, coming just days after the announcement of George the Third's coronation, was His mark of Holy Wrath against the whole sinful Hanover royal line!

Common folk and humbler men whispered that Harry, their paladin, had been done in by the rich and powerful, and the Ashe, Ramseur, Lillington, Howe and Moore names were cited often—and none too charitably, either. There was darker talk, too: of midnight vigilance meetings, of gathering weapons so armed men might find a way to exact justice, or of issuing some vague new Magna Carta for the Cape Fear against the barons and the landlords.

Constable Swann was in a bad way. No one could understand his freeing the Negro, yet doing nothing to solve the murder, as if those in power held him in check. Yet those in power harangued him to solve it quickly before those rumors of riots became real!

And there were some—the callous or the calculated—who didn't think that politics had been the reason at all. They winked and snickered lasciviously in speculation over exactly *which* outraged husband, father or jealous lover had killed Harry Tresmayne for topping his wife, daughter or *amour.* Which usually led to the much more interesting topic of which woman, or women, were prim as Prudence in their parlors, but secretly wanton and abandoned in Harry's embrace.

Damme, Matthew Livesey was forced to swear to himself in rare abandon of his own, as he watched the turmoil simmer, *now there are some as wish to blame Harry's . . . inability to master himself . . .* Livesey termed it charitably *. . . as the reason for his murder! As if he's to blame! Merciful God in Heaven, was he not the* victim?

Matthew Livesey had always lived a fairly mundane, circumspect life. His parents and grandparents had seen to that, with a rectitude worthy of Quakers, Puritans or Dissenters. Had they been on Earth in Cromwell's time, they'd have cheered his Round Heads! The Liveseys had been Lowland or Border Scots in the hallowed past, Presbyterian or Calvinist, 'til their branch had been seduced to resettle in Ireland as the Scotch-Irish, had even *dabbled* with the Church of England, before emigrating to the Colonies.

Despite the usual schoolboy capers, Livesey's life had been one of unremarked civility and probity . . . 'til he'd done that part-year at Harvard, of course, and had fallen in with the irrepressible Harry Tresmayne and some other like-minded Southern scholars. Right, Harry *had been* a wastrel in their mutual youth, who'd come back to their lodgings or the lecture halls still reeking of the past night's pleasures.

And it still made Livesey cringe to remember that he had gone out cavorting with Harry a time or two, seduced to Folly, expecting to gawp in proper Christian terror of what he might discover, then found that late evenings, music and song, wine, beer and strong spirits at-table with clever, witty fellows didn't *seem* like damning Mortal Sins! And if Livesey could never bring himself to partake in the fleeting pleasures of chambermaids or brothel inmates, no matter how alluring or coy they'd beguiled him in the taverns,

Harry had never pressed him to it, would only go off with a wink and a smile, and a girl on his arm, and never made Livesey feel less a boon companion for staying behind, and called him "Saint Augustine," as if marvelling at his restraint! In like wise, Matthew Livesey could never bring himself to feel revulsion for Harry's youthful indiscretions, his breezy explanation of "gather ye rosebuds while you may," nor had he ever chaffered him about them as a dutiful Christian ought to chide the misled. For he and Harry were, in all other respects, as alike in intellect, in scholarly pursuits, in politics, in the deeper sentiments as "two peas in a pod" and were, inexplicably, seemingly destined to be friends as dear as soul mates, evermore. They simply had different ways of going about things!

Livesey could see where Harry had gotten it, once they had come to the Cape Fear, for the region *was* licentious, its young girls what they called "obliging" or "round-heeled" and not just the lower sorts, either. The frontier, perhaps the warmer climate, so different from New England, enflamed the hotter humors of their blood, so that even the best families had their scandals, their secret jades and open rake-hells, their sword-point weddings and suits for support of unexpected offspring! At least in North Carolina, some wags chortled, it was white men and white women who cavorted. Up to patrician Virginia, or grandee South Carolina, Lord . . . *any* combination was possible, usually involving "refined" white misses and stable hands, or scions of wealthy "nobles" caught atop a house slave . . . or a fetching female cousin!

Right, Livesey thought; Harry had returned from Harvard, after his expulsion, to such a heady stew of hedonism. And, granted, Harry had more than likely been "free" among the local girls . . . *before* his first marriage, of course. Harry Tresmayne had ever been a comely fellow, tall enough, slim enough, and had always cut an air of roguish good cheer and romantic-but-dangerous allure that was all but patented to make any woman swoon. He rode well and hard, hunted and fished, gambled close and deep, and had the luck of the devil. He also could dance, converse, spin tales so enchanting . . .

But, Matthew Livesey thought, he'd married in his late twenties, as a fellow *should*—one of the Sampson girls, of a good family. Harry had made his own, and her dowried, plantings the envy of the region.

But there had been no issue from his twelve-year union with his late wife, Priscilla, Livesey realized. But again, he thought, in the two years that he had seen them together, as close to his own family as cater-cousins, had he ever seen Harry treat Priscilla with anything but doting and intimate affection? He thought not! And in her long illness, Harry had been by her side, sleeping and awake.

But . . . a year after her death, when glib Harry had lured Matthew north with him in the 2nd Regiment, their line of march had been strewn with camp followers, laundry girls, outright whores or those lovely-but-neglected "grass widows" who had borne the second heir for their husbands and were now relegated strictly to housekeeping roles, while the husbands—their duty to continue their lines over—dallied with younger mistresses for pleasure, not obligation.

As he had at Harvard, Harry had come to the officers' mess at dawn as fagged as his horse, almost every morning. And if he slept in their tent lines, or alone, it was a rare evening.

Yet, he had come back to Wilmington a little before Matthew had been able to travel, after the militia forces were disbanded, and had married almost at once. And married deuced well, too, Mr Livesey thought! Georgina was one of the most beautiful women of the Cape Fear settlements, fifteen years his junior, and had brought him even richer, more fertile acreage. After selling off some, and combining hers and his, he had founded Tuscarora, over three thousand acres of rice, cotton, tobacco, corn, hemp, indigo and timber-stands northwest of Wilmington on the far bank of the river.

Even in his pain, and his grief, Matthew Livesey had rejoiced for his friend Harry. He was once more settled, after finding himself again, with a lovely and accomplished younger wife. Harry had been outwardly fond, almost doting, towards Georgina, to the amusement of some, and the envy of others.

Matthew Livesey did not wish to think ill of the dead, but . . . had Harry *not* been able to master his penchant for fleshy diversions? Sordid as it was, would that be Harry's legacy—to be remembered as an adulterer? Would people still titter ten years hence whenever they recalled him? *God forbid!* Livesey thought.

❦

That Sunday, Constable Swann was no closer to discovery, and it had come to prey on Livesey's mind something sinful. Keeping his own thoughts to himself all week had vexed his patience, too. And, he had had another bad night. There had been little pain in his stump, but a disturbing dream had plagued him. Just a tiny snippet of a dream, but one which had brought him up short, waking with a horrified gasp, soiled and dishonorable. And made Livesey's Sabbath a shameful sham.

He had dreamt he was dining in a grand house, a rich house, one filled with art and books, and furnished fine as a duke's palace. He had sat at a polished cherrywood table long enough for twelve, with a lace runner down the center, set with compotes and servers of gleaming coin-silver. Sterling candelabras burned expensive bees' wax candles, not his usual tallow or rush dips, and everything glowed honey-gold.

He had dreamt Samuel sat to his left, dressed in silks and satin, under a powdered wig, conversing most wittily about John Locke and Voltaire with equal ease.

Bess had been on his right in a gleaming white sack gown awash in fripperies, adrip with strands of pearls, and a heavy gold necklace, bracelet and earrings set with stones which matched her eyes.

At the end of the table, where a hostess would sit, where a wife would preside, was a woman who'd made the dream-Livesey flush warm in his chest with affection and pride.

He had dreamt of Georgina Tresmayne!

Her intriguing, green cat's eyes fluoresced in the candle flames, entrancing him, drawing him in. Her lips parted, and her perfect white teeth were bared as she laughed at some witticism he had made but could not recall, as she gazed at him so fondly. Livesey was drawn closer, flying inches above the table runner, snaking around compotes, wine bottles and steaming made dishes, as if people could aviate at will, as easily as a mesmerized gnat!

Then, without knowing quite how he had gotten there, he had been seated on the side of a high bedstead, one of luxurious goose-feather mattresses and fine-loomed cotton sheets, not his normal scratchy linen, or cotton-waste stuffed pads. He could still recall the feel of heavy silk against his thighs from the bedgown he had dreamt he wore.

And there was Georgina, kneeling before him! In a retiring gown of her own so translucent only a husband should ever see. And she was massaging his stump. And he sighed with pleasure at her gentle touch as she took away his constant dull aching. Kissed it and took away all his shame for once. And made him swoon with arousal.

She stood up. Stepped close to him, close enough to breathe in her light, sweet aroma of jessamine. Her eyes were huge now, and her face peered down somber with want. Her hands went to the small of her back and the retiring gown fell away like mist before a morning wind!

Hands on his shoulders, her knees outside his. Long golden tresses teasing across his shoulders. Large pink nipples brushing at his cheeks! The musky aroma of a woman's breath as she bent down for him, as she raised his face to hers, as he reached for her to seize her flanks, stroke her round bottom, to bring her forward against his aching tumescence. And at her elbow, suddenly, a silver tray with a pair of fine German crystal wineglasses, shimmering amber with sherry held by a servant in livery.

But it hadn't been livery. It had been Colonial Militia blue-and-buff. And with the illogic of dreams, Livesey had dreamt that he reached for a glass, looked up to dismiss the servant . . .

And had come awake, thrashing, chilled to his marrow, with an inarticulate shout of pure terror for his loathsome betrayal. And, with his flannel bedgown sodden with the proof of it.

Matthew Livesey had never known another woman except his dear, departed Charlotte. Nor had ever wanted to, while she was alive. And no matter how Wilmington's "buttock-brokers" and matchmakers connived since his year of mourning had officially ended, he had saved his energies for work. Sore as he'd been tempted, he'd avoided those few jades who sold their pleasures. With iron will, he'd retained his essences, knowing, as any educated man did, that too much spending of a body's vitality sapped one's force, shortened the breath and weakened will. So that nocturnal emission left him feeling betrayed by his own weak body, just as much as he felt he'd betrayed Harry *and* Georgina.

Re-marriage was just as much out of the picture. He sorely missed his Charlotte, truly the closest and most wonderful friend he'd ever known. He had a business to save, first and foremost. And he had his and Charlotte's children to care for, in the second instance. It was a father's duty to do his best for them. And it seemed fitting to Livesey to deny himself and provide for their futures so that some part of Charlotte, of him, and of their marvelous life together, would continue down the generations as a living memorial to that good woman. So he had inured himself to a sober life which honored her memory, a life which allowed no improprieties which harmed the Livesey name. He saw his own pleasure, his own wants, as distractions he'd outlived. He had no wish to sully the times they'd shared. Still, he was a man, a widower. Georgina was now a widow. After a year of mourning, since they'd been close as cater-cousins before . . . there was Tuscarora, and security, and she was so . . . !

He shook himself, like a bear just leaving a winter den. It was a *damnable* fantasy! A whole host of mortal sins to even imagine! Thank God, he thought, that Georgina had not attended Divine Services at St James's that morning, else he'd have ended staring at her, or greeting her in the churchyard, wearing that dream, and she would have seen his rapacious designs for what they were, and recoiled in utter disgust from his pecuniary lust to gain all that Harry had, and shunned him forevermore after. Or if she laughed such hopeless pretentions to scorn . . . !

Matthew Livesey wondered how he would face Georgina Tresmayne in future, as long as that brief, uncontrolled instant of desire was in him, tamped down though it was, buried in remorse. He had the sad notion it would arise every time he saw her, forevermore.

"Ahem? Another dish of blueberry jumble?" Bess asked louder.

"Uhmmph?" he grunted, surfacing at last from pustulent musings. "No no, I've eat sufficient, thankee, Bess. Wool-gathering. Have I missed some brilliant conversation whilst I was away? I didn't give either of you permission to do something foolish in my stupor, hey?"

"No, you didn't, Father," Bess grinned.

"More's the pity," Samuel muttered.

"Should have struck while the iron was hot, me lad," Matthew Livesey replied, trying to shed his gloominess. "Too late now."

"I would ask your permission for something, Father," Bess bid him. "The Burgwyns have invited me to a tea this afternoon. May I be allowed to attend?"

"The Burgwyns?" Livesey brightened. "Hah hah, that's moving up in Wilmington Society, ain't it?" They'd had little dealings with John Burgwyn so far, even though he owned five ships that traded as far away as Barbados, London and Amsterdam. "Are they scenting about for an arrangement, with the business? Or, is it reward for the way you took that Ramseur oaf to task the other day?"

"The reward, I should expect." Bess grinned. "I leave agreements over trade to you, Father."

"And they didn't invite me. Oh, well." Livesey shrugged. "Of course you may attend, Bess. 'Tis little enough diversion you get."

"Tea with the Burgwyns!" Samuel said, almost singing. "Lick on the cream cakes, cat-lap with the latest gossip. Meow, Bess! Sweet puss! And will Andrew Hewlett be there, too, hmm? Hmm? Meow?"

"Oh, don't be so tiresome, Sam'l," Bess replied in an arch tone just snippy enough to arouse her father's curiosity, and raise a paternal brow in query. "Well, what if he may be? *I* mean . . ." she said, exasperated.

"Hmm!" Livesey japed her, stroking his clean-shaven chin.

"Meow-meow! Lap-lap!" Samuel reiterated. "Purrrr! Will our sweet puss come home with her fur aw wuffled, hmm?"

"Now you *are* being tiresome," Livesey corrected. "*And* lewd."

"Sorry, Father," Samuel coughed, though he didn't seem a least bit abashed, too intent on cocking a jeering eye at Bess, to nettle her even more with a silent "Meow" in her direction, and a licked "paw."

"And you, Sam'l?" Livesey asked.

"Ah, ahum?" Samuel answered, caught in mid "lick," and turning cutty-eyed and cautious. "Well, some of the lads, d'ye know . . . we had the mind to go birding on the far banks. Bag some ducks? Go birding, with the double gun? I know how you and Bess like a good duck . . ."

"Some of the lads," Livesey posed slowly, dubious. "Might one of those 'lads' be Jemmy Bowlegs? Is that why you don't name them?"

"Jemmy's all right, Father." Samuel blushed, defending carefully.

Jemmy Bowlegs was an "all-nations," his heritage as varied as a dram-shop: English, Irish, part Lumbee or Cherokee—part Negro, some said. And a lanky, swaggering lay-about. Hunter, fisherman, trapper, guide, idler . . . and slave-catcher, when he cared for real work. Pig-ignorant of letters, of grooming, of . . .

"Hmm . . . I've a thought, Sam'l," Livesey senior mused. "Let's go riding. Hire us three horses from Taneyhill's livery. Bess and I will fetch down our saddles whilst you do that. We'll take Jemmy with us. As our guide, as it were."

"Really?" Samuel perked up with surprise, then deflated, then perked up once more. It was rare the last two years for them to spend much idle time together, at fishing, hunting or sailing, as they had before their come-down. Work, eat together, some brief, glorious son-to-father talks, but . . . It should have been a festive rarity, elating to his starved heart. But Samuel had also been looking forward to a bachelors' holiday with friends, where he could curse, smoke, spit and share a stone crock of corn whiskey, away from disapproving eyes. And Jemmy had sworn he knew of a poor-white settler's daughter across the river, near Belleville Plantation, of the "most *obligin'* sort." And a tumbledown shack where he and the other lads could, for half a crown . . . ! Samuel shivered, torn most horrid. And picturing spending close-binding time with his righteous father on *that* sort o' hunt!

"Thought we'd ride out east," Livesey commented as he rose from the table with a grunt of effort. "The three of us."

"Oh, well, yes we could," Samuel quickly agreed, thankful that he hadn't chosen the far bank of the river, where they might come across his other friends, indulging, and how would he ever explain that? "East, d'ye say, Father? Of course! Though, I doubt there's much sport left in those woods, these days."

"Bring along the double, anyway," his father suggested, almost smirking as if he knew all from the outset; but it was just his fertile mind which gave him that probing look. "You never can tell what we may bag, Sam'l."

Chapter 8

A HARPSICHORD was being tortured by clumsy fingers, while a violin "squawrked" now and then on an awkward bowing. The flautist was the best of the three young girls who were grimacing their way through Cultured Attainments in the salon. And that was being charitable.

Bess stood by one of the floor-to-ceiling windowed doorways that led to the front porch, trying to avoid wincing in public at the sounds, since the mothers of those struggling daughters were peering about the salon to see if everybody else was enjoying the music with as much outwardly-rapt pleasure as they were. And those mothers had husbands so well off they could buy out Livesey & Son half a dozen times over if they felt slighted. Bess caught the eye of one, and widened her frozen but polite half-smile a notch more.

"Bloody Hell," Mrs Barbara Yadkin whispered *sotto voce* at her side, "but they're giving that pig a *rare* cobbing!"

Bess jerked with a sudden snort of thankfully inaudible amusement, almost upsetting her tea cup on its saucer. She flushed with embarrassment and had to turn away toward Mrs Yadkin, thinking she'd never get another invitation if she broke one of the Burgwyn's precious Meissen china cups brought all the way from Hamburg!

She stepped out onto the wide veranda where there was a bit of a breeze. Mrs Yadkin followed her, eyes blared and brows higher than most people's hairlines. "And how is your dear father bearing up after the loss of his compatriot, my dear?" she asked.

"Main-well, considering, ma'am," Bess answered, doomed to more of Mrs Yadkin's love-struck grilling. "He and Sam'l went riding."

"Bless me, he's a wonder, to get about so!" Mrs Yadkin gushed. "To take his mind off his *cruel* loss, I'm bound."

"I would imagine, ma'am," Bess replied, opening her fan to beat some coolness on her face. There were others who had no ear for music (or who did, and had escaped) seated under the trees, or walking in the shade on the small front lawn and veranda. Bess felt dawkish and dowdy.

The women wore fine gowns of the costliest imported silks and satins, velvets and cambrics. They had the latest hats, and richer women had bound up their long hair over bracings, topped them with convoluted wigs and floured them pale white. Bess was one of those few present who "wore her own hair," regretting her choice of bonnet. It was humble straw, drop-brimmed and much too wide for fashion, but with no gaudy profusion of wide (and expensive) ribands, no plumage or costly lace-work or cloth-of-silver trim to make it acceptable.

Her gown was modest pale blue taffeta, unrelieved by lace or silk ruchings. The neckline was round, higher than most, and bound from each shoulder to the bodice with pleats and folds, while other girls more daring were almost bare-shouldered, with necklines low and square-cut. She had a simple gingham apron, trimmed with scrap taffeta, while others' were so lacy and gaudy, so intricate, so . . . it was her long winter's best effort, and it seemed so . . . dowdy.

". . . so gladsome that night, with a rare night out," Barbara Yadkin was rattling on. "Three bottles they shared, and the best my house could boast, they were, too."

"I'm sorry," Bess said, coming back to reality from envious and useless perusal of the fashion parade. "You were saying, ma'am?"

"La, don't 'ma'am' me, Bess," Mrs Yadkin simpered. "I feel I may address you as 'Bess,' not 'Elisabeth,' your father's talked so much about you, and rare 'tis when he says Elisabeth. Him and poor Harry Tresmayne, you know. Their last night at my establishment."

Establishment sounded more refined than "ordinary." Her "establishment" was a log-framed cabin set back on a half-acre town lot to make room for water trough, hitching posts and mounting blocks—and horse droppings—with a few crude shacks out back which served as kitchens, scullery, smokehouse, storerooms, stables and bed spaces for weary (and none too picky) travelers. After her husband had died, Barbara Yadkin had kept his tavern license, and it was so close to the courthouse that she still had a decent trade, but the work of running an ordinary, keeping the drunks orderly, serving and cooking, were too much for a woman beyond a couple of years at best. Most went under, found a rough man to run their businesses for a share of profit, or remarried and let the new husbands have them.

"Yes, he did come home a bit light-headed," Bess agreed.

"Chirping gay as larks, they were." Mrs Yadkin sighed dramatically, lifting a mended handkerchief to touch her nose. "And who could know that that very night . . . ah, me!"

"But they parted, they said their good-byes?" Bess wondered.

"Never knowing 'twould be their last, alas," Yadkin mourned, though dry-eyed and peering with a blank stare at the middle-distance.

"They left together, ma'am?" Bess asked suddenly.

"Dear me, no, Bess," Mrs Yadkin said, turning away from pondering the aether. "Your father left first. Had to get home, he said. And the talk was getting a touch loud and raucous."

"Politics," Bess supposed.

"And horse racing," Mrs Yadkin supplied. "I would have shushed them, but they were in high form, all of them, and you know men when they're 'cherry-merry' in drink. God help me, 'tis all I may do just to maintain the *slightest* bit of decorum, and will a pack of tipplers heed a publican's warnings . . . ?"

"Uhm . . ." Bess posed, frowning until the crease between her brows appeared. "How long was it after, that Uncle Harry . . . Mr Tresmayne departed?"

"Not a candle's inch later," she informed her. "He saw your dear father to the street. The door was open, so I could see them embrace and shake hands in parting . . . so they *did* say proper good-byes, praise God! Then he came back in, had a brandy and stingoe with it, and paid his reckoning. Paid for your father, too. It was his treat, I suppose. Mr Harry was *ever* the generous soul. He joshed me some, as he paid . . ." Barbara Yadkin got misty-eyed at this revelation and had to dab with her handkerchief. "He went to his horse and rode off."

"Down the Sound Road." Bess nodded.

"Why no, he headed up Third Street, like he was going home, my dear," Barbara Yadkin told her. "I recall it clear as day. I had to follow that scamp

Pocock . . . he owed me five pence for ale and supper he hadn't paid for . . . and I saw poor Mr Harry turn his horse over to Second, down toward his house, at the corner. I thought it odd, him living so close, not to be walking, but . . ."

"Ah, Mistress Livesey," Thomas Lakey called from the corner of the veranda as he approached, with his nephew Andrew Hewlett in train. "How elegant you appear, my dear. Compared to the peacocks, I vow you're the *epitome* of simple, understated elegance and grace."

"Mr Lakey, good afternoon, sir." Bess smiled at the high-flown compliment, and under the shy gaze of the young man who stood a little behind his uncle's shoulder. "Though I fear your position in Society will suffer should you deem the other young ladies 'peacocks.'"

"That's why I didn't say it that *loud*, my dear." Lakey smiled, as he took her hands briefly. He had been close enough so his comment didn't carry. "They've done with the Purcell piece. I expect you know it so well, you didn't need to hear it again, hmm? Or, was it simply their . . . erm . . . rendition, ha!"

"What could I say, sir?" Bess smiled in reply at his droll wit.

"That wouldn't get *you* in trouble, hey?" Lakey snickered with a wicked glee. "You remember my nephew Andrew?"

"H . . . hello, Mistress Livesey." The boy blushed, doffing his hat and making a clumsy leg. "Your servant, ma'am."

"Good day to you, Mr Hewlett. Your servant, sir," Bess replied, dropping him a graceful curtsy. At least she tried. She had forgotten the cup and saucer and almost came a cropper, within an inch of tipping the cup out to smash on the floor of the veranda.

Dear God, open the ground and let me drop straight through, she groaned, mortified and red-faced with chagrin!

"Done with that, are we?" Thomas Lakey interposed, taking it from her. "Gone cold, I'm bound, anyway." He set it on the nearest table for her without missing a beat, allaying her mortification with a sly, man-of-the-world grin.

"Thankee, Mr Lakey," Bess replied with gratitude.

"Your father is well?" Lakey asked. "Devilish doin's, for our community. Bearin' up, is he?"

"He is, sir. He went riding today with my brother."

"Ah, that scamp," Lakey breezed on. "Your brother, I mean, ha! Best thing, to go about one's business. Grief shouldn't be fed, else it only waxes fatter. And goes, in time, the more it's fended off."

"I would suppose that is true, Mr Lakey," Bess told him. Thomas Lakey was an elegant gentleman, an emigré from more-worldly Charleston, one who always knew the right words to say, the proper social airs that seemed so far beyond even the best of Wilmington Society. He was garbed in a burgundy velvet coat with a fashionable stand-and-fall collar of blue broadcloth, edged in black silk, silk-shirted, awash in lace at cuffs and front, with a pale-tan satin waistcoat sprigged with embroidered vines and flowers, "ditto" velvet breeches with white silk stockings, and wine-dark leather shoes with coin-silver buckles. He sported a long, thin, walking stick, now held under a crooked elbow. His wig was a short, side-curled peruke with a be-ribboned queue at the nape of his neck, under a fine beaver tricorne hat edged with gold lace at the brims.

"For a platitude." Lakey frowned suddenly, making a face at his own statement. "And a deuced old'un, at that. In all seriousness, please express to your father my highest respects, and my deepest sympathies. 'Tis only words, an' words fail us when we try saying somethin' heartfelt. They *all* come out soundin' like old saws."

"I shall, Mr Lakey," Bess agreed, warmed by his commiseration.

"Well, will you have some punch with us, Mistress Livesey?" Lakey offered. "Hot tea on a spring day is all very fine, but a cold sip or two of somethin' sweet is even finer. Andrew, attend to Mistress Livesey, there's a good lad. With your permission, ma'am?"

"Thankee, Mr Lakey," Bess agreed again, laying her hand upon the offered arm that Andrew made for her. He really was a very fine-looking young fellow, Bess thought; Andrew Hewlett was tall and fair, with an open, honest and forthright face—when he wasn't blushing or biting his lips in nervousness. Lakey garbed him just as fine as he did himself, but there was a rawness to Hewlett's posture, as if the fine clothes wore the young man, not the other way 'round, and a gawkiness of elbows and knees and neck that made him look as clumsy as a spring colt.

Gawky or not, he was reckoned a fine catch, and Bess enjoyed the attention, and the side-long glances from the other girls as he escorted her to the punch bowl under the trees.

"You . . . uhm . . ." Hewlett stammered ". . . I cannot recall the pleasure of your appearance the last few weeks, Mistress Livesey, other than at church. You have been work . . . hah . . . otherwise engaged?"

Bess turned a cool gaze on him, seeing him stumble over what surely was a well-rehearsed speech. *Damme,* she thought, *he's as scared as I am! And he's a man!* She decided to put him at ease.

"Oh, 'tis spring, Mr Hewlett!" she said with her openest smile and perkiest airs. "Cleaning to be done, my growing brother to be re-garbed, before he comes out at the elbows and knees . . ."

Damme, why remind him how clumsy boys look! she groaned to herself.

"Preparing for a glorious summer," she concluded, rewarding him with another, disarming smile.

"Sure to be another hot one," Hewlett said, flummoxed.

"Why, indeed, sir!" Bess nodded. "But glorious, in spite of it. The smell of jessamine, of azaleas . . . the pleasure of flowers about the house. Even a humble spread of honeysuckle along a fence . . ." she enthused.

"Ever catch a bumblebee in honeysuckle?" Hewlett asked suddenly, infected with her manner. "Creep up and close it over the bee?"

"I would not *dare,* sir!" Whisking her fan in punctuation. And encouragement.

"Then pluck it, and hold it to your ear, and you can hear him buzzing like anything!"

"A feat for braver sorts than I, surely!" Bess praised, fanning herself again in mock fear. "But you've done it? My word!"

"Often!" Hewlett preened under her approving expression. "Here, allow me to dip you a glass of punch, Mistress Livesey."

"With pleasure, sir." Bess smiled. "Though we sound so formal."

"I could name you by your first name, then?" Hewlett paled with glee at that privilege.

"Elisabeth, sir. Andrew," she replied, looking away shyly.

"We have roses out at The Lodge . . . Elisabeth." Hewlett gulped at the enormity. "Not the wild woodroses, but real'uns, brought in from England! Oh, all sorts of flowers growing. Perhaps you . . . and your father and brother . . . could coach out to see them sometime."

"I would expect my father would welcome your uncle's invitation," she breathed, almost cooing as he handed her a cold glass, looking to Mr Lakey for confirmation.

"Heavens, yes," Thomas Lakey agreed quickly. "Whenever I've come to town, I've noted the improvements you've made about the yard with marigolds an' such, Mistress Livesey. Why not take cuttin's to transplant for your house, hey?"

"We would appreciate that greatly, Mr Lakey."

"Well, shall we sit in the shade yonder?" Lakey suggested.

They took seats on a white-painted stone bench which circled the girth of a tree to sip their drinks.

"Ah, the concert's ended, thankee Jesus," Lakey said, as people began to leave the stuffy salon and make for the punch bowls. "And did you smile proper, Mistress Livesey? When the dotin' mamas give you the eye?"

"I did, sir." Bess laughed.

"If one of 'em'd broken wind, their dames would have glared at the audience, as if to say 'they' did it!" Lakey sniggered. "Pardons, Mistress Livesey, but the thought did strike me, an' I'm cursed with sayin' aloud things better left hush."

"A tendency a politician should control, surely, sir?" Bess bantered back. Lakey was around mid-thirties, a real adult, but he'd always been so droll that she had few qualms about Lakey getting his back up over a comment.

"My dear, a faction man *should* say what first comes to mind, now an' again," Lakey laughed. "Bless me, but you're a sharp'un. A credit to your father. An' becoming a fine young woman. God help us, there's so few with sense enough to come in out'n the rain here. Most refreshin', I must say. Don't you think so, Andrew?"

"Oh, indeed, Uncle." Andrew Hewlett beamed whole-heartedly.

"Make a feller a fine match. *An'* never let him forget it."

"As fine a match as . . ." Andrew struggled, blushing again as he looked for an example. "As Harry and Georgina . . . hmmph . . ."

"They were a rare couple," Lakey sighed, losing his gay edge. "God, poor Georgina! I don't rightly know what she'll do without him. She's closed up the townhouse, don't ye know . . . retired to Tuscarora. 'Spect it'll be a year or more, before we see her."

"Father said that life will never be as grand and lively, with Uncle Harry gone." Bess sobered as well. "Yes, poor Georgina." Bess took a sip of punch. "And you, Mr Lakey?"

"Hey?" Lakey puzzled. "Oh, you mean the faction. Well, there is Osgoode Moore to carry on. The Harnetts, down to Brunswick. Others as sharp as Harry was."

"And you, Mr Lakey. Father thought you would inherit leadership," Bess said.

"Lordy, girl, I'm a gad-fly!" Lakey laughed at himself. "Long as Harry and Osgoode crafted things, I could shout myself hoarse from a stump, an' huzzah like the Vicar of Bray. Stir things up, an' back up their works. But leadin', though . . . I ask you, Mistress Livesey. Do you see anyone followin' *me?* With the plantation to run, most of the time, I have little *spare* time. To huzzah at meetin's, yes. But for leadership an' deep thinkin', no. Serious an' devout as I believe our argument to be, to improve the lot of all Englishmen in our colony, of all the colonies, in fact . . . Harry showed me letters of like-minded men from as far away as New York an' Boston. But it's a matter of respect an' sobriety, far as who takes over the good work. Never did I think it'd come to murder, though . . . Harry's goadin' an' all. Thought we were dealin' with gentlemen."

Against her better judgment, and her father's harsh admonition, Bess pressed him further. "So you think some of our 'barons' had him *killed?*"

"Don't know *what* to think, truthfully." Lakey frowned. "Might never know. Not official," he said, tapping a finger alongside of his nose for a sage tap. "P'raps it was someone followin' the orders from his betters. Or might've been one of the middlin' pack who sided with 'em, an' got too rowed by Harry, on the other hand, an' did it on his own. Things get hot enough, a scapegoat'll appear like a 'Jack-in-a-Box,' an' never a word you'll hear 'bout any ties to the 'barons,' an' I'll lay a serious wager on't. Best he springs up soon, though, 'fore somethin' happens. Way people are talkin' already . . ."

"And Constable Swann solves this?" Bess added.

"Swann, Lord help us!" Lakey spat. "This is way beyond him, my dear girl. A body gets murdered 'round the Cape Fear, most o' the time 'tis two-a-penny reasons. A drinkin' spree, a woman at the heart of it, two sailors goin' at each other? And too drunk and witless to get far. Most get caught at the scene of the crime, knife in hand. Or there's so many witnesses, all Swann has to do is go knock on the right door, come mornin', t'get his man. But Harry, now . . . dear God, but I think that was *planned.* Somebody cold as charity finagled to get him out on the Sound Road in the middle of the night, an' *knew* he'd come alone . . . an' that makes it a cold-blooded homicide, not a hot-blooded killin'. Your pardons, my dear." Lakey cooled, almost wincing. "This ain't a fit topic for conversation. Do forgive me, please."

"There's also talk," Bess began, "down in the market, the stalls, Mr Lakey. Well. Let me ask you something. At the funeral, when Reverend McDowell asked for Uncle Harry's sins to be forgiven, some of the people, uhm . . . well, they found it amusing."

"Ah," Lakey pondered, stroking his chin as her father did. "I see, hmm. How to best phrase this the most gently. Long as you asked, that is, an' have heard the gossip already. Harry Tresmayne was . . . ha! In his younger days, mind . . . rather more'n free with the ladies. Some, *not* ladies, but . . ." Lakey coughed, turning a tad crimson. "Fact or no, it's a repute that'll cling to a man, no matter how long, or how single-minded a man's later married. The sort o' thing that gets blown all out o' proportion, but that's understandable, 'cause Harry was champion for the common folk, an' they always wish t'make a hero's fame bigger, more colorful than it might really be, d'ye see? But for him t'be messin' about, recently . . . well, I can't believe a pinch of it. Harry's first wife . . . my cousin, Priscilla. Do ye recall ought o' her, Miss Livesey?"

"I do, sir," Bess replied. "Most fondly."

"Wild as he was, Harry was the most dotin' husband to her, an' Priscilla wasn't your average brainless twit, either," Lakey declared. "Not the sort t'be taken in by the first gay swaggerer that comes down the pike. Far too intelligent an' discernin' a woman, an' willful for her future happiness, t'let herself be beguiled by just any jumped-up rogue. 'Tis a young man's nature t'be wild, for a season, I tell you. And a young woman's t'grind the rough edges off him. Just as my dear Priscilla did with Harry. And I always deemed it a mortal pity there were no children who might've inherited her sensibility and charm, or Harry's boldness and wit. What a waste o' good breedin', that was . . . her dyin' young . . . an' so hard." Mr Lakey sighed most wistfully.

"And then, there was Georgina," Andrew Hewlett contributed.

"Lord, yes, lad." Lakey nodded. "Knew her, too, since we were sprouts, an' your aunt Priscilla's shade forgive me for sayin' so, but Georgina's even handsomer a match. Was. An' just as quick-witted an' sensible as ever Priscilla was. Neither would've let a rake-hell pull the wool over their eyes."

He took a sip of his punch, looking a bit mournful. "I called on Georgina, myself. Had hopes, at one time, but . . ." He shrugged it off, philosophically. "An' I expect every landed gentleman or landed gentleman's son in the next five counties did, too, hey? Pretty as she is? No, Mistress Livesey . . . both were the sweetest, handsomest, smartest, gentlest ladies in the whole Cape Fear. Not the sort for a rake-hell, or the sort t'suffer such a one for long. Man'd be a purblind fool who'd go behind their backs. Now Harry was a lot o' things but he was never a fool. Not once he came back from that college up north. Oh, he took a spell, right after Priscilla passed away. Went off soldierin', an' mayhap he assuaged his grief along the way. But once back, an' in his right mind, again . . . ? Only problem was, he had that former reputation to live *down!*"

"Yet, something lured him out on the Sound Road, alone," Bess pointed out. "Even so, Mr Lakey, you said you'd heard things . . . even if you put no stock in them. Pardon my curiosity, but . . . what?"

"Well, mind now . . . this is a scurrilous rumor." Lakey glowered at her, though seeming to relish being a gossip, even a reluctant one. "I've heard some say there's this girl, 'cross the river. Cape Fear an' the Brunswick, both. Biddy MacDougall, or so I heard tell she is. Pretty enough little snip. 'Bout as fair as . . . well, 'bout as fair as Georgina. Not a breath over sixteen or seventeen, younger than you, my dear. *Somebody's* been callin' on her, of late. *Somebody* dressed gentlemanly, on a fine horse."

"Taking his life in his hands, if he did, sir," Andrew Hewlett stuck in, glad for a chance to participate in such a fascinating conversation, happy to have a tidbit to share—and get Bess's attention back in his direction. "Her pa is Highland Scot. They came down from Campbelltown or Cross Creek by flat-boat. This MacDougall . . . there's talk he was run off by his own clan back in Scotland. And by others of his clan here in the Cape Fear! I *heard* . . . before he left Scotland he murdered his wife! And slew the son of his clan lord, the same time! A right-fearsome fellow to be messing with!"

"Really," Lakey drawled, winking at Bess as he put on a scowl. "And where would an upstandin' young gentleman be goin', when my back is turned, t'hear such? You been across the rivers, yourself, Andrew? You sound impressively well informed 'pon this matter."

"No, Uncle, certainly not!" Andrew blushed, protesting vehemently. "But some who *have* seen this Biddy MacDougall, and heard about it, talked to me, and naturally . . . uhm . . ."

"Ah, Andrew," Lakey grunted, as if disappointed that his ward could be so gullible. "No proof to that . . . only idle talk. An' talk is the cheap-est dish. A strange newcomer *will* get talked about. An' a promisin' lookin' young chit with him'll be thought the worst of . . . an' usually by the worst young fellows, 'til she's proved 'em wrong. Now, gossip like that's a *tasty* dish, I'll allow. But! I have heard myself that this MacDougall fellow is a cold'un, I'll grant you. Devilish black squint on his phyz most o' the time, when I see him come to town to market. Never see the girl with him, far as I recollect, so she's just as big a rumor, ha! An' may the devil take 'em for calumny, but . . ."

"What?" Andrew and Bess gasped together, intrigued by the topic, and morbidly, eagerly interested by then. Lakey sighed, looking down and miss-ing their first, secret, shared grins at each other.

"There's some black-hearted hounds do say that Harry was hangin' his hat on Osgoode's hatrack too often for innocence. Whilst he sent Osgoode off on faction business, up to Duplin or New Bern, down to Masonborough and Brunswick, far as Charleston. Gettin' him conveniently out o' the way so Harry could . . . well, damn their blood, I say!"

"God Almighty!" Bess hissed in shock. "Anne Moore? But . . ."

"Told ya it was vile talk." Lakey shrugged once more. "Slurs, not *worth* repeatin', hey? You may hear such trash from others, but just remember I *told* you it was trash, made up by trash! An' not the sort of stuff I'd care to hear you were spreadin' about for fun."

"I could not mention such, Uncle, ever!" Andrew swore.

"It's too unspeakable." Bess shivered, though her imagination swam with giddy images of lust, of Uncle Harry clasping women to his breast, enfolding them in a riding cloak. Bess tried to picture some poor, hard-scrabble farmer's daughter in home-spun, bare-legged and barefoot, without stays, petticoats or chemise pretty enough to . . . And Anne Moore, "Do" Jesus, surely not! Though she was handsome, Bess thought. Dark-haired and almond-eyed. Sleepy eyes, with breasts . . . tight as fashion-bound women, Anne Moore was pouted as a pigeon up . . . there! Darkly pretty as she was, Anne Moore looked somewhat . . . common. Trullish. Doxie-ish. Like a sailor's "Poll." But Bess also wished she was merely a tenth as endowed as Anne Moore. *Boys put so much stock in them,* she thought, *and so far, I've so little, God help me!*

She came back from her fevered fantasies, aware of fanning in a frenzy, of sipping her glass of punch down to "heel-taps" in a few gulps. *Most* un-ladylike!

"But if Uncle Harry *was* . . . Mrs Moore, I mean . . ."

"It would mean that Osgoode Moore murdered his best friend," Lakey scoffed. "Now, can you imagine anything more unbelievable than that? For God's sake, let's converse on somethin' else! Lord, here comes Mrs Yadkin, gogglin' the multitude."

"She'll want to ask me all about Father, I expect," Bess said, making a small, private *moue.* "Happens every time, and no escaping."

"You two young people go for a stroll, why don't you?" Lakey suggested, getting to his feet. "I'll beard the peepin' ewe myself."

"Mr Lakey, you are a Christian gentleman," Bess offered sweetly, kissing him on the cheek in parting.

"An' 'him whom the Lord loveth, He chastiseth,' hah! I go forth to be chastised. Scat, younkers. While you may!"

Chapter 9

FOR NINE MILES east of tiny Wilmington, to the Sound or the islands, it was a barren—a maritime forest of pines, oaks, cypress in low-lying areas, and gnarled and convoluted smaller wind-sculpted tangle-oak. Very few people lived there, and those small holdings that did exist were little larger than scrap shacks, clearings just large enough for hut, stock pen or truck garden. One road ran to the southeast to Masonborough and the Sound. Another darted east towards an even tinier settlement of fisher-folk and outcasts some deemed Wrightsville. Both roads were narrow, little wider than a wagon, hemmed in by dogwood, tangle-oak, oleander and myrtle, pine, vines and thicket bushes no one had yet classified; dirt, sand and mud roadbeds heavily rutted by cartwheels, depressed to budding fens wherever they crossed a seeping spring or rill. And the blue sky was cut off by interlacing, sighing boughs that trembled to a sea breeze blowing in off Cabbage Inlet. A breeze which didn't quite reach the ground, or the men who stood beside the Masonborough Sound Road, sweltering and still.

"Reckon 'is be where it happ'm," Jemmy Bowlegs said, kneeling several paces down a game trail which straggled off east into a grove of trees and bushes. He held the reins of his horse with one hand, pawing gently at the ground with the other, the sand and trampled grass, pine-needle detritus and dead leaves. "They's blood 'nough heah, Cap'm . . . 'less a body kill his-self a hawg," Bowlegs tittered.

Matthew Livesey kneed his horse forward for a better view, even though it felt distasteful and morbid to do so. Or to participate.

"Naw, Cap'm, keep yer horse back, 'less ya trample sign," the tracker warned him. He was distasteful to Livesey, too. While Jemmy Bowlegs was only two years older than Samuel, Bowlegs had *never* been a boy, and exuded the oily air of a man of middle years who had seen all the world's evils. And had relished them.

Bowlegs stood and walked back to them. He was part copper, and part nut-brown. His cheeks were wide, his eyes black as pitch, while the rest of his face and body were lean and lanky, tautly long-muscled. He wore Cherokee moccasins which reached his knees, much like a rider's top-boots, and a loose pair of pale-tan, red-striped "ticken" trousers cinched low on his bony hips with a hank of twine. Jemmy's shirt was a gentleman's cast-off (or stolen off the line, Livesey uncharitably suspected) of fine muslin, once ornately laced, though it now bore a pattern of faint stains, smudges and sweat-moons in the armpits, and the sleeves had been cut off at the shoulder. Over that, Jemmy Bowlegs wore a loose deerhide weskit of many pockets, patterned after a proper long waistcoat, with stag-horn toggles and sinew button loops, though he was always seen to wear it open. Said weskit was adorned with knots of ribbon, festooned with patterns of trade beads and tiny shells, in designs only he could explain. On his left hip rode a brass-hilted infantryman's hanger sword, cut down to a wicked sixteen-inch fighting knife in a beaded bearskin scabbard; on the other hip, his powder horn and bullet pouch, atop a sailcloth "possible" sack.

Jemmy Bowlegs's hair was Cuffy-dark and frizzy, but as long as a horse-tail, gathered at his nape with a rawhide lacing . . . and, like a horsetail, badly in need of combing and teazeling. And when Jemmy doffed his hat, a tricorne so old that it had sagged outwards into an awning, Livesey could espy little tufts of spun-wool in his hair.

"That's t'keep th' Cuffies I cotch f'um workin' 'witch' on me," Bowlegs matter-of-factly explained. "Haints, boogers an' plat-eyes, too. Can't be too careful with spirits, Cap'm."

"Ah hum," Livesey commented, creaking in his saddle to ease his aching rump. "What may you deduce from what you've seen, sir?"

"Mistah Harry come along heah, shore," Bowlegs replied, lifting an arm to scratch himself. "Can't tell much in th' road, 'cause folk done mess hit up, since. Over heah, though . . ." He went back to the broken reeds and the dried flecks of rotting blood, which had gone nigh black or a foetid blue. "People come fer th' body, they mess hit up, too, Cap'm," Bowlegs said over his shoulder. "See th' drag mark where they drug him out? Bare foot, over heah . . . big heels, an' wide. Fella *never* wore shoes. Cuffy 'at found him, I reckon. It do appear Mistah Harry wuz afoot when he died."

"Not shot from his horse?" Livesey grunted in some surprise.

"Cack-handed, were he?" Bowlegs asked, instead.

"Ah no . . . right-handed," Livesey told him.

"Then that's right queer," Bowlegs said, coming back to stand by Livesey's left-side stirrup, close enough that Livesey could smell old smoke and old sweat, seared meat and deer musk. "Hoof prints're on his left side, an' a right-hand man'd lead a horse wif his good hand. But he might had hisself a gun or swo'werd . . . 'spectin' trouble, mebbe. Or heard somethin' made him draw, light down an' poke in heah."

"Didn't have a weapon on him, Jemmy," Samuel told him. "Least, when they fetched him in, he didn't. Right, Father?"

"No weapons, no," Livesey sourly replied. "Oh, a jackknife in his saddle bags. None when he was at Widow Yadkin's, either, nor upon his horse that I could see. Umm, Mr Bowlegs . . . ?"

"Wasted on th' likes o' me, Cap'm," Bowlegs chuckled. "'Jemmy's' good 'nough. You kin see why." Indeed, rickets or toddling too young, riding horses from infancy . . . Jemmy was as bow-legged as a cavalryman, his toes turned inwards like a pigeon.

"Constable Swann said he was shot out of his saddle. Ambushed. Then shot a second time after he'd fallen," Livesey sadly related.

"Head *and* heart, Jemmy," Samuel supplied, standing at the head of the game trail, with a coldness that snapped his father's head about and made Livesey wonder what evil, callous effect Bowlegs's friendship had had on his son.

"Took time t'reload?" Bowlegs sneered. "I *doubt* hit! Show ya why, too. Need t'git down t'see this, Mistah Livesey." With Samuel's help, Matthew withdrew his prosthetic "foot" from the deep right-side stirrup of his own devising, and swung his bad leg over and down, all his weight for a moment on That Thing. To remount, he'd need a tree stump.

Matthew and Samuel Livesey gathered behind Jemmy Bowlegs as he took a few more steps down the game trail, tutoring over the spoor he found, using a grass reed as a pointer. "First off, you kin see boot prints, a'goin' in. First shot, I reckon, hit him right *heah,* ya see how he most-like stumbled and skidded? Over heah, th' shot spook his horse, an' hit rared back, too.

Mighta spun an' hit him on hit's way out. Left laig slid out f'um under him, he drapt t'one knee over heah, 'fore he fell. See th' blood speckles on th' bushes, thar, aside th' path? 'Bout chest-high, that'd fit, fer one shot. Belly-high, that'd come f'um th' second. An' . . . they ain't 'nough blood on th' ground. He dead when he hit th' ground, Mistah Harry wuz, sure's Fate. Took one shot on his feet. Second, he wuz kneelin'."

"You can tell all that?" Livesey queried, feeling utter confusion.

"Man git mortal-shot, he'll bleed bad *'fore* he dies, an' leave a big puddle, Cap'm," Jemmy patiently explained, gruesomely digging into the soil with both hands, sifting it like a farmer sampling land, and almost making Livesey gag and recoil in horror.

"Ain't no pellets," Bowlegs stated, sounding almost whimsical. "Did a body shoot him once't he wuz down . . . usin' buckshot or pistol balls like Sam'l said, I'd figger t'find some 'at missed or went clean th'oo him, but they ain't heah."

"*Real* close, though, Jemmy," Samuel countered, on his knees to see. "Really wicked powder burns an' speckles. Maybe none missed!"

"Naw," Bowlegs disagreed, shaking his hands clean, wiping them on his ticken trousers as he rose. "Mistah Harry git shot *'at* close up . . . after he's down, I'da found bone chips f'um his head, an' I didn't."

Matthew Livesey made a dry-retching sound.

"I'm that sorry, Mistah Livesey," Jemmy said, "but I kin only tell ya what th' sign say, an' that's why ya asked me t'come out heah."

"I . . . I . . . understand, Jemmy. He was my friend, d'ye see . . ."

"Iff'n hit's any comfort to ya, Mistah Harry went quick, Mistah Livesey," Bowlegs said, removing his hat. "Don' know jus' why he wuz out heah, or what got him down this trail, but I 'spect he didn' have time t'be afeart. Whoever done it, it wuz *Bim-Bim!* fast as that, an' he wuz gone. Mighta felt *suprised,* wuz all, then hit wuz over."

"Thank God for small mercies." Livesey grimaced.

"Amen, Cap'm." Jemmy nodded, turning to squit tobacco juice at a flowering bush. "Huh. Y'all hear that?" Bowlegs said, raising his nose to sniff the wind like a wary stag. "They's a wagon comin' 'long th' road. Best we see t'our horses, 'fore they spook an' leave us."

Chapter 10

THEY HAD LEFT their hired horses droop-reined at the side of the road, at the top of the game trail, so they went back to secure them before the clattering wagon spooked them, and left the men to walk a long three miles back to the livery stables.

But it wasn't a wagon, it was a coach, being driven four-in-hand, at a decent clip. There was a white coachee atop the box and two liveried, young black slaves riding above the rear boot, trying to keep their little egret-feathered tricornes on their heads.

"Wayull, sheeyit," Jemmy commented, spewing another load of tobacco juice on the road, like a witch-woman bestowing bad *cess.*

The coach glowed with bee's wax and polish-oils. Bright yellow-spoke wheels spun like daisies. The flat-roof, potbellied box of that expensive equipage swayed and rocked on leather suspension straps, with all the windows down for a breeze. It was very dark green overall, and picked out in gold leaf and bright crimson trim, with a coat-of-arms on the doors.

"Heah come Prince Dick. An' Sim Bates's drivin'. Reckon we oughta go down on our knees to him, hey?" Bowlegs joshed, punching Samuel in the shoulder.

The coachee drew back on the reins as a walking stick appeared to thump the driver's box, bringing the coach horses to a walk, then a stop.

"Jemmy Bowlegs!" the richly garbed man inside shouted in glee, as he leaned out a window. "Workin', are you? Hallo, Livesey. Got a runaway slave needs catchin'? Didn't hear you owned any, yet. Much held with it, either."

"Mr Ramseur, sir. Good day to you," Livesey rejoined.

Richard Ramseur, Esquire, was a hawk-beaked, distinguished aristocrat—distinguished in looks, at any rate, if one cared for eagles. While Roger Moore at Orton Plantation on the west bank of the Cape Fear owned, rented or ruled so much land he styled himself "King Roger," the unofficial lord of the long, sabre-shaped cape that curved down to the mouth of the river on the east was Ramseur. His Ramseur Hall was nigh a match in finery to Orton, though not in acreage or profits, causing most folk of the settlements to refer to him as "Prince Richard," yet secretly hoping he never inherited the kingship, recalling a distasteful royal of long ago—Richard the Third—with whom Ramseur shared more than a few faults as a hard-driving landlord or employer.

What they could see of Prince Dick was costly: a black beaver tricorne festooned with white lace and snowy egret feathers. A snow-white periwig perched above a lean, choleric face of a raw complexion, as if Carolina sunlight would never agree with him, a face webbed with a lifetime of gentlemanly tippling, too. Silk shirt and stock, and a gaudy coat of parti-colored velvet—black, gold, tan and gray, intricate as a Turkey carpet—over a fawn waistcoat. Ramseur banged his stick once more, and those postillion boys sprang down to fold down an iron step and open the coach door for him. As he descended, he showed fawn moleskin breeches, and top-boots as glossy as the coach itself.

"Not slave-catching, sir," Livesey felt compelled to answer.

"Then why have this stinky scamp with ye, on my side of the river, Livesey? Huntin' guide? Oh," Ramseur said, then paused, peering down the game trail. "Oh!" he said again, his voice rising in tone as a child's might, over an unlooked for present. "'Twas here he died, is that it?" Ramseur seemed sardonically amused.

"As if . . . !" Samuel began to bristle, then hushed.

"What, puppy?" Ramseur barked. "Did it speak?"

"Ya use 'is road, ya musta knowed that a'ready, Mr Ram-sewer," Jemmy Bowlegs drawled.

"I don't concern myself with the places all the rogues meet untimely ends," Richard Ramseur bit off short.

"Though your son did attend his funeral, sir," Livesey felt emboldened to retort, irked by Ramseur's high-handed, dismissive sneer.

"Aye, I recall him mentioning that. Since he *was* in town, and it made as fine a show as any raree." Ramseur smiled thinly. "I also recall he made mention of your daughter, sir. With the Burgwyns? An opinion over which they differed? Well, the nut doesn't fall far from the tree, does it, Livesey."

"My tree, or yours, sir?" Livesey quipped, stung to anger, but struggling to keep an even and civil tongue in his head in spite of it.

Ramseur eyed him head-to-toe intently, as if he'd never seen him before, or had never seen this aspect to the tradesman. He got a crafty leer after he was done. "So, you've come out here with Bowlegs to sniff it out, have you? Trail the killer back to his door stoop, hey?"

"*Wherever* it leads, sir, yes," Matthew answered, dead-level.

"Friend of yours," Ramseur said, making it sound like an accusation. "Like calls to like? Just like some of his faction, you think 'twas the rich men done him in, isn't it?"

"That is one of the rumors about, sir," Livesey said calmly.

"I'd put my money on one of his shiftless lawyer friends, were I wagerin', Livesey," Ramseur sniffed. "Murdered him to stir the pot. Work up the followers. Wouldn't be the first 'saint' to go to glory so the faction prospers, your Harry."

"It is a plausible rumor to believe, Mr Ramseur," Livesey responded, "that those in power had it done. The common folk adored Harry."

"And he just *adored* the common folk," Ramseur sing-songed back. "Shit, he did. Knew him all my life, and let me tell you, Harry Tresmayne didn't care tuppence for 'em! Long as they were useful—well!—play 'em like a fiddle, stir 'em up with promises of free land, or low rents, promise of the vote, for fiddler's *pay!* Thanks, and wine, that is. Aye, *then* he loved the common folk, so *he* could run the Assembly. Had his eyes on the main chance, even as a lad, as clear-headed and ruthless as Julius Caesar. And about as faithful as Caesar was to old Pompey, too!"

"Sir . . . he was my friend, and I deeply resent . . . !" Livesey said, or tried to say, stung to the quick by such a callous statement.

"Right, right," Ramseur calmed, pushing his palms at him as if to shush him. "Devil take him, though . . . ever think he might've played *you* like a fiddle, too, Livesey? Clever fella such as yourself, sir . . . level-headed I vow, just gettin' a business started. Yet you up and go off at Harry's horsetail to the fighting, leaving all behind . . . one more dewy-eyed . . . follower, to your feudal lord."

"Damn your blood for that, sir!" Livesey barked, making them all shy in stupefaction at such a sober man bridling in anger, in leveling a curse so black it surely could lead to a duel, and a killing! But Ramseur merely laughed, as if he admired Livesey for showing a sign of "bottom." Or, he *enjoyed* rowing people beyond all temperance.

"Oft as folk wish that, Livesey, I'm mortal-certain 'tis damned already," Ramseur chuckled. "Still," he sobered. "You think those in power had it done? That English gentlemen would stoop to *murder,* sir? Or, do you think anyone would be so lunatic they'd make a martyr, and run the risk of a rebellion for the sake of his memory? Crush with the power of the *word,* sir. But never the sword. No, never!"

"Unless someone badly miscalculated, Mr Ramseur." Livesey glowered. "Times change. Harry knew that. More people moving in and settling, now. A handful of 'barons' can't rule forever, nor keep the newcomers from having a voice. It does looks suspiciously convenient that he died when he did . . . for *your* faction, sir."

"Which is exactly why no one of my faction . . . not Moore or anyone else, would have thought it *necessary,* Livesey," Ramseur graveled. "We mayn't own *true* patents of nobility, as we almost did during the Lords Proprietor days, and we now have this sorry parade of Governors sent out by the Crown. But we're still an English Society, Livesey. King on his throne . . ." Ramseur ticked off Society on his long, sclerotic fingers. "Parliament for representation. Barons here . . . lords if you will, rulin' the equivalents to shires or counties. Educated men, *cultured* men of good breedin' in office under us. Tradesmen, planters, magistrates, gentlemanly tenants or freeholders under them, same as a yeomanry in the middle. An' common renters, laborers, back-woods no-accounts sifted to the bottom of the barrel, same as a keg of flour. That's English Society, Livesey, an' God willin', it will always be so. Orderly, reasonable . . . where people know the place they hold. If they work hard, save an' prosper, they rise. Become yeomanry, then get the income to qualify as voters. Hell, man! I *relish* newcomers, do they have the wherewithal, and the gumption, to make somethin' of themselves. More hands for me to shake on the hustin's! More votes for my sort or the candidates we put up.

"But not 'til they're *qua-li-fied!* Educated, prosperous and made something solid for themselves. You give the vote to any damned fool of no substance, you have inferior men who'll follow the first firebrand who shouts the loudest. Like Harry wanted. And a mob that fickle, and gullible, should *never* be encouraged!"

"Hear hear, sir!" the coachee shouted in "Amen."

"Oh, hallo, Bates," Livesey said, looking up at the sycophant. "Working for Mr Ramseur now, are you?"

"Yessir." Sim Bates nodded. He was a fairly short, thin and reedy man, knobby-featured, with a prominent Adam's Apple, a hatchet face with lank, straw-colored hair. "Got me a good p'sition. Had it some month, now."

"Wondered why I hadn't seen you outside a tavern, lately." Mr Livesey smirked. "Didn't know you were any good . . . with horses."

"Been a stableman all me life, sir. Growed up 'round 'em."

"As I recall, Bates, didn't Harry have you tied to a cartwheel and flogged when we were up north? Twice, wasn't it?"

"He did, sir," Bates admitted, his face darkening.

"Once, for drunk and sleeping on guard. Next, for drunk and disorderly," Livesey remembered. "Took a swing at him, that time?"

"Yessir," Bates grumbled, ducking his chin into his livery—which on such an unremarkable man was like gilding on a pig. "Aye, I got th' 'checkered shirt' put on me. Six dozen lashes it was." He turned away, eyes on the tangle of reins.

"Any other militia officer would have given such a sorry soldier to the Regulars' provost-marshal, and an Army court would have made you dance a Newgate Hornpipe from the nearest tree, Bates." Livesey felt inclined to sneer. Bates had been a disaster as a fellow soldier!

"What goes around comes around, don't it, sir?" Sim Bates truculently replied, stung by the idea that Harry Tresmayne had shown him a jot of "mercy," for he'd loudly despised him ever since.

Jemmy Bowlegs shot another dottle of tobacco juice under Bates that splashed, runnily ruddy, on the downturn below the coachee's bench.

"Don't go smuttin' *this* coach, nigger!" Sim Bates cried.

"Ooh, what ya *call* me, *Mistah* Sim?" Bowlegs leered back, with one hand on his hip and the other on the hilt of his fighting knife. "My Injun pap'd jus' *love* that'n. Irish kin would too, I reckon."

"Well . . . !" Bates cried, going as white as fresh-boiled linens.

"Enough!" Mr Ramseur barked. "I'll thankee to clean that off, Bowlegs. An' keep to your side o' the Cape Fear, in future. I'm the man that owns *this'n!*"

"Mean, ya won't hire me t'cotch yer runaway slaves fer ya any more, Cap'm?" Jemmy Bowlegs said with so much mock, lip-trembling distress that Livesey had to bite the lining of his mouth to keep from laughing out loud. "Ya think t'git Bates t'do it . . . when he couldn't foller smoke back to a campfire? Huh!"

"We've wasted enough of my time here, I believe," Ramseur said in an imperious drawl. "This conversation, and the company, are become boresome."

"Good day to you, Mr Ramseur," Livesey said with a doff of his hat, though it was to Ramseur's dismissive back.

"An don't you babies ever *think* o' runnin' f'um yer good ol' mastah, heah me?" Bowlegs warned the young slave boys, looming over them with an insolent thrust of his chin. "Else I come an' *cotch* ya, hah!"

The two youngsters slammed the coach door, hoisted the steps in a twinkling and leapt to their box at the rear of Ramseur's coach, as swift as if they'd seen Old Scratch himself!

Mr Ramseur angrily banged his cane to Bates, who had cringed deep into his clothes. Bates whipped up the team, making the elegant equipage rattle and sway down the Masonborough Sound Road in a sudden haste, mud and gritty sand flying in "rooster tails" from its wheels.

"Hit do appear t'me, Mistah Livesey," Bowlegs said in a slow and thoughtful drawl as he spat at the coach's fresh ruts in scorn, "did a feller take a double-barrel gun in them bushes back yonder, he'd git hit all hung up in th' branches an' such."

"Hah?" Livesey harumphed, still angry. "What do you mean, sir?"

"Look at Sam'l's, thar. Got barrels long as a musket. But if a body wanted t'do a murder in a thicket like that, he'd do better did he have a shorter-barreled gun. One he could fetch up quick, when hit wuz time? Short 'nough, mebbe, t'hide under a coat'r a cloak, so th' man he planned t'kill'd never 'spect a thing til hit wuz too late. If he had a *coachman's* gun, that is . . . hmm?" Bowlegs wryly intimated.

"I . . . well, I'm dashed!" Livesey gasped in sudden understanding, whirling clumsily to peer at the coach-and-four, now far down the road. "A double-barreled coaching gun!"

"Could be, suh." Bowlegs sourly grinned, ruminating on his quid. "Hit very might be."

Chapter 11

NOW SPURRED with a clue to the weapon, *and* a very plausible and understandable suspect, Livesey urged Bowlegs to probe further down the game trail.

"Hey, now!" Jemmy exclaimed about ten minutes later, warning them to lay back a bit. "Here's whar yer killer stood an' waited, hit look t'be." Bowlegs knelt and worked his way down both sides of the trail and the center, almost putting his nose to the dirt to smell or taste for a sign, peering worm-close and very carefully.

Samuel stayed close to Bowlegs, squatting on his heels with his shotgun between his knees, both young men mumbling together in growing excitement, whilst Livesey held and gentled all three horses, 'til their guide flopped back on his rump Indian fashion and cross-legged. "'Twuz only one more feller in heah 'sides Mistah Harry. Only one man did hit, an' I don't think he wuz Sim Bates, after all."

"*Not* Bates?" Samuel spluttered. "Why not, Jemmy?"

"Sim Bates got li'l short foots, Sam'l," Jemmy told him. "Has holes in his soles, too, didn' ya notice, back at th' coach, with him a'sittin' up thar so grand, an' both shoes on th' coach front? These heah prints, they's a lot bigger, with new-like soles. Ya think that skinflint Ram-sewer'd waste good money shoddin' him? Man's so tight, I 'spect he's still got his birth-string, haw!"

"He hated Harry enough," Livesey pointed out. "If Ramseur or one of his crowd paid him, he'd have relished it, if he didn't do it on his own."

"Might be, Cap'm, but hit warn't Bates in heah," Jemmy replied. "Oh, I reckon he *would* kill a body, iff'n Prince Dick told him to. But not by *hisself* is what I'm sayin'. Bates kin bluster all he wants, but he's got a rabbit heart, suh. Even wuz he damn hot, it'd still take him half a crock o' whiskey, an' a pack o' bully-bucks wif him, 'fore he'd do anythin'. I 'fit' him once't, an' I know. Bates'd not do hit face t'face, neither. He's th' back-shootin' kind,

Mistah Livesey. Nossuh, this feller heah wuz a *cold*-blooded man. Come down an' see. There's whar a horse wuz tied, an' th' killer alit. Then he paced, back an' forth, back an' forth, *real* slow an' patient. Didn't stray far at all. Jus' paced, diggin' his heels in like he wuz bored. Same path, up an' back, like a Redcoat sentry. Over heah . . ." Jemmy said, getting to his feet to indicate with his reed over the prints, so Livesey could spot it for himself. "Heel-an'-toe, some. Puttin' one foot ahead t'other t'amuse hisself whilst he wuz waitin'. Like a feller walkin' a 'narry' plank. Over heah . . . see 'em little clods? Musta not keered fer too much muck on his boots, after a while, so he pared 'em off. Smooth, slick sides t'some of 'em? Used a jackknife or a ridin' crop t'do hit, I reckon. Whoever he wuz, he's a patient *huntin'* man. Gentleman, too, I'd say. Crisp, well-*made* boot prints."

"Nothin' else in here, not recent," Samuel said, taking a turn at divining the sign, a little beyond where Jemmy Bowlegs stood. "He rode in from the north, looks like. His and his horse's prints are still fairly fresh . . . nobody come lookin' this far to spoil 'em, when they fetched Mr Harry out. Whoa! Deer tracks, from a big'un! I didn't think there were that many left, this side of town, or of the river anymore! Uh-oh. These boot prints look . . . different, Jemmy. Heavier on the toes, I think?"

"Runnin', once't it wuz done," Bowlegs said, sagely nodding and bestowing a wink at Samuel's father, as if proud of a good student.

"Didn't go into the glade, though . . . whoo! Deer, by *damn!*" Samuel cried. "Come look at *this!*"

At the back of the snaking game trail there was a glade in the forest, perhaps three rods across, circled by myrtles, dogwoods and scrub pine, with a much taller lone pine in the center whose branches were high enough for a man to go under without much ducking. Under it lay a hard-packed, trampled bed of pine needles the color of rust that spread at least thirty feet across, and was strewn inches deep.

Samuel and Jemmy Bowlegs scampered into the small clearing, all but oblivious to the reason they'd come as they eagerly cast about for deer sign, leaving Livesey senior to stump along in their wake.

"Nighttime hidey-up fer a whole *herd* o' deer!" Jemmy laughed as he ducked under the outermost boughs and pawed the ground. "Ain't been heah, *lately,* but give 'em a while, Sam'l, an' they'll come back. Soon's th' stink of people, guns an' horses goes away."

"Deer?" Livesey barked, sounding almost exasperated with their misplaced enthusiasm. "Deer, is it? When . . . !"

"Shy, Mistah Livesey, suh," Bowlegs explained, shuffling about to face him on his knees. "Deer, they lay up fer th' night, after a las' draynk o' water. Huddle up safe under a big tree like this'un, a ways off any trail. They'll scat a ways off, too, so they kin smell trouble comin'. They's a big herd 'round heah, *somewheres.* Haven't been heah in a while, though. Months, mebbe. But they's out thar."

"Scared off by the . . . murderer?" Livesey grumpily asked.

"Oh, long 'fore that, Cap'm," Bowlegs said with a smug leer, as he crept round the pine's trunk, then ducked out to where he could get fully erect. "Place like this, nobody livin' close-abouts? This is a place where Jacks've took their Jills, ya see? Lookee heah, underneath."

Livesey was drawn forward in spite of himself, to stoop and bend at the waist as Bowlegs pointed lurid traces out to him, smirking all the while. "Scuff marks, Cap'm. Boot'r shoe toes, *between* heel marks, don't ya know. Over heah, they's heel skids and *bare* toes betwixt 'em. An' a'leadin' in an' out, there's iddy-biddy ladies' shoe prints, wif a mess o' *hasty* men's prints alongsides. Dancin' an' a'twirling round each other . . ."

"Hmmm . . . tuft or two o' blanket wool, too, Jemmy," Samuel said, producing a few strands, looking both immensely pleased with skills that Bowlegs had taught him and secretly smug with amusement, that he, by personal experience, knew what to look for after a man and a woman had pleasured each other. "Wasn't any *woods* critters under here!"

"Dear Lord," Matthew Livesey groaned. This glade was a trysting place, a secret, but well-used spot where lovers could . . . Harry's? he wondered, and, with whom? Was that what made him rush out here? *Harry, how could you?* he bleakly thought, his face persimmoned.

"Warn't no saint, he," Jemmy Bowlegs said, guessing the reason for Livesey's evident distress. "Can't say *who* been couplin' heah, but th' sign's 'bout a week'r two old, no more. Might's well saddle up, an' head on out. Nothin' more this glade'll tell us. 'At cool man's too keerful. Might strike his back-trail, though. Hey, Sam'l . . . find whar he rode out fer me."

Once aboard their horses, again, they walked them northward, on the only other passable path. They rode single-file, Samuel and Bowlegs in the lead, swaying right or left to peer at the ground or undergrowth, though to Livesey if felt like a bootless endeavour, with nothing to see but sand, dirt and only vague disturbances in the path that *might* have been "sign."

"Last horse through here wuz 'bout a week ago, same's I said," Bowlegs called back over his horse's rump. "Pert soon, we'll come out on th' Wrightsville Road, near Smith's Creek, an' there won' be a hope in Hell o' sortin' these prints outta all th' others, Mistah Livesey."

"You did what you could, Jemmy, and for that I'm grateful," Mr Livesey gloomily replied, his mind numbed by the grievous possibilities in what they had already discovered.

"I still git m'choice o' new clothin', like ye promised?"

"I shall consider it my pleasure, and civic duty, to tog you out the same as we bargained for," Livesey assured him with a polite smile, the mental image of Bowlegs in gentlemanly finery lifting his spirits for a trice. He had long thought that Jemmy Bowlegs only took a bath when caught in the rain, only changed his attire when the old rotted away!

To the "better sorts" of the Cape Fear, the far-ranging Bowlegs was a sometimes-useful, but sordid, creature, best kept at arm's length 'til his unique skills were required. The very prim loathed him like a baby-stealing Gypsy, though most ordinary folk looked on him with faint amusement, as if he was a mysterious local legend, a character as colorful as any from a "Jack Tale." The "sporting" young men of the colony especially liked him, and wanted to associate with him, go hunting and tracking with him and learn even a little of his arcane "White Injun" arts.

It irked Livesey, and made him fear for Samuel's character, for him to run with Jemmy's roguish pack, if only on those few work-free days when Samuel didn't have his nose to the grindstone. But . . . even the sons of the "better sorts," with whom Livesey *preferred* Samuel to associate, would tramp-about with Bowlegs, and even if Jemmy Bowlegs wasn't present, Samuel and his bachelor friends would follow the same sort of pursuits in emulation. The Carolinas, the Cape Fear, *was* a frontier, the very nature of gentlemanly Southern Society was more agricultural, much closer to forest, stream and field than staid coastal Pennsylvania, and the only way Livesey could think to fend off what he feared as "bad influences" was to bind Samuel in a "croaker sack" from dusk 'til dawn, and only free him for the workday, and lead him to the chandlery with a leather leash and collar!

"Whoa up!" his son suddenly yelped, reining back his horse and leaping from the saddle. To Livesey's consternation, Samuel hared off through the thickets and brambles to the right—the eastern side—of the game trail, swishing and wading through branches, snags and vines. "Ow!" he was heard to mutter, then "Ow!" again. "Ow . . . shit fire!"

"Keep sniffin' fer *snake* now, Sam'l," Bowlegs hooted with glee, leaning back with a hand on his horse's rump. "Ye cotch a whiff o' cucumber, be ready t' skedaddle!"

"What do you think he saw?" Livesey dubiously asked. "Something to do with the rest of what you found?" He kneed his horse alongside.

"Most-like," Jemmy drawled back. "Sam'l's comin' along, quick as a whip at huntin' an' trackin'. Make a right-smart 'country boy,' ye git land t'put him on agin, an' let him."

"That is my . . . !" Livesey began to bark, before catching himself—irked that it was none of Bowlegs's business, but dreading that he just might be right. "Unless he becomes as renowned as you, Jemmy," he said instead, "Sam'l must stick to his chosen last. You're reputed to be one of the best at what you do. Else . . ."

"*One* of 'em?" Bowlegs lazily snickered. "Mistah Livesey, they ain't *nobody* better'n me in th' whole Cape Fear! An' I ain't half th' tracker my pappy wuz . . . whichever one he wuz. Ye awful hard on him, Cap'm. Sam'l won't *never* make a shopkeeper, same as you. But he's gettin' right good at what he keers fer . . . what I teached him."

"Jemmy . . . what you're teaching him," Livesey said, trying to make light of the fellow's unwonted intrusion into his own business. "It's not the tracking I *worry* about!" he said with a chuckle, which elicited a deep belly-laugh from Jemmy Bowlegs.

"Look at this, y'all!" Samuel proudly called as he fought his way out of the clinging thickets, wading chest-deep in a green surf.

He held a small bouquet of blossoms, little larger than a nosegay bunch, of oleander blooms, all white, red and showy when first cut from a bough. Now, they were limp and too long from water, crackling and wilted, though their perfume was, perhaps, even headier.

"Oleander?" Mr Livesey said as Samuel handed the bouquet over to him, almost bird-dog pleased with a fresh-shot "fetch," face abeam. "An evergreen . . . part of the dog's bane family, as I recall? Odd, to find such a trinket so far out here."

"Pizen' berries, though," Jemmy supplied. "Heard-tell of some slaves doin' in cruel mastahs wif oleander berry juice. Git yer sweet an' yer bitter, with oleanders. They just comin' inta bloom."

"Tied with a hank o' ribbon, Father. See?" Samuel eagerly added, pointing out the narrow royal-blue satin, tied in a double bow.

"Aye, and good material, too, Sam'l . . . as I'm sure you noted," Livesey said, taking time from his intense perusal of the nosegay to bestow praise on his son. He felt like a tracker, himself, on his own sort of "spoor," as he appraised the goods. "Not shoddy. A throwster in London or Paris made this. Not a slub nor a drop to the weave. It might sell for ha'pence a foot. We carry some as good as this in our own shop, son, for two pence, ha'penny a yard."

"And the ladies pay it, too!" Samuel crowed.

"Quite, ah . . . astute of you to spot it, son," Livesey further said. "I must own that I had no idea you had such a talent! The apt pupil of an apt teacher, it would appear." Which added praise almost made Samuel wag his own tail with joy; he went dirt-kicking red-faced, come over all "aw-shuckin's."

"Just looked a little further afield, like Jemmy always says to, else ya end up trackin' in circles, followin' the deer that stood right by the trail, an' walk right past him. Right, Jemmy?"

"Done good," Jemmy added, and Livesey saw that his son was not sure whose congratulations meant more to him: his father's or Bowlegs's.

"Father," Samuel said, returning to his smaller, in-town hesitance.

"Yes, lad?"

"These flowers look t'be a week or more off the branch. Could ah . . . could this've been what Uncle Harry had in his right hand, when he led his horse into the glade back yonder? If he was meeting . . . uhm?"

"Mistah Harry didn't have a weapon, so anyone said, but then he mighta not expected *t'need* one, yeah," Bowlegs speculated aloud to Samuel, almost cutting Livesey out of it, "iff'n he wuz 'spectin' t'meet a woman back thar. Mighta been, at that, Sam'l. Say some man wuz th' jealous kind, saw what wuz a'goin' on, an' laid out a'waitin' to kill him. Dragged his wife'r girl off, an' th'owed this purty as far's he could th'ow it on his way out, yeah!"

"Nonsense!" Livesey spluttered. "We don't know that at all! It could have been anyone who . . . trysted out here and threw it away. The girl spurned her wooer, the girl didn't show up and the heartbroken . . ." He *would not* accept such a sordid end to his finest friend! "Besides . . . *if* some lover were here, neither party could carry a bouquet home with them as evidence of their, ah . . . sin."

"Aw, sheeyit, Mistah Liveesy," Jemmy interrupted with a knowing leer and a sarcastic drawl. "I don't reckon you b'lieve that anymore than I do. Last signs say 'twuz Mistah Harry an' his killer th' onliest people out heah. Lemme see 'em flars." Bowlegs studied them for a long moment, then held them up for all to see. "Stems ain't brittle, yit . . . cut 'bout a week ago, give'r take. 'Bout th' same time as th' night he rode out here an' got murdered. How far off th' trail, Sam'l?"

"'Bout four or five paces."

"Man th'owed 'em, then. Gals cain't th'ow that far," Jemmy decided, spreading his hands as if it was self-evident. "'Ayr ye go, suh. Cain't say fer *shore* what these-heah flars had t'do wif his death, but they's *heah*. Mighta been a *lure*, left off the Masonborough Road t'mark the game trail, mighta been somebody decided t'kill him an' saw what he wuz about an' took advantage."

"I . . . see," Matthew Livesey finally replied, groaning as if in physical pain as he peered off into the thickets where the flowers had been found.

How blind could he have been, he asked himself, to have thought that Harry Tresmayne had changed his nature! For a moment, he bleakly considered his removing to such a fast-and-loose colony as North Carolina an incredible mistake, nothing at all like staid and proper Philadelphia, that had engendered such licentiousness into even elite Society . . . that had suckled Harry on its disregard for righteousness from his cradle, producing a man who, for all his grandeur and better qualities, had won the love of *two* angelic women and yet spurned the long-term joys of monogamy for . . . thrills! Harry had risked it all, for he was, like many Southern gentlemen, weak when it came to passion and lust. Risked his life . . . thrown it away . . . to rut with a cheap bawd. He'd died for . . . *quim!* Lived his whole life a sham, and lost it on a rake-hell's lewd *geste.* And in such a dismal place.

"God," Livesey all but moaned at last, "I wish we'd never found them."

"I'm sorry," Samuel muttered, turning sheepish.

"Oh *no,* lad, don't take on so," Livesey gravelled, reaching down to take his son's shoulder. "You've nothing to apologize for. You did well, and I'm both surprised and pleased by your abilities.

"No, 'tis me . . . for being so blind. I fear that Jemmy has the right of it," Livesey confessed, removing his hand from Samuel to rub absently at his stump, feeling very old and weary. "Those flowers *are* involved in Harry's murder. How, I don't know, but . . . That glade was a place where Harry met a woman . . . perhaps a *lot* of women over time, 'cause fine as Priscilla or Georgina are, or were, one just didn't satisfy his . . . humors. I'd thought he'd outgrown such, but it appears that all this time I was deluding myself. Perhaps as your uncle Harry deluded us all. And Dear Lord, but it's hurtsome!" he concluded with a hiss, slamming a fist on his right thigh as if to accentuate the pain he felt . . . to add the physical to the spiritual.

"Wayull," Bowlegs softly drawled in the shame-faced silence that followed Livesey's strangled revelation, "leastways we know it warn't nobody *poor* done it, Mistah Livesey. 'Twuz a gennleman on a well-shod, high-steppin' horse 'at bushwhacked him. Had hisself real fine ridin' boots. Double-barrel coachin' gun'd be dear, too. An' th' girl's shoe prints look well-made. Li'l bitty heels. Not what you'd reckon t'see this deep in th' woods. You said 'at ribbon wuz costly, Mistah Livesey. Hit 'ppears t'me whoever done it wuz th' lofty sort."

Livesey held out his hand to re-examine the rotting flowers and study the ribbon more closely. The stems had been well-wrapped, bound in a double bow, very neatly, almost prissily done—*with loving care?* he sneered to himself. Even the free ends had been snipped inwards to tiny swallow-tails. Truly, a person of "Quality" had taken great pains to make the nosegay.

"Aye, a lady's work. Or a clever gentleman's," Livesey agreed with a grimace of distaste. "Perhaps a rich lady's maid servant, at her orders. Lord, if word of this gets out, it will break Georgina's heart! Yet, puts us no closer to discovering the *why*, or the who."

"Mr Ramseur, maybe, Father?" Samuel opined. "He's lots of servants who could've tied it. And he's rich enough, *and* hated Uncle Harry. This *is* his side of the Cape Fear . . . like he told us."

"Maybe hit warn't Sim Bates, but Prince Dick has plenty other people workin' fer him who coulda done hit, Cap'm."

"One of the others in the barons' faction, too, maybe, Jemmy," Samuel stuck in. "Like Father said. Or Ramseur said, whichever."

"No call t'fash Miz Georgina, Mistah Livesey," Jemmy suggested. "We could th'ow it away, again . . . fergit we found it."

"Let's not *tell* anyone we found it," Livesey decided suddenly, peering intently into their eyes. "Else we . . . spook the perpetrator. And I'll conjure both of you to say not a blessed word about all that we did this afternoon. Say, instead, that we went hunting, found some promising deer tracks, but came home empty-handed; can you do that for me?" With a much more demanding glare at Samuel than at Jemmy Bowlegs.

"Good. But no . . . we'll not throw this away. It's evidence," Livesey declared. "Sooner or later, it may lead us to the identity of the killer, or killers."

"Feller thought he th'owed it away, he might git keerless, hey?" Bowlegs chuckled with a sly, sage look. "'Til hit lead right to him?"

"Like you always say, Father," Samuel recited, looking up at his sire with a dutiful expression, "sooner or later, the truth will out."

"Ay-meh-un!" Jemmy Bowlegs loudly added, in such a pious tone that it startled both of the Liveseys, the father most of all.

Chapter 12

"HE SAID *what?*" Matthew Livesey grunted over his simple supper as Bess related the gossip of the afternoon's gathering.

"That Uncle Harry was . . . messing with Anne Moore. Or a girl from across the river. Biddy MacDougall." Bess cringed.

"After I specifically warned you both not to indulge in idle speculation, you . . ." Livesey spluttered, as testy as Bess had ever seen him.

"Father, I could hardly avoid it," Bess rejoined meekly. "It was the *only* topic of conversation. I said nothing. I didn't *have* to. Much as folk were talking, I didn't have to say a word to hear as many opinions as I wished."

"Hmmm." Livesey frowned heavily at her, nigh scathingly.

"And you know gossip, Father," Bess tried to cajole. "Mr Lakey gets invited to so many teas and things, he hears everything firsthand. 'Tis a wonder he can bear to be out on his plantation, and cut off from fresh gossip, he relishes it so. There can't be a thing in the entire colony he *doesn't* hear of, sooner or later."

"And delights in passing on," Livesey fumed. "Vile, or no."

"Well, yes," Bess replied, adding quickly, "but he *swore* us not to repeat what he related about Anne Moore and Uncle Harry. *He* deemed it vile trash, not worth repeating. He was quite angry over it, himself."

"Mmm, hah." Livesey nodded. "Good. He has *some* sense. Though I do *not* appreciate his relating it to *you*. Goose-brain."

"Bess, Father?" Samuel snorted with glee. "Or, Mr Lakey?"

"Lakey, of course," Livesey sniffed. "Ridiculous twit."

"Mr Lakey, Father?" Bess suggested coyly. "Or, Sam'l?"

"Again Lakey, young miss." Livesey at last smiled, cozened out of his anger. "Bless me, but you're both as smart as paint tonight, far too quick on the rejoinder for me."

"Mrs Yadkin was there, too," Bess related, as she slid back from the table to fetch what was left of her blueberry cobbler. "If not for Mr Lakey, she'd have corraled me up something fearsome. She sends you her regards, Father. Again," she chuckled from the sideboard as she set out smaller plates, and fresh forks.

"Oomph," Livesey observed with a wince at the mention of that name.

"I didn't bring it up with her, either, Father," Bess went on. "But she talked about the last evening you and Uncle Harry were at her tavern. How she last saw him getting on his horse and riding off down Third Street, and turning off for his home."

"Now, how could she have seen that?" Livesey wondered, almost scoffing.

"She said she had to go outside for awhile," Bess replied as she came back to the table with the dish of cobbler, and a short stack of dessert plates from their everyday service. "When you and he said your good-byes, I think. No, perhaps twice, 'cause she said he came in and had a brandy and stingoe, then settled his reckoning after. Then, when he saddled up and rode off down Third Street and turned off for his home. Perhaps she went out twice. Something about chasing down a Mr Pocock, who didn't pay for his supper?"

"Sam'l, don't hog it," Livesey ordered as his son dug into the cobbler with a large serving spoon before Bess could even be seated. "Leave some for us, what?"

After supper, Livesey enjoyed a pipe on his front porch. It was not as grand a gallery or veranda as the Burgwyns, or other longer-settled homeowners on Dock Street had. It was pine boards, railed, and shaded by split shingles, barely deep enough for two rough, pew-like benches, some planter tubs cut down from molasses casks which held a variety of spring flowers and perennials Bess had set out, and his rocking chair. His bad leg was stretched out in front of him to ease it, That Thing propped on the rim of a planter tub. It was aching something sinful. Too much riding and walking on slippery, uneven ground, he thought; more exercise than he'd gotten in a week of work at the chandlery, or stumping about the town. He had a decanter of rum in the sideboard; a few sips might be needed to let him sleep that night, he considered. Or a willow-bark tea?

A long, clay, church-warden pipe fumed lazily in his mouth as he rocked slowly back and forth, the small white bowl resting on his now-taut upper stomach. Local leaf was good as any Virginia export lately, and he wished again they had land. Cotton was fine, but tobacco . . . now there was a profitable crop!

Dark had fallen, and the town, somnolent to begin with on Sunday, with all public houses closed, was disturbed only by the peeping of the frogs, or the faint cry of a final gull winging its way to a nighttime nest somewhere. Watch bells chimed from the ships anchored in the harbor at the foot of the street. Crickets sawed and creaked, in time to the rhythmic groan of the porch boards below his rocker's runners. Off to the west, dull red glows lit Eagle's Island, where sleepy millhands stoked the tar-pots and rendering tubs to keep the product soft for the next day's labors. And a faint smudge of wood smoke wafted across the last after-glow of sundown. Lights were springing up here and there in Wilmington. A porch lantern on the more affluent houses, brass or bronze frames with inset Muscovy mica—isinglass. Poorer homes (such as his) lit their tiny share of the night with cheaper tin lanterns set with thin-pared sheets of cowhorn. Only by the courthouse were there proper street lamps so far, or along the wharves at the foot of the hill. Often as Wilmington had suffered raging fires, the idea of emulating the grand street lighting of London or New York was looked upon with suspicion. And the cost was sure to be hideous-dear.

So how had Mrs Yadkin seen us, then? he wondered, troubled.

They'd embraced and shaken hands near the lanterns at the gate of the stable yard and court. And there were two more small lanterns on the porch of the ordinary, which lit the courtyard well enough. But the night beyond . . . ?

Livesey stopped rocking and shifted upright in his chair.

Beyond the lanterns' circular dull gloamings, the streets were doubly dark—dark as a boot! Down Third Street at the intersection of Market Street, there was one tiny lantern by St James's Church, but beyond a few paces, a rider would be swallowed by the night. Beyond that one, there were real street lamps at Third and Princess, by the courthouse yard. And, as Livesey recalled, there had been no moon to see by the night of the murder.

It had been new at the time. He leaned forward to look up from the porch overhang to confirm that the moon was now but a quarter-moon, a week later. So how *could* Mrs Yadkin have seen Harry turn his horse at *either* intersection?

Wide as she blared her eyes, Livesey had always suspected that her sight was bad, and the woman too vain to suffer the indignity of spectacles. He had even japed about her sight with their family physician, Dr Armand DeRosset, when he had come in a few months earlier to order a supply of pre-ground spectacles from Philadelphia. He had told Livesey that as men aged, they began to lose their near-sight at first, while their far-sight remained sharp years longer. Whilst the women-folk lost their far-sight first, and kept their near-sight, so necessary for neat sewing, cooking and household chores, almost as if God had planned it Himself. A man would need far-sight to explore or hunt, to labor and build, to detect approaching dangers so he could be protection to his family, and what was his, so the Good Lord had ordained male eyes for that purpose. Women, being the weaker sex meant to be protected by men, didn't need far-sight after their children had at least survived and grown to near adulthood, so God let them retain near-sight in their declining years.

And since Barbara Yadkin was of an age, certainly, to need the aid of spectacles for far-sight, then how had she seen far enough to see what she had told Bess she'd seen, without them?

"Imagined it," Livesey dismissed with a grunt, and a puff on his pipe. "Even if she did see him, the lights would be better down by the courthouse, at Princess Street. Not Market, surely."

He leaned back in his rocker and thrust with That Thing. He blew a perfect halo of tobacco smoke that ghosted away on the river wind, closely followed by another that twined and spun like a plate on some juggler's stick. If Harry *had* turned down Market, though . . .

"Dear Lord," Matthew Livesey sighed, frozen on the back roll of his rocker stiffened by a distasteful discovery.

Anne and Osgoode Moore's house was on Market Street, not three lots down from the intersection with Third!

Georgina had not come into Wilmington for Court Sessions with Harry this time. Might that have given Harry an opportunity, or the sinful urge, to canter past his lover's house—if those deplorable rumors about them were true? *And the Devil take 'em,* he most bitterly thought.

And Osgoode Moore. But he'd been at the tavern, too, right in the thick of things. But when had *he* left, Livesey wondered? And how soon before or after Harry had left? Suspicions, one atop the next, and each more vexing and disturbing—and more confusing! Livesey could not recall Moore's excited voice raised in high dudgeon against poll taxes or the system of Royal governors, in that last wine-sodden hour he himself had been at the Widow Yadkin's.

"Dear Lord," he sighed again, loosing the tension in his body, and rocking forward again. To find the answers to those puzzlers, he would have to go see Barbara Yadkin, and 'front her, direct!

And, what that befuddled chick-a-biddy might make of his sudden attention . . . he shuddered to contemplate.

Chapter 13

LIVESEY TOOK his breakfast at the Widow Yadkin's Ordinary, in hopes it would be less crowded than at mid-day. It was—at least in the public rooms. Travelers who had stayed the night were saddling up in the court and stable yard, yawning and scratching as packs were tied to muleback, donkeyback, or slung into oxcarts or pony traps. The public rooms were messy from their feeding, but blessedly silent and empty by the time he took a table freer of grease or spilled victuals than most. A sleepy, dawdling slattern mopped his table down with a dishclout stained the approximate color of spilled beer or tea, making the rough tabletop cleaner, though wetter, than before.

"Stabling for your two horses!" Livesey heard a shrill voice say from outside. "Room for the night, three to the bed. Supper, ale, two bottles o' 'Teneriffe' wine, sirs. *And* breakfast, sirs! *And* punch!"

Livesey leaned back far enough to see out the window, to behold Barbara Yadkin in a morning gown, over which she'd thrown some dressing robe that resembled a coarse horse blanket. Her own hair topped that apparition, tweaked into curls over stiff paper spills. In morning's light—bleakest of all and unkindest to women, no matter how lovely they'd seemed the night before—her complexion without artifice was like a plucked chicken's. And shouting as she did didn't help!

"Four shillings for stabling and fodder," she was demanding of the rough-looking trio of travelers who loomed over her. "Five pence a man for supper, five pence for breakfast. Four pence bed per head . . ."

"An' a rough'un 'twas, too!" the leader ranted back.

"As makes no difference, you contracted it!" Barbara Yadkin said in riposte. "Wanted cheaper, did you? I offered you the floor in front of the hearth! That's . . . five shillings altogether!"

"Five shillings *six* pence," Livesey grunted to himself.

"Ale, Teneriffe, punch, that's . . . two shillings more, sirs!" she tried to sum up. "Seven shillings is your reckoning. Seven shillings is what I want, or I sic the constable on you!"

Livesey's gaze went to the notice board over the counter of the bar, and he clucked in disapproval. Two bottles of poor port, three quarts of ale with their supper—and to his lights these men looked like the sort who'd put down more—was more like four shillings, six pence, of itself! No wonder the woman was husband-hunting as hungry as a shark; she needed someone who did sums!

The leader of the travelers got a sly look and was quick to dig into a washleather purse hung on his belt, doling out silver coinage. English money was so rare, anything would pass: French, Spanish, Dutch, even Austrian—all varying in value. *He'd* not have looked as pleased as Mrs Yadkin did, without a chance to sort it over! But back in she came, seemingly satisfied by the exchange, face grim as Death-on-a-Mopstick. And just about as handsome or desirable.

"Why, Matthew . . . Mr Livesey!" she gasped, startled to see him in her "establishment." Her hands went fluttering to her hair, to the throat of her horse blanket robe.

"Mistress Yadkin, good morrow to you, ma'am," Livesey bade her.

"Bless my soul, I never . . . !" she cheeped, blushing, midway between coy and chagrined she wasn't turned out more fetching for him. "*Della?* Girl?" she barked for the serving wench, as loud as a regimental sergeant-major, then flushed as she mellowed to a more becoming coo. "You usually break your fast at home, I do believe, Mr Livesey? Such a surprise for me . . . you will excuse me just the moment, whilst I repair my habiliment? You will take coffee . . . anything else you wish? *Della!*" she crowed again. "Just a moment, surely . . . ?"

"Of course, Mistress Yadkin," Livesey said with a cheery grin.

"Um, yes, just the moment, then," she peeped, flustered.

She came back not ten minutes later, now dressed in a sack gown with her hair un-papered and combed out almost girlish, with makeup done to a palely white perfection, and a beauty mark on her cheek, as Livesey savored his second mug of coffee with milk and loaf-sugar.

"You have not gotten your breakfast yet, sir?" Barbara Yadkin squinted in disapproval, narrowing her hugely goggling eyes for once.

"You said you would rejoin me soon enough, so I have not placed my order with your server, ma'am," Livesey told her.

"Oh," she gasped, realizing he had come to have breakfast *with* her. "Oh!" Again. Softer this time, paling as she stumbled onto the plank pew opposite him at the table.

He ordered eggs with a rasher of bacon, bread and more coffee (hoping for the best) from the slack-jawed young serving wench Della. He suspected it was she who would do the cooking, too, poor mort.

"Take more than proper care for our guest, now, Della," Yadkin warned her. She might as well have been talking to the square-hewn log walls, as the slack-wit shuffled off to the scullery

"This is *such* a surprise, sir," Barbara Yadkin began, fanning herself with one idle hand.

"Well, Mistress Yadkin, you spoke to my daughter, Bess, yesterday, at the Burgwyns . . ."

"I am *so* sorry you could not attend, Mr Livesey," Barbara Yadkin simpered. "It was the most tasteful entertainment. Though the music left a *bit* to be desired, don't ya know, but . . ."

"Bess told me you had discussed Harry's last night on earth with her," Livesey prompted.

"Oh God," Mrs Yadkin sighed sadly, realizing his presence had no personal connection with *her*, and fearing he was wrathful. "Is *that* why you came for your breakfast here this morning, then, sir? Forgive me if I caused your sweet, dear girl any anguish, *do*, please sir! She did call him 'Uncle Harry,' and you were close as cater-cousins . . . I had no thought . . ." She looked on the verge of scolded, dash-hoped, tears.

"I assure you, ma'am, you caused no pain, no," Livesey had to tell her. "I'm told talk of the murder was common coin at the party, since it happened. I know that for fact. No . . ."

Barbara Yadkin extended a fretful hand, begging for forgiveness, and Livesey felt bound to give it a dubious pat or two, in spite of himself. She hitched a breath as if he'd just put his hand up her skirts, but dared to entwine chore-roughened fingers around his. Her eyes grew even *more* disconcertingly large as she peered at him, as if she could wring some sign of affection from him.

"Well, hmm. Haa." Livesey coughed, trying to disengage himself with what would not appear to be unseemly haste. "Sam'l and I rode to the murder scene yesterday, you see . . ."

"How terrible for you!" she blurted, her abandoned hand still on the table, flopping like a landed catfish for attention.

"Aye, but . . ." Livesey nodded. "What I meant to ask you . . . you'd told Bess that you'd seen me and Harry depart, I believe?"

"Aye, I did. I had . . . I had an errand to run, out on the porch," Mrs Yadkin stammered. Livesey thought she had come to the door to peer after him with her usual calf-eyed longing.

"Then he came back inside, paid his reckoning, and had a drink, a stirrup cup, as it were?" he proceeded.

"He did."

"And could you tell me how long you thought that might have been, between my leaving and his that night, Mistress Yadkin?"

"A candle inch, I told your sweet girl, sir. Perhaps a quarter-hour. My mantel clock is not the best, but it seemed to me to be just about a quarter-hour. La, poor Mr Harry, he was so gay and chirpy when he left. Joshing and teasing, as was his wont, don't ya know . . ."

"Hmm. And did he seem anxious to leave, ma'am?"

"Anxious?"

"Eager to go? Or was he dawdling? Chatting up the others, or preoccupied with his own thoughts?" Livesey pressed.

"He was his normal sportive self, Mr Livesey. The crowd was thinning out. 'Twas about half past ten that you left. So, 'twas one quarter shy of eleven that he rode off. I'd shut off the liquor right after you departed. Constable Swann and the magistrates don't like the ordinaries to stay open too late, or get too disorderly. La, don't you recall the troubles . . . well, 'twas in '58, whilst you were away . . ."

"So Harry did not seem overly eager to be off. Yet he did not seem inclined to dawdle, either, I take it," Livesey summed up, fearing a screed from her about business, which could waste half the morning.

"About like that. His normal self, as I said."

"You did not see Sim Bates about that evening?"

"Sim Bates? Bless my soul, Mr Livesey, but that lay-about's not welcome in *my* establishment," Mrs Yadkin huffed.

"Nor in the streets that night?"

"The only time I see Sim Bates these past months is when he's driving his master's coach into town." Yadkin sniffed archly. "And a good riddance to bad rubbish, I say! He does his drinking at the New Inlet ferry tavern, or in Masonborough, now, thank the good Lord. He was *ever* a trial, Mr Livesey! Were he not ruining my floors with his spew, he was rolling in the stable muck, singing or hollering at the top of his lungs . . . picking fights with people who'd not have a chance against him—"

"Yes, well, but about—" Livesey attempted to say.

"—*and* the constable and his bailiffs summoned almost every night on *me*, 'cause of *him!* And Sim Bates *never* had enough coin for his reckoning, when the night was over," Barbara Yadkin fumed.

"So Bates was not about, good!" Livesey almost barked, putting an end to that subject, he hoped. "But Mistress Yadkin . . ." he said, steepling his fingers under his chin, "did Harry seem as if he had an errand to run? Did anyone send him a note or letter after I departed? A . . . uhmm . . . small bouquet of flowers, perhaps?"

"Flowers, sir?" Mrs Yadkin asked in return, perplexed.

"Or did he receive any note or message before I arrived?"

"Flowers, d'ye say?" Mrs Yadkin repeated. "Oh!" she cried.

"Oh?" Livesey prompted.

"You think 'twas a husband or daddy stopped his business, don't you?" she gushed in a conspiratorial voice, leaning forward so quickly Livesey almost recoiled. "Everybody's been saying it was a *faction* matter, but there's the other rumors . . . La, Harry was a handsome rogue, and a great one for the ladies, 'fore he married, of course, and well I ought to know, growing up together as we did, seeing him out, squiring t'other young ladies . . ."

She got a dreamy (and wide-eyed) look of dewy softness at that reverie, and hitched a dramatic, regretful-sounding sigh, as if she had missed out on a prime experience and felt forever cheated.

"Poor, poor Georgina," she sniffed, though. "Betrayed by love!"

"Well, we don't know *that,* surely . . ." Livesey tried to counter.

"*Did* they find flowers in his hands, Matthew?" Mrs Yadkin said with a quick flare of enthusiasm. "Oh, how . . . ! Or fresh flowers on his grave, and no one knows who placed them? How romantic! How sad, *too,* o'course, *but* . . . romantic! How . . ." she gasped, waving a hand to waft the right word down from the air.

"Lurid?" Livesey suggested dryly.

"Did they, Matthew?" she implored. "Find flowers . . . by his body?"

"No, ma'am they didn't," he answered quickly, not *exactly* lying. He hoped to hide the existence of those flowers. "But the other rum . . ."

"Who were they from?" She shuddered, all but fanning herself at such an image. Or the makings of some devilish good gossip!

"Doesn't matter," Livesey drawled, hoping to cool her ardor. He flinched at his admission. This interview was going horribly wrong! He'd wished to elicit information with the cool dispatch of the barristers he'd seen in court when he sat on juries. Now his every utterance was turning to fuel to stoke this woman's fires, and he knew she'd hare off and spread this gossip with the lungs of a town crier!

"Oh, but it *does* matter, Matthew! Mr Livesey!" she wailed, her bosom heaving theatrically. Her hand came out to seize his once more, this time in a death-grip. "Why, I'll wager any sum you like, you find who put the flowers on his grave, or who dropped the flowers by his body out there on the Masonborough Road, you have the identity of Mr Harry's lover! And the husband or father who killed him!"

"There were no flowers, Mrs Yadkin, I was merely asking if he got any sort of message or signal . . ." Livesey begged, trying to find a decent way to get his hand back before she wrung it off at the wrist! "And we don't know *what* lured him out there that night . . . ahumm! What *reason* he had to be out there, rather. We don't *know* if Harry was having an . . . *amour.*" Livesey thought the French word more apt, less sordid. *Damme,* he thought, *I should leave before I give it all away!*

"Lured to his death, d'you mean?" she hissed, flushing and fanning madly now as she hung onto her illusions. "Merciful God, how . . . !"

"Uhmm, well . . ." Livesey sighed in reply. "Ma'am . . ."

"Oh, call me Barbara, *do,* Mr Livesey!" she insisted.

I'll be dashed if I will! he thought.

"Back to the matter at hand, though," Livesey tried. "Harry got no note that you saw, no one sent him an invitation or letter?"

"No, none."

"And you saw him ride off, Bess said," Livesey prompted, hoping he'd heard the last about those damnable flowers.

"Oh, yes! Poor man." She sniffed, groping for a handkerchief tucked into the tight cuff of her sleeve below her elbow. To do so, she had to unhand Livesey, and he withdrew both his hands out of her reach. "And no flowers did I see on his saddle, either, Matthew."

Damme, we're back to those bloody blossoms! he cringed.

"And no one approached him in your stable yard?" he asked.

"Just my 'daisy-kicker,' George, the little stableboy."

"So you were standing on the porch, I presume. Bess said you had gone out to chase down a Mr Pocock over his bill, and—"

"Bad as Sim Bates when he's had a few, that Pocock!" Mrs Yadkin groaned. "Far as keeping his wits about him, that is. Two shillings and four pence he owed me, and tossed down—"

"So you were in the yard," Livesey reiterated.

"Aye, I was."

"And the boy gave him nothing, either?"

"Nothing but his reins, and a steady stirrup," she recalled.

"Ahum." Livesey nodded, satisfied. "Now, there is one thing I'm puzzled about," he went on, getting to his major query. "Bess related that you said Harry rode off north, up Third Street for home. To turn onto Princess Street at the courthouse, so he could ride downhill for Princess and Second?"

"No, he took Market Street. By St James's."

"Ah?" Livesey exclaimed. "Pardon me, ma'am, but . . ."

"Barbara!" she insisted with a coo, making as if to strike him a teasing love-pat with the folded-up fan she wasn't holding.

"Uhmm, Barbara," Livesey said with a strangled sound, at last, "there's very little light to see by. That night especially, with no moon. I would ask about your eyesight, and . . . how may you be sure he turned down Market Street?"

"Why, there's nothing wrong with my eyes, sir!" she replied with a sudden frostiness, for having been teased since childhood over her myopic expression. "As for where he turned, I *saw* him! I'd come onto the porch, and 'twas so still and warmish that night, I stayed out to get a breath of air before running the last of the topers out. Harry was the only horseman on the street. There was the church lantern lit, and I saw him by that, him in that light blue taffeta coat he had on, and the yellow plume in his hat," she relayed, adding extra details to confirm her good eyesight out of pique. "And then, there were the lamps by the courthouse. How may I say it . . . like one of those cutout black paper portraits, those profile portraits? He rode *before* the lamp-lights as he turned and went down Market. I thought it odd, him taking an extra turning or two for home, but then he may have had call to see Osgoode Moore before retiring. He lives down Market."

"Osgoode Moore." Livesey nodded, with a silent prayer of thanks that he'd not have to raise that name, or give her any *more* suspicions to bandy about.

"They'd met up before you arrived, Matthew," Mrs Yadkin related, losing her iciness and dropping back into "fond." "Let's see . . . they came in at . . . no. Osgoode was here 'round quarter to seven, and Harry came in about five 'til, and they both got a bottle of wine to share, and put their heads together over *something*. You came in just a bit *after* seven, and the three of you supped together."

"Aye, we did," Livesey agreed. "Though Osgoode moved to the long table when the rest of the crowd arrived." *That* part of his evening was lucent, at least. "Did you get the impression I interrupted them . . . or heard what they might have been discussing before I came?"

"No," Mrs Yadkin told him, with a sly grin, "but whatever it was, they seemed pleased as all get-out over it. Plotting thick as thieves, they were. Like boys planning a prank, back of the barn, and snickering before it's played out. You and Harry were dawdling over your suppers, and the singing was starting, and that's when I remember Mr Osgoode moving to the long table with Thom Lakey and them."

"I see," Livesey absently replied. But for his arrival, Harry and Osgoode Moore might have been scheming additions to Harry's speech he was to give the next morning, and Harry might have wished to speak to Osgoode that late at night about a detail they hadn't covered before he interrupted them. So Harry's reason for riding down Market Street could be totally innocent! And Livesey could not imagine an angry, wronged husband plotting a murder being able to play the "Merry Andrew" with his future victim!

Now for the last matter, so he could completely put his mind to rest about Osgoode Moore. "Ahem . . . Barbara. Do ye know, but I can't recall just when it was that Osgoode left," he said with a shrug.

"Well, he waved to both of you on his way out," Mrs Yadkin said with a matching shrug. "Remember? Ah, but you were having the grandest time with the others. That Irish sailor who sat with ya'll played 'One Misty Moisty Morning,' and you got up and sang it, alone."

I did? Livesey thought with a cringe; *How liquored did I get?*

"Can't rightly say what time that *was,*" Mrs Yadkin admitted. "We were so busy, then. Before nine, perhaps half past eight, maybe?"

"That soon," Livesey sighed. There *was* time and enough for Osgoode to ride out of town with a coaching gun and wait for Harry Tresmayne to show up at his trysting spot.

"Bless him, Osgoode Moore's nothing like his clan," Mrs Yadkin said with a fond smile. "Not the caterwauler like some of them are. Deep stuff's more his style. Books, law and politics. Philosophies? He *never* stays 'til the wee hours. Ah! Here's Della with your breakfast . . . at last. Girl, top up Mr Livesey's coffee, and fetch out the West Indies lime jam for his toast. Do you like lime, Matthew? Or do you prefer mango? We have that, too."

"Why . . . the lime, I s'pose ma' . . . Barbara," he was forced to say. Then, under her adoring but misunderstanding gaze, he pretended to relish his repast, troubled all the while with disturbing fantasies of a cuckold sporting jolly with his impending victim, all the while with murder in back of his eyes. It didn't improve the food; nothing could. The eggs were done to washleather, the bacon blackened and as tough as Indian trail-jerky, that all went down like dirt and sat on his stomach like a worrisome ballast stone.

Chapter 14

WELL I DO declare!" Constable Swann grunted in surprise as he slouched over a mug of spruce-beer at the chandlery counter. "So it couldn't have been a faction killin', not with this for evidence."

Swann swept a glad hand over the further-wilted bouquet of oleanders on the counter, that Matthew Livesey had summoned him to see. Swann had had a rough week or so, and had taken to hiding out at the courthouse, letting his bailiffs do his work. And with few leads to pursue to begin with, that work had been sketchy at best.

"You didn't search the woods about the place where Harry died?" Livesey asked him, trying to keep his expression free of adjudging.

"Just the path 'round the body," Swann admitted. "Damme, though, sir! That Jemmy Bowlegs is good as any huntin' dog, now ain't he?"

"My son, Sam'l, helped, too. He found these."

"Makes a funny picture, damme'f it don't, Livesey," Swann said with a shaky laugh of relief that he had something to go on at last. "You out there in the barrens, followin' Jemmy Bowlegs an' your son, sniffin' an' skulkin' through the weeds. Rootin' 'round like Goodyer's Pig, sir! 'Never well, but when in mischief,' hey?"

"Something like that." Livesey sighed. Constable Swann offered his empty mug for a refill, and Livesey hid his impatience with the man as he tapped another pint for him. "Some rooting about seemed needful, the way common folk have been talking lately."

He could not repress that slight reproof from coming out. Swann glowered a bit, but shrugged it off. He'd heard worse, from all sides.

"Captain Tom o' the Mob, ye mean?" Swann nodded finally. "Well, this'll take 'em all aback. Now we know 'twas some daddy or husband, they'll calm down. No more talk o' armed justice."

"But we don't know that, sir," Livesey countered. "Not yet."

"God's Teeth, Livesey, 'course we do!" Swann interrupted. "See here, now. We both know . . . well, least I did, an' ev'ryone long about the Cape Fear—that Harry Tresmayne had a fearsome itch for quim."

"Sir." Livesey scowled, tilting his head toward Bess, who sat on a high stool behind the tall ledger desk, at the other end of the showroom. "My daughter is present."

"Your pardons," Swann grunted, lowering his voice and leaning further forward on his elbows to talk more privately. "Fella like him . . . there he was married to one o' the finest, prettiest women in the settlement. But two years or so o' scuffin' could take the shine off a silver snuff box, d'ye get my meanin', hey, Livesey?"

"Umphh," Livesey replied, appalled by such low talk.

Swann picked up the faded, rotting bouquet and sniffed it and twirled it, making petals flutter away to litter the countertop. He ran a light finger over the bows and ribbons.

"Let's say the rumors were right, Livesey. Harry was sparkin' himself some shiny new lass. Oh, he could come into town on business, an' see anyone he likes. But he was doin' it on the sly, out in that glade. So that means she was either an unmarried daughter, or she was someone else's wife. Wasn't no note needin'. Ye don't put such down on paper, as could be found. No, these *flowers* were the message from his doxy, most-like. Her to him. Maybe him to her."

"Really?" Matthew Livesey perked up, raising one eyebrow.

"Harry sets out this little bundle o' blooms himself, out by the path. His wanton rides by, innocent like as all get-out, but she sees it, and knows 'tis a sign t'meet there that night."

"But he was in town all that day, Constable," Livesey refuted. "Busy at Sessions and the Borough work. And at supper with me that night. It could have been set out in town. Easier, really."

"Her to him, then." Swann leered with a worldly snicker. "So, a house slave could have trotted this 'round to his door stoop, put it by the gate post, under the porch light . . . somewhere private he'd know to look. Might have been sent right inside, an' there they were in water in his receivin' hall when he got home."

Livesey wanted to repeat Barbara Yadkin's testimony that Harry had not gone home directly, had passed the Moore house, but he let it bide for awhile longer. Swann had heard it once, and hadn't shown any enthusiasm for it. Besides, Livesey was fascinated by the machinations of adultery, and its secret codes.

"Two bows, Livesey," Swann chuckled. "Think 'pon that. Mighta been *more*'n one little hidey-hole where they could play 'rock, and roll me over,' see? One bow's one place. Two means that glade off the Masonborough Road, most-like."

"Well, I'm . . . !" Livesey was forced to exclaim. "Really!"

"His whore used blue ribbon," Swann went on. "Mighta meant the time, or the place. Mighta meant the way's clear. Mighta sent red for 'stay away, he's suspicious,' see? Or another color signifyin' 'time's short, so don't dawdle.' Damme, sir!" Swann gaped at Livesey's expression. "I swear I'd just struck ye dumb! Never heard o' such? Ye watch yer ladies at the next drum, sir. Even in church, damn 'em. See who's foldin' a fan just so, or wearin' a brooch in the odd place. 'Tis like a second language! Some older'n Methuselah, some as the whores and the rogues make up t'wixt themselves."

"Well, I never!" Livesey frowned. And he hadn't! All the years he'd lived, and never had the slightest inkling. It was a disturbing revelation. Far happier was the revelation that Swann wasn't a *total* fool, and could make something of this evidence. Why, two weeks ago, he'd not thought him capable of saying "Boh!" to a goose!

"Hmm. Then it would be obvious that someone should inquire at the other chandleries, Constable Swann," Livesey declared. "To see who imported the ribbon. Ask among the dressmakers here in town, and the milliners. Fancy ribbon like this might be used to flounce a woman's hat. See who bought it, was it a man or a woman . . ."

"Bloody Jesus, man!" Swann groaned. "Small as Wilmington is, I could spend the next *month* at that! Must be dozens. And what do we do when we do trace it down, hey? Root 'round in every lady's sewing box for scraps? Don't need to. I got a good idea who mighta killed Harry already, thanks t'this."

"You do?" Livesey stiffened in anticipation.

"Two, really," Swann dithered a little. "Damme'f this ain't a fine spruce-beer, Livesey. Delaware, ain't it?"

"Boston, actually," Livesey snapped, taking the empty mug once more to refill, denied Swann's thoughts for the moment, like a puppy being promised a meat scrap held too far over his head.

"I'm sure ye've heard some rumors 'bout Harry an' some round-heeled girl lately," Swann muttered. "Hear the name Biddy MacDougall mentioned, hey?"

"I have."

"Lord, Livesey, ye seen her?" Swann said with a hint of awe.

"Only her Father. I gather the girl is kept close to home."

"Bloody right she is, *an'* with good reason!" Swann enthused. "Like an angel, she is. Not a minute over seventeen. Long, golden hair. Big blue eyes, an' cream-pot skin. A trifle spindle-shank, t'my lights, but there's some as likes 'em slim as saplin's. Not so tall an' gawky as t'put a fellow off, though. Like a yearlin' filly colt, but woman-bountiful 'nough for any man, haw haw!" Constable Swann all but put an elbow across the counter to nudge Livesey in man-to-man *bonhomie.* Swann had revived most wonderfully from his sulky, confused state since seeing the flowers, as if he'd just glimpsed Salvation after a life of crime. He also took a wistful dig at his crotch.

"An', when ye peer at her sharp, Livesey"—Swann sobered, as he tapped his nose meaningfully—"ye could swear she resembles Georgina, but younger . . . an', Devil take me, but handsomer, too! An', I 'spect ye've heard 'bout her dad, Eachan."

"That he's a hard man," Livesey replied. "That he immigrated in '46, he came without a wife and he never remarried. Stayed a widower all this time?"

"A widower of his own makin'," Swann agreed. "There's no proof of it, but they *say* he caught his wife an' his laird's son a'playin' balum-rancum when she was no older'n Biddy, an' he chopped 'em to bits, the both of 'em, with a claymore! Settled up at Cross Creek and drifted to Campbelltown when word got out. Drifted here when his neighbors wouldn't hold with him any longer. Farmed some good land over to Hood's Creek, but his temper ruint that, 'bout the time his Biddy started sproutin' womanly. Eachan

MacDougall's as like to go off at half-cock as a one-shillin' pistol. 'Tis a wonder he had a neighbor in *cannon* range, easy as he is to row! An' when he's hot, there's no stoppin' him short o' killin' him. There's some say one black glower o' his'd kill birds on the wing, hey?"

"But he lives on the wrong side of the river, Constable."

"Used t'be, Livesey." Swann grinned. "Used t'be! He sold that farm, bought himself twenty acres for a hog-run, an' took a job workin' the Brunswick Road ferry, just t'other side o' Eagle's Island."

"But still, how could the girl get across? If her father is so protective of her, how . . . ?"

"They come into town once a week to market, Livesey. Drove in a few hogs, a bushel'r two o' truck t'sell. An' here's the best part. Biddy's a *dress-maker!* Been sewin' up ladies' gowns an' such most o' this past year! Takes measure an' orders on one Saturday, brings her finished dresses the next. *An'* buys her materials, ha ha!"

"Oh, I see!" Livesey mused, brows raised in understanding.

"Like fancy blue ribbon, hey?" Swann chortled. "Christ, think on't! She comes t'town, Harry sees her. She sees him: a fine gentleman, rich an' all, an' cock-sure with the ladies. They like the cut o' each others' jibs, if ye get my meaning? Close as Eachan watches over her, Harry's the first fancy fellow she's ever met. Maybe she sewed for Georgina herself, by God! Been right in the house! Think about *that!*"

"It seems reasonable, Constable, but there is the problem of getting away from her father's eye, after all. Of getting across the Brunswick to Eagle's Island, then across the Cape Fear to town, and three miles further east to the rendezvous on the Masonborough Road. On the ferry her father runs! Do they have horses, or do they walk to town? How could she expect to get out there to meet him?"

"Wouldn't have had to." Swann tut-tutted. "Eachan knew Harry and his reputation. Mighta seen 'em billin' an' cooin' like stable lad an' goose-girl. Mighta spotted Harry's signals to other women or trailed him out there, followin' another harlot o' his. He takes the ribbon from Biddy's sewing box, makes the bouquet and ties it just so, but 'tis him 'stead o' Biddy that shows that night. Harry's 'spectin' the girl, he gets the father. Eachan shoots him, whether the two o' them were ever *really* rantipolin' in the buff, or not!"

"But it wasn't Saturday market day, it was . . ."

"Monday, aye, but 'twas Quarterly Assizes and Court Sessions. Ev'rybody was in town for that. I do allow I ask about, I'll find a dozen people as saw Eachan an' Biddy in town, too. Then 'twould be even easier for her t'hire a horse at Taneyhill's, if she planned to meet him."

"Constable, I find it hard to believe that Eachan MacDougall would just shoot Harry dead, at first sight," Livesey countered with a fretful feeling. This unexpected tack was just a little too neat! "Wouldn't he have warned him off first? Argued with him? Taken a whip to him? Beat him with his fists? And if it was the girl sent the bouquet to Harry, even if Eachan intercepted it, or made her do it up . . ."

"Could have been he sent it to her," Swann rebutted quickly. "He's a . . . well, he *was* a cultured gentleman. Maybe he took ribbon from Georgina's sewing box, and tied those bows. Pinked the ends as they are, to make 'em neat an' even. You told me you thought 'twas a refined lady's hand did it. Could have been a refined gentleman's work just as easy! An' when Eachan saw it, he grilled her 'til she confessed who sent it, an' he set off that very night. An' as for Eachan's temper, ya don't know him! He's not the man to 'front direct' 'thout good cause. An' go well-armed when ye do! Goes red-eyed, like a lunatic, an' there's Hell t'pay 'fore he's done, an' him 'thout one mem'ry of it after. I been 'cross the river on him b'fore, sir, an' I pray hard he's not so cup-shot or daft there's no talkin' to him—an' that with four bailiffs!"

"That is one possibility, I suppose," Livesey said, disappointed. "Yet you said you had another idea, though."

"Well, there's Sim Bates, after all," Swann said with a wave of his hand. "Hell, it's his side o' town. He knows all that barren country. And he had grievance 'gainst Harry, like you said. I think your hired hound Bowlegs is wrong 'bout Sim bein' too cowardly to do it, too. That's 'cause Bates tried on Jemmy some time back, and Bowlegs beat the livin' daylights outa him. Just about the time he took that new coachin' job for Prince Richard? So Jemmy don't think Bates man enough to worry about. But you let Sim simmer on his grievances, an' he'll find a way t'do ye back, if ye prick him sore enough."

"So he could have seen Harry meeting some woman out there, as he did his regular rounds as Ramseur's man. And sent the bait to him?"

"An' got what he always swore he'd get, after we come home from the militia. After Major Harry had him at the cartwheel a second time," Swann intoned ominously. 'Harry Tresmayne's heart's blood.' Sim Bates's very words."

"He has the double-barreled coaching gun. He has a reason. He knew those trails, too, I shouldn't wonder," Livesey reluctantly agreed. "Hmm . . ."

"One o' those two're the most likely, aye. Here, gimme a snip o' that ribbon," Swann said. "I can send a bailiff down to Masonborough to nose about. Hear tell Sim's got himself a black girl, one o' Prince Richard's house servants, to share his shack. Mighta put her up t'buyin' this ribbon. Mighta had her tie these bows, too. I doubt Sim Bates could tie a granny-knot right the first time, hey? End with a pack saddle bowline, like as not! And a storekeeper'd remember him or a black girl buyin' ribbon like this, costly as you say it is."

"One would hope it isn't Bates, though, Constable," Matthew said quickly, hoping to keep Swann there, before he set off dead-set to find the killer he wished to find. "I mean, if it *was* Bates, wouldn't people believe that Richard Ramseur put him up to it? Or took advantage of his spite against Harry . . . for Ramseur's own purposes?"

"There is that," Swann admitted. "But see here; Ramseur may be a stiff-necked, purse-proud old bastard, but he'd never do anything like this behind the back. He'd come right out an' challenge an enemy to a duel. Meet you face-to-face, man-to-man. An' *enjoy* it."

"*You* believe that, sir. But the common folk—who are talking of mob justice—don't. Even if Sim is the killer, there'll always be talk. It'll fester for years. Best those rumors are laid to rest for good."

"An' *not* look into Bates?" Swann goggled.

"That's not what I meant at all, sir. I think you should delve into whether the Ramseur household bought the ribbon, and question our Prince Richard direct."

"Now lookee here, Livesey," Swann shot back, growing cold and distant.

"Would ye tell your granny how t'suck eggs, hey? There's some'd call what ye been up to meddlin' where ye got no right. Now I thankee for findin' this bunch o' flowers, an' tellin' me 'bout those prints'n all. Good shoes, shod horse. Double-barreled coachin' gun. Aye, I'll take all ye found to heart. But I told ya earlier, I doubt it was faction, at the root of it."

"You *hope* it wasn't faction," Livesey rejoined dryly. "Else we have Captain Tom of the Mob, after all, and the garrison down at Fort Johnston called out to read the Riot Act."

"There's that," Swann grunted, stifling a belch. He was cool-voiced, though, rared back on his heels, on slit-eyed guard.

"The other rumor about the town," Livesey prompted him. "The other woman mentioned. I told you about Mrs Yadkin seeing Harry ride down Market Street, past the Moore house. Will you ask about her when you hunt up the store which sold this ribbon? And who bought it?"

"God . . . hey now!" Swann growled, sounding as menacing as a cornered bear. "Lookee here, Livesey, that's nought o' your concern. An' I'll be askin' ya t'say no more, for th' time bein', 'bout that particular rumor, hey?"

"We both know, Constable, that it is implausible beyond belief," Livesey lied, with a disarming purr. "The Moores would never countenance murder or violence. They're refined English gentlemen."

Poor Swann, he thought; *can't pursue the home-grown aristocrats, can't delve too close into the* other *faction, for fear of finding one of the Moores involved—related to his masters!* Ignore *faction?*

"But if all possibilities are not pursued, people might say that justice doesn't reach to the rich and powerful, sir. The Moore name arises . . . *any* Moore is tainted, then we're back to suspicions of favoritism and faction among the common folk. And fears of mob vengeance."

There wasn't much Swann could say to that. He was beholden to the Moores, their bought man. Livesey could actually feel a twinge of sympathy for Swann's position, square in the middle. It was faction that had arranged his election, and faction that had paid out a passel of guineas for rum, beer and barbecue on the hustings. Or purchased a few key voters in the borough outright!

"It's low, dirty talk," Swann allowed at last, gulping and chewing as if he wished to spit out rotten gristle. "Baseless, too, see?"

"Talk which must be confounded, sir," Livesey suggested softly.

"Know where it comes from, hey?" Swann grimaced. "Old chick-a-biddy, chicken-chested, gossipy hens is where, Livesey. Wimmen past their prime swimmin' in their spite. Them as envy Anne Moore's features. And her figure. Lord, like a Gypsy sash-dancer, she is! And she's not a Wilmington girl, an' that'll do it every time. She's a New Bern girl. Got manners an' airs good as London, an' that don't set with our ladies either. Close as Harry an' Osgoode were—partners in their faction, him Harry's lawyer, an' both of 'em well-off—see the bile there, hey? And Harry's repute added to it . . ."

"Or idle men who might have wished to be in Osgoode's shoes?" Livesey concluded for him.

"Them, too, Goddamn 'em," Swann agreed. "Aye, I've heard that rumor. I kept my ear t'the ground, an' don't ye think I haven't! I just can't feature Osgoode bein' the kind t'kill a body, though. An' say what you will 'bout poor Harry Tresmayne . . . he was a gentleman, damn his eyes. He knew better'n t'mess with a *close* friend's wife."

"True." Livesey nodded, though he wasn't sure of anything anymore.

"We find out it's Sim Bates, or Eachan MacDougall, the better it'll be," Swann insisted. "Then all this trash talk'll go away 'bout Mistress Anne an' Harry. An' two fine young people won't end up with their lives ruint."

"But . . ." Livesey attempted to argue.

"Thankee for yer discovery, Livesey," Swann concluded for him, draining the last dregs of his pint. "Damme if ye ain't a knacky one, no error. Leave it t'me from now on, though. Can't have ye stickin' yer nose in 'thout blowin' the gaff, hey?"

"I quite understand, Constable Swann," Livesey had to answer, hiding his disappointment that he had not been able to influence the man. "Do keep me apprised, though."

"Hey?"

"Let me know how things go," Livesey translated. "If you would be so kind. No matter his faults, Harry was my friend. And finding his killer is important to me. If I could be of some further assistance, do let . . ."

"Never ye fear! And g'day to ye, sir!" Swann hooted over a cool shoulder as he lumbered for the doors.

"Dear Lord," Livesey muttered aloud after he had gone. "What a complete hen-head!"

"Sim Bates you expected, did you not, Father?" Bess inquired as she came behind the counter at last, now that the "men's business" was done.

"Hey?" He scowled. "Pardon, lass. Now he has me doing it. Hey?"

"As a prime candidate," Bess went on.

"I suppose." Livesey sighed, sitting down on a stool at last to ease his leg. "I must confess, Swann may be right. It's hard to feature Osgoode Moore as a killer. Plausible, if there's anything to the rumors, but . . . Bless my soul, though! Eachan MacDougall? There's a tack I didn't expect. And plausible as well."

"Pardon me for meddling, Father, but . . ." Bess said, nibbling at her upper lip.

"Meddle away, pet," Livesey laughed back. "Runs in the family, it seems—to hear our Constable tell it, anyway."

"Well," she posed, "it's just that Osgoode Moore never struck me as the sort to kill anybody. If his wife and Uncle Harry were . . . ahum . . . well, I'd think Mr Moore would be more likely to brood or mope if he had the slightest suspicion of her . . . affections? He's so high-minded and honorable, he would have been cut to the quick, yes, but certainly unable to laugh and jest with you and Uncle Harry your last evening together. If he knew, surely he'd have shown some resentment, or anger."

"Still, there's Harry riding down her street that night. And a husband is, they tell me, usually the last to know." Livesey reddened with embarrassment. "Dash it, but Swann's low talk . . . him knowing about adultery, secret signals . . ."

"Perhaps he practices them?" Bess said with a wry expression.

"Or understands human nature better than I ever will," Livesey replied, not rising to her bait. "I've learned a lot since Harry died. And I'm not partial to one whit of it."

"Ignorance is bliss?" Bess tried to cajole him further.

"Perhaps naivety—or innocence, rather—is bliss."

"'Cause if ignorance is bliss," Bess went on with a blithe look, "then Constable Swann must be a *very* happy man."

Livesey at last rose to her baiting and emitted a barking laugh. "Well, let's pray God he's hand-wringing miserable, then, Bess," he said, heaving himself off the stool. "And pray God he's right. Better for all that Harry died for personal reasons 'stead of politics. Better for Wilmington and its peace."

"And simple enough for even Constable Swann to smoke out," Bess agreed.

"And the *sooner* the better." Livesey nodded. "Done with bookkeeping? Good. I'll look them over this afternoon. Thankee, pet. I don't know what I'd do without you."

"I'll put them in your desk, Father," she said, after giving him a supportive hug. "What will we do with these flowers now? Should I throw them out?"

"Mmm, best not just yet. Might put them away somewhere in the office. The fewer who know of them, the better, until Swann's gotten more evidence," Livesey decided.

"So will we wait for him to discover something, then?" she asked with a slight frown. "Or will you be making any more inquiries?"

"Well, Swann is the law. Now he's on any sort of scent . . ." her father dithered. "Bless me, but I wish I could talk to Anne Moore first, or Osgoode. Ask about the rumors. No, perhaps not. I might muddy the waters for him. Still . . . I wish there was something *more* I could do."

"I'll put them away, then." Bess smiled, wrapping the bouquet in a scrap yard of calico. "Oh, Father?"

"Yes, Bess."

"Could I have ten pounds?"

"Da . . . !" Livesey began to splutter. "Ahem . . . ten pounds, d'ye say? Whatever for, my girl? A rather large sum . . ."

"For a new gown and bonnet, for the summer." Bess beamed, most waif-like. "You look at the ledgers, you'll see we're over two hundred pounds in the black, and that's with only the first three ships of the spring cargoes accounted for. And, our last debt's paid off, finally. So . . . ?"

"Well, I suppose . . ." he waffled, *wishing* to give her anything she desired, yet so *used* to scrimping, over mere *pence!*

"Nothing *too* grand, I promise!" she enthused. "And trim some of my old homemades. Please, Father? Just the one new! Swear it!"

"Well then . . . yes, I . . ." Livesey allowed, proud to indulge her.

"Oh, you're the kindest, most generous father in the whole Cape Fear!" she cried, hugging him once more, and bussing him on the cheek to seal the bargain before he turned abstemious again.

Bess took the ledgers to his office and set them out where he'd see them later, so he could savor their profit. She opened a drawer, and took out the scissors he kept to snip margin-paper off bills, which he used to make notes. She unwrapped the bouquet of oleanders and took a clean eight inches of the ribbon with the snips, off the bottom bow, which she rolled up and stuffed into a pocket of her apron.

She really did need at least one new summer gown, Bess assured her conscience. There was her blue taffeta one, too, which she'd worn to the Burgwyns's. It would look much nicer and newer were it trimmed in this particular width and color of blue satin ribbon, backed with a bit of white lace along each pleat and ruch. That blue gown, though . . .

What a perfect excuse! With this snip of ribbon, Bess meant to hunt down the original supply, and all most-innocently. It was the least she could do, to help her father. Constable Swann . . . he might ask other importers, other shops where it had originated but he hadn't shown much enthusiasm for questioning the dressmakers, or the hatmakers. It was a woman's business, a woman's trade . . . and who would suspect her of any motive other than Fashion?

And there were the flower vendors, too, she decided; how many were there in the streets or the markets? No one, not even her clever father, had given a thought to them, either!

The vendors usually tied their poseys or nosegays with a hank of rough twine, a wire-grass frond, even with a slim, dampened strip of basketing willow or white oak! This bouquet, though . . . whoever had tied this might have brought the ribbon with them, with no chance to take it home and do it up!

"Now there's a tack Father didn't suspect, either!" she whispered as she rewrapped the bouquet and hid it in a bottom drawer. She opened the cash-box, wrote a careful receipt on a snip of margin paper, and took her ten pounds sterling in two one-guinea coins, and the rest silver shillings. And set off to shop . . . for fabrics.

Chapter 15

SAM'L?" Bess asked in her best, "please, dear brother" tone several days later, after she'd awakened him, after she'd gotten the hearth-fire going.

"What," he replied, sleepy and flat between wide yawns as he stood at the kitchen window looking out on the street.

"Could you do something for me today?" She smiled.

"Oh, no," he replied out of long practice. "Terribly busy."

"Sam'l. Dear, dear Sam'l," she crooned, ruffling his uncombed hair. "You haven't even heard what it is yet."

"It ain't kindling, it ain't water, it ain't the garden, that's seen to. And you don't simper like that 'less it's something pestifyin'. Well, I won't this time, so there," he groused, ducking away as she ruffled his hair some more. "Damme, I ain't a hound, Bess! Leave my hair be!"

"I want you to go riding with me, Sam'l."

"Lord, who'd care t'be seen riding with his *sister!*" Samuel muttered with a grimace of extreme distaste. "Even *want* to, truth be told."

He faked a shiver of revulsion before he stuck his head into the china washbasin to rinse his face and neck. He came up puffing and blowing, groping for a towel, which Bess offered him as a sop. Once he scrubbed himself dry, and lowered the towel, though, his face wore a canny expression, having awakened his wits with cold water.

"Oh?" he lisped with rising glee. "Does da puss'ms wanna pway wif da widdle he-kitten Andwew Hewwett? An' big, bad daddy puss'ms might not wike it, hmm?"

"God, you are *so* disgusting," she declared with icy scorn as she turned to face the hearth and the warming skillets.

"Widdle Bess-kittums miss da widdle Andwew, do she?" he leered.

"Andr . . . Mr Hewlett has nothing to do with it, Sam'l," Bess said, more in a snooty huff than she'd planned. She took a deep hitch of breath and turned to face him, falling back on sweeter speech. "If you must know, I have to go across the rivers. Over toward Belvedere and the Brunswick Road. There's a new dressmaker over there everyone praises, and I want her to make my new gown. And you *know* a lady can't ride unescorted, Sam'l. There's no one else but you. And you wouldn't want our family name dragged through the mud if I go riding without an escort . . . or the wrong sort."

"Easy enough, then, Bess." Samuel shrugged as he ran the towel over his damp hair. "Send a note. Tell her to come over here."

"She can only come to town once a week, of a Saturday, Sam'l," Bess said, allowing the slightest hint of pleading into her voice. "I can't wait that long."

"Women and fashion whims!" Samuel snorted in dismissal.

"I'm *told* she sews for anyone, man *or* woman, and just as cunning as anything," Bess told him, falling back on her brother's vanity. "If you wished some new shirts and waistcoats, with lace or embroidery for a change? Now our debts are clear, I'd have thought you wanted to make a finer public show. At church, and such."

"Well . . ." Samuel pondered as he combed back his hair. "Ah, but my old'uns are good enough. The ones you made'll suit. So long as I keep my coat on, that is," he could not help needling her. "So folks don't see how crooked your seams are."

Damn your eyes, Sam'l! she thought, turning back to her skillets; *my sewing needs hiding, does it?* She cracked open an egg on the side of the pan and dribbled a tiny bit in the skillet to see if it was hot yet. "If the ones I made you are so shameful to you, I'd expect you'd *relish* another's handiwork." She put a hitch in her voice, portraying sullen heartbreak. "I've *tried* t'do right by you, I really have, Sam'l! I'd never let my brother be seen all patches and darns, when I could . . ." She managed a lip-quivering sound.

"Aw now, Bess, don't take on so," Samuel grumbled. "I didn't mean it. You do main-well. You cut and sew neat as . . . neat as . . ."

Hide yer grin, Bess told herself. She made as if to wipe tears away from her eyes, still facing the hearth as she cracked open eggs and began to fry them. *Half-way home,* she speculated; *go the rest!*

"Thankee, Sam," she said in a small voice. "It's just that I thought I was doing all I could to keep a good house for you and Father. So people would be proud of you. Maybe if I have enough left over, I could pick up some scrap lace, now we've a *little* money, and redo your best ones. Would you like that?"

"Aye, Bess, that'd be handsome," Samuel agreed.

"Or, I could take them over the river with me when I go today." She wound back to her aim. "Or you could come along with me. I can't go, if you don't."

"Well . . ." Samuel relented a trifle.

"They tell me the new dressmaker's very pretty," Bess tossed to him, using her hole-card to take the trick. She turned to face Samuel with an innocent smile, the sort she imagined a girl who had just been cruelly used by her own brother, but had forgiven him, might sport.

"How pretty?" he scoffed, suddenly leery again. It would not be the first time he'd fallen for one of Bess's lures, and had gotten his fingers burned.

"Well, so pretty that Constable Swann gets this strangled look whenever he speaks of her," Bess informed him with a blithe air. "And Louisa Lillington . . . who told me of her first . . . ?"

Louisa Lillington was an extremely handsome young lady, one whom Bess knew figured highly in Samuel's fantasies, for the strangled looks Samuel wore whenever he ogled her at a rout, oyster roast or tea.

"Uhmm?" Samuel perked up at the mention of that special name.

"Well, she was a little catty . . . but she did allow that she was *very* pretty," Bess said with a straight face, having made it all up on the spur of the moment. Louisa Lillington thought herself the new generation's ideal for feminine charms in the Cape Fear, and if *she* sounded pique-ish over another girl's features, then there was a *definite* challenger toeing up, barefisted but game for a bout of "who's the fairest."

"Well, who is she, then?" Samuel asked, a bit quickly.

"Bridey . . . Bridget . . ." Bess frowned, waving a hand in the air. "Something like that. I didn't catch her last name, but Louisa assured me everybody 'cross the Brunswick knows of her. She's new to the Cape, I think." Bess shrugged off, facing the skillets again, feeling like if truth was taffy, she'd have it pulled clear across the road by then!

"*How* old, d'ye think?" Samuel inquired further.

"About my age, I think Louisa said," Bess confided. "Ours or so."

"Hmm." Samuel sighed. "Damme, though, there's the mill, and the tar-pots. Father'd have my hide if he found out. Uhmm. How long d'ye expect this little errand of yours'd take?"

"Well . . ." Bess all but hugged herself in victory as she turned with a speculative, cheek-biting look. "Were you to have a couple of horses we could use, I could get across to Eagle's Island an hour before noon. There and back . . . no more than two hours, I should think. You could say you took a long dinner."

"Hmm," Samuel reiterated, waffling now.

"I could cook us a chicken for our dinner," Bess coaxed warily. "Or since we'd arrive just about her dinner time, should I do enough for three? It might be the polite thing, seeing as how we'd be interrupting her. Then we might all sup together!" she perkily suggested.

"Aye, that sounds . . . polite," Samuel agreed, and Bess could see her brother's imagination spring to life: at-table with a young, pretty dress-maker! But his face sobered, and he got on his usual wary look.

"Here now, 'tis twice we'll have to cross the Brunswick with two horses. That's five pence per man and mount, twice. That's . . ."

"One shilling, eight pence," Bess quickly summed. "Two shilling and two pence, if you count me boating over the island to meet you, and come home again when we're done."

"Uh, aye . . . aye, it is," Samuel frowned, flustered that she was quicker with sums than he. "Must *I* sport the whole cost, or just half? *And* hire horses atop of that, that'd be . . ." he said, wincing.

"There's work beasts enough on the island, aren't there, Sam'l? Not a brace of blooded hunters, but surely two saddle-broke . . ."

"Who pays for all this?" Samuel asked, again highly dubious.

"Sam'l . . ." Bess tried cooing, though she knew he'd balk if she bargained *too* close with him. "Well . . . it is my gown, so it's up to me to bear the cost, I s'pose. But I *am* providing the dinner!"

"Anything new for me? Or just trim my old togs?" he pressed.

"I don't know if my money'd go quite *that* far, Sam'l. But Lord, you'd bargain your own sister to the last groat?" she all but wailed in exasperation.

"Darned right I would!" he chortled. "I know you too well."

"Hang it," Bess relented, letting out a frustrated breath which bulged her cheeks with an audible *chuff.* "All right. I'll pay the ferry fees for you. But new shirts are your own look-out."

"And . . . ?" Samuel prodded, smug in his victory.

"*And* I'll pay for lace and labor on two of your best home-mades. But no more than two, *please,* Sam'l, or I can't afford my new gown!" she cried.

"Well . . . all right," he allowed. "Two, then."

"So you'll ride with me?" she asked. "If I *pay* you to?"

"Mmm, s'pose I could." He shrugged at last.

"Hang it! You will or you won't!" Bess thought it had come down to begging time. "Say you will? Please?"

"Oh, aye, I will," he relented. "Long as this doesn't get me in trouble with Father, mind."

She thought of flinging her arms about him and thanking him profusely, almost attained to telling him what a wonderful brother he was.

But that might, she thought, be gilding the lily. It would also re-arouse his suspicious nature. And end with her owing him a debt he'd be sure to remember, and collect on, later.

So she left it with a simple "thankee, Sam'l, I'm grateful to ye," and a warm (but not too warm) smile of sisterly thankfulness.

Chapter 16

FERRIES in the North Carolina colony were horrid. Service was haphazard, even around the larger towns and boroughs. The eastern Low Country was laced with rivers flowing from the Piedmont; some too deep to ford, or too swift; most too broad to bridge. The ferry operators were supposedly licensed, and the county courts oversaw their boats or flats, and their fees. Some few were free, the owners getting an annual stipend—they were the worst, usually: the ferrymen surlier, the boats worse maintained, without the incentive of money in hand for every passenger, horse, crate or barrel, right on the spot.

Bess took a small shallop across the Thoroughfare and the Cape Fear, a leaky tub under lug-sail whose bilge-water scepage soaked the hems of her petticoats and gown. Better to soak than pull them up to protect them, for the ferryman was a bewhiskered, toothless sot who spent his time trying to see her ankles and engage her in bawdy conversation. When he wasn't muttering to himself, chewing his beard and laughing at his own monologue, that is.

Samuel was waiting for her at the landing, a muddy slope which trailed off into the river. The lengthwise-laid pole roadbed should have been sanded, but it wasn't, so every step squelched poles into a brown soup between them, and each pole was so slick it took Bess some time to get on "dry" land without breaking an ankle or coming a cropper.

Showing no brotherly concern whatsoever, Samuel had stayed above the landing, only offering shouted advice on how to walk, pointing out the larger and deeper puddles of muck. And the two *horses* he had said he'd procure turned out to be two roach-backed *mules* who had seen better days. At least they had saddles.

I'll remember this, Sam'l, she thought, *'deed I will, you . . . oh, you'll be years working this one off with me, you!*

"No side-saddle?" she commented, trying very hard to maintain an air of pleasant adventure. She *almost* attained a smile.

"No horse, either, you'll note," Samuel said, enjoying himself. "Wanted a girl's saddle, shoulda brought it from home. Up you get, my girl. I'll take the hamper. What all'd ye fix? Bring my shirts?"

"Don't go eating it *now,* Sam'l," Bess scolded. "And could you give me a leg up? This beast must be fifteen hands if he's an inch."

Samuel left off pawing through the willow food basket to offer some assistance, shortened the stirrups for her once she was astride, then led off. Bess's mule craned his neck about to look at her with a chary expression, flicked his long ears, and shambled into a paddle-footed, slow gait that no amount of coaxing could improve.

Eagle's Island was low, marshy, foetid with swamp smells and fumey with smoke: pine kindling as it burned under tar-pots, tar and pitch giving a sharp tang of sulphurous oil to the air; sweet scent of fresh-sawn boards and sawdust, the amber perfume of resin-renderings or the aseptic smell of turpentine.

The road was better past the ferry landing, raised above the low-lying sand and mud, the lengthwise-laid poles decently covered with sand and dirt. Samuel rode silent, hugging the willow basket, a little ahead of her, as if ashamed that one of his compatriots might see him with her and tease him, holding the basket awkwardly, as if it was his sister's purse he was holding. Which was fine with Bess, still simmering over his latest crudeness. It gave her silence in which to think, too.

She had haunted the market, the produce sheds and the street vendors, but no one could remember a customer who'd brought his or her own ribbon to tie up a bunch of oleander blossoms. She had wandered from shop to shop, seeking fabrics and showing her sample of ribbon as the exact color she wished. She was sure most of them thought her daft as bats by then. Or worse. One old chick-a-biddy milliner had flat told her "now yer dad's well-off, ye've turned off miss-ish as t'rest o' them ol' gals," and speculated where her level-headed sense had gone.

In a week of giddy gushing over bolts of cloth, of comparing a spool of ribbon to "that exact color" she craved, of dashing off to a next, and then a next dressmaker or milliner in her fruitless search, she was beginning to wonder if that blue satin ribbon had sprung into existence of its own. It certainly had not come from a Wilmington or New Hanover County store! Bess hoped that Constable Swann was true to his word, and had had better luck down to Masonborough.

How to handle this, now, she mused as the mule plodded onto the plank bridge over Alligator Creek, a stagnant slough through wire-grass marshes, surrounded by the stark stumps of dead and hollow cypress. It was rare to see a 'gator around Eagle's Island anymore, but it wasn't out of the question. She peered over the low side of the bridge, hoping to see at least a swish in the water, if not a scaly back, a tail in motion, or a pair of eyes barely awash.

Bess was still pondering whether her giddy, girlish pose and her silliness would serve with Biddy MacDougall. If the girl was implicated, would she not recognize the ribbon, and suspect why she had come? she wondered. But what other sham could she play? She still wondered as they crossed Richmond Creek, the last stretch of dry land, and got to the Brunswick ferry landing.

So that's *what a murderer looks like,* Bess thought, scowling as she got her first glimpse of the man she took for Eachan MacDougall.

"Passage for two," Samuel said to the ferry keeper.

"Man an' horse, fi' pence," the dark-featured man in the Scotch bonnet grunted, peering up at them with a frown not entirely caused by the sun's brightness. He was dressed in a coarse, pale-tan linen shirt with voluminous sleeves rolled to his elbows, and a pair of well-made tartan plaid trousers, cinched with a broad leather belt. In the belt, he had stuffed a pair of clean white stockings, bagged as heavy as a duke's coin purse. Evidently, he stowed his shoes in the stockings, for his horny feet and ankles were bare.

"No discount for mules, or for a girl?" Samuel made to jape.

"Nae, thayr's not," Could-Be-MacDougall answered with a weary sigh, as if he'd heard that one so long before that he'd kicked slats out of his cradle the *last* time he'd found it amusing. "Weel ye be dismountin', then? Or air ye waitin' for Noah's Ark t'come by for ye?"

Samuel sprang down from his mule and handed his reins to Could-Be-MacDougall, who sniffed as if Samuel had asked him to lick his boots clean. Samuel came to hand Bess down.

"'Tis still fi' pence. Ten pence, in all," the man grumbled.

"Here you are, sir," Bess answered, digging into her clutch.

"Th' lassie pays th' rogue's way, is eet?" Could-Be-MacDougall smirked, all but biting the coins to assay them. "Yair feller canna be worth much, girl. Nae bargain, cheap as th' fee be, haw haw!"

"You're absolutely right, sir!" Bess chirped back disarmingly, smiling half from nervousness. "He's my brother, d'ye see. I'll sell him to you for free passage."

"Haw!" the burly man hooted briefly. "Yair brother, is he? I'd rather hae th' puir auld *mule*. Lead on, lead on, lad, an' keep yair beasties still whilst we're crossin'."

The Brunswick Ferry was a double-*piragua,* two long cypress logs split lengthwise, then hollowed out with axes, adzes and hot stones. Once laid wide and gaping, the ends had been boarded up blunt and the logs set about five feet apart, nailed or pegged athwart with timbers, then planked and railed to make a flatboat about ten feet by thirty.

"All on?" Could-Be-MacDougall bellowed at the idlers who lazed on the landing bollards or benches. "It'll nae get any cheaper. All on, air we? Right, then . . . shove off, lads."

All four ferrymen dipped their long poles into the mud of the bank and heaved, and the ferry began to move, shuffling a little on the slow current of the Brunswick.

"Left side, now! *Heave,* ye heathens!"

Working the down-river side, in the blunt bows or stern of the larboard log, the ferrymen sweated and strained, dipping and poling, as the large Scotsman tended a wide sweep-oar at the stern, aiming above the landing on the opposite bank.

Bess left Samuel to tend the mules and crossed to the right-hand, up-river, side of the ferry. Try as she might to seem incurious, Bess could not help sneaking fearful looks at the potential murderer. And after one furtive glance too many, and a too-quick look away, the man finally snarled at her.

"D'ye think I look like Auld Scratch, himself, lass?" he barked.

"Oh, why *no,* sir!" Bess croaked, desperately thinking.

"What, then?" he demanded.

"I was wondering how . . . anyone could make every line of your plaid trousers meet so cleverly, sir!" Bess lied, gushing prettily to disarm him. *Babbling will help,* she quickly told herself. "Is it a clan pattern, or just a bought plaid? Mean t'say . . . you sound like a Scot. You are, aren't you?" She threw in a bright smile, and batted her lashes rapidly enough to create a two-knot breeze.

"Och, 'tis MacDougall plaid," the man replied, grinning a little as well. "That's ma clan, that's ma name. Eachan MacDougall, miss."

"Good morrow to you, Mr MacDougall, sir!" Bess said, even dropping him a slight curtsy. "Allow me to name . . ."

"You're that sawmill feller's lass. Miss Livesey, air ye no?"

"I am, sir, Bess Livesey. That's my brother Sam'l, yonder."

"Aye, th' idle one, I'm told," MacDougall said with a slow nod and a disconcerting crinkle of sly humor round his eyes.

"The very one, sir!" Bess snickered in spite of her dread, glad that her bold, ditzy front had won the man over.

"Trews," MacDougall said.

"Sir?"

"Ma 'trews.' What we call trousers back in Scotland."

"For when it's too cold for kilts, Mr MacDougall?" Bess asked. "Pardon my ignorance, but I thought all Scotsmen wore kilts, even here in summer, and all."

"'Tis *ne'er* too cold t'wear a kilt, miss," MacDougall boasted, "nae for a real Scot. Trews be mair practical for workin' th' ferry, is why."

"Cunningly well-made, though, Mr MacDougall," Bess repeated. "Every line, every color come together, as clever as . . ."

"That's ma lass's doin'," MacDougall said with evident pride. "She's a knacky'un when eet come t'sewin'. Here now, Miss Livesey . . . ye'd not be crossin' th' rivers t'do yair laundry, that bundle o' sarks an' such ye got thayr. Ye'd be lookin' for a seamstress, yairself?"

"Well, I'd heard there was a marvelous dressmaker, the far side of the Brunswick, Mr MacDougall, aye, so . . ." Bess replied, trying to keep her teeth from chattering with sudden dread of Mr MacDougall's seemingly suspicious and leery glower.

"That'd be ma lass Biddy ye come seekin', then," he told her. "Why'd ye not say so?"

"Biddy?" Bess stammered. "Oh, Biddy! The lady who told me of her called her *Bridey!*" she extemporized, feigning brainlessness.

"Musta been ain o' th' 'Quality,'" MacDougall sneered, spitting over the side. "She does for th' rich'uns, noo an' ageen . . . them that has mair money than brains. Biddy does braw off thayr trade."

"Mr MacDougall?" Bess piped, wide-eyed and innocent-seeming.

"What?"

"What's a 'braw'?" she tittered. "What's a 'sark'?"

"Braw is 'fine,' Miss Livesey," MacDougall told her, after he'd thrown back his head for a good laugh. "So, ye look for Biddy, do ye? Turn off th' Brunswick Road, gae past th' ordinary at th' ferry landin' on th' Belville Trace, then follow th' smell o' pigs, an' that'll be my land. 'Tis thayr ye'll find Biddy, an' she can tell ye herself all about sarks an' such. Mind, now . . . about yair brother. I don't hold with a man, any man, sniffin' round ma girl, 'less I'm thayr."

"He's very well-behaved, sir." Bess grinned. "Mostly."

"Aye, that's what I'm feart of," MacDougall said with a scowl on his face. "I'll be askin' later, count on eet. Biddy says he shewed a *jot* o' disrespeck, I'll call on yair brother with ma horsewhip, nae matter who his daddy be. He's t'stay in th' yard, an' he's not t'gae further than ma porch, or I'll cut ma clan tartan on his back, were his father King George o' Hanover!" MacDougall vowed.

"Sam'l only came along to escort me, as a brother should, sir," Bess replied, getting a sudden inspiration. "As you guard your daughter's reputation. Is it very far to your lane from the ferry tavern?"

"'Bout half a mile or so," MacDougall allowed with a grunt.

"Hmmm . . . what if Sam'l saw me to your lane, Mr MacDougall, then came back to the tavern to wait for me? Where you could keep one eye out for him, would that suit?" she asked with a sly, impish grin.

"Hah! Aye, that'd do. I'd settle for that."

"I trust the ordinary sets a decent dinner?" Bess chuckled.

"Och, they do *not!*" MacDougall snickered with her, even winking as he got her intent. "'Tis swill I'd nae feed t'ma pigs!"

"That will have to do him," Bess told him. "And here I brought all this fried chicken and biscuits! Oh, what a pity."

"Good God, Bess!" Samuel urgently whispered once they were back ashore and remounted. "Do ya know who that scoundrel is you were all jolly with back yonder?"

"MacDougall, I think he said he was," Bess sweetly answered.

"Lord, Bess! That's *the* Eachan MacDougall, the meanest man in the whole Cape Fear!" Samuel ranted, reeling off the high points of a fearful reputation for brawling, fighting, maybe a once-before murder—and a fiercely protective father, too. "I heard he'll cut a man's heart out if he looks in his girl's general direction, Bess," Samuel concluded.

"He *seemed* nice enough." Bess only nodded, holding back her surprise. "Give me the basket. I can carry that, too, if it shames you."

Samuel handed it over without a thought. Bess was glad that he hadn't been told Constable Swann's suspicions yet, so he didn't know what was coming. Or had the rumor to pass among his friends.

"Sam'l, he just told me where to find my dressmaker. That was all," Bess said, lips curling in a smile in spite of herself. "I can ride the rest of the way alone, if you'll stay here at the tavern and watch me. 'Tis only half a mile on."

"Stay at the tavern?" He whirled. "Watch you *go?*"

"Just up the road, he said. On the right."

"But . . . wasn't I supposed to ride with you?" he blustered, not the sort who dealt well with surprises. "That's why you got me to come with you, wasn't it? That's why you got me away from work, wasn't it?"

"Mr MacDougall didn't think your going a good idea."

"What? Wait, what about dinner? And meetin' the dressmaker?"

"Her name's not Bridey or Bridget," Bess confessed, gaping wide-eyed as if she'd just learned it. "It's Biddy. Biddy MacDougall!"

"Oh, Lord," Samuel grunted, paling, nigh-swaying in his saddle.

"I'm *so* sorry, Sam'l!" Bess commiserated. "I didn't *know! I* can call on her, but he objected to you, being a young man and all. God, Sam'l, I really *am* sorry!" Bess swore, finding her tone so sympathetic and convincing that she half-believed it, herself!

"What's this? Didn't *know!* O' *course* ye knew. Well, the devil with Eachan MacDougall!"

"He said for you to sit on the tavern porch, Sam," Bess went on. "Where he can keep an eye on you, I expect. He was really *most* insistent. Here . . ." Bess offered, digging in the basket. "Here's a breast, a thigh and a drumstick, *three* biscuits . . ."

"Gah, you . . .!" Samuel seethed as Bess handed him his share of dinner wrapped in a napkin. He turned in his saddle to look back over his shoulder, to see MacDougall standing on the prow of the ferry, arms akimbo and hands on his hips, glaring at him. "Think you're funny, do ye, Bess? Think ye've fooled me again? See if I *ever* do ye another favor, dang . . . God, ah . . . shit *fire!*" he trailed off weakly.

He thought of leaving Bess on the Brunswick side, going back to the sawmill, 'til he realised that *Bess* had the coin for that passage, unless he abandoned the mule and rode cheaper. Counting on his sister to pay, he further discovered that he didn't have enough money to buy a *very* needful pint of beer, or two!

"Back as quick as I can," Bess said, kneeing her mule to motion. And there she went, up the Belville Trace!

Chapter 17

"HELLO the house!" Bess hesitantly called out. The Belville Trace had been gloomy enough of a hemmed-in track, but the MacDougall lane and yard were even more off-putting. Tall pines surrounded it, scrub growth beneath them pressing in as if the forest wanted to take back the interloper's clearings. There was a cornfield beyond, with a truck garden to the right, where the sun shone. The rest stood deep in shadows, bounded by zig-zag rail fences, behind which she could hear a herd of pigs snuffling and grunting. There were some sheds, a tumbledown barn, and a stock pen and pasture where a lone mule dozed, cock-footed. What passed for lawn was all but buried in long, brown pine needles and cones. The house in the middle of it all . . .

Actually, the house was the one bright spot, Bess thought. It was made from square cypress logs, the sandy mud chinking daubed with white paint. Its doors, shutters and window frames were painted a gay green, and under each window was a painted planter box full of blooms. On the deep, cool porch were half-kegs much like her own, overflowing with bright wild-flowers, or herbs. The roof was well-shingled, and a creek-stone, mud and cypress chimney drew well, lazily fuming smoke.

And, there was a pair of dogs: *huge,* bushy half-wolves, barking and snarling, of a sudden, teeth bared and slinking in dashes for her!

"Hello?" Bess called louder, feeling her mule shiver. "Help?"

"Hello, yairself?" a shy voice called back from within. A drape was pulled back, and a face appeared in a window that was only fitted with one glass pane. The rest of the glazing was paper-thin deerhides. The door opened and a girl stepped onto the porch, clapping her hands and whistling. "Wallace! Dundee! Hesh, yairselves, now! Come here, an' sit. Sit! Aye, now . . . may I be helpin' ye, mistress?"

Constable Swann was right; Biddy MacDougall was, indeed, as fair and pretty as an angel. Her hair was long and the slightest bit curly, parted down the center of her head and drawn back loosely into a single, lustrous tress. Her eyes were incredibly large, blue as cornflowers or periwinkles, and her complexion was as creamy and clear as . . . !

"I'm Bess Livesey," she managed to say at last, shaking herself before the girl thought her a mute. "Your father said I could come up to see you. About getting a gown made, and such?"

"Och, aye!" Biddy MacDougall perked up, pleased and relieved at once. "I'm Biddy. Get ye doon, Mistress Livesey, an' come on inna th' house. Ne'er fear th' dogs, thayr mair bark than bite, once they know ye. Here, let me help ye."

She came off the porch to lead the mule to a large stump, which Bess could use for a dis-mounting block. "I'm that sorry t'sound like ye fashed me, Mistress, but we don't get much comp'ny callin', d'ye see. Here, laddies! Let 'em sniff yair hands, an' they'll not be a bother. Nice lady, see Dundee . . . Wallace? Hae yairself a seat on th' porch, Mistress Livesey, an' I'll water yair mule for ye."

"Oh, that's not necessary, Miss MacDougall," Bess pooh-poohed. "You mustn't go to so much . . ."

"It's nae trouble, Mistress Livesey," Biddy smiled most sunnily as she petted the old mule's nose, cheeks and neck. "Puir auld fellah would care for a sip or twa, I'd expect, hey auld lad? An' a nose-bag of oats'd nae be spurned, either," she crooned to the mule. "Take yair ease, Mistress, an' I'll be back in twa shakes o' th' wee lamb's tail, an' th' first a'ready be shook!" she gaily chirped, then led the mule towards the barn, leaving Bess with her bundle and basket. She mounted the low porch and sat down in a caned ladderback chair, glad that the two dogs were well-behaved enough to merely sit and whine at the scent of fried chicken, not mob her and run off with it.

Biddy MacDougall . . . Bess looked up to watch her stroll towards the barn beside the mule, and felt a touch of envy. The girl was just about her age and height, but womanly, coltishly full at breasts and hips, yet willow-slim overall. Biddy MacDougall wasn't the bawdy drab that the constable's tale had made her envision, the usual poor country girl in muddy bare feet and a soiled cast-off shift.

Biddy perhaps only wore one petticoat, and no stays or corsets, but her simple homemaker's sack gown was clean, bright and well-made, and had smelled of fresh soap, starch and sunlight; she was neatly and almost primly garbed. Cotton stockings winked white beneath the hem of her gown as she strode away, and good, solid shoes with shining iron buckles were on her feet.

No one taught *her* to glide, either! Bess thought with the start of an easy smile as she took note of the purposeful, bouncy stride of a healthy, infectiously cheerful young girl. She could see why her uncle Harry might've been smitten, if that particular rumor would prove to be true. *And what man wouldn't be?* she asked herself. Suddenly she wished that she hadn't come . . . or, that at the end of her amateurish digging into the matter, she'd find both Biddy and Harry Tresmayne blameless.

"Oop!" she suddenly gasped, flinching as she felt something brush her skirt and shin! *Snake!* her already-heated imagination gibbered! A glance at the dogs showed them ready to pounce on *something*, and . . . !

But it was a cat, a large black-and-white with a speckled face and a white blotch around its pink nose. It swiped back and forth on her gown, purring madly, then got down to its real business at the food basket, pawing, peeking and fumbling for a way in.

"Naughty Flora," Biddy MacDougall mock-scolded as she came back to the porch. "Naughty kitty, that's not for you!" She bent over and hefted her cat into her lap as she sat down beside Bess, brushing its head and chops. "Ye brought vittles with ye, Mistress Livesey?" she asked. "Must've come a fair piece, did ye hae t'fetch food along."

"Only from over the river," Bess told her with a laugh. "But I thought to share, if I came before you started your dinner."

"Och, that's kind of ye, Mistress Livesey, 'deed it is! I've barely started th' tea water, an' that happy I'd be t'set out anything else ye may care for!" Biddy exclaimed, all but clapping her hands as the cat finally jumped down.

"I've enough for three, really," Bess replied. "No need for you to do anything else. My brother rode me out, far as the ferry tavern, anyway. But he, uhm . . ."

"He met ma daddy," Biddy finished for her with a wry expression.

"We've fried chicken, four-beans in sweet oil and biscuits," Bess promised. "And an apple pan dowdy."

"La, but ye provide handsome, Mistress Livesey!" Biddy whooped. "An' here I woz, fixin' t'slice some bacon an' ham for a simple soup. Bless ye forever, for fetchin' fried chicken. We've a few, mostly for eggs, an' ain fryer of a Sunday. Rest o' th' time, Gawd! 'Tis bacon, ham or pork chops, pig this an' pig that. Swear t'ye, Mistress, I've et sae much pork I think I'm growin' trotters. Aye, I *do!* Come inside, Mistress Livesey. I'll pour us both a cuppa tea, an' we'll enjoy yair generosity!"

Chapter 18

"OOH, THAT WOZ handsome," Biddy said with a sigh of pleasure as she un-self-consciously licked her fingers, and sat back with a purr of utter contentment. "Couldn't eat another bite!"

The MacDougall house was simple, neat and Spartan, but it was a clean, well-ordered place, its furnishings home-crafted, by the father's skilled hands. The chairs, tables, benches, cabinets and cupboards were very plain of line, but they gleamed with resin, pine oil or precious bee's wax polish. The large main room was half home, half workshop, for Biddy had a quilting frame against one wall on which a colorful Tree of Life was taking shape, with a pile of finished ones on top of a nearby chest. There was a shuttle loom on which a short bolt of linsey-woolsey hung. Next to the loom was a spinning wheel and wool carder. By the signs of things, when not making gowns to order, Biddy MacDougall spun or wove to make her own curtains, coverlets or clothing.

"Aye, woman's work is ne'er done," Biddy chuckled as she laid out small wooden plates for their dessert. "We get visitors s'seldom, 'tis time an' mair I hae for mine. Thank Gawd we've a sma home, else I'd be hard at it, licht tae mirk, an' not be able t'sew. That makes us a braw bit o' money, beyond th' pigs an' ma daddy's wages."

"Licht to . . . ?" Bess asked.

"Light tae dark. Sunup tae sundown."

"You've so many talents, Biddy. You should have a place in town to work at, to show your wares. Your quilts and all!" Bess gushed.

"Och, away wi' ye!" Biddy shyly scoffed. "I get to town often enoo." She turned more sober. "Father dinna hold much with towns, in the main. All reeks, dins an' jostles, he says! We go to Wilmington *almost* ev'ry Saturday, sometime a rare Sunday."

"Seems a waste that you have to keep your skill under the bushel basket, this far across the river, though, Biddy," Bess said. "Did you ever live in a biggish, settled place?" she gently began to probe.

"We once lived up-country in the Scots' settlements, with guid neighbors an' all, but ma daddy, well . . ." Biddy bleakly said, with a sad expression. "He can be a hard man t'know, with little need of others. Come south an' cleared a farm on Hood's Creek, an' Gawd, that was even worse than here! Nought but rank strangers passin' by on th' trace, but nae close neighbors. 'Tis better here, with folks settled round th' ferry landing, but . . ." Biddy frowned, and crossed her arms under her breasts.

"Father," she expounded on her theme, with an exasperated toss of her head. "Ye met him. Naebody comes un-asked, an' he dinna ask many. I 'spect this is as close as he'd ever wish t'get to a place as big as Wilmington."

"Wilmington's not all that grand, Biddy," Bess said, hoping to lighten her sudden mood. "We came down from Philadelphia, and even if I was real little when we left, it was a dozen times bigger and . . ."

"Oh, but Wilmington's grand enoo for me, Mistress Livesey!" the girl insisted. "Biggest place *I've* ever seen! Shops an' stores full o' wonders . . . to a puir lass such'z me, that is. All th' ships come in, all th' bustle an' industry? An' folk strollin' about as grandly cleed as lairds an' ladies in London. Got a fine kirk built, where a body can worship . . . e'en is Saint James's Church of *England.* Father don't hold with *anythin'* English, 'coz he fechted for Prince Charlie in The '45, 'fore we come tae th' Colonies, 'fore he gie his Bible-oath tae King George an' got his pardon."

"You must have been just a babe-in-arms, then, Biddy," Bess said, wondering if Biddy had any inkling of the rumors of her father killing her mother, or if she'd been old enough to recall it herself.

"Aye, I woz." Biddy smiled briefly. "I ken thayr's no Scottish kirk hereabouts, but that Reverend McDowell, well! With a name like that, he must be *some* sorta Scot, an' might not mind me prayin' thayr!"

"Dissenters aren't welcome," Bess told her, "nor are Catholics, Baptists and such. But we're *Lowland* Scot . . . that and Scots-Irish. We were Presbyterian, once, and no one objects to *us* being parishoners. I'm sure you'd be more than welcome, Biddy!"

"Och, that'd be grand!" Biddy declared, perking up of a sudden. "An'

I've made mahself some grand gowns t'wear, should I e'er. Might e'en make friends with some o' th' other girls ma age at kirk . . . get asked in for tea, or something after? Hear ain o' those musical *concerts* they hae. Real music, 'stead o' ma daddy's tuning-box! Gae in th' front doors a guest . . . 'stead o' th' back tradesman's entrance."

Bess was startled by the intensity of Biddy's wishing, and she shifted uncomfortably as Biddy's eyes began to moisten as she stared upwards as if voicing a heartfelt prayer.

"I'd care tae *dance,* Mistress Livesey," Biddy said in a shuddery voice. "Dance in a bonny gown I made for mahself just th' once!" Then her large blue eyes squinted shut as tears began to flow, and she shoved away from the table blindly, scooping up dirty dishes along the way, almost sprinting for the back porch. "Sorry!" she stammered from a tight throat, over her shoulder, as she exited.

Startled, and slightly ashamed, Bess rose to follow her, found her wiping crumbs, bones and scraps into an earthen slop jar near the pig troughs. Biddy set the plates down on the ground and went to the well to winch up a bucket of wash water, cranking fiercely, and dabbing angrily at her eyes with the hem of her apron.

"Let me help," Bess hesitantly offered, unsure of what to do to ease the girl. She took hold of the crank and finished the hauling as Biddy turned away to mop her shame-reddened face. "I'll do the wash-up, too. Once you . . . whenever you wish, Biddy."

"I dinna ken what comes o'er me, sometimes," Biddy said, trying to make light of her tears. "Here I fin'lly get some comp'ny, an' I make a *hash* of eet. I'm not tetched in th' head, nae matter what yair thinking, Mistress Livesey. It's just . . . !" She heaved a controlling sigh to master herself, though it sounded broken.

Bess secured the water bucket, then went to put an arm around Biddy's shoulders. "They're not all they're cracked up to be, Biddy. The dances. Once around with my clumsy brother, and that'd cure you! Everyone catty and judging how you're gowned, hold your tea cup or . . ."

"Th' ain ye left at th' ferry tavern?" Biddy asked, snuffling, trying to play up chipper, though she began to shake with stifled sobs. "I dinna know, but I . . . !" Then she started to keen, turning to bury her head on Bess's shoulder and cling to her, crying out loud.

"There, there," Bess whispered, stroking her back. "Cry it all out. Sometimes girls are due a good one, and no telling why. Done it often enough, myself. Father and Sam'l away, and none but me to cope with things. So *many* things, all at once. Half-bankrupt, poor . . ."

"You!" Biddy bawled. "Puir?"

They both sat down on a rough bench near the well and held each other for what felt like ten full minutes as Biddy had her a sorrowful cry. Finally, she leaned away, sniffing and groping for a handkerchief in her apron pocket.

"Gawd, I'm sorry t'gae all silly on ye, Mistress Livesey," she muttered. "I'm not like this, swear I'm not! What ye must *think!* We get by, braw enoo, most o' th' time, but . . ."

"It's lonely out here by yourself," Bess intuited, "and your father's so strict, so . . . prickly."

"Aye, that's th' way of eet." Biddy mournfully nodded, looking as if one wrong word would set her off, again. "None t'talk to, tell ma cares to . . . 'cept for Flora an' the dogs. An' the mule. An' th' pigs! An' thayr not guid list'ners, in th' main. Yair own mother?"

"She died a few years back," Bess admitted. "'Tis none but me, the sole woman of the house. Since I was barely into my 'tweens."

"I'm sorry," Biddy said, blowing her nose and swiping a sleeve across her eyes. "Least ye kenned her. Ma own died when I was just a wee'un, still in swaddlings. Forgive me asking, for 'tis hard t'lose yair mother, nae matter how auld ye are."

"Your father never thought to remarry?" Bess asked. "He's not that hard to look at . . . 'cept for being, well . . . prickly."

"I dinna think he e'er really tried verra hard. An' we've gaed about sae much, place t'place, job t'job, an' aye . . . Daddy's th' sort who likes keepin' tae himself. Truth be told, I 'spect he'd be happier high up into th' Piedmont, round King's Mountain or farther, with nary a neighbor by at *all,*" Biddy said with a doomed chuckle.

"You couldn't have been alone all this time. Weren't there . . . ?"

"Oh, our neighbors up by Cross Creek or Campbelltown. Daddy'd leave me with neighbor women wheelst he worked, then fetch me home in th' ev'nings. Other children t'play with, things t'learn. Letters an' cyphers. A bit o' real schooling, noo an' ageen, if Daddy could afford it, an' we bided somewhere lang enoo. Believe me, we moved a *lot!* Nae proper education, but I can read an' figure as guid as anybody I know!

"Thayr's another reason I'd wish tae get to Wilmington an' meet people, Mistress Livesey," Biddy continued, her eyes now dry, her voice scratchy and phlegmy. "Only book we got is th' Bible, an' I'd *dearly* love tae borrow new'uns! I heard talk of some folk 'cross th' river starting a library, where ye can just up an' be lent any one ye care tae read! Choose ain of a Saturday market day, soak it up durin' th' week, an' return eet th' next, wouldn't that be a marvel? That way, I could talk as smart as anybody, even do I tutor mahself, 'stead o' having a proper schoolmaster. Oh, eet might coot ha'pence or so. Och, what ye must think o' me, ramblin' on so, and you probably with ain hundred books in yair own house, Mistress Livesey . . ."

"Biddy, will you stop calling me Mistress Livesey?" Bess said. "My friends call me Bess."

"I could?" Biddy asked, perking up as if offered jewels. "Do ye mean it? E'en do I sew for ye, an all?"

"Hang that mistress-seamstress rot, Biddy," Bess declared, her heart breaking for the girl's heretofore bleak prospects and swearing that she'd find a way to change them, heart opening to a fellow young woman in need . . . and coming to like her a great deal. "Next time you come to town, come to *my* house through the *front* door. We only have about forty or so books, but you're welcome to borrow anything we have."

"I doan know . . . Bess," Biddy shyly responded. "Daddy might hae t'see them first t'see thay're uplifting, not novels or wasteful trash."

"My father's the very *same,* Biddy!" Bess chuckled. "He wouldn't let anything too salacious under our roof, either. You could come *this* Saturday! We could have dinner, go shopping and all! You could put on one of those gowns you said you'd made for yourself," Bess slyly teased, "and we could go calling at other homes, together. I could ask about, see if there's any music planned . . . well, *good* music. The last one I went to, your pigs made better, they were so . . ."

"Och, gown!" Biddy cried, shooting to her feet. "Ye came for me tae make ye a gown, an' here we quite forgot all about eet! Let's gae in th' house, an' see what I've got t'suit ye. For a promise like that, I'll do ye up a gown sae fine, ye could dance at yair wedding in eet!"

Chapter 19

BESS WAS IN TORMENT. She'd come all this way to "smoke" a possible murderer, and had found a needful friend! *How can I carry on this miserable charade?* she guiltily wondered.

"I'll wash up, Biddy," Bess re-offered, stalling. "You go take your ease on the porch. Oh! In my bundle, I've two shirts I made for my brother. No great shakes, but . . . I said I'd bring them . . . if he'd ride me out. I had to bribe him! Could you take a look at them, and see what could be done to . . . ruffle them up for him?"

Minutes later, Bess returned to the front porch, just as Biddy was polishing off a dish of the apple pan dowdy. She looked up with a sheepish smile as she licked the last morsels off her spoon.

"Lovely dowdy, Bess," Biddy congratulated. "Ye bake as guid as ye sew . . . yair seams an' stitchings air all sae neat an' fine? Fine as mine, when I've ma wits about me!" She picked up one of the shirts and held it out. "This linen sark . . . I've some guid ecru lace that'd gussy it fair enoo. Nothing fancy. This white cotton sark, though, would be perfect for Sunday come t'meeting, with layered lace ruffles, and a layered neck-stock t'go with it, above th' plaquet."

"So *those* are sarks?" Bess exclaimed. "Shirts! I didn't catch what your father was saying."

"Not many people do," Biddy snickered. "Guid as ye sew, Bess, I dinna see why ye'd need me t'do for ye."

"*Ease,* Biddy," Bess chuckled, taking a seat by her, explaining what desperate straits the Liveseys had been in, and why, the last few years. "Now we've our heads above water, again, thank God, and if He continues to bless us, we might be able to take on a *part-time* helper round the house, at least. Like you said, woman's work is never done, but I think I could cope well enough, if there was just a bit *less* of it!"

"Och, aye!" Biddy heartily agreed.

"*I'd* like to go to parties and teas and such, too, Biddy," Bess told her, "have the *time* for them, even if it's only every now and again. You wish to dance? Well, I would, too. In a gown I *didn't* make myself, in something *really* elegant, 'stead of scrimped together!"

"Ye mean it's not just me feeling dawkish?" Biddy gasped. "But . . . yair a fine lady, Bess!"

"And the other so-called 'fine young ladies' snicker when I *do* attend something, 'cause I couldn't afford their . . . flounces, and all, and had to piece together my own gown out of left-over cloth, wear the same two to everything, and . . ." Bess carped. "Well, you understand."

"Aye, I've heard tell." Biddy nodded with a wry grin. "I call on *some* t'take measures, an' I've heard 'em sneer. Swear t'Gawd, did I ever *live* in Wilmington an' be a Society lady, ye'll ne'er hear *me* say a cruel word 'gainst another body. *Ain* thing my daddy taught me, 'tis whether thayr's a guid person *in* th' gown, nae matter how grand her trappings be, an' no amount o' frippery can make th' bad guid."

"Ever and amen to that!" Bess chimed in agreement.

"Someday . . ." Biddy said, looking dreamy at a better future. "I just *might* become a lady, mahself! Ye ne'er can tell! A'doing quadrilles, sae grand an' graceful . . ."

Biddy got to her feet and picked up Bess's blue taffeta gown, put the end of a sleeve in each of her hands, and let it drape against her like a dance partner, then began to step around the porch.

Saw ye ma Maggie, Saw ye ma Maggie,
Saw ye ma Maggie, linkin' over da lea?

She sang in a pure, piping alto as she danced.

"Quadrilles an' minuets," Biddy fantasized, "an' then, we'd go all breathless at th' *contre-danses!* Dance th' night away, an' not stop 'til th' cows come home! Dancing with handsome, successful husbands, acleed sae fine, them an' us, th' other lasses'll grind thayr teeth with envy tae *be* us! Dance at our wedding's, me at yours, you at . . . !"

She wa seen wi' wir Johnnie,
She wa seen wi' wir Johnnie,

She wa seen wi' wir Johnnie,
He'll be takin' her fae de!

So wistfully said, or sung, that Bess was touched. Turning red at her own actions, Biddy stopped, held the gown out and came back to her chair. "Here, then, what ye wish tae add t'this'un? An' ev'ryday, Sunday church gown? Or"— Biddy slyly grinned– "a courtin' special?"

"Oh, ah . . ." Bess said, groping, amazed by Biddy's dreams. Had Uncle Harry dallied with her, Biddy couldn't *help* but be distraught by news of his death; she would be the sort who'd fall head-over-heels in love, with all her soul. *Was that what made her weep?* Bess speculated. But Biddy was impish-cheerful and aspiring minutes later, as if she'd met *somebody* who she thought might marry her upwards, so . . . ? One more time, Bess felt like cringing that she'd come to delve, and deceive in the process!

"'Tis the best I made all winter, and I'd like . . ." Bess stammered, growing bolder by merely speaking. "I'd like for no one to *recognize* it, frankly, Biddy. I'd thought to edge the shoulder pleats, the bodice and cuffs, with lace and ruches, maybe lace and ribbons to boot? I . . . I found a bit of ribbon the very color, but . . ."

Feeling as if it would scald her hand, Bess reached into her clutch and withdrew that snippet of royal-blue satin ribbon from the bouquet her father had discovered.

"Aye, that'd be peert," Biddy enthusiastically agreed, totally oblivious to Bess's distress, and showing no sign of distress, herself, to Bess's immediate relief. It didn't *signify* to her!

"White lace, o' course, Bess," Biddy speculated with her head cocked to one side. "White satin bodice panel, an' down th' front tae just abune th' hem, with lace flouncing round th' bottom, an' . . . oh, Bess!" she cried, gasping. "White *figured*-satin! I've some a'ready, an' less than twa yards'd do! Come on back to ma room, I'll show ye!"

Biddy led her into the house to one of the two doors in a wall to the left. "Pardon th' mess," Biddy warned her as she flung open the right-hand door to a fair-sized bedchamber, one awash in half-finished clothing hung on pegs or nails driven into the log walls. The corners were taken up by swatches of fabrics. Whole bolts of cloth stood on-end, or filled the few shelves. There was a tall wardrobe, a narrow four-poster bed, and a dressing table and mirror, flanked by—dwarfed by—stacks of wooden boxes turned into shelving that held lace, ribbons and "possibles."

"'Twoz ma daddy's, first," Biddy said with a sheepish *moue* at how cram-full it was. "But since ma sewing turned profitable he took th' other room, an' moved yon partition. He's talked o' building on off th' back porch, if things got e'en mair crowded. Take a perch on th' bed, wheelst I dig. I know 'tis in here, somewhere!"

Bess looked around whilst Biddy muttered to herself and pawed through her boxes. For being such a mercurial person, Bess thought her much better-organized than she. Each box bore painted labels for lace, ribbons, threads, buttons, quilting scraps and such. Cloth on the shelves were sorted by color or pattern. There was even an accounting ledger on the dressing table, open to show debits and expenditures *versus* profits, done in a careful printed hand, not the sloppy script that only the writer might decypher later.

"Ribbon ye brought's a tad narrow, Bess," Biddy said, single-mindedly grubbing about. "Dinna want th' trim hanging out *too* far so we could use this hat-lacing. It'd be bonny, 'gainst royal-blue, an' I'd sew it flat. No over-lapping th' pleats."

"Yes, that's quite nice," Bess answered, distracted. The door of the big wardrobe was open, and she could see that it was filled to bursting with finished gowns, from work-a-day plain to royal ball fine, plain cotton chemises to the frilliest silk underthings. Things Biddy had made for herself, Bess realized, some of the sort she seemed to dread she'd never get to wear—for company, church, afternoon entertainments, or . . . courting? Bess thought them fine enough for *Philadelphia* Society, not staid little Wilmington. Morning gowns, even cunning hats, and a small pile of babies' clothes?

Bess reached across the bed to take one of the baby gowns off the pile. It was a light, shimmering watered silk, laced and eyeleted, bibbed and ruffled, as elegant a baptismal gown as ever she'd seen . . . complete to the itty-bitty pearly buttons no bigger than ladybugs.

Her hope chest, Bess sorrowfully thought. Like any good girl, Biddy was amassing her linens and paraphernalia for the day she'd wed and start a home of her own. Yet, would that ever happen? Bess had to wonder. Not if her irascible father scared off every available young man, the upright and the rogues together, and kept her isolated so far away. And someday, in another of his huffs, Eachan MacDougall might just uproot them again, and storm west, deep into the Piedmont or the high mountains, and dutifully sweet Biddy would have to follow him and end up abandoning or scrapping her wishful finery, 'til she became the shoeless drudge that Bess had first imagined, reduced to home-spun wool shifts! A baby on her hip, wed against her will to a rough copy of her father? Or adrift and helpless, hundreds of miles from friends should her father ever pass? Old before her time, over-worked . . . ?

"It's so *pretty!*" Bess crooned over the baptismal gown.

"Och, those," Biddy almost flinched, turning shy. "Thayr, uh . . . not *mine.* I dinna have room for 'em on th' shelves, d'ye see? I'm to deliver 'em, soon."

Bess didn't believe that for a minute.

"Here it is!" Biddy gushed, sitting on the bed with her. "Th' white figured-satin. I thought I had some left! Just enoo to do, ye ken?" she said, laying the white-on-white, almost embossed fabric the length of Bess's plain blue gown. "This lace trimming eet?" she said, laying a sample at the edge. "If yair partial t'this, why, I could be done an' bring it to ye Saturday, 'long with yair brother's sarks!"

"It'll be lovely!" Bess replied, and it would be. No one could recognize it for old, once Biddy had done with it. "I am partial!"

"Guid! Now, I've twa royal blue ribbons," Biddy chattered on, reaching over to fetch samples. "Got a spool o' velvet, an' that'd be fetchin' with this narrow lace. Or, I've some satin left over, enoo t'do an' mair, I think. Ooh, Gawd A'mighty, Bess, lookee here! That ribbon ye brought, 'tis th' very same as mine. Same width an' color, th' same edges, an' ev'rything!"

Laid end-to-end, it was hard to tell where the eight inches or so that Bess had brought ended, and the remaining spool from Biddy's "possibles" began, and Bess's stomach chilled and her throat turned dry. There was no *way* she'd wear that murdering ribbon on a gown!

"I . . . I think I'm partial to the velvet, after all, Biddy," she managed to say, feeling her face turn hot as fire. "We . . . must've bought from the same store."

"Mayhap, Bess," Biddy cheerfully agreed, unaware of Bess's upset. "Though I bought it, oh . . . nigh a year ago an' mair, back when I first began sewing for others, an' used most of eet up on a special job o' work. Thought I'd got th' last spools t'be had, so . . . where'd ye get yours?"

"Uh, it, ah . . ." Bess stammered, looking up to see if Biddy was subtly probing her, if she'd ignited any sudden suspicion, fantasizing for a bizarre moment that Biddy had *sent* the bouquet, *tied* the bows . . . !

But no! Bess could see no guile in Biddy's open, honest face. Just girlish and innocent curiosity, perhaps a dab of disappointment that she might not have enough to trim her new friend's gown. Yet the ribbon was here, might have *come* from here, but how?

"Cat got yair tongue, Bess?" Biddy asked, teasingly.

"It was tied round a bouquet . . ." Bess blurted without thinking, lowering her head quickly and blushing fit to burst afire for coming so close to the truth!

"Ooh!" Biddy exclaimed, laughing. "Thayr's a bonny lad sent ye flowers? Ye've a secret beau, an' ye wished t'please him by wearing a matching colored ribbon? 'Tis nae wonder ye craved blue sae much!"

"Well, there *is* this one . . ." Bess flummoxed on, unable to meet her eyes. "We don't know each other *that* well, yet, but . . ."

"Weel, th' velvet's fair-close," Biddy chuckled, "an' when he sees ye cleed sae braw in this gown, he'll be fechting t'other laddies for a dance with ye, an' claim a knot or bow of yair ribbon. At yair sleeve ends, or over yair heart on th' bodice, I could add a wee knotted bow of th' *satin* ribbon ye brought he could claim for his own, so ye could let him know he's special."

"Yes," Bess whispered, wondering what effect that outward sign would have on the shy and awkward Andrew Hewlett if he ever *did* send her a ribbon-bound nosegay.

"Och, I fashed ye. I dinna mean t'tease, Bess," Biddy said in a soberer tone. "I won't e'en ask ye his name . . . yet!" she chirped.

"And you, Biddy . . . do you have a beau?" Bess suddenly asked, inspired with such a conversational opening, if for no other reason than to distract Biddy from too many questions fired at *her*. Just one of the hundred questions Bess wished she could ask Biddy, but this one followed the flow of things.

"Me!" Biddy scoffed, looking away for a furtive second, turning red herself. "Living way out here? What fine young gentleman would ride up our lane, if Father dinna give him leave?"

"The velvet ribbon, and the little . . . love knot, then. Pity, though, that there may not be enough satin," Bess decided, pondering on why Biddy got so shifty on the subject of swains. "Did the rest go on a particularly fancy gown? It must have been dear, and showy."

"Aye, 'twoz," Biddy told her, shifting on the bed, "though, in th' end, I dinna make money on eet. Three spools of eet, I used, that gown flummeried up busy as anything, but th' lady'd nae pay mair than ma first estimate. I dinna know any better back then, but I learned peert quick, I'll tell ye. Why, she e'en wished a bonnet made, satin ribbon-trimmed tae match, an' said I should do it for *nothing*, an' she *might* recommend me tae her friends. Show what I could *do?* Used me as ill as a shamblin' bear, she did, Bess! Like I woz low, clay-eating woods trash! 'Twixt you an' me," she said, leaning chummily close to lower her voice as if that customer was lurking outside the windows, "an' Gawd forgive me for speaking snippy, but . . . neither blue, nor pearly gray satin, were fetchin' on her. Neither woz her best color, but could I say a single thing about eet? An' by the time 'twoz done, weel . . . Gawd forgive me, ageen, but it felt like sweet revenge t'think o' her sportin' a gray gown!"

"It doesn't sound that bad, really," Bess replied, puzzling as to where she might have seen such an outfit.

"A pale lady with light hair might manage eet, but not her, I tell ye," Biddy said with a catty little laugh. "Weel, like ma daddy says, 'tis not th' trappings that make a lady . . . an' her time will come, sooner'n she might think."

"Who was it?" Bess blurted out, intrigued.

"Weel, if yair heart's set on knowing." Biddy smirked, biting a corner of her mouth. "'Twoz Mistress Anne Moore."

"Dear Lord!" Bess exclaimed. *Anne, Uncle Harry; could it be?* she thought.

"Ye must've hae dealings with her before, then," Biddy said with agreed-with satisfaction that she and Bess were of the same mind where the handsome and elegant, but arch, Mrs Osgoode Moore was concerned.

"Well, not that many really . . ." Bess answered.

"Now Mr *Osgoode,* och, he's a *fine* gentleman!" Biddy enthused. "Sae cultured an' polite tae one an' all, and la! th' *books* he owns. Walls an' *walls* o' books, an' when I woz sewin' for . . . *her,* he'd let me borrow some, then ask me what I thought of 'em, kind as anything. A tip o' his hat tae any man, e'en my daddy, once. Not like t'other Moores, an' th' barons. Not like his high-nose *wife,* the . . . !"

Biddy babbled on about Osgoode Moore's merits, and how she wished to emulate his style and erudition someday, whilst Bess's mind was in a whirl, trying to recall Anne Moore wearing a pearly, light-gray, satin gown trimmed in off-white lace with royal-blue ribbon flouncings . . . as dark-haired and dark-eyed as she was, with her slightly olive—nigh Spanish—complexion, neither color *would* enhance her. She reviewed a host of church and vestry meetings, horse races and teas, oyster roasts and "pig-pullings," yet her memory was blank.

She might have realized the unsuitability, too, Bess speculated, might have worn the ensemble once or twice, then flung it in the back of her chifforobe, or handed it down to a maid servant . . . donated it to a winter charity . . .

As a cast-off, might it have made it all the way down the cape to Masonborough, in Mr Ramseur's domains? Bess's mind boggled with the possibility that Sim Bates's live-in slave woman had ended up with it! *Just how convoluted is this snip of ribbon going to be?*

"Now, whayr's ma naughty Flora?" Biddy asked with a laugh as she wound down. "Whayr's that sly kitty?"

"Hmm?" Bess said, jerked back to the here-and-now.

"Cat's got yair tongue, *an'* yair wits as weel, I'm thinking."

"Oh, don't mind me, Biddy, I was maundering," Bess said, forcing herself to sound giddy. "Lord, wouldn't it be awful, if I really cared for the satin ribbon 'stead of the velvet, to go beard Anne Moore and beg for her scraps?"

"A shame tae th' jaybirds, aye!" Biddy whooped, bouncing on the bed in mirth. "Ah, but she's prob'ly thrown eet out lang ago, for th' magistrate's wife had one right-similar not twa weeks later. Saw her by the courthouse one Saturday. Mayhap Anne Moore saw her, too, an' couldna bear th' shame. *I* dinna make th' second, but *some* seamstress must've. What they call . . . coincidence? An' eet looked much better on old Miz Marsden.

"Weel, then," Biddy finally asked, "do ye prefer this figured-satin an' velvet? Materials an' ma work, I think . . . I could do eet for eight shillings, an' hae eet ready for ye on Saturday. Th' sarks would be two shillings each, twelve shillings altogether. If that's not tae dear on yair budget?"

"Biddy, that's perfect!" Bess exclaimed at the low cost. "It leaves me enough from the money my father budgeted me that I could have you make a whole *new* one, atop of this. You've made my day!" she could honestly declare.

"Th' Guid Laird save me, Bess," Biddy exclaimed with glee, and took her hands in congratulations, "for 'tis mortal-certain ye just made mine!"

"Och, I hate t'see ye gae, Bess," Biddy told her, after she was mounted, after the dogs had been calmed down from their own good-byes. "I'm sure t'pester Flora an' th' hounds with blather after ye've gone."

"Then come early as you can on Saturday, Biddy," Bess demanded. "So we can have as much of the day as possible for our . . . girl stuff."

"Looking forward to eet something fierce," Biddy replied. "Ma daddy'll be coming with me, mind. Doan say I dinna warn ye."

"You'll most-like meet my brother, Sam'l," Bess chuckled back in kind. "So, be warned your own self, Biddy. Well, I s'pose I'm off. Got my basket and all . . ."

"I'm that glad ye come tae call, Bess Livesey," Biddy announced of a sudden, stepping near the mule's reins to hold her there a little longer, and turning somber. "Ye ken ma situation. Since we came here, I haen't a lass ma own age t'tell ma heart to, d'ye see, an' . . . !"

"You have one, now," Bess swore. "You get lonely 'twixt those Saturdays and market days, send me a note and I'll find a way to come over and just visit. Set a spell, as my father says."

"I'd *hoped* ye'd say that. Gawd bless ye for that. An' when I come, I promise not t'shame ye," Biddy pledged in return.

"Shame me? How?" Bess scoffed.

"I ken I'm not sae fine a lass as some ye might be kenning," Biddy confessed, "an' I canna converse with manners as proper as some ye ken ought, yet. For now, I'm a puir, wee seamstress tae th' fine folk . . . but I learn quick as *anything*, I do! Do I do or say wrong, noo an' ageen, ye swear ye'll tell me or shew me what's proper, what a real lady would do? I'll heed ye, an' not shame ye afore yair other friends."

"Well, of *course* you won't!" Bess cried, startled by the seriousness of Biddy MacDougall's declarations, by how desperate she seemed to want to please, to fit in. "We Liveseys don't run with the barons and *their* crowd; we're plain folk, and most everyone we like and love are plain folk, too. You'll find a warm welcome with almost all, and . . . those few who might turn up their noses, then . . . Devil *with* 'em, I say! Don't you worry 'bout a blessed thing. Just come and be yourself, and more than welcome!"

"Yair a fine lady, Bess Livesey," Biddy chortled, much relieved. "With friends like ye tae learn from, I might just have a chance t'be *some* kinda lady mahself, someday."

"Come hungry, too." Bess beamed back, taking her hand one last time as the mule tittuped a bit with the dogs prowling round its legs. "We'll lay on a grand feed. Much better than today."

"I doubt *that!* Bye, then, Bess. Ride safe, an' I'll call on ye Saturday!"

On her solitary way to the ferry landing, Bess chastised herself for playing such a tawdry, theatrical trick on sweet, trusting Biddy, like a thief in the night prowling through her wardrobe. Yet, she *had* found a friend! Bess was tormented, too, by the existence of the leftover ribbon at Biddy's place; how did it fit in?

She couldn't imagine Biddy getting involved with Uncle Harry. There was no sign of grief in her, and Biddy just wasn't the sort who could disguise a thing like that. Neither did Bess think that Eachan MacDougall was the murderer. If Biddy *had* been called upon by Uncle Harry on the sly, and she knew he'd been killed, she'd naturally suspect her hot-tempered, hard-handed father, and wouldn't abide staying another *hour* under his roof. If Eachan MacDougall *had* done it, then why hadn't he isolated Biddy completely, denied Bess access to their house, if he had something to hide?

If he had killed a man to protect Biddy's naive and trusting honor, why wasn't he packed up and gone to the Piedmont, already? she asked herself. It didn't make sense! Yet, Biddy had wept about *something* beyond her loneliness, and had acted most cutty-eyed when asked about having a beau, about the baby clothes in her wardrobe. Was her enthusiasm for being tutored on how to be a proper Wilmington lady a thing beyond an almost pathetic need for company, or . . . ?

"God, I wish I'd never come . . . almost!" Bess muttered to her plodding mule. "But I *will* be her friend."

That put her in a much better frame of mind, picturing how she and Biddy would enjoy a free day on the town. Until she remembered that she still had to re-cross the Brunswick on Eachan MacDougall's ferry . . . and God, how long had Samuel been kicking his heels at the ordinary! What was the time, anyway?

"Oh Lord, don't let Sam'l be too cross!" she prayed aloud.

Chapter 20

THE WIDOW had come from Tuscarora.

Matthew Livesey had been surprised when a liveried, black house slave had delivered an invitation to attend her at the townhouse. He had thought, like others, that Georgina Tresmayne would stay cloistered during her year of mourning out at the plantation house. Yet here she was, uneasily seated in a throne-like parlor chair in her dark widow's weeds, her wide-brimmed hat veiled with black netting even indoors, reigning over the small gathering of close friends and relations, who just as uneasily drank her wine, and ate her cakes and light "kick-shaw" snacks off the sideboard. Osgoode Moore attended her like a royal equerry might a queen, bending down to mutter deferentially to her, or listen to her low conversation. Anne Moore stood a bit behind the throne-like wing-chair, much like a lady-in-waiting would. Thomas Lakey and his nephew Andrew Hewlett were present, young Cornelius Harnett from Brunswick, a few other leading lights of the Tresmayne faction and their ladies, and Matthew and his family. Harry had been the last of the Tresmayne tribe living, but there were some Maultsbys from Georgina's side, hovering together near a settee.

Livesey could, indeed, not face her directly: his dream about her still plagued his conscience. Yet he had to, for the only chair left was just a little in front of her and to her left, and his leg was paining him. Armed with a neat brandy, he settled himself.

"Dear Matthew," Georgina said in a soft, weary voice almost at once. "Our closest and dearest friend."

"Umm . . ." Livesey nodded to her, peering in spite of himself to penetrate her veil to read her features, or to gaze upon her beauty. "You are well, ma'am?" he asked gently. "Do you bear up?"

"'Tis hard, Matthew," Georgina barely whispered. "Wretchedly hard, but I try." A gloved hand penetrated the veil to dab her eyes.

"I must own surprise, ma'am, that you came back to town. The restful, bucolic peace of Tuscarora surely would be more . . . umm . . . conducive to . . ." Livesey stumbled, then blushed in dithered silence.

"To mourning?" Georgina supplied for him. "One would think so, Matthew. More contemplative a place, yes, one would surely suppose. But the silence, Matthew!" Georgina almost shuddered as her control slipped. "No one with whom a body may converse but servants, or the overseers. The loneliness of the estate, with few visitors . . ."

"I deeply apologize for not coaching out sooner to relieve you of such loneliness, then, ma'am," Livesey grunted with another cause for shame to contemplate. "I would not like you to think I, or any of the Liveseys, meant to abandon you. No! It's just . . ."

"Life must go on, truly, Matthew," Georgina responded. "Those who remain must cope with the mundane matters, even direct kin or the closest of friends. And, I've found," Georgina came near to jesting, for a brief moment of her former self, "people feel awkward around the widow, or widower. As if death is catching, like the ague?"

"Yes," Livesey confessed.

"When your dear Charlotte passed over, Matthew, Harry and I were just as awkward toward you for a time," Georgina admitted. "But it does pass. True companions remain true companions. I found that, in experiencing your grief. I assure myself with those recollections, that mine will pass as well. And someday, you will no longer feel so dawkish as to refer to me as 'ma'am,' when before it was 'Georgina' . . . and Harry."

"Forgive me, Georgina," Livesey said with a shy smile, and was rewarded with a brief touch of her cool, gloved hand upon his knee in assurance. A touch which wakened every damnable bit of that damnable fantasy all over again! Livesey covered his chagrin with a deep sip of brandy. "You will reside in town, then?"

"I believe I shall, Matthew," Georgina said with a firm nod of her head. "I spent less time here with Harry than at Tuscarora. We seldom came to town together. Harry's legal work, his faction and assembly duties called him away from the plantation at short notice, or at odd hours. Besides, we built Tuscarora together, whilst this house was almost entirely his planning before we wed. Odd as it may seem to you, Matthew, being here, surrounded by so many of his things, instead of 'ours' out in the country, comforts me."

"I see," Livesey answered, flinching a little at her naivety toward what "business" Harry Tresmayne could have been on when "called away at odd hours" from her.

"And Wilmington is so full of life and doings, compared to the rustication of Tuscarora," Georgina spoke up bravely, hitching her shoulders like a dray-horse breasting to its harness for a hard pull, "that I am certain grief will go quicker where I may re-enter the business of a noisier life."

"I am sure it will," Livesey assured her. "And, you will have your friends close by you for your more immediate support."

"I count on it," Georgina said, turning to peer at him through her misting veil. "As I count on you. And the others."

"And perhaps our awkwardness will pass the sooner, too, Georgina," Livesey replied, shifting nervously in his chair under her intense gaze.

"I count on that as well, Matthew," Georgina said with another desperate, fond smile, which discomfited Livesey as much as anything else she had said previously. *Damn that wretched fantasy,* he thought, *but it could yet be!* If she smiled like that. If her words implied what he deduced from them!

"Bess, good day to you," Andrew Hewlett offered as they grazed the sideboard together. "May I pour you a glass of wine?"

"I would relish that, Andrew, yes." Bess beamed back at him.

"So surprising Mistress Georgina is back in Wilmington," Andrew went on as he reached for a decanter of hock. He said it softly, after a wary look over his shoulder at the others, should he be accused of presuming too much familiarity.

"Yes, it is," Bess agreed. "To see you in town as well, Andrew. I thought your uncle Thomas would keep you out in the country 'til the Sabbath."

"He usually does." Andrew grimaced. "With a tutor. When I'm not out in the fields, riding rounds with the overseers. But then her invitation came, thank God. I hoped you would be here as well, with your father, d'you see. Well . . ." Andrew blushed for expressing his wishes to her. ". . . to continue our . . . *excuse* me for daring to pose it as *our* acquaintance! How presumptious of me. To continue . . ."

"I was pleased to know that you and your uncle would be in attendance, Andrew," Bess informed him, with just a hint of cautious decorum—the slightest lift of her shoulder and nose to tell him to not put *too* much stock in it—but with a warmth to her tone of voice that belied it, leaving the young gentleman pleasingly perplexed.

"Yes, well!" Andrew breathed, his chest expanding with triumph or defeat; he wasn't quite sure which. "Oh, hello, Mr Livesey."

"Hewlett," Samuel grunted uncharitably around a mouthful of honey and molasses-baked barbecue chicken fritter.

"Pay Sam'l no mind, Andrew," Bess almost snickered. "He's still fashed over yesterday."

"Am not," Samuel growled.

"Are, too!" Bess giggled. "I was beastly to him. Or so he believes. But it was none of *my* doing."

"Fashed?" Hewlett questioned. "What sort of a word is that?"

"Scot for 'peeved' or 'vexed,'" Bess informed him. She paused for a moment, furrowing her brow. Her *father* had not appeared half as "fashed" by her trip across the river as she might have expected. It was almost as if he was secretly pleased that she had ridden over the Brunswick to pry information out of Biddy MacDougall. While he had not praised her overly, he hadn't taken a strip of hide off her back either. He had hummed to himself over supper after her revelation, a sure sign, good as an encouraging wink anytime, that she had done extremely well.

But her father had also told her to keep mum about what she had learned, until he had had time to take it to Constable Swann. And the sudden invitation which had come after supper, almost at bedtime, had delayed that. Still, this was Andrew, after all . . .

Making it a gay misadventure, Bess told Andrew about their ride, and Samuel's enforced stopover at the Brunswick Road ferry tavern.

"Lord, Bess!" Andrew gushed when she had ended. "For a girl, I swear you've the bottom of a dragoon! To beard Eachan MacDougall on his own turf, well! After all the talk about town, too!"

"But I didn't know it was *his* daughter 'twas the dressmaker," she insisted gaily. "I'd heard Bridey, *not* Biddy. How was I to know?"

Such an inspired fib! Bess thought. *It deserves more than one airing, and 'twill suit, I'm certain!* She batted her lashes fetchingly, in punctuation to a smile of witless innocence.

"Imagine how surprised *I* was, Andrew!" Bess breathed, with a dramatic hitch of her bosom, and a reviving waft of her fan. "I showed no sign of that 'bottom' of which you spoke. I'm not *that* brave. Why, I was trembling like a leaf when I discovered who he was! And who she was. No, not brave at all . . . just giddy and silly. And ignorant."

"Amen," Samuel agreed gruffly.

"Oh, surely, sir,"—Andrew drew up, defending her with a frozen smile—"You do not own your sister to be ignorant. Perhaps mistook, at best. I'm sure she did not intend to strand you at the tavern, under MacDougall's wrathful eye."

"*I'm* mortal certain she *did.*" Samuel snorted, lifting his brows in derision for another of Bess's victims, too easily taken in by her. "You'll discover her sly ways soon enough, sir, way she's got her cap set for you," Samuel concluded with a malicious leer and grazed beyond them to a tempting platter of pork short ribs.

"Ahum." Bess reddened, fanning herself madly, screening her embarrassment. She took a deep sip of her white wine and coughed.

"Ah," Andrew Hewlett muttered, rocking on his heels over that bit of news, wondering if a fellow's heart could indeed burst with joy. "Hmm. Well . . ."

"Pay Sam'l no mind," Bess implored. "He's a heartless tease."

"Well, then . . ." Andrew deflated a little. "Biddy MacDougall, though, Bess! What is she like?"

"She's very handsome, Andrew," Bess told him as she led him off further toward the front of the parlor by gliding away from him. "Very sad, too, living that lonely out yonder. But very sweet, an incredibly sweet girl, about my age. I found myself quite liking her."

"Did you think to question her about your uncle Harry?" Andrew pressed in a conspiratorial whisper. "I mean, the rumors . . . !"

"Not really," Bess lied, heeding her father's warning. "But I didn't feel she was involved with him, Andrew. Surely, a girl who has lost her lover would show *some* grief, one would think. And she didn't."

"Ah." Andrew Hewlett blushed over the picture of an older lover with a tender young morsel of a girl. "What about her father, then?"

"He didn't appear half the ogre your uncle or the others make him out to be," Bess mused aloud. "I think there's a certain sadness about him, too. I could be wrong, but I don't think she or her father are involved."

"Why?" Andrew countered. "I would have thought him the perfect suspect."

"I know nothing of peoples' secret emotions, Andrew, but Mr MacDougall already knew who we were, soon as we were introduced to him on the ferry boat," Bess replied. "Knew us, surely, as friends of Uncle Harry's? Yet he didn't blink an eye. Didn't go 'squint-a-pipes' as a bag of nails, looking six ways from Sunday. One would think a guilty man could not meet the gaze of a dead man's relations."

"Well, there is that." Andrew frowned, disappointed. "I still say, though, that braving it out, after you found yourself in such a situation, took a *power* of bottom, Bess. You're to be commended."

"Why, thank you, Andrew!" Bess grinned, delighted, though she turned her gaze down shyly. "Immodest as I acted . . . I am pleased you think so, instead of lecturing me for playing the fool."

"Never, Bess!" Andrew declared. "Well, I mean . . ."

"Hmm," she replied, looking away quickly. "Oh, Mrs Maultsby, so good to see you again!"

"Bess Livesey?" the frail old grandmother of the widow gummed back, peering over her spectacles. "That you, my dear? Oh, come take a seat by me and the mister, here. La, poor child, your uncle taken from ye so cruel!"

Let him wonder, Bess told herself, abandoning Andrew.

"Ahum," Osgoode Moore at last announced tentatively. "Ladies and gentlemen, thank you for responding to Mistress Georgina's invitation." He stepped out into the middle of the parlor onto a fine Turkey carpet, clad in black breeches and waistcoat, and a sober mid-gray coat. "While the recently departed Harry Tresmayne was a grand neighbor and true friend to many in the Cape Fear settlements, those present here today were especially close to him, and his dear wife, Georgina. Those bound to them by the bonds of family, those others as close as family and especially esteemed. Georgina will have more to say to you in a moment, but she has requested me, as his . . . as their attorney and confidant, to preface her remarks with some of mine own."

Could he *have killed him, if Bess is correct about MacDougall?* Livesey thought, looking up at him from his seat near Georgina. Osgoode seemed no less perturbed by his own brand of grief than any of the rest. Did that signify? he wondered. How *would* a killer act in front of the widow, the mourning? Too overly grief-stricken, shedding those crocodile tears; or formally brusque, as Osgoode seemed to be at that moment? Still, he *was* a lawyer, Matthew reminded himself, a creature born to pose in any manner his client's cause required, whether he believed it or not.

"You will be relieved to know that our Harry died testate," he went on. "Soon after their marriage, Harry and I drew up his testament, with Mistress Georgina, my wife and myself as witnesses. Certain codicils were amended since, the last performed a little over four months past. The last will and testament is with the magistrate's court now for review, and those few creditors listed in Harry's ledgers are at last redeemed. The notice for any last debts will be posted tomorrow at the courthouse, and those still owing will have a fortnight from tomorrow to come forward and present their bills in good faith. He . . . Harry wrote that I should serve as his executor for the nonce, until his last affairs are cleared, and I'm happy to relate that Mistress Georgina has agreed to that arrangement."

Last affairs, my Lord! Matthew Livesey winced at the turn of phrase. He was not the only one. Livesey cocked a chary eye toward Georgina, and caught the last tiny flash of frustration or anger which had passed over her features, the last settling of a well-controlled start of alarm. Or was he imagining that? he asked himself. Good God, did *she* know about Harry's ruttings, in spite of his caution to conceal them from her?

Georgina turned her head a trifle, caught him staring, and gave him a quick, pained grin, though her expressive green eyes were narrow.

By God, I think Georgina did *know!* Livesey realized. *She's not a stupid woman; far from it.* She grew up in the same community Harry had been born in, would have known his nature of old. Hoping that he *might* have changed, as women seemed to believe of their men in spite of all evidence to the contrary—hoping and trusting that they alone would be the ones to amend a rogue's life!

". . . and testament shall be read," Osgoode concluded, turning to Georgina, pacing back to her chair to take guard over her shoulder.

Georgina slowly lifted her veil, folded it back over the brim of her hat to bare her wan face to them at last. She shifted forward on her chair to pose at the forward edge, folding her black-gloved hands in her lap.

"Of all the myriad acquaintances Harry had, you present today were most revered and cherished," she began slowly. "Dear Osgoode may be a tad retiring, and of such a gentle and ungrasping nature to say so in his preface, but all of you have been cited in Harry's will as heirs of some possession, or possessions. Some may be no more than an item of a sentimental nature unique to his relationship to you . . . but he held you all . . . us all . . . as his dearest life's companions, and would wish to be reminded to you in death, as he was in life. For . . . for my part . . ." Georgina broke off, covering quivering lips with a handkerchief, bowing her head for a moment to master herself. Osgoode put out a supportive hand on her right side and she groped for it, and seized it blindly.

Then, wonder of wonders to Matthew Livesey, her left hand came down from her face, the sodden handkerchief crushed into a ball inside her palm, and groped toward him! Fervently he offered his own, gave a reassuring squeeze as she rested her wrist atop That Thing, right atop the hateful kneecup of his shameful, shattered limb!

"I thank you, sirs," she managed at last, sitting upright and releasing them. "For my part, I have commissioned small tokens be made in remembrance of Harry. Forgive me, but I did not know your sizes, so instead of mourning rings, please accept these poor offerings in their stead. Keep them close to your hearts forevermore, as you did . . . as we all did my Harry!" she rushed out before grief overcame her again.

Anne Moore knelt to offer solace this time, as Osgoode was busy passing out small tissue-wrapped packets which had been stored in the *escritoire* at the back of the parlor. He passed among them, as solemn as a vicar distributing the Host at the altar rails.

Matthew Livesey unwrapped his. It was a sterling silver medallion, between two and three inches across. The heft in his palm felt heavy enough to have required ten shillings or better; perhaps four ounces of coin-silver. He squirmed with remorse at such a crass thought. The medallion had been cast with a milled edge. In the center was a side-view portrait, a noble bust of Harry Tresmayne's profile, with his name scrolled above it in an arc, and the dates of his birth and death below. The obverse side presented a quartered shield such as a Spanish doubloon might bear. One canton of the shield held two pine trees, another crossed swords; the third was a trading ship, and the last were crossed corn and wheat sheaves.

Cape Fear commerce and agriculture summed up neatly by those icons, Matthew Livesey thought with a firm nod of recognition. And all about the obverse rim, inside the milled edge, were the words:

Planter + Scholar + Soldier + Loving Relative + Firm Friend

Aye, Livesey nodded again, his eyes beginning to water as he clasped his fingers about the medallion to press it hard against his palm; that pretty much summed up Harry Tresmayne, too. For better or worse, Harry had been a *damned* good friend. For all his faults, he'd been a man to cherish—as he would cherish this remembrance.

Livesey swore he'd get a joiner to make a small presentation box for his medallion, soon as he could—a triptych box with a plush lining, so the medallion could be seen on both sides, and take pride of place on his mantel down through all the coming generations.

Chapter 21

SOLEMN AND SUBDUED as everyone felt, Georgina bade them enjoy themselves—take more wine, stay and have a bite more. Slaves set out fresh platters and bottles, though Georgina excused herself for awhile to go upstairs and refresh herself before rejoining them.

Bess got herself another glass of hock while her father was sunk deep in a brown study, gazing mournfully at his medallion—so intent he couldn't tell her not to—and went out onto the front veranda for a welcome breath of cooler air. Samuel was barely fit company anytime, even less so today. Andrew was over in one corner with his elegant uncle Thomas Lakey. The Maultsbys were both boresome old trots, for all their sweetness, so Bess desired just a little time to herself.

For a moment, she *thought* of joining Andrew. But after Samuel's spiteful parting shot about her "setting her cap" for him—so doubly wounding since it was *pretty* much true, she thought with a quick hissing anger—she wasn't sure how to approach him until she'd sorted out her depression and resentment, so she could appear chirpy, gay—and coyly uncommitted.

For company, though, she found Mrs Anne Moore, seated alone on the shady cool veranda on a white-painted slat settee, with her hands folded in her lap about the stem of a half-full glass of sherry, chin high and gazing out onto the sandy, sunny street.

Why not? Bess asked herself. *She's here; I'm here. I might not get a better opportunity soon. And it beats wangling an invitation to her house, or inventing another plausible lie, all hollow!*

"So sad," Bess began hesitantly.

Anne Moore swiveled her elegantly coiffed and hatted head about for a moment, and straightened her back, as if she'd been caught in the unladylike activity of slouching in public. Bess saw that Mrs Moore's eyes were pink and slightly puffy from weeping.

But the woman merely glanced at her once, dismissed her presence with the slightest squint of petulance, and folded her arms across her bodice. She returned her interest to the street's doings, which were no great shakes at that moment. One idle hand brought the crystal stem up to rest against her cheek, near her mouth, in a contemplative pose.

Mrs Moore's wide petticoats and lacy sack gown, so precisely arranged, left little room on the settee, so Bess settled herself on the edge of a matching chair nearby, and fortified her unsettled mind with a sip of hock. She directed her own gaze to the roadway.

A piebald hound on the porch opposite yawned, then rolled from its left side to its right. The tail flopped once. Then, a hind foot rose up lazily and made some vague scratching motions somewhere in the vicinity of its ribs. But that was too much effort.

Fascinating, Bess groaned to herself.

"I'm so glad Aunt Georgina's come back to Wilmington," she said finally, blurting out the first solid thought that occurred to her. "I was worried Tuscarora would be too isolated, when she needs company to take her mind off things. Distractions."

"One would suppose that is so," Anne Moore replied in a tone so distant she sounded infinitely bored with anything a mere chit of a girl might say. Bess imagined (not for the first time in talking to her elders) that her remark, and Mrs Moore's reply, had been such a rare coincidence of timing between her, and a real adult's conversation, that what had passed might actually be mistaken for a sign they were taking place at the same time, with Mrs Moore actually listening, then making an effort to respond!

Turk Janissaries are stealing your carriage horses, ma'am, Bess thought sourly; *"That's lovely, my dear," Mrs Moore might say.*

"Not balls and such," Bess blathered on. "Oh, supper among her friends now and again. Music in someone's parlor. Sewing with some other ladies. Tea and talk?"

Mrs Moore took a deep breath, held it for a moment as she pondered the idea, then slumped a little as she most unenthusiastically murmured, "Mmmm," with a faint nod of agreement. She took a sip of her sherry, then returned the glass to her cheek, near the corner of her mouth where it was caressed like a lover's fingers.

"Such a fine memento," Bess said after another long moment had passed. "The medallions."

"Hmmph," Mrs Moore commented, with the most liveliness she had yet shown.

"You did not like them, ma'am?" Bess inquired.

"*More* than a touch—as the French might say—*gauche,*" Mrs Moore sneered lazily. "I was not consulted."

Bee-yitch! Bess drawled to herself, savoring *every* nuance of the Southern pronunciation. "But Mr Osgoode surely was. Perhaps then, you and he . . ."

"Don't be so tiresome, dear," Mrs Moore said with an arch lift to one brow to underline the vexation her voice was too lazy to impart.

"Perhaps mourning rings *would* have been more appropriate, more . . . *tasteful,*" Bess simpered, posing as a social critic more attuned to Mrs Moore's tastes. And hating herself for even pretending to sneer at Aunt Georgina behind her back. "Or, had she her heart set on the medallions, they could have been . . . smaller? Less pretentious?"

"Less gaudy?" Anne Moore actually deigned to reply for once, a corner of her mouth lifting in amusement for a second. "Oh, indeed."

"I never heard it done in Philadelphia," Bess added.

"An *infinitely* more elegant and mannerly city," Mrs Moore said, turning to look at her at last. "Not a sawmill *town.*" She grimaced.

"Were you ever in Philadelphia, ma'am?" Bess asked her.

"Not that far north, no, my dear," Mrs Moore intoned. "Virginia when I was small, then New Bern. Charleston, though, many times—my family and I. One could wish that Wilmington, new as it is, could aspire at some point in its existence to such gentility and refinement."

"It was quite a comedown for us, too, ma'am. Leaving Philadelphia when I was little," Bess encouraged, matching Mrs Moore's dismissive tone, and lifting a brow of her own in sympathy. "I've never been to New Bern, but I hear it's grand. Not as large as Wilmington, but . . . !" Bess managed to squirm girlishly, and to play eager and curious. "What is it like?"

"The houses are proper mansions," Mrs Moore informed her, with a wistfulness. "Streets, the main roads, are actually paved, my dear. The General Assembly brings gentlemen and ladies of the highest merit and breeding together. When in session, there is a *continual* round of balls, routs and drums. Small it may be, but wealthy, so very wealthy! And *refined* wealth—as opposed to the tawdry flummery of Wilmington's . . . how like the French to have such a *perfect* word for them . . . *parvenus*—attracts only the finest merchandise, the most tasteful and cosmopolitan selection from London, Paris, the great capitals of the *civilized* world."

Bess could not help glancing down to her gown, a fairly new pale-yellow cambric. But so tawdrily plain!

"Present company excepted, of *course,* dear Mistress Livesey," Anne Moore allowed, with a nod in her direction, and a wry tip of her sherry glass. But the smile which accompanied that nod Bess thought denoted a hypocritical condescension.

Lyin' bee-yitch! Bess fumed to herself, even as she returned her smile with a rather beatific one of her own.

"I suppose a person must be wealthy, to appear tawdry," Bess replied, after a cooling sip of hock that lit off a slow heartburn in her innards. "Our circumstances . . . but for some color, a bit of lace now and again . . . I must appear Quaker-plain." She frowned.

"Not at *all,* my dear," Mrs Moore quipped, fully engaged now, and wholeheartedly amused. She turned her torso to face Bess, with one arm on the back of the settee. "Even a strumpet may earn the price of too much flibbertygibberty. 'Tis their stock-in-trade, hmm? *N'est-ce-pas?*" Mrs Moore actually laughed. "Besides, very young girls, such as yourself, should *never* be awash in crack-ery. Time enough to follow fashion. There *is* a line, after all."

"I've always adored your taste, Mistress Moore," Bess lied with a becoming shyness. "Why, I wager even the barons' wives, with a week to prepare, can't hold a candle to you when it comes to elegant. Oh, what *is* that French word? You're right, they're *so* apt when you need *le mot juste! Panache!* You could throw on a croaker sack with not a moment's notice, and carry it off with *panache.*"

"Why, *thank* you, my dear, 'tis a pretty compliment." Mrs Moore blushed, and dimpled prettily. "Though I fear I'm quite beyond the day when a hasty toilette would serve to carry any occasion."

"I only wish I had that sense of easy, but elegant, style," Bess pretended to bemoan. "Now our condition is improving . . . oh, I dasn't ask this of you!"

"What, my dear?"

"Your sensible advice," Bess gushed. "Before I go and do something silly. And tawdry." Bess forced herself to giggle, though it was a wrench. "Before I become so enthused over having a new gown made, 'stead of sewing for myself, that I end up looking foolish and trullish. Young Andrew . . . Mr Hewlett? Oops! Well . . ."

Well, heck, everyone else believes it, even Andrew, Bess told herself; *go all the way past miss-ish—aspire to simpering twit! A guinea to a pinch o' sand she'll believe it, too!*

"Aha, so *that's* the reason!" Mrs Moore cajoled softly. "Well, why not? He's a good prospect. Though, should you be able to travel to a *larger* city, I'm sure you'd discover a myriad better. Yes, we could get our heads together. Who are you using?"

"I haven't decided yet, ma'am," Bess lied again, quickly. "Umm . . . I'd *thought* of something much like that lovely gown you owned last winter. I recall it was pale gray watered silk, with off-white lace? And lovely blue ribbon to set it off. To match my eyes. You looked *so* handsome in that!"

"Mmm, perhaps not," Mrs Moore decided, eyeing Bess up and down like a horsetrader. "Too mature, *by years!*" She found it amusing.

"It was so funny," Bess chuckled with effort. "You wore it once, all I can recall, and then . . . Good Lord, here comes the magistrate and his wife two Sundays later, as if she hadn't a *clue!* Mrs Marsden in nearly the same gown, I swear! Poor old thing."

"I do recall," Mrs Moore replied. But her gay tone had taken its leave. She swiveled away to face the street once more, her face returning to a vacant mask. To Bess, her reply had almost sounded snippy!

"I do trust her . . . *pale* imitation did not hurt you, ma'am," Bess stumbled, wondering at her mercurial change, and if she caused it. "Or did I, by bringing it up, then? If I did . . ."

"No, my dear," Mrs Moore responded quickly, grating out her words, though, as she took a deep breath for steadiness. "It would be extremely silly for me to be upset over such a trifle, past a slight irritation of the moment. To hold a grudge so long . . ." Anne Moore sighed, waving her wineglass absently. Reminded that she still held it, she took a dutiful sip.

"But you still have it?" Bess pressed. "That gown?"

"You wish my cast-offs?" Mrs Moore queried, raising her brow in arch, but weary, amusement again.

"No, ma'am, of course not!" Bess answered, flushing hot that it sounded like she was begging. "I'd wish to see it, to recall its details for my dressmaker, though. If you no longer care to wear it. So I would not imitate you . . . I have no *need* to beg, ma'am!"

"Too old for you by half," Mrs Moore dismissed with a snort, returning her gaze again. "Best stay with youthful styles suitable to your years. Such heavy fabrics, so glittery, are unseemly for one so young. The color is more apt for an established matron, as well."

"I see." Bess nodded. "Then I thank you for that advice which I requested, Mistress Moore. You see, you have saved me from a crude error already!" Bess grinned, trying to cajole the woman with a bit of flattery.

"I have the latest sample folios, just arrived," Mrs Moore at last allowed. "Direct from London. And from Paris, no matter that we are still *technically* at war with the French. There are means . . . I'm told. I'll send you them, once I've perused them for myself. I will indicate which I deem proper for you."

"That would be very gracious of you, Mistress Moore," Bess said. "I'm grateful to you for your most experienced advice. Forgive me, if I've imposed upon you, ma'am. But with Aunt Georgina in mourning, and no woman about our house to advise me, I dasn't pester her with silly concerns at this time."

"It is no imposition," Mrs Moore intoned so dully and dutifully that Bess was sure that it, indeed, was.

"Could you advise me just the tiniest bit more, then, ma'am?" Bess coaxed, leaning forward as if to conspire. "About whom you think is the most talented dressmaker in the settlement?"

"Oh, well." Mrs Moore pondered. "There is the widow Cofer, out on

Fifth Street. I use her almost exclusively, but she is swamped with work. And *rather* expensive these days," Anne Moore informed her with a gratuitous nod to Bess, and the state of her finances.

Sneerin' bee-yitch, Bess deemed her in silence.

"There *is* a black freedwoman, Mama Trickett, who is quite good. Though one *must* keep her lazy fingers to their task. Her fee would be more . . . comfortable." Mrs Moore shrugged doubtfully.

"I've heard there's a new girl 'cross the Brunswick. Her name is . . ." Bess paused, forcing herself to simper with giddy stupidity as she got to the crux of her interrogation. "Oh, dear, I've quite forgot. Was it Goody? Bridey? Biddy? Louisa Lillington told me, but . . . have you heard anything of her, ma'am? Louisa speaks highly of her, but I would trust *your* judgment more. Have you seen any of her work?"

"No," Mrs Moore dismissed sharply. "I have not." She rose to her feet gracefully, though with a touch more haste than that languid style a lady should display. "You will excuse me, my dear." It was an order, not a polite social withdrawing sound.

Bess was forced to her feet as well, puzzled by how stern Anne Moore looked, wondering just what the connection was between her sudden vexation and that dress. Or was it the *dressmaker?* Bess thought.

"You are feeling unwell suddenly, ma'am?" Bess chirped. "Have you a headache? Perhaps I could . . ."

"A most *egregious* headache!" Mrs Moore all but snarled, showing her true feelings at last. "I have no more patience for this."

"If I have offended, ma'am . . ." Bess shambled.

"To prate 'bout dresses, and *fashion,* at such a somber time!" Mrs Moore hissed. "When *sensible* people would respect the melancholy of those who . . . I mean, really! Respect the dead, and the mourning, you silly little goose-brain! *Think* where you are, at least!"

"Ma'am, I . . . !" Bess gasped, recoiling.

Anne Moore set her sherry glass down on the porch railing and swept past her with a final crushing glare and re-entered the house, swishing her skirts in frothy hostility.

"Well, da . . . darn!" Bess muttered to herself on the empty porch.

Now what in tarnation did I say to set her off like that? Bess speculated, mortally abashed by Mrs Moore's scornful dressing-down. She felt crushed by her clumsiness, as well, when she thought she had been so clever in bringing up the subject of that gown—and Biddy.

She went to the sherry glass on the railing and picked it up. Shrugging, she lifted it to her lips and tossed it off to "heel-taps," badly in need of fortification at that moment.

"Beats hock all hollow," she told herself in a whisper as the sweeter, mellower sherry settled warmly in her stomach, muting heartburn from her more-acrid white wine, and her sense of failure.

Mrs Moore came out onto the porch a moment later, nose high, with her parasol ballooned out to protect her already-olive skin from the sun. Osgoode Moore came almost bleating in her bustling wake, expostulating in desperate whispers as she plowed her way down the steps and across the walk, toward the front gate and her waiting carriage. He tacked from port to starboard in her wake, avoiding dogwood bushes and azaleas that impeded his progress.

He handed her into the four-wheeled cart while the black coachee held the door for her; all but wringing his hands. Bess turned to stare at the middle distance, up-hill, to avoid shaming him further. And to spare herself, truth be told; such domestic hurricanes between man and wife should never be seen in public, especially where the woman held the upper hand. And it boded ill for young people to witness them, blighting their own naive prospects for a happy life.

Mercifully, Bess made to enter the house, though she could not *quite* avoid seeing Osgoode Moore sag in defeat as the coach departed.

She set her wineglass on the sideboard, wishing no more hock. Then she picked up a chewy molasses cookie and nibbled on it, pondering all the while what had set Mrs Moore off.

That gown! she thought. Biddy'd made it for her; yet she lied about knowing her work. She'd only worn it once, whatever the reason. Everything had been going just wonderfully, until she'd brought it up. Bess sighed. She cast a guilty glance over at her father, sitting by Aunt Georgina. Now, if *Anne Moore* had been seeing Harry Tresmayne on the sly, if the bawdy rumor was true . . .

Lord! Bess gulped, blushing at the fantasy which arose!

What if Anne Moore had worn that gown on one of their trysts? Samuel had told her how muddy and weedy that grove was. He'd snorted with sly, lascivious glee that the lovers' bower was beneath a prickly pine, littered with dry needles and cones. Had she ruined it? Haste, fear of undressing completely lest someone discover them . . . or the dank chill before spring had come . . . or torn it in the throes of *lust?*

Bess flushed again, feeling a need for further fanning. Proper as she'd been raised, there were *novels,* after all! And lower-class market girls, who delighted in relating their amorous adventures. She was not *entirely* naive!

And Samuel had come home with his clothing snagged on the undergrowth. If Anne Moore had ridden out alone with no coachee as witness, she might have torn the gown on the thorns and such along the narrow trails, riding in or out. Or ripped away in passion by Uncle Harry!

I'll wager she still has it, Bess thought, hitching her breath as she did so. If that gray silk gown with the blue ribbons was her apparel on their very *first* tryst, then a snip of cloth, a length of lace, or a hank of ribbon from it would be one of those silent signs Constable Swann had sneered about, an outwardly innocent token which had a covert, shameful meaning only to the "whores an' rogues" who shared it.

Of course! That gown had been hung far back in Anne Moore's chiff. orobe, too ripped or soiled for public view, too damning if her husband saw it again and asked about it. Yet, too sentimental to be discarded—until now. Bess started, withering herself with appraisal of her stupidity! Mrs Moore might be so upset about her innocent-seeming questions, she might be throwing it out, or tearing it into rags this very moment—whether she knew that her flowers, with the incriminating ribbons from that gown, had been found or not!

"Ahum," someone said at her elbow.

"Oop!" Bess exclaimed with alarm. "Oh, Andrew!"

"Forgive me if I gave you a start, Bess," he apologized shyly.

"Not at all, good sir!" Bess assured him too brightly. "I was . . . I fear the occasion has given me a melancholy headache."

If it works for Anne Moore, it'll serve for my excuse, Bess told herself.

"I am so sorry, Bess. A cool cloth, perhaps?" he offered.

"I really would feel much better if I could go home, Andrew."

His face fell at that news.

"Father will wish to stay. Sam'l, too, if God is kind to me," Bess said, attempting to cheer him. "Would it be an imposition if I asked you to escort me home?"

"It would not be, certainly not!" Andrew beamed quickly. "You do me the greatest—"

"I will make my excuses to Aunt Georgina and Father. Do you the same with your uncle. I'll meet you here on the porch?" Bess suggested, remembering to massage her brow and frown in her "suffering."

Chapter 22

YOU SET a hot pace, Bess," Andrew complained. "Surely that is bad for a headache. To stir the causative humors of the blood so . . ."

"Oh, the sooner I am home . . ." Bess puffed, waving vaguely.

"My uncle set no time limit for my return, Bess," Andrew said with a hopeful sound, fantasizing about heady visions of being totally alone and private with her, of daring to actually hold her hand with no one to see them, of aspiring to be allowed a modest kiss on Bess's bared shoulder! *His* blood was up and stirring, of a certainty!

Bess had hiked them uphill to Third Street, the main thoroughfare, thence quickly along Third to the intersection of Market below the courthouse. She slowed her pace once they reached the southern corner, after crossing Market, and came to a stop in a welcome patch of shade.

"I'm sorry for rushing, Andrew," she said, though she was too distracted to put much effort into making it sound heartfelt. Bess was too intent on the Moore house three houses down. "Let us stand and converse here for a moment where it's cooler. I'm sure you must be . . . perspired."

"I'll get us something cool to drink?" Andrew suggested, pointing to a street monger's cart which bore a barrel and a row of wooden mugs.

"Nothing for me," Bess said, wrinkling her nose at the prospect of how dirty the mugs, or the contents of the barrel, must be. "Well, perhaps a tiny sip of yours. Whatever it is." She laughed wryly.

"Here, fellow!" Andrew called as he approached the free-black monger.

The coach was back in the carriage house in the back lot of the Moore property, Bess noted in his absence, thinking it a fine pretension to need a carriage for a two-block journey she had walked in less than a minute. The pair of horses were free of their harness, and the coachee, now with his livery-coat off and his sleeves rolled up, was filling a trough for them to drink from. The front of the house was shut and mute, though, the drapes drawn snug for cooling dimness against the early afternoon sun.

Urgently as she'd wished to get a vantage point to see if Anne Moore would dispose of the gown, Bess didn't have a clue how she was going to pull it off, now that she was there. Young ladies did not loiter on the streets, even if they did have an escort. And if Mrs Moore spotted her, pacing on sentry-go in front of her house! Even worse, if she was discovered sneaking around the alley in the back, or pawing through their refuse bin . . . !

Idiot! she accused herself.

"'Tis ginger-beer," Andrew announced, returning to her side with a foaming piggin. "Fresh off the ship from Jamaica, still in the original barricoe, not decanted. Nothing spiritous. Quite good, actually."

"Mmm," Bess replied, giving him a brief glance.

"Ginger's good for settling biliousness," Andrew prated on. "If your headache was brought on by biliousness . . . well. Excuse me for my thoughtlessness. To speak of such . . . *ahum* . . . natural things with you, a young lady . . . !"

"I believe I will assay a sip, after all, Andrew," Bess decided, turning to him, and rewarding him with a smile. "Perhaps the ginger *will* relieve whatever caused my headache. I did experience a certain bilious feeling after the hock I drank."

"My pardons for suggesting it, then, Bess. Had I known hock did not agree with you . . ." Andrew muttered.

Bess took a taste, savoring the sprightly tingling of the bubbly brew, and the hot, sweet tang of the fruit-and-ginger concoction. But she could not help peering over the rim at Andrew Hewlett, wondering if he was going to apologize for his every unguarded utterance, scraping, bowing and wringing his hands should she throw him the least cross expression.

Lord help me, Bess thought, *but Anne Moore might have the* right *of it . . . even if she is an arrogant trull! Andrew's pretty, a courtly gentleman, and all, but . . . surely there's someone out there for me who can be more forthright and easy.*

"Uh, y'all 'scuze Autie, folks," the teenaged beer monger asked hesitantly, "but . . . is y'all gwine be long wit' 'at piggin?"

"Give us time to drink it, boy!" Andrew snapped with an unconsciously superior sneer.

Bess frowned, creating that furrow 'twixt her brows. "Don't be cross-patch, Andrew," she murmured, treating him to a cool glare; she said louder, and more sweetly, to the monger, "Pardon us for taking so long, but it's so sprightly, 'tis hard to drink quickly. We don't mean to restrict your trade."

"Yassum, hit sho' be, umhum!" The monger grinned back, doffing his shapeless straw hat to her.

"What trade?" Andrew whispered, after a peer up and down all the streets.

"Got me plenny mo' piggins, ma'am, y'all take yuh time, 'at'll be fine," the monger said on, bobbing like a quail. "I kin come back fo' hit when y'all done, yassuh, sho' kin! No 'fense, massa. Autie don' mean no disr'speck, sho' I don'!" he added with another doffing of his hat, and a foolish titter that Bess suspected was as forced as the one she'd used on Anne Moore. Autie lifted the cart to trundle to safer ground, dreading the risk of rowing a white gentleman's ire; but Jemmy Bowlegs came up, and stopped him in his tracks.

"Ho, Autie!" Jemmy shouted as he crossed the street. "What-all ya got thar this time, boy?"

"Got da *fine* gingah-beah, Mistah Jeemy, suh!" the monger cried happily back. "Ya want some? Ha'pence, da piggin."

Bowlegs came from the courthouse hitching rails, dodging a mud puddle or two, a squawking goose, and some piles of fresh equine ordure. He looked *almost* respectable, these days, after Bess's father had let him select new clothes. Jemmy Bowlegs now sported a clean linen shirt, a rather natty pair of nut-brown moleskin breeches, tan cotton stockings, and, wonder of wonders, a crisp new black tricorne hat with silvered lace on the brims. He'd even aspired to black buckled *shoes!*

"Ginger-beah, that's kiddy-swill, Autie," Bowlegs scoffed. "Ya ain't got no ale, like ya use'ta? Afternoon, Miz Livesey. Afternoon, Mistah Hewlett, suh." He grinned, barely lifting his hat to doff.

"Jemmy Bowlegs, how do," Bess said in reply.

"Bowlegs," Andrew grunted, gruffly ill at ease. Walking Bess to her home was turning into a street raree.

"No ale?" Bowlegs asked, turning back to Autie the monger.

"Nossuh, Mistah Jeemy. Sher'ff an' Const'ble, they say Pap an' me ain't got no li-cence t'sell no *sperrts,* 'at's fo' tavern folk, an' such. But dis heah gingah-beah be mighty good!"

"Stole hit, did'nya, Autie," Bowlegs teased straight-faced, as he dug into his breeches pockets for a coin. "Well, gimme some."

"Naw, Pap ha'dly *evah* steal no *mo',* Jeemy. We give da chandluh four shillin' fo' dis bar'coe. 'Ayr ya go, Mistah Jeemy, suh. Cold an' *tangly* gingah-beah, yassuh!"

Bess could see that Jemmy Bowlegs had not been *completely* civilized by his new togs; his new tricorne sported hawk feathers bound in a red ribbon cockade on the left front, like a military officer's dog-vane, loop and button. A white egret plume peaked over the left brim, too, and on the right side, drooping like an off-side queue . . . well, it looked like a rather *plush* raccoon's tail. And, of course, he had kept his deerhide waistcoat with all its esoteric knots and headings, and his waist-sash and cut-down fighting knife.

With an astonished grin, Bess also realized that Jemmy must have actually taken a *bath* a few days previous; he no longer gave off the aroma of an outraged skunk!

"Yer brother keepin' fair, Miz Livesey?" Jemmy inquired, after a deep draft of ginger-beer, and turning his head to "politely" let go a small belch. "I heard-tell ya put him out right-smart t'other day . . . cross th' river."

"Unfortunately, I did, Jemmy," Bess snickered. "Not really my doing, but . . . And I've heard of nothing else, since. He's in a terrible pet over it."

"Aw, he'll git over hit," Bowlegs said with a shrug.

"Perhaps we should be getting on," Andrew sulkily suggested.

"But I haven't finished yet, Andrew," Bess cooed, beaming up at him to let him back in her good graces; *if* he behaved. She took a small sip of her beer, her mind whirling with possibilities. She had entertained a vague thought that she might be able to employ Andrew in her plan, posting him as sentinel on the Moore house, which had been half the reason she'd asked him to walk her home. Now that he was so "tetchy," though, and abrupt . . .

Bowlegs, though. His appearance was almost heaven-sent. The fellow could track game through a driving rainstorm, Samuel had assured her. He'd helped her father; surely he could help her in this, too!

And, she sighed to herself, who would suspect Jemmy Bowlegs if he loafed around this part of town, when he did nothing *but* loaf most of the time?

"Besides," she added for Andrew's benefit, "Jemmy Bowlegs and my brother are inseparable friends, Andrew. They go hunting, fishing, tracking, I don't know what-all, together all the time. He's one of Sam'l's best friends."

"Wayull, thankee Miz Livesey." Bowlegs beamed, doffing his hat to her once more in gratitude. "Reckon I am, at that."

Damme, it is *a raccoon's tail!* she noted.

"Andrew," she said coyly, "would you excuse me just a moment, if I schemed with Mr Bowlegs?"

"Hey?" Andrew sputtered. "Scheme? With Bowlegs?"

"To find a way to make amends to Sam'l, Andrew," she confided. "Who would know better than his best friend what would thaw him out? So he isn't so sulky with me. Nor with you, I might add," she added quickly.

"Oh, well, in that case . . ." Andrew frowned, groping at his neck-stock in growing frustration.

"Thank you, kind sir," Bess told him. "Come here, Jemmy. Let's plot!" she demanded, leading him several steps away down Market Street. "I need some help, Jemmy," she whispered once they were apart from the others. "The same help you gave my father, the other day."

"Yes'um?" Bowlegs asked, a trifle dubious.

"It's about that bouquet of flowers you and Sam'l found," Bess went on quickly. "I think I found out who sent it, and where the blue ribbon came from!"

"Oh, Law," Jemmy said with a groan, his dusky face clouding up. "Miz Livesey, ya oughtn't be a'messin' wif such. Whoe'er it wuz that murdered Mistah Harry, they find out you been pokin' inta their doin's . . . they might jus' be of a mind t'come after ya!"

"That's why I need you, Jemmy," she announced.

"So'z *I* kin git kilt, 'stead of ya?" he snorted. "Huh! If hit were Eachan

MacDougall done hit, ya already stirred th' pot by goin' over thar, an' he'll be on his guard fer shore. Ya want me t'go over th' Brunswick an' rile him up *more?* Ya couldn't *pay* me enough!"

"Not the MacDougalls, Jemmy!" Bess objected. "Unless there's something you know about Biddy and her father that I don't."

"No, ma'am, I don't," Jemmy said, scowling. "Nor nobody else, neither. Jus' did get back f'um Masonborough, an'—"

"Sim Bates, then?" Bess hissed, her eyebrows high in query.

"Warn't Bates, Miz Livesey, nor Mistah Ram-Sewer, neither," he told her. "Bates's black gal's lucky t'have a single shift t'put on her back. An' Sim wuz cookin' at a pig roast, th' night Mistah Harry died. Got drunker'n Davey's Sow, fell in th' fire, an' come nigh to roastin' *hisself.* So . . . just who *you* 'spect hit be?"

"Mistress Anne Moore," she imparted, barely above a whisper.

"Wawwgh!" Jemmy groaned, leaning back to savor that news. "'At'd mean pore Mistah *Osgoode* . . . ? Wawwgh!" he reiterated, struck dumb with the implications.

"It *might* be," Bess allowed carefully. "But the ribbons are off one of her gowns. Now here's what I wish you could do for me, Jemmy . . ."

Matthew Livesey stumped toward home, barely fit company, though he tried to perk up talkative and cordial. The occasion, the medallion, Georgina Tresmayne's pathetic need of his support, and her almost fervent, waif-like fondness toward him to plead for that support, had him all a-kilter. And the weight of the commemorative medallion in his coat pocket weighed him down as heavily as the weight of his heart.

". . . coach in more often than is my wont, now Georgina, well . . ." Thomas Lakey sighed.

"Hmm?"

"Well, sir," Lakey drawled soberly, plying his elegant walking stick stylishly as he paced alongside Livesey—a pace very close to the languid, gentlemanly gait he usually employed. "Her plantation is close by mine own, not a quarter-hour's ride away from The Lodge. I had thought to coach or ride over to look in on her, now she needs all her old friends' comfort. Still, except for faction business, I've had too few occasions to draw me to town of late. As I get older, there's more pleasure, it seems, in rustic routine. Though I fear rusticity's made me somethin' of an Eremite." Lakey sniggered at himself.

"So do my concerns, sir," Matthew admitted charitably. "Why, I cannot recall the last time I had my boat out on the river. Business! A working plantation is even more an uncertain venture, I'm sure."

"'Deed 'tis, Livesey, 'deed 'tis," Lakey agreed with a chuckle. "Engrossin', absorbin', but barely rewardin', even when things at last go well, don't ye know. Reminds me!" Mr Lakey enthused suddenly, all but snapping his fingers for being remiss. "I extended an invitation . . . rather, Andrew, my nephew, did to you an' yours . . . few weeks back. To coach out an' visit. Your lovely daughter, Bess, wished some cuttin's of my gardens. Late in the season for azaleas, now, but roses . . . did she not mention it to you?"

"I believe she did, sir." Livesey nodded. "Though, with all the unsettled doings of late, I quite forgot. And I thankee for extending the invitation again."

"Ride out after Divine Services, dine on the grounds . . ." Lakey mused happily. "The lad's quite took with your girl, Livesey. All he talks about, I swear."

"Young Hewlett has figured in her remarks as well, sir," Matthew informed him, turning to see if the man was proposing a match. Hewlett was an orphaned cadet scion of *the* Hewletts, due to inherit The Lodge from Thomas Lakey someday. Well-educated, well-bred. It *could* be a profitable and reasonably suitable pairing.

"I trust she sounded *somewhat* fond, hey?" Lakey cajoled gaily.

"Early days, though," Matthew replied cautiously.

"Oh, my, yes!" Lakey poo-pooed. "Cream-pot love, if love it is! Andrew barely eighteen. Your sweet Bess a year shy of that. Much too young for serious spoonin', hmm?"

"Oh, of course," Livesey mildly agreed. "Of a certainty."

"Damme, Mr Livesey, I don't know what gets into our youngsters in these times, swear I don't," Lakey went on most wryly. "Not out o' their teens or barely come to their majority, an' they're courtin' an' weddin'. Now, in our day, young folk'd wait 'til they're established. Acred, educated . . . embarked in life, and securely settled."

"Mmm, in the mid to late twenties, as it should be," Livesey admitted with a sage nod. "As we and our parents always have."

"Lord," Samuel muttered with a bored sigh, rolling his eyes as he dawdled in their wake, half-stepping, almost hobbled by their gait.

"Get the wildness out of them, first," Livesey added, turning to look over his shoulder and give his son a meaningful warning glare.

"Exactly so, Livesey," Lakey chortled. "Exactly so! Still . . . for the nonce, cream-pot courtin's a way for them t'discover manners, an' which qualities most please their natures . . . for later on serious consideration. Unless you have any serious objections, sir . . . Andrew is a mannerly young fellow. Not allow him t'see your precious Bess to home, were he not, I assure you! And Bess is a most sensible, house-mannerly young lady . . . of considerable pleasin' attainments?"

Samuel could almost be heard to wheeze at that, choking off a sarcastic comment. Livesey screwed his head about to glare again.

"More ultimate promise in her little finger than in the entire borough's crop o' misses, Mr Livesey," Lakey lauded on, oblivious to Samuel's scorn. "As I say, should you have no serious objections, we could, perhaps, allow 'em more chances t'be acquainted. Many a slip, t'wixt the crouch and the leap, o' course. But . . . !" he barked happily at the auspicious prospects.

"Mmm, not encouraging, exactly," Livesey mused.

"Nor *dis*-couragin', either, hah!" Lakey bubbled. "Just so!"

"I promise I will give the matter serious reflection, sir," he allowed at last. "And—"

"Why, here's the lad himself, at last," Lakey announced, using his long walking stick to aim at his nephew who approached them. "You young scamp, you took your own sweet time. Just leavin', were you?"

"Uncle," Andrew Hewlett replied, still out-of-sorts.

"Bess is feeling better?" Livesey inquired.

"Some better, Mr Livesey," Andrew said. "She applied a cold cloth, soon as we attained your stoop. We sat on the porch while she did so. Then she decided to go in and have a lie-down so I just bade her my leave, just now."

"Very good," Livesey told him, approving his good manners, and knowing enough about the lad to know he was telling the truth. Besides, if he knew his Bess (and well he did), any caddish behavior would have been put down in a twinkling! Livesey rather suspected that Andrew *had* hoped for more—he looked rather hangdog and nettled—but it would not have been anything worthy of a switching. But any promising lad lucky enough to share Bess's company *would* aspire to more. A lad with any bottom, at any rate. Still, he thought, he could ask her in a few minutes how Andrew Hewlett had conducted himself.

"Well, the social amenity done," Thomas Lakey decided, "an' Bess seen safely home, we will take our leave of you, good sir."

"And we of you and Andrew, sir," Livesey responded, tipping his tricorne, and bowing their departure.

"Don't forget our invitation," Lakey reminded him.

"I will not, sir, and thankee again," Livesey told him. "We await your notice as to which Sunday would suit you best."

"Hang formality," Lakey chuckled. "Weather permittin', let us say *this* Sunday. Ride in my coach after church. I'll bring a horse or two, t'ease th' crowdin' in th' coach."

"You are too kind, sir. But weather allowing, yes. Let's."

"*Adieu* then, Mr Livesey . . . young Samuel. Come, Andrew."

Samuel waited 'til Lakey and Hewlett were safely out of hearing distance. "We weddin' her off, then, Father? Huzzah, I say."

With long practice, Livesey boxed his ear. "*That* for yer sauce!"

"I'm a man grown, Father," Samuel graveled, rubbing his ear and blushing hot at such a public humiliation. "Don't deserve such . . . not where all can *see*, I don't! You didn't have t'do that . . ."

"Then *carry* yourself like a man grown!" Livesey hissed, seething livid. "Such flippancy, mockery of your elders' conversations . . . at such a time, too! An occasion nigh as grave as a funeral? Yet you would sneer, like a *boy*. Keep your counsel to yourself . . . or wait on my displeasure at home . . . where I just might take a strop to you, like an errant *child* deserves!"

"I'm sorry, Father, I didn't . . ." Samuel snuffled. But Livesey, Senior, was already pacing away from him, forcing him to trot to catch him up.

Chapter 23

"YOU TAKE ENTIRELY too much upon yourself, my girl," Livesey warned her sternly.

"I realize that, Father," Bess replied, seeming chastised, in an uncharacteristically meek voice.

"Bowlegs's advice to you was correct," Livesey, Senior, went on, rasping in a confidential softness, as if he did not dare to use a normal tone of voice even in his own parlor, for fear of being over-heard. "This is dangerous business."

"I know that, Father," Bess whispered back, almost ducking her head. His harsh, confidential mutter rasped at her like a rough iron file. She cut a quick look toward Samuel, who was seated in one of their pair of decent wing-chairs. No matter how dangerous their father portrayed it, Samuel seemed to be enjoying Bess getting her "comeuppance," scowling properly judgmental when Mr Livesey saw him, yet smirking with glee when he was not looking. Despite his earlier chastisement.

"My fault, I must suppose." Livesey sighed heavily. "After your little escapade 'cross the Brunswick with the MacDougalls, I shouldn't have seemed so approving. Or encouraging."

"But it's only dangerous if the murder *was* a factional conspiracy, Father," she dared enough to point out. "If it was only Anne Moore involved, if the reason was personal . . ."

"Even so, my girl," Livesey cut her off quickly, slashing at the air between them with his hand. "Even so, you inquired too deep of her! Should you have put her on her guard . . ."

"On the *qui-vive,* as she would be wont to say?" Bess said, trying to lighten his mood, and her possible punishment.

"Do *not* attempt to jape!" her father gloomed back sternly. "You will not cosset me. Should you have put her on her guard, the gown may disappear, and with it, all proof of her involvement. Or her husband's."

"But that's why I set Jemmy Bowlegs to watch the house, Father," Bess reminded him. "To see if she throws it away."

"Maybe she threw it out a long time ago," Samuel offered up, in the tense silence which followed.

"Hmm," Livesey mused, steepling his fingers under his nose. "If Anne Moore was romantically involved with Harry, as it now appears I must admit, Osgoode . . . Sam'l, that's an interesting thought you just had, my boy." Matthew Livesey perked up a bit. "If the gown was discarded long ago, then she knows for certain that Osgoode is guilty. Has known, in fact, all this time. And is covering his crime, and her shameful link to the murder, and the reason behind it."

"But Father"—Bess frowned—"if Uncle Harry and Anne Moore were lovers, how could she stand to live under the same roof with a man who'd killed the one she loved?"

"If Osgoode is found out, her rather comfortable, respectable life is over," Matthew Livesey announced. "Even if he's innocent, she would be ruined in the Cape Fear for her adultery. And the stench of it would follow her anywhere she went in the Carolinas. Except for Charleston, perhaps. Word of it could follow her all the way to London! *If* it came out, do you see."

"Yet she could have thrown the gown out long ago, as Sam'l says, and still not suspect Osgoode of killing him," Bess said. "If she felt the gown was a danger to her reputation alone. Forgive me for judging others, but Mrs Moore doesn't strike me as a body who cares much for anyone but herself. And I've done something stupid, hoping she still had it! That she'd kept it out of some kind of . . . sentiment! I hope it's still there. Else we'll never know."

"Most perplexing, 'deed 'tis." Matthew Livesey sighed. "Bess, be a good girl and top me up with some more of yon Madeira, will you?"

She sprang to do his bidding, fetching the bottle from the open wine cabinet and pouring his abandoned glass full again. She sat on the narrow arm of their shabby old settee, near her father, as he took a sip.

"So, did Osgoode suspect them, do you think?" her father asked at last. "Maybe put two and two together? And caught them together in that glade? Is he our murderer?"

"Well . . ." Samuel muttered shyly.

"Go on, Sam'l," Livesey prompted.

"He left you and Uncle Harry *early* enough to get out there where the murder happened." Samuel shrugged, hunching into himself as he felt their eyes upon him. "But if he'd caught 'em, wouldn't he have shot him right then? Or been mad enough to have shot the pair of 'em? Or, shot him running away, in the back? But Uncle Harry was waylaid. Ambushed. No word of warning or nothing."

"Hmm." Livesey speculated, "Let's assume Osgoode Moore *had* begun to be suspicious. Bouquets coming with no card, Anne sending a servant off with a bouquet. Over time, he could have discovered where they were coming from, *and* where they were going. He might even have followed his wife and seen them engaged in . . . ahum. Well, covertly, I should expect. I find it hard to picture Osgoode Moore bursting from the bushes, bristling with indignation. I should think he would be the sort to brood, to follow them more than a time or two. He's a *lawyer.* He'd wish to make a case, after all, to satisfy his legal mind. Doubtless, he *loves* Anne. A public spectacle would harm both of them. He'd lose the leadership of the faction, if his best friend Harry had . . . ah. No one will follow a cuckold. A bill of divorcement would have to be presented in the General Assembly. Reverend McDowell would have to rule on it, as a one-man ecclesiastical court. Anne, Harry, Osgoode . . . they'd all be ruined. But a murder would solve every problem rather neatly."

"And save the faction," Bess piped up quickly.

"Hmm? Yes, it would, wouldn't it?" her father agreed, just as quickly. "If Harry had been revealed as a traitor to his best friend, he'd have lost all respect, and the faction would have fallen apart."

"So Prince Dick Ramseur was right, Father?" Samuel snickered. "In part, anyway. Uncle Harry ended up a martyr for the cause, 'long as nobody ever discovers the real reason?"

"Exactly so."

"Then, maybe Osgoode Moore threw the gown away, himself." Bess nodded. "If he recognized the ribbons or lace torn from it to make up the bouquets, it would be too incriminating to keep. If he was the murderer, if he confronted his wife once it was done . . ."

"Yet she did not seem . . ." Matthew Livesey began.

He was interrupted by a soft scratching sound at the back door of the kitchen annex, which led to a small back porch off the garden. They stiffened in dread as the scratching came again, louder this time and more insistent. The latch-string jiggled!

"Sam'l, my dragoon pistols, on the mantel yonder," Livesey ordered in a whisper. "Bess, see who it is, but don't open it until we are ready."

Bess went to the door, her arms folded across her bosom, hands clasping opposite arms hard to still her trembling. She glanced back to see her father on his feet, Samuel close by, and both now armed with heavy pistols, fresh-primed and drawn back to half-cock.

"Who is it?" Bess demanded, feeling fluttery with dread.

"Hits us'uns!" someone whispered back. "Op'm up!"

"Jemmy!" Samuel exclaimed, relieved, recognizing the voice.

"Good God, but you gave us a fright!" Bess said as she cracked the door just wide enough for Bowlegs and little Autie to slip in.

"Ev'nin', Mistah Livesey," Bowlegs said, beaming. "Hidy, Sam. Hidy, Miz Livesey. Whoa! No call fer them 'barkers,' hit's just us. Say hidy to th' folks, Autie."

"Ev'nin', y'all," Autie said, doffing his straw hat and bowing to one and all. "Boss . . . ma'am."

"Show 'em, Autie," Jemmy ordered, and the monger laid a ragged sailcloth bundle on the dining table, opening it slowly, enjoying his brief moment of importance. Under the sailcloth was a gray, watered-silk sack gown, now much the worse for wear!

"Dear God, it's . . . it!" Mr Livesey exclaimed in wonder.

"Whoo!" Bess whooped in glee, giving Bowlegs a hug for reward. "You're marvels, the both of you! It was still *there!* But how did you get it?"

"Wayull, I put Autie out front, Miz Livesey," Jemmy proudly said, "sellin' ginger-beah on Market Street. Weren't nobody goin' t'care much, t'see a black feller vendin' in front o' their house. Most folk don't even *see* black folk half th' time, anyhow, nor pay 'em no mind."

"'At's right, suh, hit *sho'* be!" Autie confirmed with a wry look.

"I got me a full piggin and went an' had me a sit-down in a bit o' shade," Bowlegs went on, preening a little at his cleverness.

"Knowin' you, Jemmy, they took it for rum," Samuel joshed.

"Yeah, reckon so, Sam'l," Jemmy agreed. "Got me a second, then follered th' shade to th' alley back o' th' Moore house. Pertended to take me a li'l nap . . . folk'd 'spect that o' me, too . . . an' then a bit after dark? Wayull, heah come Miz Moore her ownself, sneakifyin' out her back door, lookin' six ways f'um Sunday! Slanky-slid over th' trash barr'l an' stuffed this-heah dress in. That's why hit's a tad ripe on th' nose. Sorry . . . they wuz all sorts o' slops in thar, afore, an' some chamber pot, uh . . . stuff. Once't hit got real *good* an' dark, I jus' hopped right over an' snagged 'er. An' here hit be!" he crowed, thumbs hooked into the armholes of his waistcoat.

"You're a marvel, Jemmy," Mr Livesey declared. "It seems your backwoods skills are just as useful in town. Sam'l, fetch the wine. These lads have earned a glass, and our gratitude!"

"I can barely remember her wearing it," Bess said, busying herself by pawing over the soiled gown despite its ripeness. "And, it's not as flouncy as Biddy MacDougall described it, either, Father. See how much lace and ribbon has been removed? Carefully, but . . ." Bess reached into her apron pocket and brought out that eight-inch sample off the bouquet and laid it atop the remaining ribbon on the gown.

"Is it a match?" her father pressed impatiently, bustling over.

"To a Tee, I think," Bess announced, her enthusiasm mysteriously vanishing, leaving a void in her soul. "Take a look yourself, Father. I'll fetch the candles so you can see better."

Livesey bent over the table and butted ends together, peering closely at them, frustrated that *he* might have need of spectacles at last, as if he was falling slowly apart. Too close and it all became a blur. "Well, da . . . tarnation," he muttered.

"Here, Father," Bess solicitously offered, bringing him a magnifying glass from the *escritoire*.

"Uhm, better. Confound it," he grumped. Under the lens, though, the enlarged ribbons were a perfect match, identical in all respects.

S'pose I should see Doctor DeRosset for specs, he ruefully told himself, *or* fumble *through mine own stock at the chandlery for a pair.*

"They match, as you say, Bess. Perfectly," he sadly said as he stood erect. "Sweet Jesus. Poor, poor Osgoode Moore."

"Match whut, Mistah Jeemy?" Autie whispered to his confidant.

"Never ya mind, Autie," Bowlegs cautioned. "Th' less said, th' better. Less ya know, th' less trouble ya git inta. Rich white folk's doin's. Murder, an' such."

"Ooh, Lawsie!" Autie said with a stunned expression. "Mistah *Harry's* murder?" he asked, quickly surmising the situation with a wit most folk would not have expected. "Mm, mm, *mm!*" he concluded, dropping back into his witless, safeguarding, public pose.

"I quite forgot!" Mr Livesey exclaimed. "The curfew bell has already rung. Can you get your friend, Autie, home safely, Jemmy?"

"Don' worry 'bout that, Mistah Livesey," Jemmy assured him, all but twinkling. "Autie an' me know more'n a few ways 'round Wilmington. Ain't th' first time we had . . . doin's after dark."

"Gosh, no!" Samuel attempted to add. "Why, once . . . !" He stopped short of a sudden, fearful of revealing his own dealings in the night.

"I will not enquire as to why you are so confident, Sam'l," his father said, sternly frowning. "Nor where such knowledge came from." Which veiled rebuke, and warning, made Samuel cough into his fist, and try to look innocent. "We must detain you no longer, Jemmy. For this, I owe both of you a debt, not just in fiddler's pay . . . thanks and a jug of wine, hah. A monetary award, or . . ."

"Best we hide Autie's pushcart in yer shed fer th' night, suh," Bowlegs suggested. "Makes fer easy skulkin'. Nigh half a barr'l left, an' I'm shore Autie'd say yer welcome to hit. T'other chandler asked *five* shillin's for't. Now, could ya sell Autie an' his Pap bar'coes o' ginger-beah fer *less,* they'd . . ." Bowlegs slyly hinted. "Say three, or somewhars in thar . . ."

"Five shillings for each of you, this very night!" Mr Livesey firmly declared. "And any time I have ginger-beer to wholesale, Autie and his . . .

Pap, may have a barricoe for three shillings, six pence."

"Lawsie *Muh'cy,* thank ya, Mistah Livesey, suh!" Autie cried.

"Kin I s'ggest ya put yer extry candles out, Cap'm?" Jemmy further hinted. "That way, we kin sneak th'oo th' back door better. We don't wanna be seed. Safer all 'round."

"Do you think anyone might have seen you take the gown, tried to follow you here?" Mr Livesey asked, with a worried frown.

"Huh!" Bowlegs sneered. "I'da *knowed* iff'n a body wuz trackin' *me,* Mistah Livesey. Y'all give it a li'l time, put some lights out, an' once't hit gits right quiet, Autie an' me'll be goin'."

And, a few moments of peeking and listening later, they went, slipping away past the shed and by the truck garden on cat-feet. Like a most-capable pair of chicken thieves.

"Well!" Mr Livesey gloomed once they were gone. "Now we know. Or, we *believe* we know."

"Perhaps." Bess sighed, sitting down on the settee.

"Why so glum, girl?" her father asked, stumping to take a seat beside her. "You were right, after all. The gown was still there in her house. And your probing forced her to throw it out. I was wrong to chaffer you about it. Once more, I stand in debt to your wits."

"She doesn't suspect Osgoode." Bess frowned. "Else why would it have still been in her wardrobe until tonight?"

"Perhaps because he was very methodical and clever in his spying them out," Matthew Livesey decided. "If he was in love enough to kill Harry to keep her, then he must have been smart enough to realize that throwing the gown away himself would only raise her suspicions if she missed it. Leaving it in her wardrobe, though, Anne must still think Harry's killer was hired by the barons, or the motive had nothing to do with her affair with him."

"Yet, if she knew, do you think she would tell anyone, Father? If telling would cost her so much?"

"Truly, I don't know." He shrugged. "Perhaps she threw it out to protect the *both* of them, as we thought earlier. Well, tomorrow will settle it, I hope. I'll go see the constable with the gown, and let him decide, once he's seen the matching ribbons."

"Oh, Father, you know Swann won't want to know anything damning about the Moores! What can we expect him to do?" Bess fretted.

"That's up to the law, Bess, imperfect as it may be. S'pose it would go down better if Mr Marsden the magistrate was present, too. I believe I'll insist on his presence, yes. Well," he said again, "this has been an exciting afternoon and evening. But it's time for bed."

"Yes, Father," Bess agreed dutifully, though she was certain a good night's sleep would be impossible.

"Blow out the candles. I'll light my own way. And keep this mysterious bundle in my room tonight. Sam'l, do you escort me to the chandlery in the morning, and we'll fetch the bouquet from my desk so we may take both to the courthouse."

"Yes, Father. Goodnight, sir."

Chapter 24

MATTHEW LIVESEY wasn't having much luck falling off to sleep, tossing and turning and punching his pillows in frustration, long after the last glim had been extinguished. Samuel could be heard snoring deeply across the hall; the mattress ropes in Bess's chamber squeaked now and then as she tossed and turned as well.

Finally, except for the loud clacking of the mantel clock, the house was still. He yawned widely, stretched and turned his mind to another topic, one less fevered and dubious. Bess and Andrew Hewlett: should he put too much faith in that alliance? They were very young, still, though people in the Carolinas seemed to marry young, as Mr Lakey had pointed out. He fell asleep at last, dreaming of what the future might be like.

CRASH! The tinkling of glass! Ominous thudding noises!

Matthew Livesey jerked awake, found himself sitting up in bed of an instant, imagining the worst. Wishing he'd kept a pistol from the mantel on his bed table! It sounded as if someone, or a pack of someones, had just burst through the front door!

"Sam'l!" he yelled. "Get a gun!"

His door flew open, making him gawp with fright! It was not an intruder, but Samuel in his long nightshirt.

"Go! Protect the house!" he ordered, rolling to sit on the side of the bed and grope for his prosthetic. "I'll be along!"

"Father?" Bess screamed.

"Stay in your room, Bess!" he wailed in reply.

"There's a *fire!*" she howled back.

"Oh, God!" he moaned, shoving his stump into the cup. "Get out! Get out of the house, this instant!" He looked up long enough to see a ruddy fluttering reflected from the cream-painted wooden walls of the hallway. His fingers lost their sureness on the buckles and straps. A *fire!* Wilmington's plague!

At last! He swung to his feet, lurched for the hallway, peeking round the doorjamb toward the growing, hungry flickerings. There were flames eating at the porch beyond, at the front door. Bess was flinging a bucket of water at it.

"Careful, Bess!" he ordered, thundering down the hallway. "I'm coming! Sam'l, get the fire buckets! Bess, wake the neighbors! Get out the back door!"

Every house was required to have water-butts and buckets ready and filled, against this very calamity. Few did, though, and no one ever seemed to be fined for their lack.

Matthew Livesey reached the kitchen and picked up a full wooden pail as Bess went haring out the back, clad only in her nightgown, to raise the hue and cry. He saw that the small kitchen window facing the street was broken out, and flames licked at the bottom sill. He threw up the sash and began dousing the flames. Samuel came lurching from the side garden and the well with another bucket, which he threw onto the porch.

"Just the porch so far, Father," Samuel puffed. "Hasn't reached the roof! Damme!"

The water only seemed to spread the fire! Though some was out, it seemed to slide to some new place to sprout again!

"*Sand,* Sam'l! Get the shovels! It's a lamp-oil fire!"

Livesey went out the back door himself, to the tool shed. They kept garden spades there. He and Samuel collided at the shed's door, tangled for a terror-filled moment, before Samuel entered the shed.

"Dig, boy!" he snapped as Samuel dashed off for the front of the house ahead of him. "Smother it like a ship's fire, down low!"

Bess's frantic screams had awakened some of their neighbors at last. There were people in the street, dashing to help with buckets, some with shovels and tools of their own.

"Water aloft!" Livesey shouted to them. "Keep it from climbing to the roof!" He began to dig into the sandy roadway, flinging great, hopeless showers of soil onto the porch boards, gasping and panting as he quickly wore out. Wishing he was *half* the man he used to be!

Finally, he could do no more than lean on his shovel and shake with exhaustion. But the fire was subdued. The roof shakes were wet and dripping, the charred porch columns only smoked, and the boarding across the front of the house, around the doors and windows, was shiny, treacle-black, but saved. With pry bars and crow-levers, axes and more water, the porch boards were got up, so every last lingering spark was extinguished.

"Lantern turned over?" Constable Swann asked, gulping for air by his side. He'd thrown on a pair of breeches and shoes, and a heavy dressing robe to rush to the scene. "Smells like oil."

"No, Constable," Livesey groaned. "We'd put it out before we retired. 'Least I think we did. Sam'l, did you put out the porch lamp?"

"Yes, sir! It was out, sure enough."

"There it is, though," Swann pointed out. "Ya use whale oil?"

"Yes."

"Was it full?"

"I don't know. At least half full, I think."

The cheap lantern now lay on its side on the porch, far from the bracket which usually held it. Swann picked it up and felt inside.

"Empty now," he said. "Bung's out. Musta fallen."

"But the bracket's on the other side of the door, Constable. It couldn't have fallen *that* far," Livesey disagreed, now that he had his breath back. "And it was extinguished, hours ago. What time is it?"

"'Round two o' the mornin', or so." Swann shrugged. "I didn't stop t'look at a clock."

"And thank God for your alacrity, sir. Thank God for you all, to come to our rescue so promptly!" he told his gathered neighbors.

"Wasn't just f'r you, Livesey," Swann allowed, scrubbing his unshaven chin with a rough hand. "Your place took alight, th' whole damn side o' the street'd gone up like kindlin'."

"We went to bed a little after ten, sir," Livesey informed him in a softer voice. "And the lamp was *out*. Sam'l knows better than to leave it burning, I assure you."

"Lucky y'all woke up, then. Somebody hallo ya, when they saw the fire?"

"No. It was breaking glass," Livesey told him. "Sounded like someone was breaking in. You can see the front door glass broken out."

"Fire sometimes does that." Swann sighed. "Usually not so *small* a fire, though. Has t'get really roarin' first."

"Father?" Bess said, coming out onto the porch from inside.

"You went back *in?*" he demanded, aghast.

"I had to see if it had spread inside, sir!" she cried. "Just now. And I found this."

She handed them a large lump of rock, bound in paper and tied with rough twine. Several corners were square, like a brick scrap.

"It was in the middle of the carpet," she said. "Someone threw it through the door glass, I think."

"This was a set fire, Constable Swann," Livesey announced.

"Aww, now . . ."

"And here's proof of it, sir!" Livesey snarled. "Someone tried to burn us out tonight, sir! Had they not thrown this through the window, we'd have roasted in our sleep!"

"Hang on, hang on," Swann cautioned, using his teeth to undo the knots in the twine. "Let's see what we got here, 'fore we go off half-cocked."

Constable Swann got the twine off and unwrapped the pale brick shard. The paper was stiff and new. "Feels like good stuff. Costly," Swann commented. "Hmm. Got a light inside? Best if we . . . ye know." He shrugged dramatically at the milling neighbors.

They went inside the house, and by the light of four candles, read:

Newcomes!
Keep Yr. noses out of
our Business. or
we will Stop yours!
Call off your Bitch
& sing small!
This is your only
Warning!

"Do you see *now,* sir?" Livesey demanded hotly. "The fire *was* set. Good God! The chandlery! The millyard!"

Livesey dashed back to the porch, fearing that the arsonists had torched his other properties. Thankfully, though, there was no smoke or light beyond the dull glims of night lamps along Chandler's Wharf, and no greater glow across the river beyond the usual dully red night fires under the rendering vats. He heaved a huge sigh of relief that he'd not been ruined again. Yet. Deadly as the fire could have been, it had been meant as a brutal warning. But by *whom,* he fretted?

If the arsonist had meant real harm, there would have been no note through the window to wake them before the fire had gotten so well-fed they would have smothered on its smoke, and died unknowing, or woke too late to escape, girded by a thousand tongues of flame.

And why tonight, he wondered? What made some person, or persons, so desperate? The *dress!* In spite of Jemmy Bowlegs's proud boast, *could* someone have followed him and Autie? Could someone have been standing watch over the Moore house, seen them recover the damning evidence, and decided to act to protect the Moores? Or Osgoode himself, glancing out his window by happenstance, the very moment Bowlegs was at the trash barrel, knowing the game was up if that evidence was found?

Shaky as the scrawl on the note appeared, it could have been just about anyone who'd written it—a barely literate tough, or a cultured gentleman using his cack-hand to disguise himself. A lone perpetrator thinking he was covering his tracks—or a desperate cabal of faction men. It did say "*We* will stop your business," after all!

Yet, *which* faction, then?

"So you've warned me, by God!" Livesey muttered to himself. "We get your message!" Teeth clenched, hands fisted so hard his nails almost cut his palms, he shivered with late-blooming anger. "Why not the shop, though, or the mill, or . . ."

The chandlery still stood! he gaped. Whoever, whichever faction, had done it, didn't know about the bouquet of flowers! Yet the dress had called forth this violence! Why? Or had it?

The ribbon off the bouquet led to the gown. Yet if the person who'd warned them didn't know about the bouquet, then what possible threat could the gown pose to them, which would have demanded such a dire threat?

He stumbled back inside, past Samuel, who was doling out mugs of ginger-beer in gratitude to his thirsty, smoke-blackened and now much-relieved neighbors.

"Constable Swann, let me have another peek at that note, will you, sir?" he bade. "There's something pow'rful queer . . ."

Chapter 25

"THIS . . . SHITE, is goin' to cease!" Magistrate Marsden swore, squinting so angrily at a much-chastened Constable Swann that he might be mistaken for a one-eye. Evidently, before Livesey had been called to the courthouse, Marsden had had some rather scathing words with him. "My word 'pon it, sirs!"

The magistrate turned to hawk a juicy dollop of tobacco juice into a wooden pail he used for a spitkid by his chair. The magistrate despised smoking as a heathen practice, fit only for pagans, meaning Indians and back-country bumpkins—or for indolent, ignorant Spaniards, meaning Catholics. Chewing, Mr Marsden thought, was the proper, Christian manner God intended tobacco to be enjoyed by Mankind—which meant Protestant, Church of England Christians.

"I'm much gratified to hear that, sir," Livesey replied as the magistrate turned the one recognizable eye in his black glower on him. "This affair must, indeed, be brought to a speedy conclusion."

"Pretty much what my marchin' orders were from King Roger," Marsden grunted, crossing his legs and irritably flicking at the damp grass cuttings on his silk hose. "Settle it, by God. Settle it for good an' all. No more o' this shilly-shallyin'. 'Fore anyone else is killed. If it takes martial law in th' borough to do it!"

"Martial law, sir?" Livesey puzzled. "Won't that . . . ?"

"Got packs o' hotheads, on both sides, ready to tangle, Mr Livesey," Marsden mumbled as he shifted his cud from one side of his mouth to the other. "Here 'tis Saturday market day, that'll bring 'em outa th' woods like yer hound'd fetch a herd o' ticks. People are hot, *damn* hot, 'bout yer fire last night. 'Fore trouble breaks out, we'd best overawe th' bastards. Why I sent down to Fort Johnston for men, to keep th' borough quiet whilst we sort this out."

Marsden leaned over to spit again, wiping his chin with a silk pocket kerchief. "Swann, go see if they're here yet. Do *somethin'* useful, for once."

"Troops in the streets, sir?" Livesey paled.

"Aye, if that's what it takes." Marsden nodded affably. "Now, let's see what all th' fuss is about. Show me yer stuff, Livesey."

Livesey laid his bundle on a side table. Marsden got to his feet, leaned over to inspect the evidence, and sniffed.

"Damme, the wife's got a gown damn-near th' spittin' image o' this, sir." He smirked. "Didn't look half so fetchin' as Anne Moore in it, though. I tell ye, Mr Livesey, this doesn't look half so imposin' as I thought it would, either. Not a reason to kill for this note . . ."

"We think it was a warning, sir."

"Aye." Marsden nodded, peering at the note briefly. He tossed it back onto the bundle and stalked back to his spitkid to release a cheekful. He settled himself back into his high-backed chair like a man with no cares in the world, shot his cuffs, crossed his legs, and began to hum a tune to himself.

"That part about 'newcomes,' sir," Livesey began in the uneasy silence. The magistrate promised action, and a quick solution, but he looked as witless and breezy as Swann did!

"Hmm?"

"That could mean it was written by someone long-established on the Cape Fear, sir," Livesey commented. "And the plural 'we,' well . . . it could mean a faction."

"Umhmm," Marsden agreed, tugging at his periwig to settle it straighter on his head. "It could."

"Forgive me for saying so, Mr Marsden, but that could mean *either* faction," Livesey dared to hint. "Harry's, or the barons."

"Granted," Marsden said with a sage nod.

"Well, then . . ."

Squit, Marsden commented into his spitkid.

"I mean . . ." Livesey prompted, shrugging.

"Means we question everybody, Mr Livesey, faction be-damn," Marsden said at last. "Look ye, though. A lady's gown . . . Anne Moore's gown, in point o' fact. Flowers, tied with ribbon from that gown. I ask ye, does that sound like faction? Or does it smack o' sinful fornicatin'? Adultery, sir! Heathen, willful adultery!"

Squit, went another dollop; the prim old stick's baleful opinion of such doings.

"Yes, but the wording of the note, sir . . . it . . ."

"Words written to throw us off th' scent, sir!" Marsden hooted. "To lay suspicion away from th' murderer, I warrant. Th' murderer who was in town yesterday, last night. Th' one who saw yer minion Bowlegs fetch this up, an' tried to burn ye out. To warn ye off, maybe even to destroy th' gown into th' bargain!"

"That could be, Mr Marsden," Livesey had to allow at last.

"Ye'll stay for th' questionin'." The magistrate said, raising an eyebrow to make it appear a request. "Ye've delved deeper than any. Swann, well . . . he told me what ye told him, but damme if I wasn't just as confused when he ended as when he first started."

"Um. Just whom will you be questioning, then, sir?" Livesey inquired.

"Thought I'd begin with yer ferryman, MacDougall. Then Anne Moore an' Osgoode. See where it leads." Marsden shrugged, waving his hands with what seemed an airy disregard. "Ye'll stay?"

"I should be honored, sir," Livesey replied, putting a hand to his breast and dropping the magistrate a short bow of thanks.

There was a soft rap on the door. "Come!" Marsden barked.

"Sir!" the Army officer snapped as he entered, trailed by one other. "Captain Buckles, sir . . . 16th Regiment of Foot. Your servant, sir. Leftenant Sturtt, sir . . . my second-in-command."

Introductions were made, all round. Captain Buckles was a florid man, his gingery complexion red as his scarlet coat or crimson rank sash. Lieutenant Sturtt was darker, wirier, one of those idly too-handsome sorts to be found in any regimental mess—a second son from an average family of the squirearchy. Livesey thought him about mid-twenties, or so.

"Well now, Mr Marsden," Buckles sighed at last. "I've my troops waiting at the wharf. What exactly is it we're to do, sir?"

"A whole line company of sixty men?" Livesey puzzled, worried.

"Two files of ten, sir," Lieutenant Sturtt supplied with a grin. "We have no more than a half-battalion, the entire colony! Served, did you sir?" he asked, glancing down to Livesey's artificial limb.

"Fort Dusquesne." Livesey nodded, gruffly prideful for once.

"My admiration, sir." Sturtt bowed. "And my condolences."

"Bloody Hell," Buckles groaned with impatience. "What sort o' bother have you rr . . . mean t'say, what need have you of troops?"

"Have you rude or raw Colonials," Livesey thought he'd meant to say, feeling a quick flash of resentment.

"We're goin' to be solvin' th' murder o' Harry Tresmayne today, Captain Buckles," Marsden informed him, squinting a little at the imperious tone the soldier used. "Could be trouble. Faction trouble . . . when they learn one o' their own is to be arrested for questionin'." He gave him a head-to-toe look-over. "Are you prepared for such?"

"The Levellers, you mean, sir?" Buckles snorted with distaste. "The late Tresmayne's faction."

"Exactly who I mean, sir," Marsden drawled. "Gonna fetch people to th' courthouse here. I want it protected, lest somebody goes off half-cocked."

"Perimeter 'round the courthouse, aye," Buckles agreed.

"Not *that* blatant, sir," Marsden scowled. "Just . . . be present. On hand. A man or two t'guard th' entries?"

"But . . . !" Capt. Buckles said, mouth agawp, and Livesey, who had been *some* sort of soldier, thought he looked irritated. No wonder, if Buckles had been rooted out of bed in the middle of the night, mustered and sent off before dawn. Boats from HMS *Cruizer* at the river's mouth would have ferried Buckles and his troops up-river in the fogs at "first sparrow-fart." A cold breakfast, if any, and it was no wonder that Buckles looked miffed! Here he'd come, keyed up to order Fix Bayonets, Load and Level on armed insurrectionists, now this vague, idle duty!

"File o' men to go with my constable an' his bailiffs to fetch th' ones we want," Marsden continued. "Not so much a press-gang as . . . "

"A sign of government interest in the matter?" Livesey offered.

"Exactly." Marsden smiled. "No strong-arm work, 'less some do offer resistance. Courtesy above all. I'll insist on courtesy."

"Courtesy," Buckles muttered, as if trying to remember what that outlandish custom might be, tucking his outraged, disappointed chin into his neck-stock. "Very well, sir. Courteous, it'll be. So, who's the murderin' bastard we're to help your man arrest, then?"

"The constable will point him out t'ye, never fear. Prepared, are ye, sir?"

"Of course I'm prepared, sir!" Buckles blustered. "Soldier's always ready . . . the 16th Foot more than most, damn my eyes!"

"Then let's get yer redcoats afoot, hey, Captain Buckles?" the magistrate all but cackled. "With luck, we'll have this murder solved by sundown, th' guilty in irons, an' your men swillin' th' beer of a grateful borough."

"Uhm, yes, of course, sir. Sturtt?"

"A moment, Leftenant?" Livesey whispered, taking Sturtt's arm.

"Sir?" the young man replied stiffly, disliking being touched.

"One of the people you'll be arresting will be a man named MacDougall, a rather hard-headed Scotsman," Livesey explained. "He and his daughter will be coming into town today. Coming to my house. His girl is to see my daughter. I would greatly dislike anything . . . untoward in behavior done at my home, sir. MacDougall will most-like resent being taken, and he can be violent. You will take especial care?"

"I see, sir." Sturtt nodded. "Never fear, sir. I'll handle his arrest myself. And swear to protect the tranquility of your home."

"More courteously than . . . ?" Livesey grinned, inclining his head a trifle to Captain Buckles.

"Oh, *indeed,* sir!" Lieutenant Sturtt whispered back with a sly grin.

Chapter 26

THE BEST was laid out in expectation of Biddy's visit; fresh scones waiting in a napkin-covered bowl, tea things set out on a fresh tablecloth. The front rooms were as clean as they were going to get, considering. Bess scanned the room one more time in an anxious pet, wrinkling her nose for the hundredth time at the sour smell of fresh-burned wood and paint. All the camphor in the world couldn't disguise it, nor all the sluicing and scrubbing she'd forced Samuel to do on the front of the house restore the appearance.

"Too grand, do you think?" she asked her brother, whirling to face him as he came in from the back porch off the kitchen, scrubbed and in fresh clothes.

"Oh, for God's sake," Samuel breathed.

"Sam'l, don't blaspheme," she chid him with a deep sigh.

"Oh, for . . . !" He grunted. "It's not like we're havin' King George over!"

"I don't want them put off by having it too showy, but . . ." Bess moaned, all but gnawing on a thumbnail. "If we don't make *some* effort of welcome . . ."

"Serve 'em on the porch, then, why don't you?" Samuel smirked. "Maybe that'll make 'em feel more at ease. Now *that's* showy, hey?"

"Oh, Sam'l!"

"Scatter some pig shit, so MacDougall'll feel right at home."

All she could do was growl at him, else she'd blaspheme herself! A tempting thought of hurling something heavy at him crossed her mind.

"You want to meet her, or don't you?" Bess said instead.

"After finding out who her daddy is, it don't signify to me," Samuel sniffed. "For ha'pence, I'd rather go huntin'! Damned foolish, if ya ask me. Here we almost got murdered our ownselves last night . . . house half burned to the ground, and you're boilin' tea water and got out the good china like it's nothing! Didn't get a wink o' sleep, I didn't. Up all night with the pistols, lest the bastards come back to finish the job. Had me fetching and scouring since the crack o' dawn . . ." he ranted, waving his arms and striding aimlessly about the room.

Yet, Bess noted, he had shaved what boyish stubble he possessed and had taken more than usual pains about his appearance. He'd donned his Sunday best. And he continually fiddled with his neck-stock, like a lad working up his courage to abandon his sniggering cronies, cross a crowded salon, and ask a likely lass to dance.

Bess glanced at the mantel clock, willing it to advance hands to speed Biddy's arrival. And end her nervous waiting. She drew a deep breath, took one last look at the room, and thought that it would have to do.

Am I welcoming an arsonist? she asked herself. She doubted it. Once her terror had subsided, and she had retired to her bedchamber to toss and turn and drink in the cleaner air from her one small window to escape the wet, charred stench, she had pondered the identity of the person who'd tried to burn them out.

Not Eachan MacDougall, she'd convinced herself. He'd not ever think to call them "newcomes" when he was so new to Wilmington himself. He wasn't part of any faction that she was aware of, so he'd have not made threats in the plural. And, far as she knew, he didn't have a clue that she'd been snooping—few did beyond her family and the constable. So why had the writer warned them to "call off your bitch"?

The only conclusion she could make was that she had roused suspicions, or fear, when she questioned Anne Moore too closely the day before. Hard as it was to picture, gentle, cultivated Osgoode Moore had seen Jemmy Bowlegs take the discarded gown, and . . . and set fire to their house to cover his tracks? It *still* didn't make sense. Samuel joined her a minute or two later—studiously trying to look above it all.

She went out onto the porch for a breath of air, down to one of the unburned corners, where the paint was still white. Saturday market day, and Dock Street thronged with country-folk, with mongers and pushcarts. She looked down toward the wharves, where the cross-river boats landed, hoping to espy Biddy MacDougall's lustrous golden mane, or her father's hackle-feathered bonnet, head and shoulders above the rest.

A file of ten soldiers came marching by, with a handsome young officer in the lead, headed for the docks. With the constable! She raised a hand to wave at Mr Swann, but he merely lifted his hat to her as he passed. The officer smiled and removed his, laid it on his chest below his rank gorget and bowed his head.

Bess bowed her head in reply, blushing at the unexpected attention, trying hard not to smile so broadly that the young man might misconstrue politeness for . . . Heavens! He was talking to a sergeant, and coming right up to the porch!

"This is the Livesey household, mistress?" he asked with a glint in his eye.

"It is, sir, but . . ."

"Leftenant Sturtt, 16th Foot, your humble servant, mistress," he said, making a formal "leg" to her and clapping his cockaded tricorne to his breast once more. "You are the daughter of a Mr Matthew Livesey, that worthy to whom I had the honor to be introduced at the courthouse not ten minutes past, mistress?"

"I am, sir. Elisabeth Livesey. My brother Samuel," she said with a giddy feeling as she rose from her curtsey.

"Terrible doin's, mistress," he said, scowling at the seared porch. "Your magistrate sent for troops, whilst he concludes his investigation, ma'am. Something to do with a murder, I gather? You must pardon my lamentable ignorance of Wilmington affairs, but Brunswick—and Fort Johnston—is rather removed, I fear. I could post a brace of men to guard your house for the nonce, if you deem such needful."

"Troops?" Bess frowned. Had things come to *that?*

"No need," Samuel spoke up, sounding uncommonly gruff. "We've our neighbors, after all."

"Unless, lad, 'twas one them *done* it, hey?" Lieutenant Sturtt chuckled with a superior expression. "Your father bade me see that the tranquility of his house was protected, sir . . . Mistress Livesey. I promised I'd see to it personally. Your magistrate, Mr Marsden, is of the opinion that there may be some factional unrest today. Once we've made some arrests." He shrugged in idle speculation.

"Perhaps our businesses, Leftenant Sturtt," Bess decided. "Do you not think so, Sam'l? Surely not the house again in broad daylight. Arrests?" She started. "What arrests?"

"I will post a man at your business, then," Sturtt promised. "Where is it?"

"What arrests?" Bess repeated. "Whom?"

"Why . . ." Sturtt began to reply, but there was some shouting down the street that drew his attention. Then a feminine scream and a harsh bellow of a deep male voice, rising above the undecipherable chorus of a great many people trying to get out of the way—or the angry mutterings of Englishmen instantly outraged by the sight of soldiers exercising any military authority upon free subjects of the Crown.

"You must excuse me, Mistress Livesey," Sturtt snapped, clapping his hat on his head so quick his powdered hair gave off a puff of flour, and turning his knuckles pale on the hilt of his small-sword as he took it in a firm grasp. With long, impatient strides, he was off the porch and heading down the roadway for the docks, plowing a path through bystanders who didn't know enough to take sides yet.

"Soldiers, by God!" Samuel muttered darkly, convinced, as everyone else, that a large standing army was an oppressor's instrument, the armed servants of darkness that should be hidden from sight until a foreign foe threatened. "Redcoat lobster-heads!"

"Och, ye bastards!" the stentorian male voice bellowed louder, even above the rising tumult of the crowd. "Sassenachs!"

"Oh, God, they've gone to arrest Mr MacDougall!" Bess cried, clattering down the steps of their stoop to the street.

"Thank bloody Christ, at last!" Samuel muttered, thundering in her wake in spite of heartfelt misgivings.

"Scots, tae me!" MacDougall cried from the center of a melee, bounded by redcoated, white pipe-clayed soldiery. "Usurpers! Tyrants! Och! Come, laddies, come! Defend th' right! Will naebody come?"

"Biddy!" Bess screamed to be heard as she neared the melee.

"Bess!" Biddy screamed back from the far side. "Och, ma Gawd, Bess! Geet yair father; they're murderin' 'im! Help us!"

Howling and growling, puffing and grunting, part of the mob fell to the ground in a heap, red mostly on top, with Eachan MacDougall beneath, droved pigs squealing and fleeing to the four winds, insulted geese hissing, flapping and pecking at all and sundry to escape.

"Bind him!" Lieutenant Sturtt shouted, emerging from the fracas.

"Garrgh!" MacDougall howled under the press, his face trampled into the sand and muck. Bess skirted the throng to Biddy's side, and shouted for her again. The girl flung herself into her arms, weeping and shaking like a sapling in a high wind.

"Eachan MacDougall, I take you . . ." Sturtt puffed for air, his hair awry and his uniform soiled ". . . in the King's Name! For the . . . murder of . . ." He paused, forgetting who MacDougall was supposed to have killed. He looked to the bruised Constable Swann for help.

"Harry Tresmayne!" Swann concluded for him.

"Wot?" Biddy shuddered. "Mr Harry?"

That silenced the crowd a little. People who had been ready to join in on MacDougall's side as fellow Scots, those with rocks in their hands eager to punish government brutality—or those with an urge to participate in a good brawl—quieted. The ones closest to the scene had to murmur this startling turn of events to the ones on the fringes, and their comments soughed like a breeze through a pine grove.

"Now for God's sake," Bess heard Lieutenant Sturtt mutter harshly to the constable as he found his hat, "let's frog-march the devil away, before this rabble finds mind enough to make up against us!"

"He ne'er!" Biddy wailed. "He ne'er killed *anyone,* ah swear!"

"Leftenant Sturtt!" Bess called after him. "Wait! You have the wrong man!"

"Pardons, mistress," Sturtt replied, all business now, flirtations forgotten, as he skirted past the pair of them, though his step faltered a bit as he saw Biddy and Bess together, as if trying to make up his mind which of the two he found the most appealing.

"Need redcoats t'buck up yer bottom, Swann?" someone groused from the so-far-subdued mob, reviving their dark mutterings.

"Yair, wot ya got *sodgers* doin' th' magistrate's work for, hey?" another called out. "Fer shame, man!"

"Got any nutmegs a'tall, Swann?" jeered a third. "Ye *skeert* o' MacDougall, air ye? He have 'em off, last time ye took 'im?"

The crowd liked the wit of that one, and began to hoot and cry out their appreciation as some of them rediscovered their outrage, and their courage.

"Left 'em home with th' wife, he did!" a mastiff-faced old woman from the markets crowed, emboldened. "He's King Roger's pet ram-cat. Bet *Moore* had 'em off so he don't stray!"

While they were chuckling over that bit of wit, someone found the nerve to fling a fresh horse turd at the soldiers, scoring a hit square on the tempting target of the sergeant's snowy crossbelts in the center of his back. The sergeant swung about, the half-pike with which he had been setting the march pace now held like a weapon, and his face ruddy with rage. But a harsh word from his officer made him face front again and growl, "By the center, quick—march!"

A dozen or so of the worst of the mob flowed up Dock Street behind them, to either side of the way like fearful boarhounds: baying, but not too close, yet.

"Yair Father, Bess!" Biddy reminded her, tugging at her sleeve. "He'll ken what tae do! Ye told me yair ownself, he's up-standin' . . . folk'll heed 'im! Please, Bess!"

"He's up at the courthouse," Bess had to confess. "Biddy . . ."

"Let's gae thayr, then!" Biddy pleaded, as pale as milk as she gulped for breath. "Ma daddy dinna kill Mr Harry Tresmayne, *swear* he dinna! Yair father can get him a lawyer, he . . . Och, o' course!" Biddy cried, all but slapping her forehead. "Osgoode! Mr *Moore,* I mean! Och, he's th' fine gentleman, an' th' quickest lawcourt man of all! Why I dinna think of eet . . ."

Now that'd be interesting! Bess thought, boggling at the idea.

She turned red with embarrassment and shame, ready to blurt out how she'd connived and snooped, sure that her delving had *caused* Mr

MacDougall's arrest, that her father's call on the magistrate with the gown and the flowers and ribbon had set all this in motion.

Osgoode Moore, the attorney for Eachan MacDougall? When he was the better suspect? What help would *he* render? Bess giddily wondered. If he avoided all suspicion and doomed MacDougall to hang for his own crime by putting up a poor defense, to save his own neck from "Captain Swing's" noose . . .

"Sam'l?" Bess said in a terrified croak, putting off the moment when she'd *have* to confess all to Biddy. "Do you run and fetch Mr Moore to the courthouse."

"What?" Samuel nearly screeched in astonishment. "But ain't he . . ."

"Just go, Sam'l!" Bess snapped. *"Please."*

God forgive me, she silently begged, hitching a deep, stiffening breath and taking the distraught Biddy's hand. "We'll go to the courthouse, Biddy, to find my father. He'll straighten this out for you!"

Chapter 27

"YE WENT TOO FAR, ye black-hearted rogue," Mr Marsden mused as he beheld Eachan MacDougall, bound to a hard ladderback chair before his desk. "An' now, ye've murdered Mr Harry Tresmayne."

"I dinna do eet," MacDougall growled back, rattling his chains and manacles. Even bound, with a soldier to each side of him, he was still defiant.

"Don't waste our time, MacDougall, of course ye did," Marsden accused. "Or don't ye recall? As oft as Constable Swann an' his bailiffs been 'cross the river when ye were in drink? How oft they fetch ye back, everyone bloody from th' fracas, and ye never recall *that* the next mornin', either, hey?"

"I dinna do eet," MacDougall dully repeated.

"Ye're a nasty piece o' work, MacDougall," Marsden said. "Bane o' my existence. Hard, brutal . . . a cold-hearted, violent bit o' Scot scum. An' now, ye're a murderer, to boot!" he taunted.

"Damn yair eyes, Marsden!" MacDougall exploded at last. "Ye an' all yair redcoats! Yair sort trampled ma country with yair guns an' slaughter. Pissed on th' dyin'; och, I seen yair sort *do* eet! Bayonet th' wounded, laddies, lassies an' th' auld folk t'gether . . . murtherin' *pris'ners* with out a *jot* o' mercy! Burnin' out puir crofters, rapin' th' women, an' laughin' fit *t'bust,* why . . . !"

MacDougall saw the amused glint in Marsden's eyes and settled, of a sudden, sensing the uselessness of defending himself, or of opening old wounds.

"An' now ye've none t'blame for Mr Harry's murther, sae ye seek a likely scapegoat, 'fore th' other folk come after *ye!*" Eachan MacDougall almost sing-songed in weary derision. "I 'spect no less . . . from an *Englishman!* Truth bedamned, justice bedamned, for thayr's not a drop of either in ye!"

"Ye make it sound too convenient, MacDougall." Marsden chuckled as if the Scot's outburst was an amusing Punch & Judy show. "'Twere it that easy, why'd we not come after ye weeks ago? We have evidence of it, now, though. I know why ye killed him, an' I have proof!"

"Och, ye do not!" MacDougall sneered. "Murther Tresmayne? Why, I'd've *voted* for th' man, did ye skelpin', purse-proud bastards *e'er* let a puir, honest man such as me hae th' *right* t'vote! Why would I kill him?"

"Your daughter, Biddy, made a dress for Mistress Anne Moore," the magistrate stated, changing tack suddenly. "A pearly gray gown, with lots of royal-blue satin ribbon flounces and such?"

"Aye, I *s'pose,*" MacDougall answered, confused by such a question. "She sews for lots o' th' Quality th' last year or sae."

"You recall it?" Marsden pressed.

"Can't say that I do, she does sae many. Why? What's that . . . ?"

"There's some say there's a *likely* lass, lives down the Belville Trace," Marsden went on, leaning back at ease, one leg crossed over the opposite knee, "a very *obligin'* lassie. Got th' round heels . . ." He smirked, shifting his quid. "Obligin' to Quality men like Harry . . ."

"Damn ye!" MacDougall screeched, bursting from his chair in a leap for Marsden's throat. The chair, round which his chains had been wound, and both soldiers, followed him to drag him down. "'Tis *nae* ma Biddy, that slutty girl! Say nae more, or I'll rip yair lyin' tongue out. I'll hae yair heart's *blood,* ye . . . get off me!" he wailed as he was swamped under to the floor, one soldier striking him on the skull with his brass-footed musket butt. "Nae ma Biddy, nae ma girl . . . !" he cried, muffled, from beneath the pile. "'Tis a lie, I tell ye!"

"I say she is," Mr Marsden continued as if nothing could shift him from his comfortable chair, as if nothing had happened. "An' I say that Harry Tresmayne was one of her . . . customers. Met Biddy when she came to town with Anne Moore's new gown, an' started puttin' th' leg over her, an' that sent ye daft. Ye saw how they sent nosegays, an' such, wrapped in that ribbon whene'er they wanted more o' th' blanket-hornpipe, an' ye finally sent him one, yourself, lured him out to th' Masonborough Road an' shot him down like a dog."

"Nae!" MacDougall whuffled past a split lip as the guards slung him back onto his uprighted chair.

"Sent him oleander blooms, night o' Quarterly Assizes," Marsden further accused, "bound in a hank o' blue ribbon ye filched from your girl's sewin' box, so he'd know it . . ."

"Ne'er!" MacDougall cried. "I dinna ken what yair sayin', ma Biddy's pure as snow! 'Tis nae *ma* girl a'whorin', that's that tenant Perry girl, on Belleville *Plantation* . . . !"

"You'd murder to protect her, though, MacDougall. We just got proof o' that!" Marsden snapped austerely. "Ye've killed before . . . in Scotland, so th' tale goes. A murder or two up-river's what drove ye t'Wilmington, too, I'd guess. Any missin' neighbors, MacDougall?"

"Thayr's *ne'er!*" MacDougall snapped. "In Scotland, ah . . ."

"There ye see him, Livesey," Marsden sneered, turning his head to spit. "There's yer friend's murderer, sure as Fate."

But it was Mr Marsden who received Matthew Livesey's queasy stare, for the way he'd gone after MacDougall so brutally. He sensed that MacDougall had a point, about the urgent need for a convenient scapegoat.

"Livesey," MacDougall croaked, dry-throated, glowering at him with hatred. "I heard better of ye, man. When yair lass come t'see Biddy, 'twoz *t'spy* for ye, woz eet?"

"I did nothing of the kind, Mr MacDougall," Livesey rushed to declare, feeling greasy to be associated with this sort of questioning, to be tied, somehow, to a rush to justice, and with the accusation that he'd been a willing participant in a framing. "'Twas Bess, well . . . Harry Tresmayne was her adoptive uncle, and his death tried her sore, so she, on her own, d'ye see . . ."

"Och, save yair wind," MacDougall spat. "I can see yair shame as plain as anythin', an' bedamn t'ye."

"Why not confess, an' spare us bags o' trouble?" Marsden asked.

"I canna confess t'somethin' I dinna do," MacDougall said as a trickle of blood escaped his nose from his pounding. "An' I won't!"

"The gown, the ribbon, the rumors . . ." Livesey said. "Surely you must see, with your intemperance into the bargain, how it looks, Mr MacDougall. Your daughter made the gown for Anne Moore. We've found it, and there's ribbon and lace trim missing from it, ribbon and lace of the very sort used to bind a bouquet found near where Harry was killed! Biddy still had some of that ribbon in her sewing box. What else must the magistrate think?"

"He'll think what he likes, damn his blood," MacDougall sniffed, raising one hand with a clank to wipe his nose. "His mind's made up, a'ready, that I'm t'hang, nae matter what I say."

"Mr MacDougall . . . do you own a pair of riding boots? Or a saddle horse?" Livesey asked, of a sudden. "A coaching gun?"

"What? Boots?" MacDougall scoffed, trying to raise a foot despite his chains. "*Thayr's* ma best *shoes,* man, an' puir work they be, I tell ye. Boots're for folk wi' horses, an' I've nought but ain plowin' mule, Cumberland. I work—I work an' walk—*barefooted,* as anyone'd tell ye, did ye e'er bother *t'ask* feerst!"

"And you never ride your mule to town?" Livesey continued.

"Cumberland, he's a guid worker, but he'll hae naebody on his back, not e'en Biddy, sweet as she is with him," MacDougall answered, his confused look back on his face—a match to Marsden's. "I ne'er *learned* t'ride. 'Twoz but th' high folk back in Scotland could afford *t'feed* a horse, an' we woz puir crofters. Why, some years, twa sheep woulda *starved* tae death on th' braes *we* farmed!"

"And what firearms or weapons do you own?" Livesey went on.

"I've an auld musket frae th' militia arsenal, ma granddad's claymore . . . a *skean dubh* for ma stockin' top, an auld dagger come down frae ma fam'ly," MacDougall slowly itemized, still dazed by the blow to his head, most-like. "No fowlin' gun, nor coachin' gun, neither."

"Why 'Cumberland'?" Mr Marsden demanded, his head cocked over to one side in puzzlement. "Wasn't the Duke o' Cumberland th' one who beat ye Scots so bad at Culloden?"

"'Coz, now an' ageen, I hae *t'beat* Cumberland tae make him work!" MacDougall shot back, slyly amused. "He's *English,* ye know."

"Ah, Culloden!" Mr Marsden drawled, almost happy-sounding. "I s'pose ye slew English soldiers by th' score, did ye, MacDougall? Or did ye run like a rabbit? Heard-tell ye're rumored to've slain yer own clan lord's son. What was th' matter, did he get in yer way when ye all skedaddled?"

Surprisingly, MacDougall didn't fire back defiance, but lowered his head and turned red as a ripe cherry, gulping down anger, or indignation. He strained against his bindings for a second, then slumped with a defeated clanking sound.

"Slew yer own wife into the bargain, hey?" Marsden intimated. "She get in yer way, too, hey?"

"Now, that's a damned *lie!*" MacDougall roared, stung to wrath again, held down from a new attack by the soldiers' hands atop his shoulders. "I dinna kill ma Rosie; she woz dead, a'ready, a'fore we marched awa' tae Culloden, that sonofa . . . !" And, incredibly, tears began to flow from that hard-handed man's eyes, making Livesey squirm with embarrassment again.

"Really, Mr Marsden, why . . . ?" he asked, but was cut off by an angry glare from the magistrate, and a finger against that worthy's lips to sign him to keep mum a bit longer.

"Ye *did* kill yer lord's son?" Marsden demanded. "A man who'd kill once'd kill again. Th' son o' th' man ye swore Bible-oath to . . . it doesn't get more shameful for a Scot than that, does it, hey?"

"Aye," MacDougall barely was able to say. "I killed him. But I hae guid *reason* t'kill him! Donald MacDougall. Youngest son o' *The* MacDougall, ol' Bruce Hammerhand, his ain self. Aye, I killed Donald. But I ne'er slew ma wife, for that woz Donald's doin'. An' I ne'er slew Mr Harry Tresmayne, neither."

"Why?" Livesey had to ask, distastefully fascinated by being in the same room for the first time in his life with one who'd actually committed a murder.

"'Coz Donald forced ma Rosie, an' hae his way with her 'gainst her will," MacDougall snarled, angry even after all the years since.

"So you say," Mr Marsden goaded, though it didn't sound as if his heart was in it—unlike the goading and taunting that Livesey now understood as a way to row the short-tempered MacDougall beyond all temperance, and get him to blurt out his sins.

"Donald woz a bonny lad, coulda had any lass. *Did*, Gawd help his black soul," Eachan MacDougall snuffled in weary recollection of the old times. "E'en Edinborough's colleges weren't guid enoo for him, nae, he woz sent tae Oxford . . . an *English* school," he scoffed. "Flick o' his cloak, a smile or twa, an' ev'ry lass in th' country'd lift her skirts. Then, though . . . he clap eyes on ma Rosie. Hae ye seen ma Biddy, Mr Livesey?"

"I must confess that I have not, sir," Matthew replied.

"Yair girl can tell ye, Biddy's th' very spittin' image of ma Rosie," MacDougall said with a certain air of wistfulness. "Biddy's e'en 'bout th' same age as Rosie woz, then, too. We were puir folk, like I said. Ne'er gae t'gatherin's much, nor gae t'town, 'cept for tradin' what little wool or barley we raised. Th' Risin', though . . . th' gatherin' o' th' clan afore Culloden. I *had* to gae t'that, 'twoz ma duty to Th' MacDougall, d'ye see.

"Rosie's mother was a widow-woman, year o' th' '45, nearby th' gatherin' glen, sae we went t'her croft, an' drove our sheep an' cow thayr fer safekeepin'. Rosie an' I, we went tae th' camps just so she could see eet," MacDougall muttered, with his head thrown back to one side, as if bemused, or seeing it all over again. "She woz t'bide with her mother, did things get rough, but . . . Donald saw us, an' *Gawd,* but what a fash he made over me, like I woz a newborn Willie Wallace, when he dinna ken me from Adam, b'fore! Made me a sergeant, bade me eat at his elbow with th' high folk, an' ev'nin's, when they woz music an' dancin', Donald made sure he danced th' once each night wi' Rosie, praisin' me to th' skies. Presented us both tae Th' MacDougall, guid as any in th' Highlands. Biddy woz a'ready born, d'ye see, nursin' still. Left her at Rosie's mother's most ev'nin's. Th' last night, 'fore we marched awa' t'war, though . . ."

MacDougall's ancient rage resurfaced, as the old scabs on his heart were ripped off.

"Posts me sentinel, he did, th' lyin' bastard! 'Eachan, lad, I ken that I can count on ye t'keep th' camp safe,' he says! An' like a fool, I stood ma post. Och, but it come over me somethin' hellish t'be wi' Rosie just *ain* mair time, so I slunk awa', nae matter I woz a trusted sergeant, nae matter if they flayed me on a cartwheel for't!

"I got tae her mother's croft . . ." He shuddered as he recalled the worst, raising Livesey's hackles in dread of what the man had yet to say. "Donald's been an' gone, wi' a tale o' me bein' hurt sinful-bad in camp, an' rode Rosie off on his horse. Her mother's a'wailin' banshee-like, like I woz a'ready dead.

I'd not gaed by road, lest I woz spotted, but I *run* th' road back t'camp. An' 'twoz on th' roadside I found her, all busted up inside 'coz she'd fechted him guid as she could, but it weren't guid enough, an' he'd beaten her down so he could hae her. Said he couldna ride off without he had her. An' so he did."

"Dear Lord," Mr Livesey whispered in horror.

"Dumped her near th' roadway," MacDougall told them, rocking back and forth on his chair, his hands clasped white together. "Got her lifted up, t'carry her tae her mother's, but halfway thayr, she . . . she passed over an' went limp in mah arms, sirs. Time I got her home, she woz turnin' cold a'ready. Raped an' killed th' wife of an oath-sworn man, ain o' them he woz *bairn* tae, *sworn* tae protect, hisself! A bastard Donald woz, nae matter he was t'be th' laird I woz sworn t'follow. An' he done eet with nae muir feelin' than crackin' a louse!"

"So, ye killed him that very night?" Marsden asked. Gently.

"Och, nae!" MacDougall said in a rasp. "I went back tae camp an' took up ma post, 'coz I couldna catch him alone, not without a mount o' ma own. Twa days . . . twa days an' nights, I bided ma time. An' all those twa days, Donald's twittin' me, japin' how bonny it'd be tae come home t'such a fine lass as Rosie, such a fine fam'ly, all victorious, an' how gladsome they'd be for me t'be a hero, th' damned hound!"

Officers! Livesey thought one of the soldiers guarding Eachan MacDougall mouthed quietly to himself, in disgust.

"Nicht afore th' battle o' Culloden, I crept in his tent when he woz sleepin'," MacDougall confessed in a harsh whisper which held everyone hanging on his every sibilance. "Och, how I wished tae wake th' dog an' 'front him, wanted tae make him suffer just a *wee* bit . . . ! Know why he woz dyin', an' who done eet, but . . . I had Biddy t'fash about, so . . . I cut his throat as he slept, an' took his . . . what th' sailors call his 'weddin' tackle,' an' left 'em on his breast, sae The MacDougall'd know why eet woz done. An' then I scarpered."

"So, you weren't really at the battle of Culloden?" Livesey asked in amazement over such a fell deed, no matter the justification.

"Nae, I wozn't," MacDougall said, finding that fact more shameful than slaying a rapist and murderer, "an' thank Gawd I wasn't, for I heard about it later. Wouldna mattered tae th' English soldiers if I woz or nae, for they were slayin' any puir Scot, caught under arms or not. Th' slaughter they did at Culloden ainly whetted thayr appetite, like. I went home an' fetched Biddy an' her gran, saw Rosie to th' ground proper, then snuck down tae Loch Linnhe an' Fort William. 'Twoz thayr I give me Bible-oath t'King George. Took a boat down tae Glasgow, then th' feerst ship tae th' Colonies, it dinna matter which. Ended here," he tiredly concluded.

"If someone raped yer daughter then, MacDougall," Mr Marsden mused after a long, uneasy silence. "If a rich, powerful man just took *advantage* o' her, turned her head to have his way with her . . . wouldn't ye kill that man, too?"

MacDougall cocked his head to puzzle on it, sucking on a tooth for a moment, then answered him direct. "Ye brought me here t'hear th' truth, sae here eet is, yer honor. Gawd save me, but I probably would. But thayr's nae man messed with Biddy, I tell ye. She's pure, nae matter she's a puir girl. I raised her right, an' kept ma eyes on her an' ev'ry man who come around. Fer sairtain-*sure* Harry Tresmayne ne'er laid a finger on her, so I'd nae reason tae murder him. And so I dinna!"

"Ye came into Wilmington durin' Assizes?" Marsden puzzled.

"I did not! Too busy ferryin' others who did. Kept th' boat workin' 'til lang after dark. T'other ferry hands'll tell ye that . . . tavern keeper t'other side o' th' Brunswick'll tell ye th' same. I've ne'er cared for towns, 'specially when thayr sae mobbed. Ask me that b'fore, ye'd ken I'm not yair murderer."

Squit! was Mr Marsden's reply to that, as he leaned over his spitkid to release a juicy dollop.

"We're gonna keep ye a while longer, MacDougall," Mr Marsden announced, unable to look the man in the eyes, and fiddling with the desk's inkwell and pen tray for a moment. "We let ye out now, with the townfolk thinkin' that ye did it, they'd lynch ye in a trice, so . . . think of it as fer yer own good, hey? Got others to question . . . see if yer tale hangs together. Mind now, my man . . . I catch ye in a lie an' there'll be Hell to pay. Noose'd be too good fer th' man who killed Harry Tresmayne. Corporal, put this feller in cells."

"Sir!" the soldier said, snapping to attention before hefting MacDougall to his feet and steering him roughly out.

"Poor man," Livesey sighed once the door was shut. "He never remarried, after. Lest someone rich and powerful take the next wife away from him. To avoid losing a second woman to another, even in . . ."

"That why *ye* haven't remarried, Livesey?" Marsden asked with a wry chuckle as he shot his cuffs, fiddled with his lacy shirt front. "Or . . . is it because ye cherished th' first'un so much, ye can't imagine a replacement?"

"Ahum, I, ah . . . !" Livesey blushed, stammering to silence.

"My wife is a dumplin', Livesey," Marsden said with a sly grin. "An' a chirpy ol' hen, vexsome as she can be sometimes. But I can't imagine tradin' her in, for a shipload o' silver. An' I do expect our MacDougall still feels th' same way about his long-dead Rosie. An' . . . with his daughter, Biddy, so much her mother's spittin' image, well . . . it'd seem logical t'think he'd kill to protect her from th' same fate. Rumor is, *someone* was courtin' her. Doesn't mean it was Harry."

"So, you don't think he's guilty?" Livesey marveled, all asea. "Then why did you go at him so . . . !"

"In the first place, no I don't," Marsden confessed, cackling at Livesey's stricken astonishment. "But I *had* to question him, fer he's th' likeliest, at first glance. An' . . . ponder this for a bit, Mr Livesey," Marsden said, tapping the side of his nose, winking as if amusing his grandchildren. "Wouldn't th' *real* killer be over th' moon t'think that a very plausible suspect had already been slung in cells an' hard-questioned? Hmmm?"

"But the way you went *at* him, sir, wasn't that just a . . . ?"

"Lord, Livesey!" Marsden hooted as he rose from his chair and paced about, all but prancing. "Lookee here, man. We got ourselves a crime o' passion, an' most times, th' hot blood that led to it's not quenched yet. A murder ain't like a bucket o' well water! Nine times outta ten, ye rowel 'em with *spurs* on, ye stir up that unslaked passion an' shake 'em to their very bones. Takes a clever, cold-blooded sort t'play th' game back. MacDougall, he ain't clever."

"But what if the real murderer is, sir!" Livesey demanded of him. "We'll have stirred up the whole *town,* and be no closer to solving this. MacDougall might go on trial for lack of a better, and we would never know who did it?"

"Oh, we'll crack this nut, Livesey; we'll get to th' meat, ye mark my words," the wiry old magistrate said with a smirk. "So. We got Osgoode an' Anne Moore coolin' their heels outside. I'll confess th' evidence ye found points closer t'their stoop than MacDougall's. Which first, d'ye reckon? He or she? Could've been a woman done it, ye know, sir. Or *had* it done to cover her whorin' tracks."

"Osgoode," Livesey announced, then thought deeper, chewing on his thumbnail for a second. "No. Anne, first. Set the scene with her, so when we do question Osgoode, we might have proof of her and Harry having an affair with which to confront him—if affair there was, though I can *not* fathom a reason why she was so eager to dispose of this gown," he said, waving a hand at the wrapped bundle residing on a large side table, "unless there was," he concluded. "And you intend to ah . . . shake *her* to her very bones, Mr Marsden?"

"Damme, but yer a quick'un, no error, Mr Livesey," the magistrate cackled again, returning to his desk and his spitkid.

Squit!

Chapter 28

MRS ANNE MOORE required no manacles, nor escorting soldiers, either. She was shown into the magistrate's office with dignity and decorum—almost primly dressed in a sky-blue and white morning gown, sprigged with embroidered pink roses, highlighted with maroon ribbons. Her color, and her nose, were high, though.

"Pray, do be seated, Miz Moore," Mr Marsden bade, indicating the ladderback chair, onto which she gracefully swished, though with an impatient flounce or two.

"Mr Marsden!" Mrs Moore snapped. "I wish to lodge a *most* vehement complaint of your high-handed actions. The very idea of you suspending civil law, arresting innocent Crown subjects upon unfounded charges, exposing them to public ridicule. To *frog-march* people from their homes, to invade their private residences . . . As if Osgoode or I could have had *anything* to do with . . . !"

"Sounds just like Osgoode when *he's* on a righteous tear, don't she, Mr Livesey?" Marsden asked with a wry wink. "Humors high, feathers ruffed out, an' flappin' like a cock-partridge. Ye do that some better than Osgoode, though, Miz Moore, I must avow."

"Sir!" she cried at his easy contempt. "I reiterate that—"

"Osgoode tutor ye t'spout all that? Guess he would, him bein' a lawyer, an' all." Marsden all but cackled in snide amusement.

"I need no lessons from my *husband* to express my outrage over being . . . *ravished* by that crude Captain Buckles and his low brutes. They practically *smashed* into my home, my *bedchamber*, and *dragooned* me . . . nearly man-handled me. *Ogled*, as I was ordered to dress, then marched here 'twixt armed men . . ."

"Shouldn't think that's anythin' *new* to ye," Marsden smirked.

"What? Oh, how *dare* you!" Mrs Moore screeched in disgust.

"So many men besides Harry Tresmayne ye were tuppin', there's *sure* t'been some danced ye round rough before, an' saw ye undressed."

Anne Moore reeled back in her chair, her high color paling for a second to blanched white. "*Mr* Marsden!" she shot back, though. "*Never* have I been subjected to such vile calumny. I *thought* you to be a gentleman, *above* such filthy speech and low behavior, but you reveal yourself as being as low and common as . . . him!" she accused, casting a brief, furious glance at Livesey. "A magistrate cannot—"

Dirty tradesman, am I, you . . . ! Livesey angrily thought.

"First of all, Miz Moore," Marsden confided, after he leaned over to spit, "a magistrate can do pretty-much whatever he wants. We ain't in a law court. Call it an inquest, if ye must. English Common Law lets me conduct my bus'ness any way I see fit . . . arrest anybody I suspect, hold 'em 'til Hell freezes over, put th' *screws* to 'em 'til I get th' truth. Prisoners only got th' rights I *say* they've got. If I d'termine ye're t'stand trial, I don't even have t'show ye witness lists nor evidence, even let ye have a barrister 'til trial day."

Marsden chewed for a moment, spat into his kid, and let all of that sink in for a second or two, before continuing.

"Bein' a lawyer's wife, I'da thought ye'd know that," he said. "Ah, Osgoode must've got ye confused, rantin' how he'd *like* things to be, did him and his Levellers ever get charge o' th' courts . . . but that ain't th' way things work round here, *now!* Ye're here to answer questions 'bout a *murder*, woman. And ye'd best answer straight, or it might be a woman hanged!"

Mrs Anne Moore compressed her lips, and pinched her high-nosed nostrils so snug it was a wonder she could breathe; but they could hear her do so in deep, angry surges, watch her chest heave. Blushy spots of color appeared on her cheeks and brow.

"Now, here's what I say happened, Miz Moore," the magistrate almost blandly began to lay out. "We say pore ol' dead Harry was your lover . . . yeah, yeah we *do!* Can't think why ye wished t'put cuckold's horns on a feller like Osgoode. Vexsome as he is, he's a good, decent man. We got th' evidence, we got ye dead to rights, so ye might save us th' trouble an' come clean about it."

"I do not know what you mean . . . sir!" Mrs Moore retorted, her initial shock over, and her anger becoming the slow, simmering variety. "You use me as ill as so many . . . bears! I will not sit here and—"

"Yeah, ye will, if it takes chains an' a couple o' soldiers to hold ye down," Marsden informed her, unimpressed by her arch attitude. "Damme!" he said, scratching under his periwig for a moment. "Here it is nigh on eleven, an' Captain Buckles fetched ye th' better part of an hour ago. Rousted ye from yer bed, did they? What's a homemaker woman *doin',* lollin' round in her bed that late in th' mornin' anyhow? Yer womenfolk ever lollygag a'bed so late, Mr Livesey?"

"Never, your honor," Livesey told him with genuine surprise, and the slightest sense of . . . revulsion. Perhaps it was *envy,* Livesey could imagine—or general disgust for Anne Moore. Such idleness perturbed his rock-ribbed Presbyterian soul.

"Mine, neither," Marsden said with a mystified shake of his head and all but a clucking tsk-tsk. "It is yer *custom* to lollygag, ma'am?"

"If you *must* know, Mr Marsden, gentlefolk of means do *not* have to rise at the first cock's crow," Mrs Moore replied, sneering a little. "One takes tea or chocolate a'bed, with toast or rusks. In cultured Society, one may even receive in one's private chambers."

"Other hens of yer acquaintance come callin' whilst ye're still *horizontal?*" Marsden pretended to goggle with wonder. "Never heard th' like. Ye did such back in Williamsburg, down to Charleston, New Bern?"

"As one would in London or Paris." Mrs Moore all but simpered over their lack of true culture. "And in all innocence."

"Gotta understand, Livesey," Marsden said, turning to look at him for a second, "Miz Moore's been schooled an' bred in Virginia an' *South* Carolina, then fated t'reside between, in th' last-settled, raw piney woods. Compared t'them two places, North Carolina's a dark vale o' humility, set down 'twixt two towerin' mountains o' conceit! So . . . Miz Moore. Might a lady even receive *men* callers like that?"

"With proper circumspection, yes, of course," she cooed back.

"Hmmf!" was Livesey's comment.

"Or, with a *power* o' circumspection . . . an' *care* as t'when yer husband's away, I s'pose a lady could do a lot o' receivin', hmm?" Mr Marsden sneered.

"Ever receive Harry Tresmayne in yer bedchamber, did ye?"

"I most certainly—"

"I can have yer servants in an' put 'em to a Bible-oath in th' Slave Court if I have to," Marsden cautioned her. "Fear of a master's beatin' is nothin' compared t'hangin' for false witness. Was Harry a caller in yer bedchamber, Miz Moore?"

"Yes," Anne Moore angrily had to confess with a spiteful hiss. "But he called on both Osgoode and me, many times, and—"

"Ever call on ye, alone, when Osgoode was out an' about? With yer door shut?" Marsden pressed.

"I . . . he *might* have, I cannot recall, he was a frequent—"

"Stay long, did he?" Marsden probed, looking off at the bookcases as if he already knew the answer.

"Occasionally," she finally allowed. "But it was only to chat, to gossip, nothing more, and I resent—"

"Yeah yeah, we know." Marsden waved off with a weary tone. "So when Osgoode rode away on faction or law bus'ness—Brunswick, New Bern or Duplin—when Osgoode was away fer th' night . . . did Harry ever come callin'? Say on a night when he slept in town, too, 'stead o' ridin' back to Tuscarora and his wife, Georgina?"

"Harry Tresmayne, sir, was a dear friend, that was all, I tell you!" Mrs Moore spat. "He might have supped with me, but he slept in his own bed. Really, sir, to accuse me of . . . ! I cannot bear it!"

And, quite fetchingly and piteously, Anne Moore dug a lace handkerchief from her sleeve and dabbed at her eyes, lowering her face and gaze, her shoulders beginning to heave.

"Let's have it out, Livesey, if ye'd be so kind?" Mr Marsden bade, pointing to the bundle on the side table, still wrapped enigmatically in its sailcloth.

Livesey fetched the bundle and laid it on the desk, eyeing Mrs Moore as he did so, noting how she shifted her head and peeked 'twixt her fingers, taking a furtive, wary look despite her "tears."

"We'd admire did ye take a squint at this, Miz Moore," Marsden said.

"A moment, *please,* sir!" she moaned, as if wracked by grief or insult beyond all civilized custom.

"*Now,* woman! *Look* at it!" Marsden bellowed, flicking the sailcloth open to reveal the light-gray gown.

Mrs Moore raised her head and sat up, glaring utter scorn at them, before lowering her eyes to the bundle.

If they expected a gasp or a cry, they were disappointed, for Mrs Moore merely lifted a corner of her mouth in a wry grin, as if it didn't really signify anything to her—though her outraged "tears" had evaporated too quickly for credence.

"Your gown, Miz Moore," Marsden accused.

"Why, yes it is," she archly replied. "I cast it out, just last evening." A cleverer smile crept over her features as she lazily cooed on, "I do believe someone's pored over my trash. What of it, sir?"

"Tell her, Livesey," Marsden snapped.

"Uhm, of course, sir," Livesey agreed, though his mind went as blank as new stationery, and he wished he could *damn* Marsden for putting the onus on *him,* without the slightest warning or fore-planning. "It *is* your gown, you admit, Mistress Moore."

"Have I not *said* it, Mr Livesey?" she drawled back.

"Odd, that," Livesey said, pacing clumsily whilst striving for words, a thread of cogent probing. "This gown had been in your possession for nigh a year, or so? Recall, do you, ma'am, when you had it made and who did the making?"

"A year or so, yes, Mr Livesey." Anne Moore seemed to dither and pore over her memories. "The exact date I cannot recall. Nor can I bring to mind the seamstress. Someone 'cross the river, I think."

"Biddy MacDougall, was it not?" Livesey asked.

"Perhaps," Mrs Moore allowed, with a wary, helpless shrug.

"And when was the last time you wore it?" Livesey further asked.

"Dear me . . . nearly a year ago, I'd think," she answered, with a flutter of her lashes and her hands, as if such specificity could not be demanded of a "mere woman" like her. "That quite escapes me, too."

Flirtatious with me? Livesey silently fumed; *Hussy!*

"'Cause my wife showed up in church in a new gown similar," Mr Marsden growled, supplying thankful aid to Livesey's pursuits. "'Bout a year ago, aye. We could see yer face flamin', Miz Moore, soon as ye clapped eyes on her."

"As you say, Mr Marsden." Mrs Moore actually had the nerve to chuckle in agreement. "Much too similar."

"So it's spent the last year entire in the back of your chifforobe, the bottom of a chest, and you only thought to discard it last night, Mistress Moore?" Livesey demanded.

"I'd quite forgotten its presence 'til then, sir," she replied.

"Biddy MacDougall surely did make it for you," Livesey told her. "Four or five trips 'cross the river she made, each time you demanding more flounces and fripperies, a matching hat, before you thought it was grand enough . . . and then you cheated her. I fear the young lady wasn't the least bit complimentary of you, ma'am. Mistress MacDougall thinks herself ill-used."

"What hired help of low estate thinks doesn't signify," Mistress Moore archly sniffed. "Does she wish half a crown more for her shoddy handiwork, then let her demand it herself."

"How *odd*, though, ma'am," Livesey pointed out, his temper awake and his blood hot, "that we see so *few* of the fripperies you demanded she add . . . lots of this pale gray lace gone, most of this ribbon . . . a particularly costly royal-blue satin ribbon!"

"One trims invitations . . . one adorns wrapped gifts, sir," Mrs Moore rejoined, crossing her legs and shifting on the hard chair, as if bored. "Surely, the way I manage my housewifery—"

"Binds bouquets of flowers, too, ma'am?" Livesey shrewdly coaxed. And was elated to see her stiffen her spine and lift her brows in seeming puzzlement, at last!

"Constable Swann and I speculated whether 'twas the color of the ribbon, or the variety of flowers sent, that conveyed your secret messages to Harry," Livesey finally dared to pose, rankled by her calm and derisive shams. "Was it the number of bows you tied, the choice of a lace binding or ribbon, that denoted when or where, ma'am?"

No response, merely a taut and wary glint; pent breath, but . . .

"We'd also like you to look at this, Mistress Moore," Livesey snapped, feeling as if he was playing his last, poor, hole-card, with the fingers of one hand almost crossed to make it claim the trick, as he went back to the sail-cloth bundle and fetched out the rotting, wilted bouquet.

Got you, by . . . ! he crowed to himself, to see her start.

Anne Moore's cool demeanor shattered in a single inrushed gasp of air and sudden blotches of red on her cheeks. She could not have acted more frightened at the production of a copperhead snake!

"*This* was found near where Harry was murdered," Livesey roared, actually bellowed, deciding it was time to take a page from the magistrate's book and go all-in. "Note the blue satin ribbon, the same as came off your gown, ma'am! The same as Biddy MacDougall used when she made the gown—her remaining snippets, your gown, and this bouquet all of a perfect piece, not found anywhere else in the Cape Fear. We *looked,* Mistress Moore! *You* threaded it off, to send bouquets which conveyed your and Harry's private code. *This* bouquet lured Harry to his death . . . to that private forest glade of yours beside the Masonborough Road! Under that tall pine in the center of the glade we've found tufts of blanket wool, *your* shoe prints, the scuff marks of . . . your exuberance. Did you bring the blanket, too, Mistress Moore? Or was that Harry's duty? Your entrance to the glade was off the Wrightsville Road, his off the Masonborough, hmm? So that no one would ever guess that you and Harry engaged in . . . congress?"

He'd extemporized a little, but whichever of his stretches had gotten to her, something had broken down her facade. Anne Moore was now visibly quaking.

"I note this gown is *torn,* ma'am," Livesey went on as his prey went even paler, her expressive mouth hanging slackly open. "A button or two missing in back, too. Look like thorn or bramble snags, to me. Or . . . was that more of your and Harry's . . . eagerness?"

"An' ain't it int'restin', Miz Moore," Mr Marsden evilly muttered in her right ear, after ambling about the offices so casually and seemingly indifferent to Livesey's questioning—a closeness and harshness that made her jump as he laid a hand on her shoulder, "that th' very afternoon Bess Livesey asks ye 'bout this gown, ye go home in a huff an' toss it out as soon as it's dark. 'Fraid th' hunt was comin' too close, did ye, woman? Figured ye'd keep it as a memento of Harry, 'til somebody come near learnin' yer secret? *Tarnation,* ye high-nose *whore!* Did ye think ye'd hide *for-ni-catin'* on th' sly in a place as small as Wilmington forever? Shamin' Osgoode . . . shamin' Georgina! Yer own fam'ly's good name an' *honor?* Ye think yerself too elevated t'get *caught?* Well, ye're caught now, woman. Your *a-dul-tery* . . . your *fuckin'* . . . got Harry Tresmayne D-E-A-D, dead!"

"No!" Anne Moore screamed, drawing up her legs, shying down in her chair with her hands over her ears. "I *didn't!* I didn't send him any . . . not *that* night! I . . . !" She gulped, on the edge of swooning, and almost thrashing in terror. "I *loved* Harry. He . . . ! Wasn't me!"

"Th' Hell it wasn't!" the magistrate barked, so close that his quid left tiny splatter marks on her morning gown. "He get tired of ye? Feared Georgina'd found ye both out? Did ye *hire* someone t'kill him that night, told 'em right where he'd be, for spite?"

Anne Moore's only answer was a fevered whine.

"The ribbon, the lace . . ." Livesey snapped, close to her left ear, dissatisfied and puzzled. "The ribbon meant the glade off the Masonborough Road?"

"It *did,* but I didn't *send* it, not that night, no no no!"

"The lace meant . . . ?" Livesey pressed.

"An abandoned cabin . . . off the Sound Road," Mrs Moore wailed.

"Along Smith's Creek? Why *two* bows, then?" Livesey queried.

"For *evenings,*" she blubbered. "One for mornings . . . when we'd have *time!* Oh, God have mercy, have either of you *any* mercy . . . !"

"Not for a murderess, I don't," the magistrate spat.

"But I didn't kill him, I didn't hire anyone, I had no *reason* to!" Mrs Moore snufflingly protested. "No more, please, I beg you."

"Any other hidey-holes where ye played balum-rancum?" Marsden scoffed. "A safer place to 'rock, and roll me over,' hey? In yer bedchamber, even? Wouldn't put it past ye," he disgustedly sneered. And both gentlemen were appalled to see her weakly nod "yes" to that.

"God's sake, yer own marriage bed?" Marsden marvelled, standing back from her as if repelled. "Damme, that's gall! An' Osgoode never smelled a rat?"

"We . . . we keep separate chambers," Mrs Moore admitted in a dull stupor, her panic departing after her confession, which, as the reverends always said, truly seemed good for the soul. "He comes and goes at all hours . . . bad as a physician's hours," she sniffled.

"Convenient," Mr Marsden snickered. "Seein' as how Harry had a say in settin' those hours, an' absences, *fer* him. Don't sound that lovey-dovey t'me. Ye planned t'leave Osgoode fer Harry, did ye?"

"No," she dully replied. "That would have been impossible."

"Too much to lose, financially," Livesey imagined aloud, with a feeling of disgust for her. "Your good *names.* But would Harry have left Georgina for *you?* Did he declare that he loved you that much?"

"Love, well . . ." Anne Moore said with a weary sigh, and a hint of her old arch coyness and condescension. "No, Mr Livesey, I'd no expectations. Love and passion . . . love is what one plights, to *excuse* passion." She dabbed her eyes, blew her nose, and slumped on her elbows, most ungracefully and unladylike. "Harry and I were in passion, for the moment. It was . . . pleasureable, and exciting. We might have lasted years, or but a few months more if Harry discovered a fresher challenge. Neither of us had any complaints or lack of satisfaction. So, I had no reason to break things off, *certainly* not to kill him, or lure him to his death. My only fret . . ."—she paused in sorrowful thought—"was our lack of . . . opportunity."

"Seems t'me, ye shoulda fretted more 'bout th' dishonor ye'd bring to all involved," Mr Marsden said with a snort. "Or fetchin' up a baby. Or would ye just claim it was Osgoode's?"

"Mr Marsden, I wager you gentlemen know that there are . . . devices? . . . to prevent such a calamity," Mrs Moore replied, coming close to amusement at their seeming naivety. "With Harry, though . . . how may one phrase this? . . . there was no need to employ such joyless and cumbersome things. I was grateful for that. And Harry sometimes was, as well."

"What?" Marsden tried to puzzle out. "Wasn't a whole man, are ye sayin'? Speak straighter, woman."

"Harry was *wholly* a man," Anne declared, simpering for a little in sweet reverie, "with but one . . . failing. It was his lot never to quicken a babe, alas. And our world is sadder for it."

"Damme! Of course!" Matthew Livesey exclaimed, ready to slap his forehead in delayed understanding. Twelve years Harry had been wed to Priscilla, his first wife, with no issue! He and Georgina had not yet brought forth children, either. And Livesey could not recall a single chambermaid or town girl in Boston, nary a camp follower or local girl turning up at headquarters with a "belly plea" on Harry, either! And, sadly, he wondered if that could explain his foolhardy, intemperate lust for women, so *many* women — his neck-or nothing lack of fear in the field, on horseback, in combat.

Harry Tresmayne might have begun to suspect that it wasn't his bed-partners' fault that he had no son and heir, dear as any man would wish for such; yet all the years he'd tried (and how *energetically* he had tried, God help him!), only to find that *he* was the barren one!

"How cruel," Livesey muttered, "to be so blessed with so many manly attainments, yet . . ."

"Or," Mr Marsden sarcastically imagined, "Harry didn't think he was firin' mere salutin' charges. He still thought it was ye, so he dropped ye like a toe-sprung stockin', an' found himself some new mutton, and ye weren't ready t'be dropped."

"He *knew* his lack," Anne Moore wearily insisted. "Even japed about it, a time or two. There was no new woman to catch his humors, Mr Marsden. I didn't do this, I tell you! I'd never have sent a signal during Quarterly Assizes, most certainly, not with hundreds of people in town—so many who could not afford lodgings camped out near our . . . places. The risk of exposure was too great. I will swear to you on a cartload of Bibles that I sent no flowers."

"What of Osgoode, then?" Marsden shrewdly queried.

"What of him?" she almost dismissively shot back, too fearful of her comedown in local Society. "I do love him, in a way. Though . . . when we met in New Bern, I had hopes for better, before he moved me here. He's one of *The* Moores, after all! Yet, his faction, his politics, the way he deliberately alienated himself from those who rule, his own kinfolk as well . . . I fear our marriage did not develop as I expected . . . though I made him a fashionable home, tended to his social standing, cultivated and espoused his circle."

"Then went whorin' behind his back. How cultivatin'," Marsden commented with a nasty chuckle of mirthless amusement.

"I never meant any harm to Osgoode!" Mrs Moore declared, back completely to her old self, sitting up straighter and impatiently jiggling one silk-slippered foot. "Though our marriage was never of the best, does he *have* to learn of my indiscretions? Better he filed for a Bill of Divorcement on *any* grounds but this."

"Oh, it'll come out soon as we put ye on trial," Mr Marsden promised her.

"For complicity in Harry's murder, at the least," Mr Livesey added. "*And* for siccing someone on me and mine last night, who tried to burn us to death in our sleep!" he fumed at her. "Because you saw the gown retrieved and got frightened your secret would come out?"

"No, that wasn't my doing!" she exclaimed. "You *couldn't* think that I could do such a thing! I put the gown in the slops, I looked most carefully for any witnesses, and *saw* none. I thought it was gone for good and had no reason to fear you'd—"

"Who *else,* then?" Livesey barked. "The gown, the ribbons, the lace and bouquet, all lead back to you!"

"I can't imagine. There's no one!" she desperately insisted.

"Explain yer doin's, th' night o' Harry's murder," Mr Marsden demanded, headed for his desk for a fresher quid of "chew."

"I . . . I dined with the Lillingtons," she answered. "Osgoode wouldn't go, so I went alone. My coachee can tell you that, and my maids who helped us both dress for the evening. I sent no flowers!"

"When was your last . . . tryst?" Livesey asked. "You and Harry."

"The week previous," Anne replied. "I told you it was much too risky during Quarter Days!"

"What time did ye depart? Before Osgoode, or after?" Marsden pressed.

"About half-past six," Mrs Moore declared. "Osgoode handed me into the coach; he saw me off."

"An' then?"

"I don't know what you mean, sir! We *dined!* There was music, and *'ecarte,* some dancing and lively conversation . . . ghost stories of 'haints,' hags and such. For Wilmington Society, it continued rather late, nearly to eleven!" Mrs Moore stated, sneering a trifle at the local tendency to retire round nine, to the dismay of gentlemen visitors from more sporting towns and cities. "There's a round dozen who may vouch for my every minute."

"An' yer return home?" Mr Marsden asked.

"Half-*past* eleven, sir," Anne impatiently snipped back. "I'm certain of it. We've an excellent London-made mantel clock, sir, and it struck half-past eleven as I entered our house."

So there! Livesey thought, picturing Anne Moore sticking out her tongue to "cock a snook" at the magistrate in spite: *the whore!*

"Then?" Marsden reiterated.

"Why, I retired. Went above-stairs to my chambers. Must I account for each minute, sir? I was home, as my slaves may attest!"

"Do it!" Marsden hissed, masticating his quid furiously.

"I undressed, if you *must* know," she all but snarled. "I donned a bed-gown . . . sent down to the pantry for a demi-bottle of sherry. I lit more candles and read for a while. Does the book's *title* matter? After a glass or two, a chapter or two, I had the candles doused, and retired. I fell asleep soon after, nigh on a quarter to one. *Alone,* Mr Marsden."

"Was Osgoode home?" Livesey probed, striving to make it sound an off-handed question, though he shared a meaningful look with the magistrate. If MacDougall was most-like innocent, of *this* crime, at least, and Anne Moore would not confess, then . . .

"No," she said, shaking her head. "Nothing new about that, I promise you," she lightly scoffed. "He stayed late with you and your faction men at Miz Yadkin's Ordinary, as he ever does. I heard him come in, I think. Before I fell fully asleep. He might have wakened me; I can't recall."

"And when was that?" Livesey said, taking up Marsden's chorus.

"It might have been *after* one, really," Anne Moore considered. "I'd had more than my usual share of wine, so . . . I *know* he looked in on me. Opened my door for a moment, and I dreaded that he'd . . . Well, we'd had a bit of a spat earlier, whilst we were dressing, over his not accompanying me to the Lillingtons, and I thought that he would insist on . . . surely I do not have to relate how married couples resolve an argument, must I, sirs?" She acted almost miss-ish, and coy.

"I feigned sleep," she admitted, after a moment. "Through my lashes I saw him. He had a candle. He could vouch for my presence, and the hour. *Ask* him, why don't you, and leave off abusing me!"

"You're quite sure he came in that late," Livesey pressed with a mournful feeling under his heart. "Past one in the morning, or so."

"Reasonably sure, yes," Mrs Moore decided. "He closed my door and went 'cross the hall to his own chambers. Yes, I recall that as I dropped off again I heard the half-hour strike, so it *must* have been half-past one, or near to it, when he came home. Why?"

"Time an' enough," Mr Marsden sorrowfully said.

"Time for what?" Anne Moore asked, intrigued by their reticent air. "I've accounted for my time!"

"*Someone* with access to your chifforobe, Mistress Moore, to the gown, the lace and ribbons," Livesey sadly explained, "someone who had knowledge of your secret lovers' code, who knew the significance that two ribbon bows implied . . . *knew* it meant the glade, knew the route to it that Harry would use . . . *Someone* knew every detail of your doings. Watched you, followed you, witnessed . . . ! Someone who tasted the deepest dregs of betrayal, and wished and plotted and schemed to slay him, or you, or both, perhaps . . ."

"Osgoode, you're saying?" she gasped in utter amazement. "Shot Harry? Dear Lord, sirs, he couldn't have! He hadn't a *clue!*"

Anne Moore took a moment to picture that premise. And then, to their complete revulsion, she cracked a smile and began to snicker to herself. "Osgoode a murderer? Don't be ludicrous!" she laughed.

Chapter 29

THEY FINALLY EXCUSED the much-sobered and somewhat repentant Mrs Moore, the magistrate giving orders to the soldiers in the passageway that she was to be kept separate from her husband. Mr Marsden dragged out a brass-case watch the size of a flattened apple, and grimaced at what it showed.

"Past my dinnertime," Marsden said. "We might leave Osgoode in abeyance 'til we've et, hmm? Care t'stroll down to th' Widow Yadkin's fer a bite with me, Mr Livesey?"

"I hope you'll not think me ungracious, Mr Marsden, but I find that I have no appetite," Matthew Livesey somberly said. "After all we heard from that . . . woman! I'm not the least bit peckish." His recent experiment with a breakfast at Mrs Yadkin's, and the idea of further goggling from the poor mort was enough to put him off his feed, as well.

"Sillitoe?" Marsden called down the hall, and a moment later his manservant entered. The Marsdens had taken on a married couple's indentures, one as their cook, the other as their butler and Mr Marsden's "catch-fart." Buying indentures was a lot more expensive than purchasing trained slaves, *and* they were newcome English, hence white, and gave the Marsden house a greater social *cachet*.

"Aye, sir?"

"We'll head down t' Widow Yadkin's an' eat. 'Tis such a pretty mornin', we'll stroll," Marsden proposed, "'stead o' coach, an' . . ."

"Wouldn' be a'doin' that, beggin' yer pardon, sir," Sillitoe cautioned with a tooth-sucking wince. "There's faction men ever'where ye look, an' their blood's up, d'ye get my meanin', sir? Yadkin's is full of 'em, an' them full of Yadkin's drink."

"Well, damme!" Marsden grumbled, leaning over to spit into his bucket. "Send out, then, along with th' pris'ners' meals. I s'pose I can survive a two-penny ordinary, if they can."

"Uh . . . yessir," Sillitoe warily said, realizing that it would be him, patently and recognizably Mr Marsden's "man," who would have to risk the streets—and the upset mob.

"I shall return in an hour, sir?" Livesey asked, swaying a bit from a rising urgency.

"Hey? Oh, yes, o' course," Marsden said. "We'll begin again at one."

Livesey fetched his hat and cane, went out into the hall, and took a left down the corridor that passed the actual courtrooms on one side and the wooden doors to the cells on the other. There was a back entrance beyond, which led to the coach yard, a shell drive and turnaround, and several large shade trees . . . beneath which, behind a log-cabin shed, lay the jakes, the "seats of ease." Livesey put on a little more clumping haste, since by then his back teeth were well "awash."

Instead, though, he found his daughter, Bess, sitting on a wood-slat bench in the trees' shade, looking as miserable as a lost puppy, with a cloth bundle by her feet.

"Oh God, Father!" she wailed, springing up to hug him fiercely.

"Dear girl, Bess . . . what's amiss?" he comforted, patting her back and attempting to soothe with a few "there, there's."

"I'm so miserable, I wish I could die!" Bess declared.

"You do not! Never wish for such!" Livesey cosseted, turning her toward the bench to sit down together. "Now tell me about it."

"It's Biddy," Bess moaned, wiping her eyes. "When the soldiers took her father, she begged us to help them, get them a lawyer. But when she heard you were in there helping the court, I *had* to confess: about my prying and all, and the ribbon, and why they suspected that her father, and . . . ! I couldn't keep on *posing,* could I? This is all *my* fault, and now she won't *speak* to me, called me a false friend and a betrayer, and she . . . flung my new gown right *at* me, and . . . !" she gulped, as a fresh onslaught of remorse came over her.

"Dear Lord," Livesey said with a perplexed sigh. "Well, Bess, it would have come to her, sooner or later, but . . ."

"I *tried* to explain, tell her I never meant for her father to be suspected and arrested, but she wouldn't hear a word of it!"

"He isn't," Livesey was quick to assure her. "He was over the Brunswick the night of the murder, and I'll wager he'll soon be free, completely exonerated. Perhaps she might listen to that, if you think it would help."

"Could . . . could you tell her that, Father?" Bess wheedled.

"Ermm . . ." Livesey wavered, wondering if a father's burden from children—daughters especially—*ever* eased. "At the moment, I doubt if she'd care to face either of us, Bess. Not listen to a word *I*—"

"Perhaps not, but could you *try*, Father? Say you will, *please?* She's in her father's cell, and has to come out this way, so . . ."

"Well," he said, sagging in surrender. "Let me study 'pon it for a moment. A moment only. Excuse me." He awkwardly got to his feet and fairly dashed to the jakes. Had Gabriel blown the Final Trump that moment, it was doubtful he could have paused to listen.

"Mistress MacDougall," Livesey began to say a few minutes later, after he had cozened the girl to join him under the trees and take a seat *somewhat* near Bess on the bench. "I cannot even begin to express how sad it makes me that you and your father became involved in this. A great wrong's been done the both of you for which, through Bess's . . . zeal . . . I must and will own a portion of responsibility. Bess spoke so well of you, that I was happily anticipating the making of your acquaintance as a welcome guest in our home. You *and* your father, did he wish to accompany you. As I understand he would insist, hmm?"

Biddy MacDougall coolly gazed back at him, unmoved by his words and showing only a tiny tic of well-suppressed rancor. Livesey heard that she was striking, but seeing her in the flesh confirmed everything Bess had told him. Well, not the feckless exuberance and cheery, outgoing personality at the moment—and no wonder!

"You must believe me when I say that your father's arrest was the magistrate's decision, none of mine. Nor was it ever my daughter's intent that he should be."

"But ye were thayr, sir," Biddy dared accuse, somewhere between dutifully meek to "betters" and outraged. "Questionin' him? Ye were thayr when th' redcoats hit him with thayr muskets, sir."

"Mr Marsden had him in to clear up some things, not accuse him as the only suspect," Livesey extemporized, shading the truth of it, if only to erase Biddy's angrily cold regardings. "The magistrate made some insulting statements about your ah . . . honor," he said with a cough into his fist, "and your father went for him. You know about his temper best, I'm bound? Had he slurred Bess, *I'd* have leaped for his throat as well, Mistress MacDougall. Your father will be free in a few hours, once we've delved into the last disgusting matters anent Harry Tresmayne's death and those actually responsible for it. He'll be exonerated, so ease your heart on that score."

"But yair Bess come spyin', an' arrested he *woz,* sir," Biddy sharply reminded him, serving Livesey some well-earned "sauce."

"Aye, she did," Livesey confessed, wondering if anything could heal the rift. "Not at my bidding. To discover where that particular sort of ribbon came from, certainly, but even more importantly, where it *went,* d'ye see! To find her Uncle Harry's murderer. Would you not do the same in Bess's place, Mistress MacDougall? After that, we had to call in everyone with even the slightest involvement with that gown you made for Anne Moore, to discover the ah . . . trail, wherever it led."

"If ma father's innocent, why d'ye not release him *now,* Mr Livesey?" Biddy said, after a long, silent contemplation of his words. "A puir man or not, he dinna deserve such."

"It wouldn't be safe for him 'til we can definitely name the one, or ones, who did it," Livesey assured her, sensing that she was coming 'round, at last. "Harry Tresmayne's murder's been the talk of the whole Cape Fear, and you've seen the faction firebrands, surely. Barons' men, Levellers and Jacobites, Harry's supporters, all ready to boil over like an unwatched pot, and lynch *someone* for revenge. Your father's much safer in cells for a time more, believe me, Miss."

Biddy nodded her head slowly, grudgingly understanding him at last. She tossed back her lustrous long hair, with her chin up, and prepared to rise and go.

"Biddy . . . may I so name you?" Livesey said, to hold her there longer, to say all of his piece. "I know my Bess, and I swear, there isn't a mean bone in her body. She's a sweet and caring girl . . . but for being a trifle too clever for her own good sometimes, hey, Bess? She came back from her first visit with you in the highest of spirits . . . not because she thought she'd found evidence to convict your dad, but because she'd found a *friend.* And when Bess pledges friendship, she *means* it! I know 'tis hard for you to accept, but she *is* heartbroken that her actions caused you such pain and turned you against her. Her invitation to you of our house and hospitality is genuine, and still stands," Livesey assured her. "Though . . . that may not be quite so fine as Bess intended, after someone tried to burn down our house last night, and us in it. Because we'd found the gown with the ribbons and lace on it, had it hidden in our house 'til—"

"Burn ye out?" Biddy gasped. "Och, I walked right past eet an' dinna see! Sae busy with ma own fears . . . sae selfish of me."

"Hurt as you were, Biddy," Bess felt confident enough to chime in, with a warm tone of comfort, "it wasn't selfish, at all."

"Sae Mizziz *Moore's* gown had somethin' t'do with eet?" Biddy marvelled, tentatively accepting Bess's shyly offered hand.

"Ah, I regret to say that Anne Moore and Harry Tresmayne were, ah . . ." Livesey stammered, clearing his throat. "Your pardons, Miss, for crude speech, but there's no other way to phrase it. They were having an . . . affair, d'ye see."

"Gawd!" Biddy breathed in awe. "Mizziz Moore an' him?"

"I fear so," Livesey almost blushingly confirmed.

"Laird o' Mercy!" Biddy gushed, her lips pursed for a moment; then, to their surprise, she began to beam, to silently chuckle!

"There'd been a few salacious rumors, but . . ." Livesey hesitantly allowed. "You know how cruel people—women especially—can be, Biddy. Rumors 'bout you and your father, too, that led some to think that your father might've . . ."

"What?" Biddy gulped, quickly turning red-faced. "'Bout *me?*"

"That Harry had been, ah . . . going 'cross the Brunswick." Mr Livesey blushed some more as he treaded warily round that point. "To ah . . . visit *some* younger lady, not his wife, d'ye see how you—"

"Me an' Mr Harry Tresmayne?" Biddy exclaimed, cocking her head over, stupefied by the outrageousness of such an idea. "Och, I canna *believe* folk'd say such a thing; Mr *Harry* . . . Gawd, he woz sae *auld* a feller!"

"Not that old, surely . . ." Livesey harumphed, reminded of how semi-ancient he was becoming.

"Och, I'm *sorry*, Mr Livesey," Biddy quickly amended. "Beg yair pardon, for I ken ye an' he were of an age t'gether, but . . . th' verra *idea!* Mr Harry woz auld enoo t'be ma *father!*" Biddy found the rumor so ludicrous that she began to giggle, throwing her head up and laughing right out loud. None of which did Matthew Livesey's own bruised, *elder*, feelings a whit of good, especially when Bess hooted right along with her, just as loud.

"Well, I will leave you two to sort things out, howe'er y'will," Livesey said, levering himself afoot once more. "As friends, I hope."

"I thankee for that, Mr Livesey," Biddy said, getting to her own feet and dipping him a grateful curtsy. "An' for assurin' me that ma father'll soon be free."

"Tell your father he's welcome in our house, if he finds it in his heart to forgive us our amateurish meddling, Mistress MacDougall," Livesey offered one last time. "And express to him my regrets for any hurts he took today. They were not my intention, or my wish."

"Aye, I'll tell him, Mr Livesey," Biddy more-soberly said. "Though for all th' guid that'll do, I canna say, for he's strong when eet come tae grudges."

Livesey departed, and Biddy and Bess sat down on the bench in slightly closer proximity. They shared a sheepish glance, then a second. They looked separately at the slow coach yard's doings: a horse staling 'twixt a cart's shafts, the birds, the high-piled clouds borning to the east beyond the barrier islands, the fluttering leaves . . .

"I . . ." Bess tried to start, clearing her throat and flopping her hand in a helpless gesture on the bench between them.

"Ye swear ye meant nothin' by eet?" Biddy tentatively asked.

"Cross my heart and hope t'die!" Bess vowed, turning to face her. Biddy reached up to sweep back her hair, and returned her hand to the bench, beside Bess's. "Aw, Bess!" she sighed, at last, taking hold of Bess's hand as she did so.

"Forgive me, please, Biddy, for I never . . . !"

"Aw, Bess, o' *course* I do!" Biddy declared as they fell on each other's shoulders, back-patting and sniffling. "'Tis hard, I'll grant ye, but sometimes, makin' guid friends is. I just wish when ye came th' feerst time, ye'd been able t'say what ye were after."

"I wish I knew that I could have, too, Biddy!" Bess swore.

"That *damned* Mizziz Moore!" Biddy sniffed in aspersion as she leaned back at last, holding both of Bess's hands. "Carryin' on with Mr Harry, an' shamin' Mr Osgoode? I knew 'twoz guid reason to dislike her from th' beginnin'. Is thayr *nought* that woman'll stoop tae, sendin' someone t'burn ye out, try t'murder ye an' yair father? Howe'er did ye lay hands on that gown I made for her, anyway?"

"You know of Jemmy Bowlegs? Aye, he does reek a tad. Him and a friend of his . . ." Bess brightly began to lay out, right chipper to her new friend. "Well, I set him to watching her house, and—"

Her clever tale was interrupted, though, by a stirring in the courthouse halls, the jangle of large iron keys on a ring, a stout lock being opened, and the scraping of a thick wood door on the plank hallway floor, the creaking of unoiled hinges, and Biddy hopped up, hoping it would be her father Eachan being released, but . . . it was Osgoode Moore the redcoats were fetching out of confinement, and Bess felt Biddy's hand contract and claw into her own, heard Biddy's gasp of fevered breath.

"Och, I dinna ken, Bess!" Biddy all but whimpered in a sudden dread. "If 'twoz Mizziz Moore th' culprit, why's th' magistrate still wish tae hold Mr Osgoode?"

"Well, I suppose . . ." Bess flummoxed, trying to find a gentle way to suggest that if Mrs Moore, whom she'd witnessed striding out of the courthouse homeward, in high dudgeon and without any soldiers or bailiffs for escort, might *not* have been the guilty party, and if that was so, then where else could they look but to Mr Moore? He *was* that witch's husband, *and* an offended party, Bess realized. Her uncle Harry and Anne Moore *had* been . . . well!

God, could they think Osgoode *killed Harry?* Bess thought, with a sudden lurch under her heart. *Betrayed by his wife and one of his best friends, both?*

Mr Moore turned his head to look out at the coach yard with a desperate intensity, like a felon on his way to the gallows might for his last sight of this Earth, and Bess cringed to imagine that *he* had done the deed; he was too cultured, too civilized, so genial, and . . .

Yet Osgoode Moore lowered his gaze to Bess and Biddy, his mouth opened as if he would say something to them, as if to plead innocence or curse Bess for snooping—but how could he have known *that?*—just as the brace of redcoats turned him about and led him down the gloomy hallway towards the magistrate's office, and Bess was grateful for his gaze to be forcefully averted, for she could not meet his. Not with a murderer, not with a fine man she might have accidentally betrayed and publicly shamed, if he *wasn't* the killer!

"*Why* do they want Mr Osgoode, Bess?" Biddy pressed, again.

"To . . . ask of his wife's doings, I think," Bess finally could stammer. "See if he knew anything going on 'twixt his wife and Uncle Harry, perhaps? About last night, too, when she threw the gown away. Whether she saw Jemmy Bowlegs take it and fetch it to our house, then set fire to us, even!"

"Och, o' course. That *must* be eet!" Biddy exclaimed, sounding nigh-giddy with relief. "Cairtain-sure, no one could think that Mr *Moore* had anythin' t'do with eet! He's t'nail th' coffin shut on that evil wife o' his, an' thayr's nae tellin' but eet might'a been her did set yayr fire t'cover her tracks, did she think someone'd caught her out! Aye, that must be the right of eet. But, ye'd think they'd shew mair courtesy to a gentleman as fine as Mr Osgoode."

"The way *soldiers* are, I expect," Bess was quick to assure her, "soldiers from down below Brunswick, who know nothing of his standing."

"Redcoats!" Biddy all but snarled, expressing her father's long-held hatred for the barbarian "Sassenach" horde that had ravaged dear Scotland. "*English* redcoats, aye!"

Yet . . . her father had *said* that the trail would lead inexorably to the guilty party, step by logical step, and that they'd soon *name* the murderer, and that suddenly made Bess fearful that Uncle Harry's death lay *very* close to home. She squeezed Biddy's hand at that troubling thought, finding that Biddy was squeezing back just as hard. The day might end with *both* their illusions, and their respect for that genial and seemingly gentle and erudite man, in tatters.

Chapter 30

THAT'S . . . IMPOSSIBLE!" Osgoode blanched as they presented him the last of their proofs. He stared at the gown, the ribbons and the bouquet in abject horror.

"Don't play-act with me, Osgoode," Marsden snarled. "Seen ye in court do much th' same fer yer clients. Mean to tell us ye never had a clue 'til *now?*"

"No." He sighed. "Never! It's too . . ."

"Knowin' Harry well'z ye did, *really?*" Marsden scoffed. "Don't tell me ye're that big a cully! Harry Tresmayne would've mounted an alligator, if somebody tied down th' tail, an' well we all knew that. Wish us t'have yer wife in to repeat her confession?"

"No," Osgoode Moore stated, heaving a bitter sigh. "All this time, they . . . how long, did she say?"

"Nigh on a year," the magistrate bluntly told him.

"Lord," Osgoode breathed, shaking his head in wonder, though with less surprise this time. "All that time she . . . ha!"

Livesey suspected it was something about being a Moore. Anne had found amusement at the most inappropriate moments, and now, here did Osgoode!

"Ain't funny, Osgoode," Marsden cautioned.

"I know," Osgoode replied, though he looked as if he was biting his lips to keep from breaking into a braying, hysterical laugh.

"Your marriage wasn't of the best, she told us," Livesey felt bound to ask, no matter how loath he was to tread on such a topic.

"No, Matthew, it wasn't," Osgoode answered, after he'd managed himself. "Anne, well . . . I suppose she expected better, but the Cape Fear, and Wilmington, were just too raw and small for her. Had to go down to Charleston or up to New Bern at least once a year during the social seasons to keep her happy."

"Didn't care for your politicking . . ." Livesey coaxed.

"Though, 'twas politics that threw us together," Osgoode said. "She'd seen me speak in the Assembly, and . . . you know how it is when visiting assemblymen lodge on the kindness of the New Bern residents? I stayed at her kinfolk's, and people were praising me to the skies as the newest up-and-comer . . . pardon my boasting . . . and, one thing led to the next, d'ye see."

"And she'd heard how grand King Roger Moore and his kin are," Livesey suggested with a slightly sarcastic tone.

"Another disillusion for her, I fear," Osgoode said, chuckling a little. "She expected to dine at Orton Plantation, at least *once!* Didn't see she was marrying into the *poor* side of the family. Might have done better had she taken up with the Ramseurs! A traitor to my *class,* she told me! As if we were peers of the realm."

"Resented your many absences . . . ?" Livesey posed.

"Oh Lord," Osgoode rejoined with a mirthless snort. "Anne resented a great *many* things, those being but a small part, Matthew. But I *never* thought she'd be so base as to . . . !"

"Kept sep'rate bedchamber," Mr Marsden luridly pried.

"Our personal arrangements I would prefer to remain *private,* your honor," Osgoode said, stiffening with prickly pride. "There is no relevance."

"Too damn bad," Marsden pitilessly griped, "fer 'twas *private* doin's led to Harry Tresmayne's murder."

"You actually suspect *me?*" Osgoode objected. "Why? I didn't *know,* I tell you, sir!"

"An' all those bouquets in yer hall never made ye suspicious?"

"There were *always* flowers in our hall, Mr Marsden. Coming in, going out, the salver piled with invitations and chatty notes, I don't know what-all," Osgoode countered, shaking his head.

"And the gown?" Livesey prompted.

"That one, out of dozens?" Osgoode Moore carped. "I never gave her wardrobe much thought, but for the expense. Anne loved one, one day, then despised it the next. Next I know, her body-slaves had 'em on, they went to church raffles or the rag sellers, to charities . . ."

"Own a double-barrel coachin' gun, Osgoode?" Marsden enquired.

"A single-barrel fowling gun, sir, from Philadelphia," Osgoode answered. "But then, so must an *hundred* gentlemen, hereabouts."

Livesey was disappointed that Osgoode Moore had recovered from the shock of his wife's, and Harry's, betrayal and the accusation leveled against him, and was now becoming the organized *attorney,* ready with cogent explanations for everything.

"What d'ye carry, then," Mr Marsden asked, "when ye're abroad on faction bus'ness on th' lonely wilderness roads?"

"I own a brace of pistols, your honor."

"Double barrel 'barkers'?"

"Yes, they are, but—"

"What caliber, Osgoode?" Marsden snapped.

"They're sixty-seven caliber, French-made. Harry . . ." Osgoode paused, the memory shaking his serenity. "*Harry* brought them back as a gift from the war."

"Sixty-seven . . . wide enough t'load with buckshot, or a paper twist o' fifty-four caliber balls," Marsden mused aloud, ruminating on his fresh quid. "Saw a fifty-four caliber fusil-musket over to your house once, as I recall. Still own that fusil, Osgoode—its bullet mold?"

"Yes, I do, but I swear to you, I—" Osgoode insisted.

"That'd be pretty damn ironic, wouldn't it?" Marsden hooted. "Killin' Harry with his gift pistols."

"Why would I, though, Mr Marsden? I didn't know, and even if I had known, I'd've—"

"Sure of that, Osgoode?" Livesey interrupted, leaning on that side table to ease his aching leg, too eager to end the sordid affair to sit. "Your dearest friend in the whole world, going behind—"

"Yours, too, Matthew," Osgoode reminded him.

"Aye, mine, too," Livesey sadly agreed. "But *your* mentor and confidant in the faction. Faced with such a betrayal, you still say you'd *not* have felt a murderous . . . whatever?"

"Matthew!" Osgoode gasped to have the accusation come from him. "You *know* me! You must know that I'd never murder *anyone,* no matter the provocation. Were he still with us, had I just learned—"

"Yes?" Marsden drawled.

"Well, I'd deny him my hand, my house," Osgoode fussily said, clutching his turn-back lapels closer together. "Make an open break with him! Damn his soul to the fires o' Hell, and Anne with him, I would! Divorce that . . . ! and bedamned to her, too. That's ruin, and shame *enough* in my life and career, Matthew!"

"Shootin'd *feel* a lot more satisfyin', though," the magistrate slyly commented. "Keep yer name outta th' muck. Anne's name."

"Was it shooting I wished, your honor, I'd have done it face-to-face in a duel not waylay him," Osgoode declared. "As for a fear for Anne's good name, hah! Our marriage was pretty much a sham, and why deny it? Better I'd have shot *her*, if I wished revenge."

"Fact remains, though, Osgoode," Mr Marsden pointed out, "ye had both motive an' grievance. An', it would've been easy fer ye to discover what they were up to, figure out their sparkin' places, how they sent their messages, an' plant a lure t'get Harry out in that glade that night. Who *else* has enough access t'yer household to've done it? Who else close enough t'Anne could've? An' for what *cause?*"

"But I didn't!" Osgoode cried, sounding exasperated.

"Anne says you looked in on her when you returned home that night, Osgoode," Livesey said, trying to fill out the missing pieces of the mystery. "Half-past one in the morning, as she recalled."

"Hmm, yes?" Moore hesitantly answered, swiveling around on the hard-seated ladderback chair. "I s'pose I could've been out that late. Assizes, political talk . . ."

"Yet, you left Harry and me a little after eight, according to Missiz Yadkin. It took you four hours to go a few town blocks? With nearly five hours in hand, a *circumstantial* case could be made that you had ample time to borrow a horse—take one from your own stables, with your groom or coachee already a'bed—and ride out to the Masonborough Road," Matthew Livesey wondered, chewing on a thumbnail for an anxious moment, and hoping for the best, praying that Osgoode had the most innocent of explanations. "This is so easily solved, Osgoode, if you could, pray, tell us where you were all that time and the name of a witness who could vouch for you."

"Faction work . . . wagers and horse racing prospects," Osgoode stammered, wheedling, and crossed his legs at the knee, his arms on his chest, and Matthew Livesey felt physically *ill* and evilly chilled.

"Names! Places, an' times, Osgoode!" Mr Marsden growled.

A fine sheen of perspiration broke out on Moore's forehead, and he seemed stricken, his mouth agape as he tried to speak.

"Oh, *God,* Osgoode!" Livesey sorrowfully groaned, stumping over to a chair to plop down, bereft of all illusions.

"Speak up, Osgoode, or there's a noose in yer future," Marsden demanded, slamming the flat of his hand on the desk.

"I wish to God I could, your honor . . . Matthew," Osgoode managed to croak, turning fish-belly pale, "but sadly I cannot."

"Hang an' bedamned then, ye murderin' bastard!" Marsden cried.

"As God's my ultimate judge, sir, on my honor as an English gentleman, and as a Christian as I *hope* I've lived, I am innocent of Harry's murder," Osgoode formally, but shudderingly, avowed. "On my sacred word of honor, I knew nothing of the affair. But as an English gentleman, circumstances will not allow me to breach mine oath."

"Ye dance *that* into my court, an' *ye'll* dance th' Newgate Hornpipe b'fore th' jury's *tea* time!" Marsden screeched, shooting to his feet. "Ye're a lawyer, fer God's sake. Surely, ye can come up with a better tale than that!"

Osgoode Moore, Esquire, set his visage to nigh a Roman's stoicism, bit his lips to hold back a sob of self-pity—or fear—that could unman him, but would say no more, bowing his head in resignation.

"Osgoode . . . !" Matthew Livesey tried to cajole. "Whether you go a gentleman, or a murdering rogue, hung is *hung!* Without a word for yourself, how do you think people will remember you?"

"Matthew, I wish that I . . . no," Moore stubbornly replied.

"*So* Anne put horns on you, and you'll look like a fool!" Livesey growled in unnatural heat, and closer to Billingsgate rawness than anyone could recall him uttering. "Divorce the bitch, and take your comedown like a man. Is it the faction you're concerned about? That Harry's gone, Thom Lakey's a languid twit, and if you're shamed, it'll all fall apart? Are you too . . . *bloody* embarrassed that people will *laugh* at you and death's *better,* ye damned great *fool?*"

Osgoode left off looking half-strangled but noble, and gawped at Livesey for a second before attempting to reply, and when he did, it was with the same sadly stoic tone. "It's none of those, Matthew. Believe me, I don't *wish* to be tried, or hung if found guilty. But I gave my word, my sacred word, and what's a gentleman without honor?"

"Alive!" Mr Marsden all but howled. "Ah, ye're fulla *shite,* Moore! I think ye really *did* kill Harry, ye know ye'll be convicted, but ye want folk t'always wonder 'bout yer silence!"

"I am innocent, Mr Marsden," Osgoode wearily insisted. "My God knows that, and I trust that He will take me up, but . . . to shew myself untrustworthy of the vow I made to . . . would He, still?"

"Made to a person!" Livesey cried, leaping on the possibility. "A man, or a woman, Osgoode? It *is* a person, isn't it!"

Osgoode Moore only shook his head, doggedly silent.

Livesey took a deep breath and began to think that Osgoode *was* innocent. But God Above, he was the *stubbornest* sort of stiff-necked fool, as bad as a Charlestonian when it came to his tetchy honor! He was the sort who'd die for it . . . unlike the majority of so-called gentlemen who swore they might . . . if it wasn't inconvenient!

"Listen, Osgoode," Livesey said in a softer taking, getting to his feet to go and all but purr in Osgoode's ear. "No one doubts you are honorable. But think about *Anne,* man. You swing, and Anne is shot of you, gets away Scot-free with no consequences. There's not enough time for a Bill of Divorcement in the Assembly," Livesey said, leaning heavily on the back of Osgoode's chair. "You're hung, buried unmarked in a crossroads . . . and who gets to spend your *estate,* hey? A convicted murderer *has* to die intestate, that's the right of it, is it not, Mr Marsden? Anne's your closest *heir!*

"Anne's a *wealthy* widow, up to her old tricks among the elite, Osgoode, with hundreds of young hounds baying for a chance with her, to help her spend her 'clink' . . . *your* 'clink,' me lad, among people who think adultery a *trifle* compared to your crime!"

That prompted Moore to mop his face with his sleeve and waver.

"Finally, Osgoode, there's the matter of who *really* murdered Harry," Livesey beguiled behind the man's head, "and if you take the blame, well . . . we've run out of suspects. You die as the likeliest, and the one who did it—the one who tried to burn me and mine to the ground—just might show up at your execution, Osgoode, watch you take the high-jump proper, then go home, laughing up his sleeve at what a witless *cully* you were. Do you *want* that, Osgoode? Harry betrayed you, yes, but think of the love you had for him once. Don't we owe Harry *justice,* Osgoode? No matter his sins?"

"Oh God, Matthew," Osgoode muttered, swaying, almost delirious. "It's so tangled. *I've* sinned as much as I was sinned against, but . . . 'tis such a *wondrous* thing! Never meant it to happen, but . . ."

"Mean ye're *confessin'* t'Harry's death?" Marsden goggled.

"*No,* not *that,* Mr Marsden!" Osgoode blurted out, finally. "It's ironically funny, really . . ."

"Not from where *I'm* sittin', it ain't!" Marsden acidly said.

"You see—" Osgoode began to say, on the cusp of revelation.

But there came a rapping on the door.

"Bloody burnin' *Hell!*" Marsden bellowed. "*Not* bloody *now!*"

The rapping came again, softer, as if chastised, but insistent.

"Suff'rin' *shite!* Get yer arse in here, damn yer eyes!"

The door creaked tremulously open, and there, to Livesey's mortification, stood his daughter, Bess, with Biddy MacDougall shrunk back halfway behind her, and both their faces gape-mouth embarrassed!

"Father?" Bess cringingly said, all but whispering.

"Garrh!" Marsden gravelled, bending so low over his spitkid behind his desk that it appeared he was hiding his chagrin over shouting crude Billingsgate at girls.

"Bess, this is hardly the time; we've serious matters . . ."

"We *have* to speak with you, Father," Bess said, putting a supportive arm round Biddy MacDougall and dragooning her into the office. "Biddy has vital information that you must—"

"Osgoode?" Biddy wailed.

He'd snapped about at the mention of her name, and risen from his chair.

"Biddy, you mustn't—!" Moore began to say, before the girl broke free of Bess's arm and dashed right at him, to fling her arms about his neck and dangle, with her shoes inches off the floor!

"What th' bloo . . . pry that girl *off* him, somebody, an' tell me what in Tarnation is goin' on!" Marsden fumed, chewing vigorously. "Who th' . . . what's yer name, girl?"

"Biddy MacDougall, yair honor, sir," she piped up shyly, once she had been lowered to her feet with Osgoode's hands on her waist. "An' I've come tae tell ye that Osgoode Moore couldna killed Mr Harry Tresmayne, sir."

"Speakin' to his character, are ye?" Marsden snapped, "Or do you actually know somethin'?"

"Both, yair honor, sir," Biddy responded, between an adoring glance or two 'twixt the two of them. "I ken that Mr Osgoode's too fine a gentleman t'be doin' such, an' . . . t'tell ye that he woz 'cross th' rivers with me th' nicht Mr Harry woz shot."

"Saw him 'cross . . . Oh, *Hell!*" Marsden exclaimed, plopping into his chair in surprise when he twigged to her meaning. "Well, damme! No *wonder* ye'd go t'yer grave mum, Osgoode. 'Twas a young lady's name ye were protectin'."

"Mum?" Biddy suddenly fretted. "He kept *mum?*"

"Would've hung fer Harry's murder, 'fore he'd say where he was, nor who he was with who coulda cleared him," Marsden explained.

"Guid Gawd, Osgoode!" Biddy said with a shiver, torn 'twixt adoration, terror and exasperation. "Ye wouldna save yairself all tae guard ma name? Och, ye wondrous fool, ye'd've *died* for me? Osgoode, ma dear, I love ye mair than life itself, but . . . let's hae nae mair o' *that!*" She giggled, throwing herself on him again. "I ken ye said ye love *me* mair than life, as well, but . . . well, I ne'er expected ye'd try tae *prove* eet!"

"Ah, Osgoode . . . Biddy," Livesey finally had the temerity to intrude on their mutual, blind-to-the-world bliss. "Just how long ago did this, ah . . . ?"

"Last year, Matthew," Osgoode beamishly, proudly, told him, at last. "When Biddy came to the house to take measures for that damned gown, yonder. At first, you understand, it was only . . . talking when she called, sharing some books and such. It began so innocently."

"Most fool things do," Mr Marsden wryly observed. Not that anyone was paying much attention to him.

"Even after the gown was done, we'd meet," Osgoode went on.

"Ev'ry Sat'rday when I come t'town, sirs," Biddy further said. "I'd call at his law office . . . returnin' books I borryed, gettin' a new'un or twa . . ."

"I'd find a way, did business take me over the Brunswick, to stop off, was Mr MacDougall tied up at the ferry. Suggested that others should use her talent for dressmaking, ordered some things for mine own wardrobe," Osgoode chimed in. They left off embracing, but sat close together on matching ladderback chairs, hands still firmly clasped. "I was smitten, sir . . . Matthew, but I couldn't help myself. Nor, after getting to know Biddy, did I *care* to. After a few years of plodding, dull indifference and *conditional* affections from Anne, well . . . you can see why I was, ah . . . I couldn't dare hope that we could ever *really* change our situations but . . ."

"'Twoz ma fault, I fear, sirs," Biddy happily confessed. "Oh, I woz sae fashed over Osgoode. Churnin' in ma boudins when I woz tae see him, frettin' th' times betwixt. Silly weepin' spells sae bad I dinna think I'd live did I hae t'miss him ain mair hour. Bess got th' bitter end of ain o' those, th' day she come callin' on me for a gown. Then, came a day when I thought I'd bust if I dinna tell him how I felt . . . sae I did! Thought I'd lose him, him bein' wed, but och, when we saw how we *both* felt, weel . . ."

"You got across the Brunswick? Past Eachan MacDougall?" Mr Marsden puzzled.

"There's one-hull *piraguas* a'plenty up-river on Eagle's Island, sir," Osgoode told him, "and lots of people use them late at night after the ferry service shuts down. And I have a little shallop of mine own, docked at the north end of town. You can sail across the Cape Fear, then pole through the marshes to the Brunswick, north of Eagle's Island, where the rice fields aren't planted yet."

"And ye *never* took a ride t'gether this side o' th' Cape Fear?" Marsden asked, if only to put the matter to a final rest. "Out the Wrightsville Road, the Masonborough?"

"Once we knew how we felt, sir," Osgoode Moore swore, "we never took a risk that could harm dear Biddy's name. Never, in Wilmington."

"It *is* kinda ironic," Marsden mused aloud, leaning far back in his chair, at his ease at last. "Yer wife off sportin' with Harry, th' two of ye, well . . . no wonder ye didn't have a clue o' th' affair 'til we told ye."

"I thought *I* was the betrayer, frankly, your honor," Osgoode replied. "Too *busy* to look for clues, even if I *had* known of their doings. Didn't spare Anne a second thought."

"Night that Mr Harry woz killed, yer honor," Biddy firmly vowed, "ma Bible-oath an' word o' honor on eet, too, Osgoode woz with me in Daddy's hayloft, past midnight or better. Ma daddy woz down tae th' ferry tavern, dancin' whisky reels an' playin' his tunin'-box with th' others nigh 'til mornin'." Biddy snuggled up, arm-in-arm with clasped hands, to Osgoode, beaming with such joy that the both of them seemed to depart the magistrate's office in spirit, and Osgoode almost purred with contentment that their secret was out.

She slowly lowered her gaze from her adored one's face to her lap, and stroked her free hand over her middle, which gesture forced Mr Marsden to cough, nigh-strangling on his chaw! Bess, had noticed it too, and she jerked her gaze to the magistrate's sounds, eyes wide in shock. Marsden, a father many times over, knew that gesture's significance, and . . . after he got done hawking his disbelief into his spitkid, sat back up and tipped Bess a cheery wink, putting a finger to his lips to urge her to say nought.

"Hah!" Marsden hooted, relishing the surprise that awaited Mr Osgoode Moore, Esquire. "Seems we've two corroborations in one, then. One fer Osgoode, one fer Eachan MacDougall, as well." And Mr Marsden wore, for an instant, an equally sly grin at the thought of what *that* worthy's reaction would be. "Hmm, though . . ." Marsden sobered. "That leaves us . . ."

"Oh but . . . I say!" Matthew Livesey exclaimed. "Biddy's father cleared, Osgoode as well, and Anne Moore *involved* but not guilty of it, either . . . just who the devil *did* kill Harry?"

Chapter 31

THE MAGISTRATE'S OFFICE featured a spindly-legged settee over to one side, and Matthew Livesey made for it, for his stump was aching something sinful by then, having paced to aid his thinking for most of the morning. Bess slid in beside him, looking concerned for him.

Does it come down to faction, after all? he had to ask himself. It hadn't been Sim Bates's revenge, and now Harry Tresmayne's sinning with Anne Moore, shocking enough in itself, led nowhere. Anne had had absolutely no interest in politics, or her husband, Osgoode's, strivings to open the franchise to more of North Carolina's potential property owners and voters, even to win more autonomy for the colony from the Mother Country, or at least its London-appointed Royal Governor.

Yet it had been Anne's gown, its trimmings about the flowers, that had lured Harry to his death, and how could the rival barons of the Cape Fear have gotten their hands on *those?*

"It still hinges on the ribbon and the flowers," Livesey said in a heavy, disappointed voice. "Jemmy Bowlegs's scouting for me . . . 'twas a man waited for Harry, a man on a well-shod horse, shod himself in new-ish riding boots, who owns a double-barreled coaching gun."

"An', 'twas probably a man set fire t'yer house last night, as well," Mr Marsden gloomily added from behind the desk. "Women don't go abroad much after dark, not after th' curfew bell. Not unescorted. Arson *can* be a woman's crime, but I can't see Miz Moore doin' that."

"She went out near dark to dispose of the gown," Livesey said. "Did she go to check on it and found it gone . . ."

"Osgoode, were ye to home last night?" Mr Marsden asked him. "What-all went on at yer place, anyway?"

"Well, I had court papers to review, things to read up on, and . . . Harry's final debtors' list to go over," Moore answered. "We both were home the rest of the day, after the gathering at Georgina's. Anne was above-stairs most of the afternoon, nursing her headache, and only came down round the time that supper was ready. She went out just the once, to the . . . ah . . . necessary, I supposed, after we dined."

"When she most-like disposed of the gown," Livesey decided.

"It now appears so, yes, Matthew," Osgoode agreed. "I did not see her, exactly. We had little to talk about, so right after supper I went back to my library. She might have gone to her bedchamber to fetch the gown before she went out, then."

"An' th' rest o th' evenin'?" Marsden idly probed.

"She might have read," Osgoode answered, frowning heavily, so he could recall exactly, "in the parlor. Oh, she did come in to get some stationery from me, after Thom Lakey left . . . had some letters to write, or invitations to answer, I'd guess."

"Thom Lakey came by?" Marsden harumphed.

"For a bit. Dropped by to pay his respects. Stuck his head in to say 'hello' to me, then spent most of the time chatting with Anne," Moore related. "I could hear them in the parlor, singing gossipy as a pair o' mockingbirds."

"Rest o' th' night?"

"Hmmm . . . I think it was around ten that she told me she would retire, and went to her chambers. I worked another hour or so, then went to my own round eleven," Osgoode breezed off. "It had been quite a stern day, altogether, so I went to sleep quickly. Anything after, oh . . . a quarter-past eleven, I couldn't say. But for Anne to rise, dress and go out to commit *arson* . . . ! That would've roused the house slaves, and that to-do would've roused me."

"Might ask o' them, I s'pose," Marsden grumpily allowed. "Or there may not be much point."

"Father," Bess piped up, shifting on the short settee to face him, "I thought Mr Lakey and Andrew had coached home right after the gathering at Aunt Georgina's."

"I'd assumed they had," Livesey replied, perking up a bit. "We walked halfway home to our place, Thomas and I, to fetch his nephew after he'd seen you home, aye." To the rest of the room he said, "We were to go out to

Lakey's Lodge tomorrow for dinner after church . . . get some cuttings from their flower gardens. Was Andrew with him, do you recall, Osgoode?"

"Didn't see Andrew, no, Matthew."

"Did he come by coach, then?" Livesey wondered aloud.

"Didn't hear one," Osgoode told him. "First I knew, Thom was rapping on the front door, and a maidservant went to admit him."

"Odd," Livesey mused. "Oh, but I suppose he sent Andrew on by coach, and he could have hired a mount at Taneyhill's Livery."

"I'd expect 'twas Thom's social rounds boring young Hewlett to tears, Matthew," Osgoode said with a faint chuckle. "When he comes to town, Thom makes the most of his time, calls on as many as'll have him in. And, with his fount of gossip and wit, there's none would refuse an hour here, an hour there, with him. Anne always relished his droll wit. More her sort of gentleman than most in these parts."

Something was nagging *Livesey's* wits, something out-of-place or half-forgotten, something he'd missed, that they'd all missed, a line of questions that had to be asked, no matter how ludicrous.

"Ah!" Livesey suddenly erupted, all but slapping his forehead to punish himself for being a "jingle-brains."

"Smith's Creek, Mr Marsden! Smith's Creek! Look you, Anne and Harry had a second hidey-hole where they trysted . . . a tumbledown log cabin along the creek on the north side of the Wrightsville Road, a mile or two east of their glade, we must assume. Far enough from town to avoid prying eyes but close enough to make it a short ride. Is that not on Thom Lakey land?"

"Well, aye," the magistrate allowed, scowling. "He owns it all right down t'Smith's Creek, an' he did have some tenant parcels along th' road, b'fore he let 'em go back t'woodlots, but . . . damme! Where ye goin' with this, Livesey? I know we're stumped t'find th' villain, but thinkin' Thom Lakey might've had a hand in it's *dev'lish* desp'rate! Man's a gadfly! Did he murder anybody, I expect it'd be a *tailor* who run him up a bad fit!" Marsden hooted in wicked glee.

"He could have ridden down that way and seen Harry and Anne at their play, sir," Livesey pointed out, admittedly spinning very wispy spider webs out of Marsden's very suspicion . . . desperation. Even *he* had trouble picturing it, like a very dry and *old* spider that had not snagged a fly in weeks. "Was he so disillusioned by Harry's adultery—did it come out and destroy their faction, Harry and Osgoode, and all their good work with one blow—wouldn't a *dead* Harry serve better as a martyr, not a disgrace, sir? *Or,* had he ambitions to lead . . ."

"Thomas Lakey had no such aspirations that I ever saw, Matthew," Osgoode Moore quickly dismissed. "He's the most supportive fellow I know, always encouraging. Had good ideas, I admit, but he was always content to *serve.* Took minutes, corresponding secretary, treasurer."

"Then, might've Thomas Lakey had . . . feelings for your wife on the sly and felt badly let down . . . ?" Livesey fumblingly posed, losing enthusiasm even as he did so, knowing what a stretch he was making.

"Bachelor Thom?" Marsden cackled. "I doubt it. I ain't sayin' Lakey's *p'culiar,* fer he's ever adored women's comp'ny, but he doesn't stray off th' porch on his home ground, d'ye get my meanin'."

"Uhm . . . perhaps I don't," Livesey said, at a loss; that happened now and again, when confronted by a particularly impenetrable and esoteric Low Country folk idiom.

"Meanin' uh . . ." Marsden gravelled, shifting his quid from one side of his mouth to the other to find a polite way to say it plainly in mixed company. "In my lifetime o' knowin' him, Thom Lakey doesn't need *continual* feminine comp'ny. Never married, but never goes without ah . . . congress, whene'er th' need arise. Th' *hired* morts?" Mr Marsden added, as Livesey continued to gaze at him, still unenlightened. "A fetchin' servant girl?"

"Ah!" Livesey exclaimed, at last.

"Outta town," Marsden said further. "Mostly. Charleston, an' places like that. Osgoode can tell ye more o' that."

"Uhm," Osgoode stumbled, stiffening to be put on the spot, and with Biddy by his side looking up quizzically. "When traveling with him in the past, Thom was of the wont to be . . . entertained . . . only in the best ah . . . houses. Willing widows and such. Ever *discreetly.*"

"Meanin' he'd tread a hen in another pen, but he's not a cock-rooster who'd *crow,* after, either," Mr Marsden added, quite perkily, as if relishing Livesey's prim Northern perplexity. "An' safer with local ladies an' girls than a tonsured Dago monk. Why Thom's so well trusted by local men. Respected, too, after all th' profit he's had from his plantation an' bus'ness int'rests."

"Hmmm . . . I suppose, then," Livesey said with a sigh, sinking back against the settee back, having played his last card and lost.

"Excuse me, again, gentlemen," Bess shyly spoke up, with her hand up as if trying to respond at her schooling. "When Andrew walked me home, yesterday . . . he was with me when I met Jemmy Bowlegs and his friend, Autie, the ginger-beer monger . . . they were the ones who kept watch on Mistress Moore's house for me, the ones who saw her dispose of that gown yonder, and fetched it to us. Andrew was . . . peeved that I spoke to Jemmy, as if I was snubbing his presence?"

"So a boy's cross with ye. So?" Marsden impatiently fumed.

"Well, sir, were Andrew's feelings hurt, isn't it possible that he might have made at least *passing* mention to his uncle?" Bess added. "I have gathered that Andrew Hewlett is ah, *some* fond of me, and . . ."

"Why Thomas Lakey invited us out to the Lodge," Mr Livesey grumbled. "Spoke of allowing Andrew and my daughter to see what sort of future relationship might come of it, d'ye see."

"He did?" Bess gasped, "Oh . . . my!" She blushed, wishing for a hand-fan to cool her features— or hide behind.

"Could he not have . . ." Livesey speculated with his fingers at the tip of his nose in a steeple. ". . . stayed in town on his social calls, *seen* Bowlegs and his friend purloin that gown, by accident, perhaps, and . . . that brick thrown through my window last night! The note on it *did* warn me to call off my . . . daughter, though that wasn't quite the scurrilous term used! It said 'newcomes keep out of our business' too. We *are* newcomes to Thomas Lakey's lights. Osgoode! When Thom called on Anne, did either of them seem noticeably out-of-sorts?"

"Well, no, not really." Osgoode tried to remember: "Anne *was* out-of-sorts and a trifle tetchy for a time, but I put that down to a headache and the gloomy occasion of Georgina's memorial gathering. She brightened considerable after Thom arrived. Thomas, well . . . he was his usual droll self. Didn't stay as long as was his custom, but . . . coming in and going out, he *did* seem as if he had other calls to make that night, so he *might* have seemed a tad rushed, in fact."

"Calls unbidden, long after supper and dark?" Livesey asked. "I'd have thought the demands of a successful planter's life wouldn't allow for late-night rambles in town, nigh ten miles from home. Would he take lodgings somewhere for the night, d'ye think?"

"He'd usually overnight with me, Matthew," Osgoode informed him. "At Harry's, too, even was Harry and Georgina away."

"Now that's da . . . *deuced* interesting!" Livesey exclaimed. "If you were absent, he'd still stay at your house, Osgoode?"

"Well, of course! Most times, though, when I was away on the faction work, Thom would ride with me, d'ye see, but when I was away on *law* business, we'd give him a spare bedchamber. God, Matthew, he is the *perfect* gentlemen. I've known him all my life!"

"Knew *Harry* yer whole life, too, Osgoode," Marsden dryly said.

"And besides Harry, when he called," Livesey enthusiastically continued, levering himself to his feet again, despite the dull ache in his right thigh and stump, "was Anne in the habit of allowing Lakey to call upon her in the mornings, in her bedchamber?"

"Well, yes, he was the only other I know of that—"

"There's only three men with access to Anne Moore's bedchamber, and *wardrobe,* sirs!" Livesey all but shouted. "Osgoode, here, Thomas Lakey, and Harry—and Harry's dead. Had he known, somehow, the secret this gown holds . . . had he spied them out when they met on his land, perhaps even watched Anne make up her coded bouquets, and smoked out the significance of lace, or ribbon, or flower variety . . . ?"

Osgoode was, by then, almost goggle-eyed in surprise, and Mr Marsden had left off chewing his quid, scowling as was his wont, but with a shrewd cast to his eyes.

"Mr Marsden, we have no other possibility to pursue," Mr Livesey urgently proposed. "*If* Thom Lakey was in Wilmington when someone tried to burn me out, at the least he might have *seen* something, someone's, or several someones, doing odd things. It seems queer to me, though, that he has so many links to the evidence we've gathered, so . . . might it not be worthwhile to ask him a few questions, sir?"

"Well . . ."

"For instance, God forbid, where was Mr Lakey the night of Harry's death?" Livesey dared demand. "Osgoode, he came to the Widow Yadkin's, didn't he? What do you recall of his doings that night?"

"Thom turned up at the ordinary a bit after I did, a bit after you," Osgoode related, now frowning in concern, himself. "We chatted for a moment. Said he'd come by the house, but we'd already gone out, that he'd wished to speak to Anne before she went to the Lillington's supper party then walk with me to Yadkin's, but missed both of us. I . . . I *particularly* recall that when I left, just a little after eight o'clock, I felt hellish relieved that Thom's horse wasn't in the yard. I was on my way to my shallop, then, to be with dear Biddy," he said as he turned briefly to bestow the girl a doting smile, and a pat on her hand. "The last thing I needed was to give Thom grist for his gossip mill."

"Rode in from The Lodge, not coached?" Livesey asked, with mounting excitement.

"Wanted to show off his new mare, I think," Osgoode told him with an easy laugh. "Lovely coffee-brown beast, 'bout fifteen hands high. Wouldn't race her, but . . . hmmm. Matthew," Osgoode said more soberly, shifting uneasily on his chair, "I think I japed him over his *clothes,* that evening. Not his customary frippery. Thomas wore a suit of bottle-green ditto, coat and breeches the same, a plain black tricorne and black waistcoat. Asked him, had he found religion, or was he going . . . *hunting!* Oh, God." Osgoode blanched, then squirmed uncomfortably again. "Why, when he shewed me his new mare, he even had a cloak behind the saddle, though it was a warm evening."

"Umhmm!" Livesey commented, stamping his cane on the floor.

"You were there, too, Matthew," Osgoode said. "Did you note when he left?"

"Ah, no," Livesey had to confess. "Harry and I were by then . . . cherry-merry. Quite betook by wine. Sorry. Mr Marsden, sir—" he said, turning to that worthy, "knowing this, don't you think that we *must* speak with Thomas Lakey? No matter how ridiculous it seems?"

Marsden chewed on that idea for a second or two, mouth working as if he'd found a tough stem or a pea-gravel in his tobacco quid, in a black pet. "I will own t'havin' a hellish curiosity 'bout what ol' Thom might have t'say 'bout all these . . . coincidences. Why not?" he said, disposing of his chew into the kid, and rising, calling for his hat and cane.

"Sillitoe, I'll have me coach fetched 'round," Marsden ordered, "an' I'll thank that Captain Buckles or whatever his damn name is to accomp'ny us . . . with a brace o' his redcoats, just in case. What th' devil happened t'ye, man?"

Sillitoe had, in fetching the magistrate's dinner, been treated rather roughly by some of the hotheads; he now sported a livid bruise on his cheek, and his usually immaculate attempt at formal livery had suffered, too.

"Never mind, Sillitoe, we'll speak of it later," Marsden said. "Best hunt up Constable Swann while yer at it. Mr Livesey!"

"Sir?" Livesey replied, much relieved that he had been able to convince the magistrate to continue looking for a suspect.

"Care t'be in at th' kill . . . if killin' there be?" Mr Marsden offered. "Clever wits such's yers might think o' somethin' I don't. Though if this notion of yers don't work, God help ye, an' us."

"I would, sir, indeed," Livesey eagerly answered.

"Don't want t'ride back t'Wilmington an' find it up in flames," Mr Marsden said with a droll snicker to the others. "I'd admire did ye stay here in th' courthouse 'til I'm back, Osgoode. Healthier for ye. Same goes for yer father, Mistress MacDougall, 'til I can assure th' gath'rin' mobs that he's innocent. Knowin' Eachan, it's best he's still in cells a while longer."

"Amen t'that, Mr Marsden, sir," Biddy said with a knowing shrug, and a grateful curtsy.

"Whilst he's still in there, Osgoode," Marsden gleefully suggested, "so he can't get *at* ye, might be a good time t'tell him how ye been courtin' his little girl . . . an' what-all yer intentions are, an' I do trust I'll see ye at Services t'morrow, Osgoode . . . 'mong th' quick, not th' dead. Need a soldier or two t'help with that, hmm?"

"Uhh . . ." Moore replied with a gulp, suddenly realizing what he faced, but putting a determined arm about Biddy MacDougall's shoulders.

"Miss, I'd offer regrets t'yer father, though I doubt he's of a mood t'hear 'em," Marsden gently said. "My pardons for any rough treatment, anyway, though he brought most of it on himself."

"Och, I'll try, yer honor, sir!"

"Think Anne'd be at church tomorrow, Osgoode?"

"Doubt it, sir . . . not in our pew box, at any rate."

"Damme, but I'd *love* t'see th' look on her face when ye spring yer handsome s'prise on that hussy! Well . . . come on, Livesey. Let's go try our wits on Thom Lakey, an' see what he's got t'say."

Chapter 32

A WARM, Low Country afternoon burned bright as brass, the winds unaccountably still, and the lushly vibrant-green leaves on the deciduous trees, and the boughs and needles on the towering, spindly pines, stood motionless. High-piled, convoluted cloud heads stood tall over Cabbage Inlet and the Sounds, but here, a few miles inland, what sea breeze might develop was muffled by the vast forests.

The magistrate's coach-and-four turned off the Duplin Road onto the graveled and oyster-shelled drive of Lakey's Lodge at last, leaving a much worse-tended public road of ruts, puddles, sandy patches and mud. On either hand of the long drive, crops of corn, flax and hemp, of tobacco and cotton, sprouted springtime knee- or shin-high, brighter green than the woods, and brilliant with promise against the backdrop of rich umber and sand soil. A few thin files of men and women, with children here and there, grudgingly, slowly, toiled in the planted rows—field-slaves—with here and there an overseer or gang-boss keeping an eye on them from horseback: either a Free Negro or trusty slave bossing his own kind, or a White who was used to bossing.

Between each planted field stood windbreaks of hardwoods: trees and shrubs, spared for the purpose when the forests were clear-cut, or woodlots of mixed trees and secondary growth to be used for firewood, pine resins and turpentine, or later construction . . . places where the pigs could root, and livestock could find cooling shade. Other fields in the distance sprouted lawn-like cover crops, where animals grazed, and the grasses and their ordure would be turned under to re-nourish the land. Others, stoutly fenced off with zig-zag pine fences, stood fuzzy with varieties of hay.

Though he had never *exactly* aspired to being a real farmer, Mr Matthew Livesey knew just enough of the new, scientific ideas about rotational agriculture to be impressed, as he leaned his head out from his side of the coach, ducked and peered across Constable Swann to see out the other side to take it all in. Had he not been a fool, had he not gone gallivanting off with the militia to lose his leg, *this* was what he might have hoped his lost acres to become . . . somehow. *Perhaps at Samuel's hand?* Livesey enviously thought, *am I wrong to press him into following my trade? For which, he's sometimes so inapt?*

He sat back on the bench seat, flushed with the heat, and with a guilty idea that his pride was in the way of clearer thinking. Did Pride, indeed, "goeth before a fall," would Livesey & Son go under with Samuel at the helm, or should he face the sad reality, take a partner who was knackier at business . . . ? He firmly pushed that thought away, saving it for later cogitation and forcing himself back to the matter at hand.

Mr Marsden had been leaning out his own window of the fine coach, and suddenly thumped his cane on the roof as he hauled himself to the door and opened it to lean out, waving his cane horizontally to summon someone. "Here, boy! Whoa up a minute," he ordered.

A Negro in pantaloon-like trousers and loose, sleeveless shirt astride a saddle horse appeared alongside the coach on Marsden's side, leading a second saddled horse by the reins. "Yassuh?" he shyly said, quickly doffing a ragged straw hat.

"Where ye goin' with that horse, boy?" Marsden asked.

"Takin' 'im back t'Mistah Taneyhill's Liv'ry fo' de massah, suh."

"Yer master rented a horse in town last night, did he?" Marsden further enquired, sharing a brief glare of certitude with Livesey and Constable Swann.

"Uh, yassuh," the young stableman replied.

"Come home late? When, d'ye know?" Swann spoke up.

"An hour'r two 'fo' sunup, Massuh Thom did, yassuh."

"Roused ye out, hey?" Marsden asked with a cheerful tone.

"Ah, yassuh, I sleep in ober de stables, suh," the lad answered, put at his ease by Marsden's sunny, teasing enquiry, and perking up a tad from a slave's customary wary deference.

"An' Mr Thom's to home, do we call on him?"

"Uh, yassuh, bot' de massuhs be up t'de house, umhmm."

"Well, that's mighty fine, then," Marsden said, sounding happy, if only for the lad's benefit. "Get along t'town, 'fore it gets too hot on ye." Marsden leaned back and shut the coach door as the slave clucked his tongue, shook reins and tapped his bare heels along his mount's flanks to continue his journey at a sedate, time-eating gait that might give him a whole afternoon of at least *seeming* freedom.

"Shouldn't we have asked him how Lakey acted, or . . . ?" Livesey dared to suggest, as their coach got into motion again, as well.

"Wouldn't o' known much more'n he did, Mr Livesey," the magistrate easily dismissed, working his mouth in what looked to be a fretful grimace of distaste. "Gettin' dirt on their masters from th' Negroes is worse'un pullin' back teeth, lest they get flogged t'death for talkin' . . . or knowin' too much. Mind now . . . keep mum an' glum, like I bade ye, just nod and grump a little, an' let me direct things 'til I tell ye. Keep that bundle hid 'til I call for it. Constable, ye stand ready in th' background, too, 'long with Captain Buckles, here."

"Yessir," Swann mumbled, looking ill-at-ease with his tiny role, and mopping his face with a florid-printed calico handkerchief.

Their coach squeaked and jingled as it turned into the circular drive about a decorative round garden in front of the house's elegant stairs, at last. Livesey was again impressed, even a tad envious, to see what Thomas Lakey had wrung from the wilderness in so few years.

The Lodge was a two-story house of white-painted wood outside, raised off the damp ground and the threat of storm flooding on massive ballast-stone or "tabby" pillars, elevated about shoulder high on the average man, and the gaps between the pillars screened with latticed slatting and home-made brick. The whole house was fronted by a deep veranda or gallery that spanned its entire width, with a brick-fronted landing that bore two sets of stairs before it, with another, wider set of stairs leading to the veranda itself. Round, smooth-milled columns held up a smaller, covered veranda on the upper floor. Live oaks stood all about the house proper, shading it from all weathers, with lush gardens to either hand and out back, giving separation from slave quarters, cooking shed, smokehouse, stables and barns. Massive trees had been left in place, girded by white wood benches and sitting areas, with brick or oyster-shell walks leading to them, and the lawns under those shade trees were so neatly kept that the whole resembled a parkland of a great and titled English lord.

Andrew Hewlett was sitting on the first floor veranda, with a book and slate in hand over some studies. As they departed the coach he got to his feet, beaming in pleasure, and only a slight bit of confusion, dressed in a loose, ruffled shirt tucked into fawn breeches, and a pair of everyday white cotton stockings. He fumbled teenaged-awkward with his toes to put his old buckled shoes back on as they came up the two-stage stairs.

"Mr Livesey, I thought you were coming tomorrow!" Andrew declared. "What brings you today, sir? Did ah . . . is Bess with you?"

"No, she's . . ." Livesey replied, feeling almost pained.

"What is . . . ?" young Andrew pressed, flustered to see the pair of redcoats clamber down from the postillion seats behind the coach, their sheathed hangers and bayonets and Brown Bess muskets clinking, to see the stranger—Captain Buckles of the 16th Foot—the constable and the magistrate all together . . . He made but perfunctory answers to the somber introductions.

"Something the matter, Mr Marsden?" Andrew asked, peering from face to face as if he might divine the cause for their presence.

Such a good, gentle lad, Livesey sorrowfully thought, unable to look Andrew Hewlett in the eyes. Within minutes, did things take the turn they all now suspected, they might have to arrest his uncle, his guardian and practically his only living kin.

"Got bus'ness with yer uncle, Andrew," Mr Marsden said gruffly, getting to the meat of the matter, as he cut himself off a small chew of tobacco. "He to th' house?"

"On a brief ride, sir, but . . . what sort of business, if I may ask?" Andrew Hewlett dared demand, shifting from one foot to the next.

They didn't have to answer that question for Thomas Lakey came round the corner of the house, mounted on a coffee-brown mare of fine conformation and proud, young, high-stepping gait. When he got to the corner of the house, Lakey drew rein, and Mr Livesey was *certain* he would put spurs to her and bolt, yet . . . Thomas Lakey merely gave them all a wry smile, then kneed her back into a walk. A Negro groom came to take her reins as Lakey dismounted, and lead her to the stables.

"Mr Marsden, sir," Mr Lakey said once he'd attained the veranda's coolness and shade, slapping a weathered tricorne on his thigh before being relieved of it, and his riding crop, by one liveried servant, and presented with a cool, wet towel by a female servant, which he used to carefully, genteelly dab at his neck, face, brow and wrists. "Constable Swann . . . Mr Livesey. An' you must be Captain Buckles from down by Brunswick Town, I s'pose. Must've had a warm drive out here. Seat yourselves, an' I'll send for refreshments. An' you can tell me what brings ya out here on such a humid day," he invited as he took a sprawling seat in a big rocking chair, swinging a booted leg over one arm as if he hadn't a care in the world.

"Got some bus'ness with ye, Thom," the magistrate graveled. "We speak private, may we?" he added, with a jerk of his head towards Andrew Hewlett. Marsden used none of the usual Low Country Carolina social amenities, no joshing, no prefatory pleasantries or any round-about inconsequentials that Livesey, frankly, had found maddening those first couple of years after moving to Wilmington, before learning to adapt.

"Well, o' course, gentlemen," Lakey said with a hospitable grin and a spread of his arms as if in welcome. "Andrew, you go on into th' house, now. You can finish your studies in th' parlor, or on th' back porch, if that's cooler."

"Uncle Thom, is there something . . . ?" Andrew uneasily fretted as he all but wrung his hands.

"Go on in th' house, Andrew, hear me?" Lakey said more sternly.

"Yessir."

"Now," Mr Lakey genially asked, once his nephew had obeyed him and had slunk into the house's dim interior, "what is it that plagues y'all . . . Mr Marsden?"

The magistrate finally took a chair for himself, prompting the rest of them to sort themselves out on padded benches or spindly cane chairs, Captain Buckles and Constable Swann wedging themselves side-by-side on a short slat settee more suited to a single lady and her wide skirts.

"Got a few questions t'put to ye, Thomas," Marsden slowly began. "No call t'drag this out longer'n it should take. We *know,*" Marsden baldly announced, peering at Mr Lakey intently and waiting for a sign of upset. "Just about ev'ry li'l bit of it . . . 'ceptin' fer th' why."

If Mr Marsden had hoped to ruffle Thom Lakey's calm demeanor, he was badly let down, for Mr Lakey only cocked his head and raised a brow, with the tiniest bit of clueless but polite smile on his face. A bemused robin listening for a worm, Livesey thought of him.

"Ya know what, an' th' *why* o' what, sir?" Lakey said, seemingly at a loss, but willing to indulge the older man.

"That ye murdered Harry Tresmayne, Thomas," Marsden gravely accused, hands folded over the handle of his cane between his legs. "All about Harry an' Anne Moore havin' at each other, an' ye knowin' all o' their doin's, too. Knew their secret signals . . . lace or ribbons, off a dress o' hers. One ye got th' ribbon off of, so ye could send that last bouquet that got Harry out where he was killed. An' we know how ye set a fire at Mr Livesey's house last night, tryin' to scare him off when th' gown got retrieved."

"Your *honor!*" Lakey replied with a genteel shudder, almost giggling in surprise at the outlandishness of it all. "I surely *don't* know what in th' *world* you're *talkin'* about, sir!" he went on in one of those soft, quavery and high-pitched voices, with his vowels slurred, that Livesey had come to recognize as a Carolinian's way of being excruciatingly polite; the syrupy sort of façade that cloaked outrage, anger, fear or nerves—the sort of sing-song that usually preceded an invitation to a duel, or a fist-fight, once a man's honor was touched.

"B'lieve th' sun's got to you t'day, Mr Marsden, I sure do." Lakey smirked, plucking at his shirt ruffles and shooting his cuffs. "You sound badly in need o' somethin' cold an' wet. Some wine I've had chillin' down in th' springhouse, and we've some Massachusetts ice in the root cellar . . ."

"Oh, don't play genteel, Thomas. We *know,* I tell ye," Marsden insisted. "Ye can't weasel out. Can't put it off on Eachan MacDougall or Osgoode Moore, nor no one else. Y'always did think yerself so damn clever, an' I'll allow ye are, most times . . . but ye slipped up, Thom. Didn't watch close enough, ye o' all people, who us'lly watches things so close, takes such a keen int'rest in others' doin's, so yer gossip's juicier than others'."

"I'll ring for that wine," Mr Lakey announced, regarding Mr Marsden with a faint look of alarm, as if his supper guests had begun to rend their clothes and talk in tongues. He picked up a tiny china bell on a side table and summoned a servant.

"Mr Swann, I'd admire did ye fetch us that bundle outta th' coach, sir," Marsden directed, forcing the heavily perspiring Constable to heave himself out of the bench settee and plod down the flights of stairs; Captain Buckles shifted enough to preclude Swann's return alongside him, looking relieved, and just as sweaty and florid.

An older Negro servant came to the veranda from the house, slowly shuffling his slippered feet, to stand by Lakey's rocking chair.

"Lijah, we'll have two bottles of th' Rhenish from th' springhouse," Mr Lakey instructed, paying no attention to Swann's plodding down, then back up, the stairs. "Slivers o' ice with it, an' enough glasses for all. *Sure* you'll have none, Mr Marsden? None either, Mr Livesey, tsk tsk? I *know* Swann'll wish some, an' Captain . . . ?"

"Buckles," the Army officer pointedly reminded him.

"My pardons, sir. A glass for Captain Buckles, too. Go along, then, Lijah," Lakey directed.

"Yassuh."

Constable Swann regained the expansive porch, puffing a little. He offered the bundle to the magistrate, but that worthy grimaced, gave a sign with a finger lifted off his cane handle, and Swann dumped the bundle on the painted boards, pulling the sailcloth from beneath the contents, and using a toe to spread the gown out for better viewing.

"That's th' gown Anne Moore threw away last night," Mr Marsden grimly intoned. "Th' one ye saw Jemmy Bowlegs filch from her garbage barrel. Ye talked t'Anne last night, saw how distressed she was that Mr Livesey's daughter'd been pressin' her 'bout it. But ye knew all about it long ago. That bouquet of oleander blossoms is what ye sent t'Harry th' night ye killed him. Used ribbon 'stead o' lace for bows, 'cause ye'd already figured out that lace'd mean t'meet at that abandoned cabin on *your* land, an' ye couldn't have any o' that, an' ribbons meant a deer glade off th' Masonborough Road. *Two* bows, tied nice an' neat, meanin' ev'nin', not mornin' . . . so there'd be no witnesses. Ye see what I mean, Thomas?"

"I really don't understand a word you've said, Mr Marsden," Lakey said back, faintly chuckling and shaking his head in confusion.

Matthew Livesey had been holding his breath and peering at Mr Lakey closely to see what his reaction would be, and he let his wind flow out in a rush and took a fresh breath at last when he witnessed Lakey's face betray him. The man's mouth pinched, only the slightest, but it *did,* as two faint spots of color arose on his cheeks, even as his "genteelly" suntanned flesh transformed to the color and texture of a virginal piece of parchment. His eyes, *yes,* his *eyes!* A pained squint—part of his studied dissembling, perhaps—but he could not avoid his eyes from shifting, his lashes from too-rapid blinking!

We've got him! Livesey silently exulted to himself. *And who'd have ever guessed in a thousand years!*

In a bit of impeccably bad timing, Elijah, the old house servant, returned with a silver tray, on which rested a chilled bottle of white wine and three glasses, and Livesey imagined he could hear Mr Marsden's remaining teeth grind in fury as the old man took his own sweet time to pour the wine, dropping a sliver of ice in each glass, and damned if glasses given to Captain Buckles and Constable Swann weren't readily accepted, the old man shuffling between Livesey and Marsden!

"It was you," Livesey blurted, just as soon as Elijah's backside was through the doors, "who started those rumors about Harry crossing the Brunswick to call on a fetching girl. You told them to my girl, Bess, even if you did swear you put no credence in them, and that she wasn't to, either. But as we all know, that's the *best* way to assure that they're believed—and spread. You thought to make people think it was Biddy MacDougall Harry was spooning, 'cause everyone would suspect her father, Eachan, who's a reputation for violence and a past killing. After all, Biddy *made* that gown, there, and you knew that as soon as it was finished, a whole year ago, Mr Lakey!"

"But I *didn't* put any credence in . . ." Lakey attempted to pooh-pooh, turning to face Livesey with a top-lofty condescension.

"You started the rumor of Anne Moore seeing someone, too," Livesey quickly added, hoping to regain that rattled look on the man's patrician face, "'cause you'd *seen* them at . . . clicket . . . you knew *that* rumor was true. Did you plan to taint Osgoode with the murder of his best friend and mentor, if Eachan MacDougall wouldn't wash?"

"Aye!" Mr Marsden harumphed from Lakey's other side, regaining his own thread of thought. "But ye know somethin' Thomas? All of yer skills at watchin' folks, an' ye still slipped up. Ye were so busy at yer plottin' an' schemin', ye plumb forgot to keep an eye on Osgoode! Know where he was that night, Thomas . . . th' night ye killed Harry?"

"This game's gettin' boresome, your honor," Lakey responded with a weary sigh, "but I'll play up. Where *was* Osgoode, th' night *someone* murdered good old Harry?"

"'Cross th' Brunswick his own self, Thom." Marsden cackled with glee to relate it. "In Eachan MacDougall's hayloft, with Biddy! Can ye beat that? Both prime suspects spoken fer, an' ye th' only busybody in' th' middle of it all remainin'."

"I see," Lakey said, with a severe expression. To Livesey, it sounded as if Lakey had been gut-punched, though. He took some time at his wine, taking several small sips, his eyes shut as if savoring it.

"Always callin' on Anne, right in her bedchamber," Mr Marsden went on, looking more at ease, even a trifle amused. "Ye knew o' that gown, an' had easy access to it. Did Anne ever *confide* in ye, Thomas? Swear ye t'silence 'bout her affair with Harry? What'd Harry ever do to ye that set yer mind t'killin' him?"

Lakey only glared at the magistrate, his eyes now frosted. Mr Marsden got to his feet and went to the veranda railings to squit a dollop of tobacco juice into a bed of azaleas and dwarf magnolias.

"Might as well 'fess up, Thomas," Marsden snapped. "Dammit, be a man! For we ain't leavin' without ye."

"Harry," Lakey said at last, pursing his lips after a sip from his wineglass, as if the Rhenish was too sweet, or had an acid finish. He looked at Marsden, contemplatively, for a moment, then let his gaze wander past them all, as if did he ignore them, they would all go away. He looked out at his rich, productive fields, his elegant gardens, as if to fix them in his memory.

"Why did you do it, Mr Lakey?" Livesey impatiently demanded at last. "Harry was your *friend,* your partner in your faction for the betterment of *all* small holders and common folk. *Why,* for the love of God?"

"For the love o' God," Lakey mused, shaking his head as if the idea was mildly amusing. "Well, perhaps that, in th' end."

"Ye confess to it?" Marsden snapped, pouncing on his statement.

Lakey looked up with a sickly, quirky smile flitting over his face, then, amazingly, gave them all a slow, grave nod of confirmation.

"Why?" Livesey exclaimed.

"You asked what Harry ever did t'me, Mr Marsden?" Mr Lakey answered, with a sadly amused pout. "He slowly, bit by bit, took my life from me, ruined or stole th' best parts of it . . . turned rotten everything he ever touched! Would've gone *on* taintin', spoilin' an' stealin' until somebody put a stop to it.

"So, yes, Livesey." Lakey nearly smirked as he turned to face him, lowering his cocked booted leg to the floor at last, as he said, "At th' last, perhaps puttin' a stop to him *was* for th' love o' God."

"*How* did he . . . ?" Livesey indignantly spat. No matter what he had learned since Harry's death to diminish his respect for him, yet he could not accept such a vile calumny on his friend's memory.

"His first wife, Priscilla," Lakey calmly stated, pouring his wineglass full again with a prissy exactness, even to the way he set the bottle back onto the coin-silver serving tray and snowy napkin. "A lovely, *decent* young lady. Finest, sweetest girl who ever drew a breath. Priscilla was my first cousin, if you recall, an' when I came t' th' Cape Fear as a lad, she became as dear as a sister to me. I was a touch leery when she fell for Harry, but we all hoped he'd mended his ways . . . sewn his wild oats an' was ready to settle down. Had my reservations, but Priscilla was so over the moon for him, an' Harry could be so *damned* charmin' an' play-act upright, that I put my fears aside. B'sides, what did *I* know, a 'Johnny Newcome' up from Charleston, damn near an orphan. Harry had us all fooled, an' still does.

"Before I saw what a rapacious, two-faced, lyin', cheatin' . . . *brute* he was!" Lakey spat, exercised at last. "Priscilla was *closer* t'me than *real* kin, an' my dearest *friend.* And I had t'watch her go down, little by little, as Harry cheated on her, an' broke her sweet heart, year after year. Twelve years, it took him, 'til she couldn't stand any more, an' turned her head t' th' wall an' died. I watched it happen. An' I'm *good* at watchin', you know, hah!"

"Good God!" Mr Marsden spat in disgust.

"Priscilla sick an' on her deathbed, an' Harry could *play* th' grievin', faithful husband. But he still whored as hot as ever. New Bern, Brunswick, Duplin, Rocky Mount? An' goin' through the servant girls when he couldn't get away. Shoulda killed him, then, spared us *all* from his vileness," he said, slugging back his wine.

Captain Buckles sat wide-eyed in sick amazement, rapt upon the tale, though, whilst the others queasily listened, squirming in embarrassment, never knowing 'til now, only suspecting . . .

"He ran off to th' fightin' after she died," Lakey sourly went on. "I prayed he'd stop a musket ball. Wished him bad *cess,* as the Irish say, an' hoped his *corpse* would stay north o' here, but . . . like all bad pennies, he turned back up, a *hero,* for God's sake! Th' Devil looks after his own . . . gives 'em th' devil's luck. Hah! At least, I thought th' Good Lord'd get him poxed, an' his plow would rot off him . . . all those camp followers an' Army whores I heard of? No luck there, either, an' more's th' pity. Then, he up an' marries Georgina!"

"And you had hopes yourself with her, is that what you say?" Livesey softly intruded. "Didn't you call upon her before—"

"That was *near* th' last robbery, Livesey," Lakey snapped, "But faction came before. Christ, you want a confession? Shut up an' give heed t'me!"

"The faction?" Livesey interrupted, too surprised to be daunted. "I thought . . . Harry always told me *he'd* begun the faction, because of how we were treated by the British up north."

"It was *my* doin', *my* correspondin', never Harry's!" Lakey sneered. "Even if I would alienate myself from lifelong friends an' neighbors who held t' th' King, an' their power . . . th' old Goose Creek an' first-come settlers. Never *was* in their graces, no matter how much I made o' myself, nor how wealthy I got. Have t'be circumspect if you want t'preach great changes in old ways o' doin' things, don't you know. Harry was ruttin' like a bull with th' militia, it was *me* who wrote to th' leadin' men I read about in ev'ry colony who thought we could run our own affairs better than London, or any Royal governor-general they send us. Start our *own* Parliament, each colony sovereign, like a small *country* . . . mark my words, gentlemen, it's comin', ye'll see it in yer own lifetimes."

"Never *heard* th' like!" Captain Buckles grumbled. "What rot!"

Lakey withered Buckles with the sort of smile one bestows upon a blithering idiot child.

"Brought Osgoode an' a few younger men in 'bout '57 or '58, an' let their enthusiasm run free," Lakey chuckled. "Less t'lose, those. Th' young're *supposed* t'kick at th' traces. Well-connected young men. *Long* before Harry. Oh, he dabbled, 'round th' edges. Came back from th' fightin' an even grander figure than before . . . a hero! I thought he'd be useful. Useful! Thought t'use him, an' he sparkles so bright like he always does, next thing I know I'm scribblin' *his* words, doin' *his* errands. Just th' secretary," Lakey gloomed.

"So Harry had to go, if you wished to reclaim the leadership?" Livesey muttered. "But you wished to keep arm's distance of upsetting the barons. You didn't wish to be ostracized by your fellow—"

"'Fore I saw how widespread was th' sentiment for change," Mr Lakey allowed with a shrug and a wry cock of his head in Livesey's direction. "Expandin' th' franchise to small holders, shopkeepers an' th' sober laborin' folk. An' more'n a few rich men catchin' th' fever, as well. Harnetts, Howes, even Ashes an' Waddells? Osgoode, at least he had his heart an' soul in it . . . not like that . . . *that* sportin' bastard!"

Lakey turned in his wide chair, leaning on the arm closest between them to put his face closer to Livesey's. "'Twas just a game for Harry. Reason t'be th' center of attention. Cause t'give him a crowd t'lead. He'da led a pack o' chipmunks if they chattered loud enough . . . an' fed him th' best o' their nuts!"

"Still, Osgoode and the other younger men, they'd take over if Harry was gone," Livesey grumbled, his blood chilling to be seated by the man who'd murdered his longtime friend, and was now crowing about it! "How would you think to regain control, if . . . oh! The ribbons and lace. You *could* have carried the bouquet home to dispose of it, with no one ever the wiser, but you didn't. You threw them away where they *must* be found, sooner or later! So people would learn that Anne was sporting with Harry, and Osgoode did it! With Osgoode gone, with the faction disrupted, *you'd* be the one to put it back together again! How *very* clever of you!"

Thomas Lakey bestowed upon him a sly grin, almost the sort that a clever schoolboy would evince when relishing a witty exploit against a rival.

"Why not just leave them on Harry's doorstoop?" Livesey asked.

"An' be taken for a mourning offering? No," Lakey pooh-poohed. "For a bit, I thought I'd have t'move 'em somewhere more easily found, or pretend to've discovered 'em myself. By his body would've been th' best, an' I *did* think o' goin' back out there an' movin' em, but after his corpse was found, it was too late. Thank you, though, Livesey . . . for takin' that damned Jemmy Bowlegs out there. I knew *Swann* was too hen-headed t'even bother t'look. So you did me a favor . . . for a time. Too bad yer girl an' you got so nosy."

"And last night," Livesey asked, getting angry again. "Why did you stay in town? Visit Anne? Try to murder me and mine?"

"Bess an' Jemmy Bowlegs, whisperin' an' schemin' together, an' Andrew in a pet over not bein' th' center of her attention. Once we'd said our good-byes, I strolled past that alley an' saw Bowlegs at the trash, an' that Cuffy an' his cart out front, not sellin' much, no matter how he cried his wares," Lakey related, almost casually serene, even going so far as to wave the wine bottle in Livesey's direction with a quizzical lift of his brows as if to tempt him to partake. "No? Oh, well . . . More for me, then."

"Eachan and Biddy. Were they your first choice?" Livesey spat.

"Well, they'da served main-well, wouldn't they have?" Mr Lakey chuckled. "She who made th' gown, Eachan an' his bad repute, rest o' th' ribbon an' gray lace still out at her place . . . That surprise you, sirs? And doesn't a man have a right t'new shirts an' waistcoats for himself? Saw her in town one Saturday, knew she'd be taken for just th' sort o' bait for Harry. Rode out there, once—comin' back from Brunswick an' th' cape, th' back way to MacDougall when he was workin' th' ferry—an' ordered some things. Suggested gray lace an' royal blue ribbon for a hat, an' got t'see her supplies, since I'd already known where Anne got her gown made an' how she was usin' it.

"I even *praised* her to Harry, don't you know," Thomas Lakey said with a pleased little sniff. "Damme, that would a been toppin'-fine if he'd risked it . . . an' Eachan MacDougall'd done for him. Can't fathom why Harry *didn't* try her on, but he didn't, more's th' pity, 'cause I was set t'tip MacDougall th' news soon as Harry'd bit. Saved us all a power o' fuss, that. Either way, slap-dash as justice is done here abouts, ya *almost* thought he did it, for a time, hey?" Lakey laughed.

"But for Osgoode's own affair," Marsden pointed out.

"Aye, an' damned if I thought he had it in him!" Lakey hooted. "Osgoode's a *dry* stick, prim as a parson, an' too educated for his own good, he is. Nice-enough fella, but I can't imagine him attractin' a bed-some young chit like Biddy MacDougall . . . impressionable though she be. Too, ah . . . conventional when it comes to *amour.* Too honest, an' upright t'fall off th' wagon, d'you get my meanin'."

"What d'ye mean, Thom? Ye sayin' his wife, Anne, told tales to ye 'bout their . . . ?" Marsden asked, goggling in disbelief.

"Well, Anne an' I *did* come from a better set," Lakey lazily informed them, even daring to wink at the magistrate, to Marsden's utter revulsion. "A faster, sportin' set."

"Ye always were an arrogant, simperin' bastard, Thomas!" Mr Marsden accused. "Amusin', in yer own way, but . . . You an' Anne, are ye sayin'? Did Harry steal *her* from ye, too?"

"We, ah . . ." Lakey reddened in anger. "A time or two, before Harry came back from th' militia," he confessed, actually looking out of sorts for a change. "Only as sport!" he suddenly insisted, as if that excused it, or salved his reputation. "Up in New Bern, when she met Osgoode . . . after. Never could trust that sort o' baggage out o' sight, but she was pleasurable. Anne found out there's poor Moores an' rich, powerful Moores, an' she'd saddled th' wrong color o' horse. Well . . . call it consolation. Mutual consolation."

"'Cause you'd had hopes of marrying Georgina," Livesey quickly inferred. "Hah! You told Bess you'd once tried to court her. With your lands and hers so close together, and combined, you'd have been a *real* power."

"Aye . . . Georgina, too, damn Harry's blood," Lakey admitted as he squirmed on his chair, crossing his legs and pouring more wine, the last of the bottle.

"Georgina . . . a woman so sensible and charming," Livesey said in the appalled silence that Lakey had made. "Younger than Harry . . . closer to your age. How could a woman so bright not see the sense of a match with you?" Each statement drew a faint nod of agreement from Lakey, as if they were discussing the weather, not this bizarre insanity. "But she chose Harry. By God, sir . . . did you *mean* to cause her grief for her . . . *mistake?*"

"I did nothin' o' th' sort, Livesey, an' I resent you characterizin' it so!" Lakey growled, as if he would, given different circumstances, leap to his feet and challenge him to a duel with a slap on Livesey's face. As if he had time to face him over a pistol, in the shade of a dueling oak!

"Ye're as big a rogue as Harry, damn yer eyes," Marsden growled. "As big a whoremonger, if Anne an' ye were knockin' knees t'gether even after she an' Osgoode wed. Were ye jealous o' her, too?"

"That cow!" Lakey scoffed. "Good for tuppin', that's all she's worth. Th' mornin' I rode down t'that turfed-out tenant's cabin, an' saw 'em goin' at it . . . I coulda been miffed, but it s'prised even me I wasn't. That gown, right there. What she wore, th' first time. Oh, in weak moments I'd considered takin' her on, but . . . Anne's th' sort who'd cheat on Jesus, an' I didn't really need th' grief. No, it was *Harry* I despised, that moment. Even more than I thought I could! An' I do thank God there's no *more* Tresmaynes t'do away with. Harry's kind vastly outnumber my sort, you know, an' oh! but th' ladies do love 'em!"

Thomas Lakey drained his wineglass and regarded the empty bottle—perhaps even thought of ringing for another—with a petulant expression on his face. "Thank God, too, he cornered th' lambskin cundum market. Prob'ly kept it profitable all by himself! I doubt Harry even wanted children . . . his kind can't *stand* t'be outshone. Couldn't take th' competition, hah!"

"He couldn't," Livesey blurted out without thinking. "He was barren. Couldn't sire. Anne Moore told us that. It must explain why he strayed so far afield, as it were. Hah!" Livesey cried as well, as he saw the startled look spring up on Lakey's face. "D'ye mean, sir, she never confided *that* to you? That's why she preferred him, 'cause there was no need for clumsy appliances, no risk!"

Lakey looked appalled, seeing the reason why Anne Moore hadn't taken him too seriously, perhaps had used *him,* for *entree* into Wilmington Society. Then he, inexplicably, began to laugh.

"Mean t'say he was only firin' blank charges? Oh, how grand!" Lakey guffawed. "Th' big, bad, swaggerin' lout! A sham at ev'rythin' in life, an' nothin' but a facade in th' end! Oh, thankee, Mr Livesey, for such a marvelous revelation. God is, indeed, just!"

"Sorry I pleased you . . . sir!" Livesey growled back.

"So ye killed him, Thomas," Marsden demanded, having heard more than he could stomach. "Fancied up a match of Anne's nosegays, then sent 'em to him? Left 'em where he could find 'em, or what?"

"Yes, tied t'his townhouse gate-post, where he was sure t'see 'em," Lakey confessed.

"Waited for him out there in th' woods, knew he'd come ridin' in on that trail, an' shot him down like a dog," Marsden prompted.

"Pretty-much like that, aye," Lakey muttered, looking outwards on his acres, again, gaze almost unfocused, as if weary of his guests and their questions.

"Set my fire . . . wrote that threatening note," Livesey added. "Called us 'Newcomes.'"

"You woke up when I broke th' window with th' stone. You didn't *die.* Only meant t'warn ya off," Lakey said with a shrug. "I saw that Bowlegs creature take it to you. Told you I'm a good watcher, an' him never suspectin' he'd been followed. Not as good as he thinks he is, Bowlegs."

"Christ!" Marsden exclaimed. "*That* does it! Good enough for y'all, Constable . . . ? Captain Buckles . . . Mr Livesey? Do yer duty, Swann."

"Mr Thomas Lakey," the constable formally cried, hitching up his stomach and tugging down his waistcoat as he lumbered up from leaning on the veranda railings. "I arrest ya for th' murder of—"

"You'll surely give a gentleman time t'dress for th' occasion," Lakey brusquely interrupted, looking at Swann's official demeanor like he was watching a trained bear dance. He rang his little bell to summon a servant. "Mr Marsden? I'll not go in my shirtsleeves. Hmm?"

"Don't be too long, Thom," the magistrate said after a moment, nodding gravely in the affirmative. "Don't make us come up for ye."

"No need. Ah, Lijah!" Lakey brightly said, rising to his feet. "Took your own sweet time, you slow-coach. I'll be goin' into town with these gentlemen. Please lay out my new burgundy suit, with th' white silk stockin's an' th' sprigged waistcoat. Fresh shirt an' stock an' all. You know my wants."

"Yassuh," the old servant replied, looking concerned.

Lakey pursed his lips in a *moue* and stretched his arms, going to the edge of his veranda to sniff the wind and peer eastwards. "I do b'lieve it's gonna come a good rain 'fore sundown. Don't want to get you gentlemen soaked on my account. You will excuse me, sirs? I won't be but a few minutes."

He bowed from the waist, made the slightest "leg" in departure, then turned and went into the house, and they could hear him *trotting* up the handsome staircase to the upper floor, as if they had invited him to a horse race or a cockfight, not a set of chains.

Swann sat down and fanned himself with his hat, looking miserable and cutty-eyed. Captain Buckles placed his hands in the small of his back and paced about, mostly looking at the glossy toes of his new top-boots. Mr Marsden screwed his mouth into a lopsided grimace and stumped to the edge of the veranda, taking off his hat and wiping its leather band with a handkerchief; he spat out his old quid, and took the tobacco plug from his pocket, thought of cutting himself fresh but decided not to. He drew out his watch and looked at it, instead.

"Uhm . . . shouldn't we post Captain Buckles's soldiers out back?" Livesey at last proposed. "I know he's a gentleman, but . . ." He had a horrid picture in his mind of Lakey fleeing for the western wildernesses with a handy traveling bag of coin. "Might he be tempted . . . ?"

"No need," Mr Marsden somberly told him, putting his pocket watch away. "Thomas'll do th' right thing."

"He's an arsonist and a murderer, sir," Livesey objected. "If he can do those things, perhaps . . ."

"Be *easy,* Mr Livesey," Marsden soothingly said, studying on the coming weather for himself, rocking on the balls of his feet, both hands clasped behind him, one flexing upon the other. "Bide but a bit, an' we'll be on our way."

Matthew Livesey felt a rising unease, as if suspecting they'd all agreed, these Carolinians whose nature and inflexible sense of honor sometimes seemed so alien to him, to *allow* Lakey to flee, sparing everyone involved and both factions the embarrassment.

"I don't see . . ." he began.

Buh-Blam!

Muffled. Above them. Lightning-stark and sudden!

"What?" Livesey yelped, ready to bolt inside the house, before languid, old Mr Marsden almost sprinted to his side to block his way.

"Thomas knew his goose was cooked, soon as he saw us coachin' up his drive, Mr Livesey," Marsden carefully, patiently, explained, waving one arm to steer Livesey back onto the veranda.

"You *knew* he'd shoot himself? *If* he did, and it isn't a *sham.*"

"No sham, Mr Livesey," Marsden almost sorrowfully assured him, "an' aye, I did. Captain Buckles, ye're experienced with wounds. I'd much admire did ye go above-stairs an' see t'things?"

"Of course, sir," the Army officer replied, sounding more relieved than shocked, as if he'd known what action Thom Lakey would take, as well. He doffed his hat and began to walk inside.

"I'd imagine ye'll discover a double-barreled coachin' gun," Mr Marsden added. "We'll need that fer evidence in town. Did ye fetch it down, I'd be more'n grateful."

"You let it happen, sir?" Livesey gasped, awestruck.

"Well o' course I did, Mr Livesey," Marsden confessed. "We had him dead t'rights, an' Thomas knew it. God above, man! There's no way he'd ever stood th' shame of a *trial!* He could go t'town in irons did he resist, under close escort an' paraded fer all t'see did he go at all . . . or he could go a gentleman with bottom. He won't be church-buried . . . couldn't o' been as a murderer *or* a suicide, but dyin', he can be put under th' ground on his own acres 'stead of unmarked in a crossroad."

"Dressed in his best finery," Livesey dazedly realized aloud.

"All of it his choice," Marsden intoned. "The crimes, his way o' goin', an' his newest suitin', yes. Recall what I said this mornin', sir?"

"Uhm . . . concerning what, sir?" Livesey had to ask, too shaken to think clearly, or recall much of anything. The magistrate, sensing his shock, gently led him to the edge of the veranda, where a puff or two of much cooler air could revive him from his pallor.

"About crimes o' passion, Mr Livesey." Marsden came near to chuckling. "That, long after th' foul deed's done, th' hot blood that caused it—th' passions—are never completely spent? Thom, though . . . once we got t'pressin' him close—for yer fine assistance in such regard I truly thankee, Livesey, for ye're a knacky sort!—I saw that pore ol' Thomas wasn't just quenched for a spell, he was *utterly* cooled off. Cold an' empty as that spent bottle o' wine yonder. He *saw* that he was finished. Onliest reason he answered all our queries, an' told us so much, wasn't *boastin'* on his part. He just wanted things explained, laid out an' done for good, so there'd be no need for him t'be shamed an' cussed in a court o' law like a piney-woods *no-tooth!* It'd have hurt his pride, d'ye see," Marsden said, almost attaining to a soft laugh. "Clever feller like Thomas Lakey, humiliated that he'd been caught-out so easy after layin' such a grand scheme? Pshaw!"

"But what of Justice being done, sir? Surely . . ."

"T'my lights, it just *was,*" Marsden declared. He held out the wide wings of his coat's skirts to cup a cooling breeze off the Sounds, as trees and the standing crops began to stir, and the harsh sunlight was dimmed by darker, taller cloud heads. "We can't do much tomorrow, a Sunday, but . . . day after next, I'll convene a very public inquest, have ye, Swann an' Captain Buckles testify. Save th' damn flowers an' gown 'til then. Might even have Anne Moore in th' dock an' force her shameful doin's to be known."

"Lay grounds for Osgoode to divorce her, you intend, sir. Hah!" Livesey said, seeing the need, and gaining new respect and admiration for the cagey old fellow.

"Exactly what I mean t'do, sir, an' Osgoode's a damn fool does he not make *hot* haste o' th' doin'," Marsden almost cackled in answer. "Biddy'll be *showin'* soon, an' 'tis best th' thing's done so they can wed *b'fore,* not after. *What,* sir? Did ye not notice? Yer dear wife never gave ye this broad hint?"

Marsden hooted, stroking his hand down his own little gotch-gut. "Some husband *ye* were! An', the Cape Fear is shot of Anne Moore. She'll never show *her* lyin' face in these parts, again, an' good riddance t'bad rubbish. Altogether, don't ye conclude we're doin' Justice main-well, Mr Livesey?"

"I, ah . . . indeed imagine that we are, Mr Marsden!" Livesey agreed, after he'd gotten over his shock at *that* news. "Though . . . none of it bodes well for Harry's—now Osgoode's—faction. Nor for his law prospects."

"Well, th' levellin' faction'll have t'lay low an' sing small, fer a piece," the wily older man said with a shrug as he took off his lace-trimmed tricorne to air out his scalp, too. "The powers-that-be in th' colony will trundle along as they've always done, fer a spell. Mind now, Livesey, things *will* change. Sooner or later, all that poor Harry an' Osgoode . . . an' Thom Lakey, God rest his soul . . . worked for *will* come about. Oh, we *call* ourselves Englishmen, but sooner or later we *must* have more rights t'rule ourselves, an' not stand hat-in-hand on word from London. *Or* th' sorry pack o' governors they send us."

"You really think so, sir?" Livesey marvelled.

"I'd not wish ye t'come away from all this thinkin' what I did was me bein' King *Roger* Moore's cat's-paw. I'm not th' *barons'* pawn, no matter did they urge me t'settle things quick. What was best for us *all,* th' peace o' the region, was more my intent," Marsden imparted with a sly wink. "As fer Osgoode, well . . . I 'spect sympathy fer what Anne did behind his back'll be more help than hindrance in his career prospects. Th' whole world loves young lovers, an' managin' t'put th' leg over Biddy behind Eachan MacDougall's back is a feat worth a laureate's ode in praise o' *darin'!*"

"Poor Georgina, though," Livesey sighed, after a long moment.

"Aye," Marsden sadly agreed, looking as if he'd bitten into a green persimmon. "But . . . a year or two o' grievin', an' it's amazin' what powers of recuperation th' womenfolk own. None of it *her* fault, after all, an' ever'body'll be sympathetic . . . the womenfolk most especially . . . t'be th' victim of a connivin' two-faced man. Either way, she has Tuscarora, an' set fer life. Good friends, carin' kin . . ."

She would feel burning shame, Livesey imagined, to have been a fool for Harry's lifelong sham. God knew, *he* was! And once burned he thought she would be doubly shy of ever trusting a man again, certainly not a man like himself so closely tied to Harry Tresmayne, and Matthew Livesey felt a sudden, intense relief that Georgina would be so unapproachable of her own volition! That damnable dream was *so* unattainable!

He *could* be a good friend, not a rival for Harry's memory; his whole family could be a blessing, not a cringe-making burden—after a decent period of mourning, of course. Even then, there would always be an unbridgeable, unspoken-of gulf between them, and that Livesey thought both he, and she, could abide as nothing more than supportive *friends.*

"Damme, but Thom almost pulled it off, didn't he, Livesey?" Mr Marsden said, marveling. "He'd been but a wee bit smarter, an' he'd have been able t'brazen it out, no matter what evidence we discovered. But he was a 'gone gosling,' once ye set t'diggin.' I do b'lieve that ye mighta missed yer callin', sir. I expect I know yer political persuasions, but . . . Constable Swann needs replacin'. Lord, doesn't he, *just!* Come next by-election . . ."

"I don't see how I could, sir," Livesey flummoxed, stunned by the suggestion of taking public office. "Though I thankee for thinking I might . . . ah . . . do better. My chandlery, though, our hopes of farming again, do we get a bit ahead. Never read at law, and . . . I might be too old to start," he allowed with a soft laugh.

"Law readin'!" Marsden scoffed. "Never did much meself 'fore I become magistrate. Common sense counts more. Somethin' t'keep in mind. Someone t'sit over th' Slave Court, if just t'spare my pore ol' bones a day'r two a week. Ponder on it, once we're back t'normal."

"I will, I promise, your honor," Livesey gravely said.

"Damned if it don't look like a good rain comin', at that," Mr Marsden commented, looking upwards again. "Thank God fer a new-tarred coach-top, fer it's gonna be a gully-washer do we not get a move on."

They turned to see how things were progressing and saw Captain Buckles emerging from the house with a short, double-barreled coaching gun in his hands, Constable Swann with the damning gown and flowers re-bundled in its sailcloth . . . and Andrew Hewlett standing in the doors, his shoulders heaving, copious tears running down a face that was screwed up into a hideous death's rictus.

"He couldn't have!" Andrew wailed, looking as if he wished for someone to run to for comfort—but none of them; not then.

"Prob'ly can't bring th' body t'Saint James's, Andrew," Marsden muttered, looking bashful, of a sudden. "Him takin' his own life, o' his own hand, an' all. S'pose ye'll be layin' Thomas t'rest, here? I could have th' Rev'rend McDowell t'speak comfort with ye, though. Or, might ye have other plans . . ."

"Bury him here!" Andrew shouted. "Where he's safe! It can't be so, what they told me! It's a lie! He'd never . . . !"

"Got anybody t'see after ye fer a spell, Andrew?" Marsden plugged on, anxious to get a polite duty out of the way and quickly finished. "Some folk t'stay out here, some folk ye might wish to go to . . . ?"

"I have *no one* anymore!" the twice-orphaned lad accused them. "Damn you! Damn you all!"

"You could come into town with us, Andrew," Livesey offered as he fumbled with his own hat. "We could . . . you'd be more than welcome."

"Never with *you*, sir!" Andrew shot back. "Nor *any* of yours!"

Andrew spun and dashed back into the recesses of the house, his curses lingering and fading as he dashed up the stairs and far away.

Livesey heaved a great, regretful sigh. Andrew was a sweet boy, with a promising future—or had been. Now, no matter how blameless he had been in all this, there would always be that taint on him from his uncle's crimes. Livesey looked into the magistrate's eyes, as if in search of some answers, some solutions—but Marsden could but do as Livesey had: heave a bitter sigh, and toss his shoulders upward to Fate, or God's will.

They left the veranda, almost slinking shamefully down the wide stairs to the mid-landing, then the brick walk and into the coach, just as the pine tops began to lash and flag to a strong gust of wind from the Sounds, as a pall of storm-weather gloominess swept the skies dark, and Livesey could smell the fresh-water dampness of the rain, shiver as the temperature plunged.

Andrew Hewlett, such a *trusting* lad . . . now blighted, Livesey sadly thought as they bustled into the coach, making a tight foursome once more. He supposed he'd have to break the bad news to Bess that Hewlett would have nothing to do with Liveseys the rest of his life.

And there was Georgina a widow . . . Anne Moore blighted, too, of a certainty, and Osgoode and his rectitude, leadership of the faction, perhaps even his law practice blighted as well. Biddy? How would she be received in Wilmington, at Saint James's? Another rumor of hot-blooded murder laid on her father Eachan MacDougall—no matter if they acquitted him as totally blameless, the rumor would stick, no matter where he drifted.

"There were a few more things I'd have liked to ask Lakey," he mumbled, half to himself, looking at Marsden. "For instance, how was he so sure . . ."

"It's over, Mr Livesey," Marsden suggested, his eyes tight shut in attempted repose as the two soldiers boarded the postillion-bench and the coachee whipped up. "Over an' done. Let it be."

Over? Livesey thought. It didn't look, to him, as if it was even *close* to being over. The repercussions, the people scarred, the shame of it! The anger he felt for being so well-fooled most of his life—along with everyone else, which was no comfort to him—by a witty and clever dissembler who'd had no real affection for anyone but himself, well . . . that might be hardest of all to bear.

No, this wasn't over yet, he told himself. He imagined that he could hear a mourning bell tolling, one that could ring 'til the next Epiphany, fifty Epiphanies, 'til he and all his children were dead and gone, and would never quite cease its doleful echoes.

With the hiss of waves rushing ashore on the barrier isles, the rain arrived, great dram-sized dollops that battered on the coach top like liquid hammer blows, seething and splashing in the fields beside the road and spurring the overseers into gallops for shelter, and the slaves to shambling runs for their cabins with their precious iron implements protected from rusting under their shabby shirts or aprons.

And with their old master gone, would the mourning bell strike for them, too? What distress in dispersion might await them as well?

Matthew Livesey laid his head back on the high leather bench on which he sat, one hand extended out the open coach window to be soaked by the rain. *As Pontius Pilate washed his hands,* he sourly imagined.

Cool, cleansing, sea-born, early-summer Carolina rain.

Chapter 33

MATTHEW LIVESEY bade his children as fond a goodbye as he could muster, levered himself down off his front porch, and stumped through the damp, sandy soil of Dock Street, in the brisk coolness of a workaday Tuesday morning, a little after sunup. He tugged down his waistcoat, shot his cuffs and peered about for taunting children or angry geese—wearing his "Publick Phyz" for the world to see, that of a respectable, upright gentleman, a credit to his family and his community.

Thankfully, the few children present seemed strangely subdued, as somber as their parents surely must be since Mr Marsden, the magistrate, had revealed the identity of Harry Tresmayne's killer at his inquest the morning before . . . and all the sordid details that accompanied that revelation, too. Wonder of wonders, even the most impish lads seemed awed to silence by his presence; though he doubted *that* would last.

Livesey stumped along, head down in a bleak study, with no eyes for the Thoroughfare and the wharves and ships at the foot of Water Street, for a change. He felt no pleasure this day, for so much had been on his mind that he had barely gotten a wink of sleep once the truth had come out.

Plans and contingencies, possible responses to the crises thrust upon him the last couple of days, the duties which must be borne with a willing Christian's endurance, had put him in the "blue devils."

Biddy MacDougall to shelter, for one—'til Osgoode Moore ousted his wife, Anne, and laid a Bill of Divorcement with the General Assembly, complete with inquest testimonies and the approval of Rev. McDowell. *And* further convince that worthy minister to let them attend Services, even as non-communicants for a time, before McDowell performed a quick marriage ceremony . . . before the next Moore offspring was born "on the wrong side of the blanket"!

Samuel, with help from that free Negro, Autie, and his Pap, would take a hired dray 'cross the rivers today and fetch off Biddy's things, some that would end in his house, or be stored at the chandlery for a while before Osgoode could move her under his own roof as a legal wife.

A *wedding* to plan, which almost made Mr Livesey twitch with annoyance, for he knew little of how such things actually got arranged, though he fearfully suspected that Bess and Biddy *did,* and would plague his household for months on end!

Biddy's father, Eachan MacDougall, well . . . there was another thorn. Livesey had offered both abject apologies and a better-paying situation at his works on Eagle's Island, as amends for the way he had been treated, and to soften the blow of Biddy leaving his hearth—and her fall from Innocence. Both offers, and him, MacDougall had damned to Hell. Still, Eachan *might* come 'round . . . for Biddy's future happiness, and for his coming grandchild. Weddings *seemed* to mellow people.

Bess to cosset, too, Livesey sourly pondered as he neared the riverfront. Her sympathetic letter to Andrew Hewlett had been returned with its wax seal unbroken. Ah, well, even did young Hewlett stand to become the master of Lakey's Lodge, there probably had been no future in it, after all. Bess, to his mind, was still much too young to make binding commitments . . . to leave *his* hearth! Perhaps the giddy doings of Biddy's wedding would engross her, then . . . a season to mourn, as the Good Book said, then even more seasons to dance, mature and meet more-promising lads, before . . .

Matthew Livesey stopped his slow stroll and turned to look back up Dock Street to the front of his ravaged, simple house. They needed a new facade soon as he could arrange it, but . . . what style, what color paint? Could he afford brick or ballast stone this time, or dare they risk wood again? And it *was* small. His gaze swept uphill toward the east of the town. Beyond Fifth Street, the eastern boundary of the borough so far, a new batch of larger lots had been cleared, the pine forests and wilderness shoved back just a bit further.

Had they sufficient profits come winter, when the shipping-trade abated, might the Liveseys aspire to it, and did Providence provide the means, could they build a whole *new* house? he fantasized: a *modestly* grander house, something substantial, more respectable and sober . . . a sign that they had sunk their transplanted roots just that much deeper into the soil of the Cape Fear.

A little uphill from St. James's, with a grand view of the Thoroughfare, the river and the sunsets! Matthew Livesey imagined deep porches and balconies where he could rock in the coolness, of having separate parlors and dining rooms to entertain neighbors and friends, host parties . . .

"Blast," Livesey growled at his own imaginings, then turned back to face the river and resume his awkward stroll. After all that had happened, would Liveseys *have* friends; would anyone accept their invitations? Might he have blighted his own, and his children's, prospects in the region by exposing Harry's sins and failings? Shattered so many folks' illusions, brought a progressive faction low, and . . . brought a smear of shame, and heartbreak, upon dear Georgina's name?

With a physical shake of his head and body that would have done a waking bear proud, Matthew Livesey *refused* to meekly accept the onus, for it had been *Harry's* doing, Anne Moore's and Thomas Lakey's sins and deceits, and crimes, that had brought them all to this despicable condition! And could he find it in his nature—might God excuse him the blasphemy just for once—he would have, at that moment, succumbed to weakness and heartily damned them *all* to the hottest fires of Hell . . . and right out loud, too!

Had he been able, but . . . he couldn't.

He reached the sturdy, grey, cypress-timbered wharves along Water Street and turned south to thud his cane and the foot of That Thing on the weathered boards, but . . .

There, in the Thoroughfare, was a saucy packet-brig, just let go of her moorings and beginning to stand down-river for the sea, ghosting on the cusp of a high tide's ebb, with only her spanker, a flying jib and a foretopmast stays'l standing to give her steerage way. Gulls wheeled 'round her and mewed, and Matthew Livesey stopped again to watch her go, the faintest hint of release from joylessness taunting the corners of his mouth and brightening his dulled eyes.

"Little Sally Rackett!" the bosun sing-songed from leather lungs as a lone fiddler climbed atop the forecastle and began to play.

"Haul her away!" her crewmen on lifts and halyards roared back.

"She sailed off 'board a packet!"

"Haul her away!" Sailors aloft were freeing tops'l canvas, hauling on braces to angle them about to cup a breeze. Men on deck pulled to hoist tops'l yards from their rests on the top platforms.

"An' she never did re-*gret* it!"

"Haul herrr awwayy!"

"With a hauley heigh-*ho!*"

"Haul her away!"

And for Matthew Livesey, who'd grown up 'round ships and the sea since he'd left swaddling clothes, that call-and-response, pulley hauley chanty was nigh to a celebratory *hymn*. And to stand and watch a ship come to life and stir, almost of her own volition, was nigh equal to a mystery as old as Time, and a miracle, every time to him.

Livesey stumped his way to the very end of the wharves—scaring up a nodding pelican, being scolded by a pair of black-headed laughing gulls—suddenly rapt by this small and fleeting pleasure. Yet it made him achingly wistful, too.

God, how different things would have been if he *had* managed to run away to sea when he was young. It was what less-constrained lads of harbor towns *did!*

"Farewell to th' Dram Tree!" the bosun bellowed as the sailors had enough sail spread for the brig to manage, for a moment, and boys dashed about to serve out small tots of neat rum or brandy as she came level with the gigantic old cypress just a bit down-river, where ships' crews had established a tradition particular to Wilmington for entering or leaving port.

"Haul her away!"

"Th' Cape Fear girls so *care*-free!"

"Haul her away!"

"Sure, they swore they'd miss ye!"

For one daft moment, Livesey wondered who would care if he got aboard her and just sailed away. Or had gotten away to sea, the time he'd tried . . . and why hadn't he ever tried again? He'd never have gotten dragged back to his father's trade, and the penury and troubles that had befallen him as that concern failed.

No call to the militia, no losing his leg to *that* brief stupidity of his; he'd still be a *whole* man, most-like a captain on his own ship, perhaps captain and *owner* by now, of her or several other ships!

No wasted term at Harvard, never to meet Harry, hence no cruel disillusionment, no depravity to break his heart in *that* future. He'd never have become an aging, one-legged widower, so fettered by Duties and Responsibilities!

Yet . . .

He'd never have met his dear, departed Charlotte, not on equal terms, at least. Her parents would never have let her marry a sailor, even a mate or captain; they wanted her wed to someone "substantial and sober"! There never would have been a Bess, never a Samuel . . . well, *there* was a thought, for a wry instant. Which instant fled, replaced by his concerns once more . . . what was *demanded* of him!

Was the Lord kind to them, allowed them a year or two more with their debts cleared and the firm profitable, they might also aspire to *farmland* again. It still went for no more than sixpence an acre. If Samuel really *didn't* have the heart and head for dry, indoor Commerce, as that rascal Jemmy Bowlegs had boldly stated, then he could try his son on the land, let him sow and reap . . . perhaps as Providence always had intended for the lad. A year or two more of chandlery and sawmill work to prepare and groom him, of course, but . . . perhaps it was not God's will that Livesey & Son continue after his own passing, either.

Despite the bleakness of that thought, and the fear of leaving little mark of his existence, Matthew Livesey sadly decided that he could not deny Samuel his heartfelt yearning—as his own father had quashed his so long before. Why else, perhaps, had they been caused to move to the Cape Fear and its whole new ways of life, to a wild and raw frontier where staid people were shaken and challenged to new *lives,* but by the Almighty's mysterious ways, His miracles to perform?

"Up, my fightin' cocks, boys!"

"Haul her away!"

"Up, an' split her blocks, now!"

"Haul her away!"

"Up, an' stretch her luff, lads . . ."

Gloom departed again on sea-birds' wings, as Livesey put idle musings away and turned his attention back to the packet-brig. She was beginning to curtsy and bow a bit alee to an offshore wind that sighed over the miles of woods of the cape to the river, and tobacco-brown waters began to chuckle under her forefoot and cut-water, to murmur about her rudder and stern-post. Almost all her canvas was now set. In three or four cautious hours, she might briefly come to anchor down at Brunswick, Oak Island or the point, and wait to choose Old Inlet or New Inlet as the best course through Frying Pan Shoals, then be off and abroad on the free and open ocean.

Flying sails bought new from *his* business, or patched from *his* replacement bolts! It could be *his* paint and oils that made her look so saucy and fresh, *his* hemp and manila that made up her standing and running rigging, and a part of her outbound cargo was most-likely *his* lumber and barrel staves, *his* resin, turpentine, pitch and tar!

"We'll plow th' wide world *oh*-ver!"

"Haul her away!"

The call-and-response chanty was thinner, now, farther off and down-river than before, the brig shrunk to a child's toy, yet Livesey knew that chanty of old, and cocked an ear to savor the last morsel of happiness from it.

"Like proper deep-sea rovers!"

"Haul her away!"

The brig was fully under way, fully under sail, willing to trust herself to wind, reefs, storm and tide, for that was her wondrous purpose in Life, her fate in God's hands. Could he do any less? For the first time that morning, Matthew Livesey felt call to smile, to whisper, "Thankee, God . . . I bow to Your will for us."

"One more, an' up she rises!"

"Haul hherrr awwayy!"

"With a hauley heigh-*ho!*"

"Haul her away!"

"One more pull, and . . . *be-lay!*" the distant bosun called, and Matthew Livesey whispered it with him. Then, to his lights, it was acceptingly, most pleasingly, done.